UNBREAKABLE

Of Gods and Dragons
Book 1

Willow River Press is an imprint of Between the Lines Publishing. The Willow River Press name and logo are trademarks of Between the Lines Publishing.

Between the Lines Publishing
1769 Lexington Ave N, Ste 286
Roseville MN 55108
btwnthelines.com

First Published: February 2024

ISBN: (Paperback) 978-1-958901-66-3

ISBN: (Ebook) 978-1-958901-67-0

UNBREAKABLE

Of Gods and Dragons
Book 1

Colleen McMillan

This is for Eva and Christine, and they know why

Nothing is eternal but the gods

Prologue

The Sun God does not love.

And no one knows his true name, if he has one. Each year, when the sun shines brightest in the sky, the Sun God accepts offerings, tributes from those who worship him. Long ago, he opened his temple twice a year, but he is a fickle and temperamental being, so he closed his doors except for one day. So, once a year, his followers make a pilgrimage to the Temple of the Sun nestled high in a tall mountain that used to house a volcano. It gleams with the dawn, spilling golden light across the valley below the mountain, its pillars flashing with radiant energy, its roofs arched and graceful. Legend says the Sun God built the temple with one wave of his hand; such is his power and strength.

But another story speaks of a human with wild red hair and laughing eyes—a master architect, who was inspired by the Sun God's magnificence and bestowed the temple upon him. Upon completing his greatest achievement and proclaiming his undying love for the Sun God, the architect was stricken with a wasting sickness and passed away from the world. The Sun God was left with a beautiful home, but the light had fallen from his life, and he remained locked inside, directing the day from afar.

This story is told in only one village.

Alaric Shina was born blessed by the Sun God, the only person with crimson eyes in his village. He had his mother's pointed teeth and sonorous

1

voice and his father's broad shoulders and dark hair, which his parents lamented: if only he'd been given fiery red hair to match his eyes. No one in the village had red hair though it was said to emerge every other generation or so. Their village was truly the most favored of the Sun God for their offerings were the most celebrated, the most lauded. Their tributes returned from the temple every year, which couldn't be said for other villages.

When he turned twenty, Shina won the privilege of tribute, chosen for his sturdiness and unflappable spirit. The villagers wouldn't go so far as to call him "the sun"—or risk godly vengeance—but a day never went by that he didn't help bring in crops from the fields or carry water home from the nearby spring. If he frowned, only his parents witnessed it because the villagers received blinding smiles when he passed through the market. He was the ideal choice to bring the village offering for the year, for how could the Sun God resist that ready smile and shining red eyes. They would pack the offering into Shina's cart and send him through the forest, along the river, waiting for him to return from the mountain. To give him even more of an edge, his parents suggested an old tradition: dying his hair red.

Chapter One

Alaric wasn't sure about his hair. He'd gone along with it but only because his mother was adamant.

"You'll charm the Sun God, no matter what," she said, fawning over him, "but imagine if you had hair like no one else."

"I'm sure other tributes dye their hair, Mom. Trying to suck up isn't really my thing. Aren't I just leaving the offering then coming home? It's not like the Sun God invites everyone to a banquet and a sleepover."

His father laughed at that. "You've got a point, but we might as well make use of your looks. I'd rather he look favorably on you, so you *do* come home."

What his father alluded to but didn't mention outright was that the neighboring village's tribute hadn't returned last year. Alaric's mother tutted and fretted over his robe, unsure about the deep aubergine color, and she ignored what his father hadn't said.

"You look so handsome," she said and wiped a tear from her cheek, folding the soft purple fabric after slipping it off his shoulders. She dusted stray threads off his shirt with her hand, humming.

"That's great, but do I really have to be naked underneath?"

"Only once you reach the temple; it's tradition!" she said as though scandalized by the thought of him wearing clothes.

"Someone could try and change the tradition," he mumbled, and his father chuckled softly so his mother couldn't hear.

Now, Alaric knelt by the river, looking down at his reflection and flicking his fingers through the new red hair. It suited him, but it was so different, blazing around his shoulders like flames. It made his eyes stand out more, and the scar across his forehead did too, visible when he tucked the hair behind his ears. Maybe the Sun God only liked his tributes unblemished…but it was too late now. He'd had the scar as long as he could remember.

He was also tender from the fresh piercings, which were customary when a man in his village turned twenty. He peeked down his shirt collar at the double nipple bars and rings, golden and sparkling, connected by a hanging gold chain. Most of the men had silver chains; gold was saved for the tributes.

His father had been so proud, saying, "The chain of gold represents the everlasting bond between our village and the Temple of the Sun, and you're part of that lineage now."

Alaric was proud too; the honor was immense, but for some reason his heart ached when he looked at the chain. Was it nerves, the anticipation? No tribute spoke about what they saw at the Temple of the Sun. They added their contributions to the village ledger, but few were allowed to read it.

Was he afraid?

Beside him at the river, the family horse dipped her head to drink, swirling Alaric's reflection with small ripples. He sighed and patted her neck.

"You're just a horse, Ichigo, so you aren't afraid of an old god, are you?"

She looked at him, dark eyes blinking languidly as though saying, "Obviously not, foolish human."

Alaric snorted and stood up, stretching his back muscles.

His village was close to the mountain but more than a day's ride with the cart. They set out before sunrise, everyone waving as they departed south. His parents at the front of the crowd, beaming as he left, watching him lead Ichigo on foot. It would tire her too quickly if he rode, and Alaric didn't mind a long hike. Stopping for the night was a must, so he set up camp after a long day's journey, checking the precious cargo in the cart before settling in to sleep under the stars. He stopped the next afternoon to let Ichigo drink at the river after he took the cart down from her harness. She deserved a rest as much as he did.

"We'll be there at the perfect time," he said though Ichigo ignored him. "Not too early, and not too late. Don't want to seem too eager. And it would be rude to be one of the last tributes to arrive. Can you imagine what Mom would say?"

Ichigo's ears barely moved, and her head dipped to nibble grass near the water.

"Okay, fine, don't talk to me, but you're really missing out."

He sighed and went to the cart, pulling out his bag. He packed extra clothes, some food, and a book on plants and herbs his father gave him, but he wasn't hungry because a giant pit settled in his stomach. It was time to get naked. He didn't understand why it was necessary, but if it was expected of him, Alaric would do it. He looked around to make sure no one was nearby, then pulled off his shirt and pants. Ichigo finally looked at him, disapproving. She whickered, laughing at his misfortune. Birds high in the trees sang along with the horse.

"I know I look ridiculous," he said. "No need to rub it in."

He donned the purple robe before taking off his underwear and marveled at his mother's sewing skill. The garment was old-fashioned but cut beautifully and very soft. The folds fell around his lower body loosely, but the sleeves were tailored to his arms, showing off his defined biceps and shoulders, and it closed tight across his chest. Alaric caught more than one village girl appreciating the view as his mother draped the robe over him when it was finished, making him parade around outside their house. He'd worn pants that time. No need to give the neighbors a free show. Alaric had to admit that girls were interesting, but he hadn't minded when his attractive male neighbor checked him out too. It was nice to be looked at.

He was about to peel off his underwear and tie the matching purple belt around his waist when a loud scream and splash scattered the birds above him. Panicked voices filtered through the trees, and Alaric spotted a small form bobbing in the river's current. For the first time, he was glad he had to be naked under the robe.

Diving into the river, his body tensing from the icy water, Alaric swam with the current, searching for the person he'd seen from the bank. Twigs and leaves swirled in the water, and Alaric hoped he wasn't too late. Had the person gone under? He stopped for a moment to drift and saw a small hand a few feet away. Kicking wildly, desperate to reach that hand, Alaric prayed to the Sun God for speed and strength. Alaric rarely needed to pray to other gods, but his thoughts went to the various water gods, begging to aid him.

Alaric tore through the small waves, reaching, straining for purchase, and a child's head bobbed into sight. Just a kid! He saw Alaric, his eyes widening in fear, and water seeped into his mouth, causing him to cough and sink beneath again.

Shit! Alaric dove down and opened his eyes, seeing the child's terrified face, his eyes closing, tiny fingers still searching for help. He could do this. The river was strong, but if anyone could save the child, it was him. He couldn't let someone's life be snuffed out so soon.

Muscles searing, Alaric swam, surging forward with the last of his breath. And the boy's arm was in reach. Alaric broke the surface with a gasp, the boy under one arm. His fingers jabbed into Alaric's arm like claws, but Alaric didn't mind. Pain meant the boy was still alive, and the boy wailed, dragging in air. Alaric swam to shore, hearing panicked shrieks.

"Rolf! My baby!" A woman appeared, tearing through the reeds on the bank. Her cheeks bloomed red with anxiety as she reached for the boy, grabbing him from Alaric's grasp. She wailed, "Why did you get so close? I told you to be careful!" Peppering the boy's face with kisses, the woman took him further inland and sat him down, placing a shawl around his shivering shoulders.

"Ma'am," Alaric sputtered, staggering out of the water. "You should get him home and warm! Don't want the little guy getting sick."

She flung herself at Alaric, weeping. "Thank the gods you were here! I don't even want to imagine what would have happened."

"I'm sure you would've gotten there in time," Alaric said, grinning.

"I'm his mother! I should have been watching him closer. Rolf! Say thank you!"

The poor boy shuddered under his mother's shawl, his teeth chattering as he said, "Thank you, mister. I fell in."

That was fairly obvious, but Alaric couldn't blame the boy for wanting to explore and try new things. He ruffled the boy's wet hair, flinching at the cold water. He'd need to dry off quickly or risk a cold himself.

"Just be more careful next time and listen to your mother." Alaric winked at the boy and heard Ichigo whinnying.

Oh. No.

"Please be careful in the future!" Alaric shouted to the mother and son as he tore off through the reeds.

Alaric was in big trouble. Massive. Huge. Why had he gotten involved? It wasn't his job to help everyone in the damn world. He wasn't obligated to offer a hand to every person who needed it. And yet, when he'd seen that shape in the churning water, he didn't hesitate. But what could relieved motherly tears and shivering, grateful child eyes do for him now?

At least his hair wasn't soaked anymore, but it danced around his face like fluffy clouds, dried from the sun but not combed or brushed. He could still feel the freezing water as it hit his body, the pull of the undercurrent as he grabbed the small boy, seeing terrified eyes. With a shiver, he pushed the thought away. He didn't have time to think about if the kid would be okay.

He was going to be late.

Ichigo didn't mind when he jumped on her back, only in his underwear, sopping wet from head to toe. Maybe she knew he saved a life. Maybe she felt his panic and wanted to help. Either way, she followed his lead on her reins and raced down the forest path, cart bouncing behind her, cargo secure. If Alaric was going to be late, at least the offering would be intact.

They pulled away from the forest, flustered crows cawing behind them. Alaric cursed himself as the mountain loomed ahead but still so far away. He would probably make it in time, but the sun was lowering in the early evening sky, not the best impression for himself or his village. What would his parents say if he came back to the village, offering in the cart? What would it mean for everyone who lived there? Nothing so shameful had happened in hundreds of years. Had it *ever* happened? Not wanting to think on it too long, he urged Ichigo onward, and she galloped faster. No. He would deliver the offering if it was his last act on earth.

They were so close. Foam leaked from Ichigo's mouth when they burst from the trees, but she didn't slow. Alaric wouldn't make her suffer for his mistakes, so he pulled back gently on the reins and said, "Whoa, girl, whoa."

They could make it if they walked the rest of the way. He rubbed her nose as he dismounted, praising her speed and perseverance, and she nuzzled his shoulder.

The mountain was immense and elegant, black volcanic rock crowned with glittering snow, a sight Alaric had only dreamed of, and now, he was there. He passed young people on the road as they left the valley, all with empty carts. Some chatted animatedly with each other, but many were somber, their eyes downcast. They stared at Alaric as he went by, chest heaving from the ride, sweat trailing down his face and body. Then, they gazed at the sky, checking the sun's position. They gave him concerned expressions and a wide berth as if touching him would bring disease and famine upon them.

It might, he thought and swore under his breath. He looked like a damned fool, not prepared at all to meet the most glorious of the gods.

His village had chosen poorly. He didn't deserve the golden chain that hung across his chest.

When Alaric finally reached the base of the mountain, he took a huge breath and let it out. He needed to pull himself together. He was a little behind, but the sun was up. He had time. And the offering was a good one.

As if his body realized it could relax, pain shot through his limbs and across his feet. Looking down, he realized that he hadn't put his sandals on after climbing from the river. He wasn't sure if they were even in the cart. The skin on the inside of his thighs screamed from chaffing, but that would be covered by the robe. His feet on the other hand... He blinked rapidly, unsure what to do. It wasn't the worst thing to walk into a temple barefoot, but he would be the only tribute who did. Another mistake, which were piling up quickly.

A harried-looking man with a shock of pure white hair materialized as if from nowhere and stumbled over to him, muttering under his breath, a huge book under his arm. Another man followed behind, shorter and much livelier, carrying a pedestal. The second man grinned at Alaric with needle-sharp teeth but said nothing. He slammed the pedestal down on the ground, and Alaric stepped back, eyes wide. No one mentioned this part of the ceremony.

The older man, his hooded eyes screaming exhaustion, placed the book on the pedestal and opened it, sighing. The short man flashed another grin, almost predatory, and he looked Alaric up and down before saying, "Pretty."

"Insufferable," said the white-haired man.

"Pardon?" Alaric asked, taken aback by the two men.

"Not you. Although the hour is...late." The older man glanced at him with disdain, one eyebrow barely lifting in his lack of concern. Red fractured lines flared out from his pupils. When had the man last slept?

"I know. I'm really sorry," Alaric said and ruffled the hair on the back of his head. "I—"

"I'm sure you will be very sorry but no matter," the man said and flipped one more page in the book. "I am Draiden, Scribe to the great Sun God." His tone was flat and disinterested as though he wished to be anywhere else.

"I really am sorry, sir. I'm sure it's been a long day, and I've made it longer for you. I wish there was something I could do." Alaric hung his head as he spoke, wishing he could also be anywhere else. Maybe the volcano would erupt and end his embarrassment.

"Mmmmmmmm, and pure," the shorter man hummed, teeth clacking, and he stooped to sniff Alaric's unshod feet, which were filthy now that Alaric looked closer. What a damned mess.

"Don't mind him," Draiden said, his voice lifting slightly. "He's not used to interacting with...people." Draiden produced a pen from one long sleeve and a pot of what had to be ink from the other. "Village, offering, and name?"

Alaric looked up, holding in tears that threatened to fall. He could do this. This had to be the last step. Draiden's eyes remained tired, but there was kindness behind them, and Alaric bowed as he answered, "Yes, sir. Togarashi Village, Yatsufusa peppers, and I'm Alaric Shina."

Draiden's eyebrow inched up further. He cleared his throat and his eyes darted up the mountain for a moment. "He'll be pleased."

Alaric sighed and said, "I sure hope so. These are the best spicy peppers in the world."

"Indeed," said Draiden, a small smirk dodging across his face. "Do you intend to look like...this when meeting the Most Incandescent One?" Draiden motioned to all of Alaric's body. Damned the seven hells, he was still naked but not the right kind of naked.

Ichigo snorted when Alaric returned to the cart, and he patted her back, muttering soothing comments. He pulled the ornate wicker basket from under the tarp on the cart and filled it with glossy bright-red peppers, the hottest in the land. He knew this part: he only brought a sample of the offering to the Sun God. The rest would be taken by servants, and Alaric would come back to an empty cart and finally be able to leave this cursed mountain.

After putting the basket down, he grabbed the purple robe, which he had secured lovingly before making the mad dash through the forest. Thank the gods he'd remembered the robe. The gold chain on his chest tinkled as he pulled the robe on and closed it with the belt, and Alaric finally pulled his underwear off. He jammed it into his pack when he saw the shorter man edging toward him, nose in the air as if scenting a fresh kill. Alaric skirted around the short man and ran a hand through his hair, trying to comb out the tangles. He only succeeded in making it wilder.

Draiden remained by the pedestal, leaning on it, chin in his hand. He watched Alaric approach with the basket of peppers in hand, and Alaric thought he might have winked as he tapped the pen against his cheek.

"Well, this is as good as it's going to get, I guess," Alaric huffed and bit his lower lip.

"Passable," said Draiden, but he sounded happier than before. "If I may?" He pulled another item from his coat sleeve, a pencil this time. "This is kohl."

Alaric looked from the pencil to Draiden and back. What was he supposed to do with a pencil?

When Alaric didn't respond, Draiden breathed out, exasperated. "Put down the basket and come stand here. Attempt not to move."

Alaric obeyed immediately and stood next to Draiden. Luckily, the man was almost as tall as Alaric, so he didn't need to stand on his toes to look into Alaric's eyes.

"Close your eyes." Alaric did as ordered and felt the odd sensation of Draiden drawing on his eyelids. He wasn't sure whether this was part of the ritual or not, but he didn't want to hassle the poor man more than he already had.

After a few moments, Draiden said, "There. Now you don't look like common forest trash."

"Um, thanks?" Alaric said. His first instinct was to rub his eyes, but he had a feeling that was a bad idea. "Will my horse be okay here?"

Draiden was apparently finished with their interaction. He flipped a hand, unconcerned with Alaric's question, and took the large book in hand.

"You're the final tribute of the year. Try..." He didn't continue for some time. "Go up the path with your offering. When you come to the temple doors, say the words and enter."

Alaric flashed a confident smile. He knew this part too. Draiden didn't have to worry about that. "Yes sir! I'll do my best!"

More people, servants, appeared to take the offering from the cart, and one woman brought a food bag for Ichigo. Alaric nodded to her, thankful, and she inclined her head after staring at him for a moment. Alaric grabbed the basket of peppers, conscious of his naked body under the robe, and marched up the path. He may have been the last tribute, and there may have been no one else in line with him, but Alaric finally felt like a tribute.

As he made his way up the mountain path, Alaric wasn't aware that Draiden watched his ascent. The shorter man shuffled away with the pedestal, knowing his role, not caring what Draiden did once that job was done. The older man didn't take his eyes off Alaric until he was well up the mountain. Then, he looked up at the sun, which was fading toward the horizon.

He whispered to himself, "That young man...looks just like..." He didn't finish his thought and spun on his heel to finish the final offering ceremony task of the year.

After the arduous journey, walking up a mountain path was nothing. Though his feet hurt a bit from the scattered pebbles and rocks, and he knew his hair was a red mess, the peppers weren't heavy, and the path was even and true. Did Alaric miss the conversation he would have had with the other tributes as they waited on the path? Of course! It was one of the things he looked forward to the most. But being alone was also thrilling. He wouldn't be competing for the Sun God's attention.

Thinking about the Sun God brought his heart plummeting again. Oh gods...what would he be like? Would he be angry that Alaric arrived so late in the day? What if the peppers weren't enough? What if he was deemed unworthy to be in the Sun God's presence and the doors wouldn't open?

He tried not to think about his messy hair and dirty feet and wondered instead what Draiden had done to his eyes. They didn't feel different. Could you actually draw on people's eyes? It hadn't hurt like getting a tattoo; it just tickled a bit. Oh no! What if the Sun God didn't like his tattoo?

Relax, he thought. His tattoo was under the robe. Everything was going to be fine.

It took about twenty minutes to reach the temple, which was carved directly into the mountain. Made mainly from ebony volcanic rock, it didn't look like it was a temple to the Sun God until light hit it. When the sun rose in the morning sky, it struck the temple full on, and the rock glistened and shed its skin. A master illusion, when hit with sunlight, the black rock faded to stunning gold, amber, and honey tones, nearly blinding those who looked upon it. The night gave way to morning, the beautiful night sky welcoming the sun, ushering in the day.

It was said to be the most balanced building in all existence. Though Alaric did not witness the dawn breaking upon the temple, it was equally stunning in the early evening, for the day must give in to the night, and gold must fade to black.

The doors were enormous but simple, pure gold in color and cool to the touch. They did not soak up the sun's energy and so did not burn anyone who might knock. Alaric stared at the doors for a few minutes, steeling himself.

Unbreakable, he thought to himself, *remember that you're unbreakable*.

He set down the basket and reached out, stroking the metal, expecting it to be warm. When it wasn't, he smiled. The Sun God was a thoughtful god who cared about his followers.

As though powered by an external optimistic source, Alaric lifted his head, made a fist, and knocked three times, saying in a clear voice, "I have come from across the rivers and through the forests just to seek you. I have come bearing gifts to lay at your feet. I shall beseech your favor for one more prosperous year. I have come." He whispered the last sentence, and the doors shuddered before opening.

The quiet was unnerving, but Alaric felt strangely at peace. He was more comfortable with noise, the sounds of the village spilling through his window in the mornings: children giggling, the blacksmith smashing her anvil, dogs barking, his parents making breakfast together.

But here. Here was silence.

He saw no one open the massive main entrance doors, and no one bustled about the temple hall either. Maybe the servants were only at the foot of the mountain, but Alaric thought it was odd. Was there anyone inside to serve the Sun God?

If there had been any doors off the main hall, Alaric might have gotten lost, but there were only two directions: forward or back. He clutched the basket and walked down the hall. His feet were soothed by the cool floor tiles, shining black obsidian. The ceiling soared above him, deep blue and adorned in intriguing artwork, etched outlines of constellations giving it an ethereal glow. Because of the dark color, candles were laid throughout the hallway in shallow alcoves. Scents of clove and citrus fruits permeated the air, giving Alaric renewed energy. He wondered if the doors stayed open, letting sunlight in, if the golden constellations would provide enough light for the hall. The candles flickered along his path, urging him on.

He reached another massive door and stopped. This was another part of the ceremony, but he didn't have to knock or recite an incantation here. It was said that the Sun God could feel the person's intentions who stood at his door, and he would let them in...or send them away.

Alaric hoisted the basket up and gulped in air, trying not to hold his breath. The Sun God would think he was worthy, or he wouldn't. Either way, the main offering was already in the Sun God's coffers, so it didn't matter if he allowed Alaric into his presence.

Seconds ticked by as Alaric stood before the door, trying not to shake. His muscles screamed at him now that he was at rest again. Hadn't he done enough? Hadn't he taken the ceremony far enough? Surely it was time to rest, to lie down on the tile and sleep.

No. It wasn't over. It wasn't done until he looked upon the Sun God and presented the offering. He could wait as long as it took. He was the strongest in the village, the one chosen to represent them. He couldn't let them down, couldn't wander home with downcast eyes and a humbled attitude. He needed to be the best tribute. He would make those others who passed him on the way to the mountain feel guilty for pitying him. He needed to show he was worthy. He would not budge.

And the door swung open.

Alaric clung to the basket for dear life. A moment ago, he felt powerful, invincible. Then the door opened, and there was a literal god on the other side. A massively tall throne lay ahead of him, and a person lounged upon it. No, not a person. An actual in-real-life god. And he shone like a blazing star, too bright for Alaric to look at directly. He swallowed his lingering self-doubt and strode forward though he dropped his eyes to the floor.

The light became brighter as he walked, forcing his eyes down. Would he even get to look at the Sun God? Or would he only be able to stare at the floor as he made his offering? He was alone for this part, he knew. There would be no servant present, no Draiden to arch an eyebrow or offer a tired remark. It was only the Sun God. His god.

That's right, Alaric thought. *He's my god. He loves me, even though I'm just a human. We worship him and everything about him. He's perfect. Untouchable. Rarefied.*

But he's mine.

As Alaric reached the foot of the throne, he inclined his head in respect and held out the basket of peppers. "I have come."

A short, barking laugh came from the throne. Startled, Alaric lifted his eyes and saw the most beautiful man in the world. The god's mouth was set in a bored scowl, lips pursed but appealing.

"I saw you look at me," came a gruff, annoyed voice. Alaric was *still* looking at the Sun God though the god wouldn't notice anytime soon. The god picked at his fingernails, paying them more attention than the human in front of him. It wasn't what Alaric thought the Sun God would sound like, but the voice matched the god.

The Sun God sat on his throne, haughty shoulders set at an angle against the back, right foot resting atop his left knee. Hair the color of sun-kissed wheat flew around his head like an explosion, eyebrows arched like daggers. A glittering black and gold mask covered his eyes, finished with a twin sunburst headpiece that gleamed behind his head. He was pale, his skin almost translucent, which struck Alaric as odd, considering he was the Sun God, but his skin glowed, lit from within with divine power. Alaric could tell the god was strong though he was lithe and slim; muscles flowed with each body movement.

His clothing barely hid anything, and Alaric looked down again, blushing. This was definitely the Sun God, but not the one Alaric expected. He looked around Alaric's age, but the Sun God was eons old. Alaric thought the god would resemble his father, weathered and proud. Perhaps he enjoyed looking eternally young.

"I...I apologize," Alaric squeaked out.

"Whatever," the god muttered. "Hardly anyone looks at me anymore, especially someone this fucking late."

"I'm sorry about that too."

"Ugh, just shut up." The voice was bored, and Alaric pictured the Sun God relaxing in a hot bath as soon as the last human idiot tribute of the year left his presence.

"I'll just leave this here for you," Alaric said and placed the basket of peppers on the ground. He wasn't sure what else to do. Was there anything else? No one talked about meeting the Sun God, but they should have mentioned he was terse and ill-tempered. And really attractive.

Alaric didn't want to leave with such a meager greeting. He needed the god to acknowledge him. It was his duty to the village, to be memorable.

He picked up his voice and said, louder than he meant to, "They're the spiciest peppers in the world, and I know you'll like them." His words echoed around the room, bouncing off the walls and reverberating. He thought that last part sounded lame and resigned himself to a quick dismissal.

As though awakened by Alaric's audacious vocal tone and volume, the Sun God deigned to raise his gaze to his final tribute. Alaric felt like he'd been run through with a spear. The Sun God's eyes blazed like solar flares piercing the sky. Bright orange and ringed with gold, they glittered behind the mask, and Alaric couldn't stop staring. He might fall into those eyes and never return. Maybe that's where all the missing tributes were: lost in the Sun God's fathomless eyes.

The Sun God stared brazenly at Alaric for a long time as though consuming his entire soul. It felt like a billion stars had turned their attention on him, making his skin prickle with goosebumps, causing his heartbeat to skyrocket. Had anyone ever looked at someone else like this? He tried to break eye contact, but he couldn't. He was drawn into those eyes like a mesmerized animal caught in a snare. Was he holding his breath?

In less than a breath, the Sun God stood before Alaric, eyes boring into him. Alaric had not seen him move. The basket flew to the side, scattering peppers around their feet. The Sun God didn't care. Alaric started shaking but did not look away, blinking slowly. He knew it was important not to let the god think he was afraid. Somehow, he knew that. And he had thought the razor-toothed man with Draiden was threatening.

This man—god—before him was the one to worry about. He could tear Alaric apart by snapping his fingers. He could do it on a whim with a quirk of his mouth, a blink of his eye.

And Alaric's feet were so dirty.

Alaric held in a whimper though he wanted to scream.

The Sun God was shorter than Alaric, but not by much, and his aura crackled around him like a lightning storm, energy beaming off his skin in a display of dominance. Up close, he was even more terrifyingly stunning; skin smooth, eyelashes spun from pure gold. Alaric felt for a split second that he should lean down and capture the god's lips with his own, and he nearly choked. What was he thinking? That would be the most egregious overstep in the history of the world.

They remained in that position for a long time, Alaric's fisted hands at his sides, the Sun God's never-blinking stare drilling into Alaric's soul. Then, Alaric bit his lower lip, exposing his pointed teeth. The Sun God blinked and took a step back, shoulders rolling as if to strike out. He didn't move any farther and narrowed his eyes.

"Who are you?" the Sun God growled. Alaric wasn't sure he was supposed to answer, so he stayed still and didn't speak. The Sun God cocked his head to the side, and a feral grin spread over his face like an oil slick. "You've got some balls at least. When I ask a question, you better fucking answer."

"I'm the tribute from—"

"Too late," sneered the Sun God.

Alaric felt the warmth drain from the room as though the god sucked it all into himself. He stalked around Alaric like a panther, bare feet silent on the tiled floor. He hissed and snarled, and Alaric felt the room's lost heat pouring from the god's body. This was the power of the sun, which the god could harness in a millisecond. Alaric realized that he was about to die, burned from the inside out, his skin charring away to bone, no time to scream, but he couldn't give way. If he did, his death would mean nothing. He'd been taught to stay on his feet no matter what, to stay strong if adversity found him. He saved a life that afternoon. Someone was alive because of him.

Not even a god could make him beg for his life.

When Alaric failed to cower, the Sun God ceased putting out intense heat and stopped in front of him, contemplative. He reached out and pushed a lock of hair out of Alaric's eyes, finger gleaming with sunlight. His fingernails were painted black. He cocked his head again.

"Why aren't you on your knees?" whispered the Sun God.

Something triggered in Alaric's brain, and his knees hit the floor, his hands outstretched to stop the fall. He hadn't meant to kneel that fast, but self-preservation won out against stubbornness. His breath came out in gusts and sweat trickled down his brow. But this wasn't over. He wasn't going to be devoured without putting up a fight even if the god had a magical voice that could bend him at will. He looked up, defiant, and took in every inch of the Sun God.

In truth, Alaric had imagined a more resplendent icon. The Sun God was stunning, but his apparel was fairly simple. A fluid kilt lined in cloth of gold with slits cut up to his angular hips, banded in black at his slim waist. Golden cloth gauntlets stretching from wrist to bicep—his biceps might ruin Alaric completely—held in place by golden armbands and bracelets. Gleaming golden bands around strong thighs and slightly more ornate ankle cuffs, sunburst pattern echoing his headdress. The chest piece was more intricate, a large and thick gold necklace held in place by a black harness draped across his back, adorned with delicate golden chains no thicker than a few strands of hair. One nipple pierced in gold as well. Alaric fought the urge to reach out and twist the nipple ring with all his strength.

The Sun God smirked at Alaric's challenging expression and leaned down, nose almost touching Alaric's. Not wanting to give in, Alaric sat up straighter, though still on his knees. A piece of paper could have separated their lips. The purple robe pooled around Alaric like a shield, and it shifted when Alaric moved. Something caught the god's attention, and his gaze flicked down Alaric's robe to his chest. Anger, or some similar emotion, flared in the god's eyes.

"What village did you wander here from?" he asked, voice venomous.

This was not the god Alaric worshiped. The gods weren't contemptuous; they were giving and kind. They provided for people and gave comfort when they could. This being was something old and cruel, uninterested in doing anything but scaring him, making him submit. The god might want to kill him, but he intended to play with Alaric first. Alaric vowed to make every moment until his death difficult for the Sun God. He spit on the floor before saying, "Togarashi."

The Sun God whooped with laughter at Alaric's insubordinate action. Then, he padded behind Alaric and knelt beside him, grasping the back of Alaric's neck with one hand, and pulling his head back by the newly dyed red hair, exposing Alaric's throat. He sniffed up Alaric's neck, covetous, and licked his top lip, tongue darting out like a cat's.

"You smell like peppers," the god said, a grin in his voice. The Sun God tore the purple robe from Alaric's shoulders and let it fall, and Alaric didn't bother to grab it. There was no point.

The burning presence loomed over Alaric's back, and the Sun God stood, reached down past Alaric's shoulder, and gingerly grabbed the gold chain that hung between his nipples. He let it slide back and forth between his fingers, making Alaric's nipples tingle, stimulating him with little effort. Alaric held back a moan and bit his lower lip again. The god breathed harder and tugged the chain, making Alaric sniffle.

"You know, if you wanted me to believe that hair was natural, you should have dyed everything."

This time, the Sun God took the bar and ring in Alaric's nipple in his fingertips and twisted, and Alaric groaned, hoping the bar would rip right off his chest if only to end the painful pleasure.

The last thing Alaric heard before he fainted was, "This will do."

Chapter Two

Alaric woke to something or someone poking him in the face. He didn't want to open his eyes and hoped that the day before had been a dream. He must be back home in his room. His parents must have hugged him unconscious upon his return and tucked him into bed, and today, he would write an accurate account of his journey in the village ledger, mishaps and all.

Something kept jamming into his cheek, so his eyes fluttered open, and he groaned.

"Please, stop that," he said, voice hoarse and unrecognizable.

"Your eyes are really pretty, like the master's, but also different," came a curious female voice. "What's that black stuff all over your face?"

Next to Alaric sat a girl, maybe ten or twelve, with short dark hair cut close to her scalp, brown eyes, and heavily freckled cheeks. She stared at Alaric, expression quizzical, but she didn't seem hostile. Her hands were folded in her lap, but she had an excitable energy and quivered as though she wanted to touch Alaric's face again.

"Who? Uh," he started, then paused. "Where am I?" *Where* seemed the easiest question, though he had a pretty good idea.

"In your bedroom," the girl said and smiled. Her eyes sparkled, and dimples formed in her cheeks. She was adorable but also making no sense.

"You're gonna need to elaborate on that," he said and tried to sit up. Blinding pain filled his head, and he slammed back down onto soft pillows. They definitely weren't the pillows from his room at home. They were plush and smelled slightly of oranges and spices.

"Oh, you shouldn't move. You were pretty tired. And hurt a bit. Your feet are really tough though! And your hands too. I noticed when I was watching over you this morning." She sounded smug and way too proud of her observations as most children were. She continued, "The healer gave you a potion. You've been sleeping forever."

"Forever?" Alaric gasped and tried once again to sit up. This time, the girl gave him a gentle shove. She was much stronger than she looked, and Alaric fell back. His breath came out ragged and fast, and the girl stared down at him, concerned. He asked, "How long is forever? Where am I?"

Alaric heard a door open, and his eyes darted around. He couldn't see much from his vantage point, flat on his back, but he was on a bed surrounded by pillows in varying shades of violet and red. The room was painted pale gold and shimmered in the candlelight, but the decorations were sparse. A small table sat off to one side, a single purple vase atop it with a clutch of red flowers. He wasn't sure what kind; he would need to check the book from his father. His father! How long had he been gone? His parents would be so worried!

"Emilia. Stop bothering him and get back to work. You're needed in the kitchens," a stern voice demanded from the door. The girl waved at Alaric and slipped away, quiet as a shadow. A great, heaving sigh came, and the voice said, "My apologies. She volunteered to keep watch on you, but we always forget how inquisitive she is."

"Can you please tell me what the hellis going on?" Alaric asked and turned his head toward the voice. This didn't cause him pain, which was an improvement from the last few minutes.

A man of medium height and build sauntered into view, eyebrows like bushy black crows flying over black eyes. All black, no whites or irises, just bottomless pupils. He took in Alaric's appearance with obvious disdain, appraising every inch. Alaric chanced a look down at himself and was very glad his robe was closed, preserving his modesty. His mind flashed back to hungry flaming eyes, and he clutched the robe tighter across his body.

"No need for theatrics," said the man, his voice a pleasant drawl that didn't match his hardened features. "I have absolutely no interest in that." He indicated Alaric's entire body, and Alaric felt a bit offended.

"I...I don't mean to be rude," said Alaric, trying to relax his body. His arms and legs didn't feel nearly as sore as they had when he arrived at the mountain, and his feet didn't hurt at all. His head pounded a painful beat when he spoke. "I'm sorry, but my head..."

"Hurts? I'm sure," said the man. "Healing potions are tricky for humans. You should be fine in a few hours."

Humans? Alaric wasn't sure what the man meant by that. Wasn't he also human?

"Please, I just want to know where I am," he pleaded, averting his gaze so the man couldn't see the tears forming. Alaric flexed his fingers and toes just to be sure he was still in one piece.

"If you don't remember yesterday, that potion must have done more than we expected," tutted the man. He moved around the bed and muttered something Alaric couldn't hear. He stopped at the small table and touched one of the flowers, a petal coming away in his fingers. The man rubbed the petal between his thumb and middle finger, staining them red. As though recalling that he wasn't alone, the man straightened up and said, "You are currently the guest of his most esteemed grace, the Sun God. Congratulations." His last word dripped with condescension, and the tears dried in Alaric's eyes.

"His guest? What the hell is that supposed to mean?"

"You've been given chambers off the throne room," the man continued. "Be grateful you're alive."

Alaric bit back an angry retort. He needed this man on his side, or he might not get more information until he could walk and take a look around. He didn't trust that he'd be up and about in a few hours like the man said. Nothing had gone according to the ceremony Alaric envisioned. Everything seemed wrong and off balance. Although the little girl had been kind of nice.

"Good, you've learned to hold your tongue," said the man, crossing his arms. The red petal fell from his hand and drifted onto the bed, Alaric's bed, apparently. "My name is Kuroi Ryu, and I run this household. You will not see much of me after today. I have more important things to do than watch over a random tribute from nowhere consequential who stumbled into this temple. I shall send someone to attend to you this afternoon. Until then, get as much rest as you can."

Kuroi spun on his heel and made to leave. Alaric thought quickly; he needed an ally, and this guy wasn't going to be it. "Wait! Can it be that little girl who was just here?"

"Little girl?" Kuroi raised an eyebrow then nodded. "Ah, Emilia. Yes, I suppose she is a little girl to you. I'm sure both you and I will regret this, but yes. I can send her to you once her chores are finished in the kitchens."

"I know I'm not welcome here," Alaric said, apologetic. He didn't want to be anyone's burden, even if Kuroi was unpleasant and sharp. "But it's not like I chose it..." he trailed off and Kuroi's abyssal eyes looked him over once more.

"Indeed," was the only thing Kuroi said as he strode through the door and closed it lightly.

Everything went quiet in the kitchens when Kuroi entered, his posture straight and severe. After a moment, the chef glared at him and said, "And now I have to cook for a *human*? As if I don't have enough on my plate with the master and feeding this lot."

Imposing as the dormant volcano itself, Shefu had the face of a hardened criminal but the voice of a lark. Although it still stunned when her beautiful voice skewered you. She towered over everyone in the temple, well over seven feet tall, with muscles like large hams. Her staff scrambled away not wanting to be in the blast zone of the incoming argument.

"You're under the false impression that I also have time to deal with this," drawled Kuroi. "We all have full schedules, Shefu, not just you."

Neither broke the stare until a small head insinuated itself between them.

"I have time!" Emilia squealed, cheeks bright and teeth on display.

"You absolutely do not. You have plenty to do here," scoffed the chef, glaring down at the small servant.

"Actually, the human requested Emilia," said Kuroi. "So, we shall have to move some things around to accommodate him."

The staff paused to watch, and Emilia's head practically spun around on her neck, trying to catch the nonverbal words that flew between the chef and Kuroi. Finally, the chef threw up her hands and banged a heavy cast iron pan down on the long prep table.

"Accommodate a human? What has this temple come to?" She spat the question out as though it tasted vile.

"I think it's cool," said Emilia, and the chef bopped her on the head.

"That's because you're young and don't know any better," she said.

Kuroi rolled his eyes and cleared his throat. The chef turned away, muttering about humans and what they ate and how disgusting it was and how was she supposed to get meat of all things.

Emilia beamed up at Kuroi, unconcerned with his piercing gaze. "Should I go right now?" she asked.

"Yes," Kuroi said, "but be sure not to tell the human any details about the temple that he doesn't need to know. You're old enough to know your responsibility is to the master."

"Like, what shouldn't I tell him?"

"The human doesn't need to know anything," said the chef, brandishing a large copper ladle. "He should stay in that room unless he's called for."

"That's enough, Shefu," said Kuroi, and he returned his attention to Emilia. "If you think it's something the master wouldn't tell someone, then keep it to yourself."

"The master doesn't tell anyone anything," Emilia said, frowning.

"Exactly," answered Kuroi. "Let's get you back up to the main level. You can take the human on a standard temple tour when he's able but stay away from the master's chambers."

"Even I'm not brave enough to go in there," she said and looked at her feet.

"As you should be."

"Unprecedented," the chef mumbled as Emilia scooted out of the kitchen in Kuroi's wake.

When Alaric woke up, Emilia was staring at him, perched on a stool next to the bed. He nearly leapt from the bed, clutching his robe closed.

"Ohhhhhhhh are you naked under that?" she asked. "That's pretty embarrassing."

"That's none of your business and also really unhelpful," Alaric said, eyes wide, but he was happy that his head wasn't aching after his mad lunge away from the girl.

"I'm not known for being helpful," Emilia said, an odd pride in her countenance. So that's why Kuroi said Alaric would regret asking for Emilia.

"Fair enough. But could you maybe help a little just this once?"

"I suppose. No one's ever asked for me before." She moved back and forth on the stool, enraptured by Alaric. "We should probably find you some clothes if you're gonna be all snobby about being naked."

"That's not fair! You're not naked."

Emilia pondered his answer for a moment then said, "Are all humans this finicky about things?"

"What's with the 'human' talk? You're human, right? At least, you're not a god..." Emilia looked like a normal person to Alaric. Her skin didn't shine, and she didn't have any extra limbs or eyes. She wasn't a rare creature from what he could see.

"Oh, I'm not human. Not anymore. No one else in the temple is. Most of us are sentient spirits. I guess people call us shades? There are a few god-touched too, and one demigod who comes and goes as he pleases. He's a lazy, good-for-nothing waste of space." She said everything so matter-of-fact that Alaric had to categorize each sentence and decide what to ask next. He had no idea what she was talking about.

"It's not nice to call someone a waste of space, you know."

"That's just what Shefu always says," Emilia said, biting her fingernail. "He seems all right, just really quiet."

25

"You shouldn't repeat that kind of stuff even if you think it's funny." Alaric rubbed his eyes. This wasn't where he had expected his day to go. Had no one bothered to teach the girl—the shade—manners?

"Okay but why not?" She wasn't upset by what he'd said. On the contrary, he had her complete attention.

"Because it could hurt someone's feelings," he explained.

"Oh, those. I don't think Oken has feelings."

Alaric choked on his reply. "Everyone has feelings!"

Emilia studied him, assessing his answer. "Humans don't know everything."

He opened and closed his mouth like a stunned fish, unsure what would convince her to be nicer. "Moving on," he began, and she tilted her head, dancing in place on the stool.

"This is way more fun than work," she said.

"You're a...a shade then?"

"Yup! I died a long time ago. But I didn't want to stay in the Underworld, super boring, so I petitioned for a spot in the temples. I was really lucky to get the Temple of the Sun. Hardly anyone gets to work here." Her eyes shone when she mentioned the temple, and Alaric scrunched his nose. The temple wasn't his idea of a great place.

"Wait, so you're a soul! And you can just leave the Underworld? That's wild."

"No, silly, you can't just leave," she rolled her eyes and nearly fell off the stool. "You have to petition. And it can take a really long time to get permission. I was down there for hundreds of years. The Lord of the Underworld is fun though. He's so cranky!"

Alaric didn't think a cranky deity sounded fun, but he didn't question her. Instead, he asked, "You're solid?"

Emilia's hand darted out and pinched his arm, and she giggled when he jumped. "We're solid when we're in the human world at least. You could see right through me in the Underworld. We wouldn't be much good as servants if we couldn't touch things."

"That's true," Alaric murmured. He reached toward Emilia, and she grabbed his hand, looking over each finger. It felt like being touched by a normal human, and Alaric smiled. But he thought about his mother's hand on his cheek, calming him after a bad day, and his father's strong grip on his shoulder, complimenting him for some minor task. A lone tear trickled down his face, and he sniffled, getting Emilia's attention. He looked at her then rubbed the tear away. "Sorry, I just…how long do you think he's going to keep me here?"

Emilia's pupils expanded, and she hummed to herself. "No one tells me stuff like that," she said and put his hand down on the bed. "But I don't think he wants to kill you!"

Alaric chuckled. He wasn't so sure about that, but he didn't contradict the girl.

"Don't you want to stay here? The temple is really nice! We've got everything you could want. Chef's making human food for you even though she doesn't want to."

"I hope so; otherwise, it wouldn't matter if he didn't want to kill me. I'd die pretty fast."

"You're funny. I like you," Emilia said and jumped off the stool. "Can you stand up? It's been about the right time according to Kuroi."

Alaric tensed his body, checking for discomfort, and he moved his arms in wide circles. "Might as well give it a try," he said. Alaric grabbed each of his legs and swung them off the bed, bending the knees up and down a few times. No lasting pain there either. Whatever potion they'd given him was a wonder. "Wow, I feel a lot better."

"The Forest God has the best potions," said Emilia, inclining her head. She grasped his hands and pulled before he could inquire about the Forest God and dragged Alaric to his feet.

"Whoa! You're strong for how little you are."

"Shades are much stronger than humans," she said and pulled him around the room. "This is your room. It's not very big, but it's bigger than mine. Mine is really small, but I don't have to share. There's a window over there, but Kuroi covered it for now. I'm sure you'll get window privileges soon."

"Uh, window privileges?"

"There's a trunk at the foot of the bed—you need a large bed, because you're tall—and I think your bag is in the trunk. They brought something up from your cart last night. That has clothes in it right? We don't really *wear* clothes; this is just what we're assigned when we leave the Underworld and get a specific temple." She picked at her tunic and leggings, which were black with orange and yellow swirls. "We can't take them off since we're not fully corporeal. That means 'real.' Ours are the best uniforms. You should see the ones from the Temple of Lightning, so ugly."

Alaric couldn't get a word in as Emilia continued, telling him every detail about his room down to the paint and the pillows. She stopped at the table and looked askance at the vase and flowers. "I'm not sure about those. Master doesn't really like flowers." She shrugged and sat back on the stool, watching him. Alaric wasn't sure what to do, so he forced a smile.

"Your pointy teeth are really cool too...Didn't you want to put clothes on?" Emilia asked, pointing at the trunk.

"Oh! Yeah."

He knelt beside the large trunk and traced the sunburst carvings with a finger. The wood was dark, almost black, and Alaric wondered where it came from. No trees like that existed in the forest outside. He opened the lid, biting the inside of his cheek. It smelled good, that spicy citrus perfume again. His bag was inside but so were stacks of clean shirts, folded trousers, and stretchy leggings, all in neutral colors. Alaric didn't recognize the material, but each item flowed through his hands, supple and warm. He didn't like the look of all those clothes.

Placing the bag on the bed, which *was* fairly large now that he could see the whole thing, Alaric pulled out the spare long-sleeved tunic, pants, and underclothes he'd packed for the return trip. Maybe he would be able to get out of the temple quickly...but he felt a twinge in his chest, remembering how the Sun God had touched him. He wasn't going anywhere without the furious god's permission.

He started to disrobe before recalling his audience. He caught the purple robe at his hips. Emilia sat on her stool, staring at him, grin plastered on her face. He bit his lip, gestured at his clothes, and said, "Do you mind?"

"Nope!"

Alaric chuckled and made a spinning motion with one finger. "Turn around."

"Oh fine," she said, covering her eyes and turning on the stool. "It's not like I've never seen someone naked before. Master walks around all the time without clothes on."

Alaric sputtered and nearly fell over, his foot catching in one pants leg. "What?"

"Don't worry. He never does that around humans."

"But you said there aren't any humans here!" He pulled up the pants and laced them tightly, glancing around, blushing. What if he ran into the Sun God prowling around his temple, completely nude?

"I suppose humans *are* only here during the offering ceremony," Emilia said and spun around. "So, I have no clue what he might do with a human around all the time."

"Hey! I'm not done!"

"Your important bits are all covered," she said and stepped over to him, eyeing the gold chain across his chest.

"Don't even think about touching that," he warned and pulled the tunic over his head.

"Wasn't gonna touch it," she said, disgruntled.

"Uh huh, sure." He reached out and tapped her head, making her giggle. "Shoes…"

Emilia rushed past him and grabbed some soft-soled sandals from the floor and handed them to him. He sat on the bed to put them on.

"There weren't any shoes in your cart," she said. "I guess you can wear these around the temple. They shouldn't wreck the floors. Most of us just walk around barefoot. Especially the god-touched. They love having bare feet."

"That's the other thing I wanted to ask you," said Alaric, snapping his fingers. "What does 'god-touched' mean?"

"They don't teach humans much, do they?"

"Hey, I might not be the smartest guy in my village, but I was good in school." He patted the bed next to him, and Emilia hopped up. "But we don't know about this stuff. It's not like we live with a god."

"That's a good excuse, I guess," she said and sucked her teeth. "You can't help what you don't know. God-touched people were human once, but now they're not."

"That's it?"

She snorted, as if she knew a troublesome student when she saw one. "Let's start with the basics," she said and ticked things off on her fingers as she spoke. "First, there's the gods. They are the oldest beings in the universe and can't die."

"I got that much," he laughed.

"Shush. Let me finish. Next you have the demigods. They're usually half god and half human. They can live forever, but they can be killed even though you wouldn't want to try. They don't have specific powers usually, but they're almost indestructible. Oken, the one who lives here but is never around, he's got two powers: fire and ice. That's really rare."

"That's awesome," said Alaric, covering his mouth when Emilia glared at him again. "Sorry. Keep going."

"The god-touched are a weird offshoot of demigods. They can die, but they live a long time, and they don't usually get any powers besides living longer unless they already had a power or skill. They've got at least a little bit of godly power inside."

"How do they become god-touched? Are they born?"

"Nah, they have to be around a god for a while. Something about too much sex or drinking a god's blood."

All the color drained from Alaric's face, and his hands clamped down on the bed sheets.

Did she just say, "Too much sex?"

"Are you okay? Your face got really pale."

"I'll be fine."

30

She gave him a doubting look, probably thinking him frail and stupid. Alaric couldn't have that. She might be hundreds of years older than him, but she was still a kid.

"Really, I'm okay. So long as I don't have to drink anyone's blood."

"I don't think it's that bad," she said, finger on her bottom lip. "Kuroi, Shefu, and Draiden are all god-touched, and I think they did the blood ritual with the master."

Not knowing how to respond, Alaric stared at the wall and tried to mentally teleport himself out of the temple and off the mountain.

Emilia ignored his shell-shocked expression and said, "We shouldn't take the tour until we fix your face."

"Tour? I get to leave this room?" Maybe he did have chance at escape. "Wait, what's wrong with my face?"

Emilia jumped off the bed and opened a hidden drawer on the bedside table, pulling out a silvery mirror. She held it in front of his face, and Alaric's jaw dropped. His cheeks and eyes were covered in black smudges, like soot.

"Did you rub ashes on me or something?" He squeaked, pushing his fingers into his cheeks.

"That won't help! Let me get the cleaning oil. When that's done, I can do your eyes again."

On another spindle-legged table in the corner sat a globular ceramic pitcher, a large ceramic bowl, and five blown-glass containers each smaller than the last. Lavender-colored towels lay next to the bowl. Emilia opened each glass container and sniffed before deciding on the smallest.

"This is the cleaning oil. It will take almost anything off your skin and make it silky and smooth."

"Great," Alaric said. *Good thing I'm so obsessed with my skin*, he thought sarcastically.

Emilia sat next to him, towel in hand. She dabbed oil onto the towel and told him to close his eyes. The oil smelled like wisteria in spring. She drew the towel down his cheeks and across his eyelids with care, touching his face with gentle fingertips to wipe away the excess oil.

"What is this obsession with drawing on my eyes?" Alaric asked. "That Draiden guy did it before I came up to the temple."

"I should have figured that's what was all over your face. It used to be fashionable. Draiden's just really old. He probably thought the master would like it."

"Would he?"

She shrugged, unconcerned as though whether the Sun God liked his looks was immaterial.

Alaric glanced through one eyelid, and Emilia was hyper-focused, tongue peeking out through her pink lips. "I'm gonna put kohl lines on your eyelids right above the lashes. Makes your eyes look bigger."

"My eyes are already big."

"Bigger is better."

"All right! I'm sick of arguing."

Emilia made him wash his face when she finished with the oil, but the water was cool and refreshing, so Alaric didn't mind. There were worse things than being bossed around by a little girl. Next, she told him to sit on the stool and close his eyes. She penciled in dark lines above his eyelashes, but this time, Alaric got to see what he looked like. She held the silver mirror aloft, preening at her flawless technique, and Alaric had to agree: the kohl liner made his eyes nearly pop right out of his head.

"I look..."

"Pretty!" Emilia shouted, throwing her hands in the air. "At least your face looks pretty. Your clothes are a little common."

He chuckled. "I am a little common, Em." She vibrated in place at the nickname, eyes widening in pleasure. Alaric made a little bow and put out his hand so she could pull him up from the stool. "Now. What was that about a tour?"

It took the rest of the afternoon for Emilia to lead Alaric through the temple. Alaric suspected that he wasn't getting the deluxe tour, but he didn't mind. He hoped she would take him closer to the main entrance, but she skirted around that hallway and avoided the throne room as well. Maybe because it was the Sun God's territory.

The temple had every room imaginable and seemed to go on forever. There was a solarium with massive glass panels that let in the fading sunlight, a library overflowing with books and scrolls, an enormous indoor swimming pool filled with crystal clear water. Baths filled with steaming water that smelled of the sea.

They met a few servants on their way through the common areas, but they averted their eyes or giggled when they saw Alaric. Emilia shrugged when he asked about them and said, "Not like they've seen a living human in a thousand years or anything."

Alaric stopped asking after that. Did he remind the shades of their former lives? Was he making things harder for them?

"Why do you look so sad?" Emilia asked when they stopped in a verdant conservatory overfilling with shrubs and herbs.

Alaric crouched down by a flowering fern and pointed at it. Emilia sat down next to him, waiting for an explanation. Are shades like these plants?" he asked. "You can't leave, right? So, you're stuck in the temple, and even though it's huge and beautiful and they treat you okay, you're still stuck. It doesn't seem right."

Emilia patted his knee and shook her head. "That's just your human brain talking. When you're like me, you'll understand better," she said. "Remember, most of us who work here are dead. If we weren't here, we'd be in the Underworld working for Lord Veles or in some other temple. There's no eternal rest for us, not like in the stories."

She paused and poked the fern. "Don't look at me like that!" she said. "It's not like the gods sit around doing nothing all day while we do all the work. They have jobs, really tough jobs, and it's an honor to help them."

Alaric laughed but with no humor. "It didn't seem like the Sun God was doing that much."

"That's one day a year," Emilia scoffed and took his hand. "It takes a lot of focus and power to keep the sun where it's supposed to be and move it at the right time. Master has to be especially careful on ceremony days because his attention is split." She stood up and pulled him with her. "Do you understand?"

Alaric nodded, but he didn't truly understand what she meant. The other day in the throne room, Alaric had felt boredom from the Sun God, then arrogance and a perilous rage.

As though she knew Alaric hadn't gotten her point, Emilia sighed and tugged at his hand. "It doesn't matter. You don't need to know the particulars anyway. Now that you're his—" She clamped her lips shut and dropped his hand.

"Now that I'm his what?" Alaric asked, unsure he wanted to hear the answer.

A chime sounded deeper in the temple, and Emilia looked relieved. Alaric didn't press the question. He had a pretty good idea what was expected of him.

"That's the dinner chime," Emilia said, wiping her brow. "Not your dinner, for the shades. We eat before the master because he's busy until the sun sets."

"Do I eat at the same time as you?" Alaric asked, curiosity returning. His stomach rumbled as he spoke, and Emilia giggled. He laughed too. "I guess I'm hungry."

"You haven't eaten in a while. You're not supposed to eat anything on a healing potion." Her eyebrows crunched together as she thought. "I'm not sure what we're supposed to do about your food. Shefu was experimenting with things in the kitchen, but she hasn't needed to make human food for a long time."

"Well, what do you eat?" Alaric asked, concern for his empty stomach rising.

"Usual shade stuff, intangible energies made to look like food."

"Ah. Okay. I don't think I can eat intangible...energies?"

"That would be really funny if you tried!" Emilia exclaimed. "I'll take you down to the kitchen and see what we're supposed to do. Kuroi didn't give me a schedule or anything."

Kuroi's black eyes glared side-long at Alaric and Emilia after the chef howled for him to appear. The god-touched woman was massive, taller than Alaric, and built like a stone wall. Alaric doubted that any man in his village could have beaten her in an arm-wrestling match, and he stood before her massive bulk, obviously in her way and ruining her evening.

"Kuroi," she said when the man slid into the kitchen. "Remove this obstruction at once so I can get back to work."

Alaric didn't like being called an obstruction or being talked about like he wasn't in the room, but the chef was almost scarier than the Sun God.

"I'm really sorry. I don't mean to be a bother," he said and bowed at the waist before her. The rest of the kitchen staff gaped at him, and Kuroi's mouth twitched in what might have been a smile.

"Well, you ARE a bother," she said, and slammed a rolling pin into one hand. "I don't have the faintest idea what to serve a human anymore. Spending the entire day researching human food was not what I had planned. I'm a very busy woman. Do you have ANY idea what it takes to run this kitchen?"

"I apologize for my presence, ma'am! If it helps, I can eat almost anything," Alaric said, gulping, still bowed. "Vegetables, fruit, bread, cheese, eggs, fish, meat—"

"Meat!" shrieked the chef. "What has this temple come to?"

"I don't need meat," he assured, leaning back up and waving his hands in the air. "Whatever you have, I'm sure it will be wonderful! It smells really good down here, and Emilia's been raving about your cooking." The chef's heated face remained stagnant, the rolling pin still clutched in her hand.

"You see, Shefu? The boy is perfectly willing to eat whatever you have to offer." Kuroi turned to Alaric as the kitchen staff's trance was broken. They bustled away, flour-covered faces hiding smiles. "If you're finished with this minor theatrical, please allow me to lead you to the dining room," Kuroi droned.

He gestured out the kitchen door and Alaric retreated, thankful. Emilia was close behind, not about to be roped into kitchen duty. Alaric winked at her as she fell in step beside him, and she covered her mouth, giggling.

"I told you that you wouldn't be seeing much of me, and yet here we are," Kuroi said without looking back at Alaric and Emilia. Both of them straightened their backs and looked ahead, trying not to laugh harder. "Really, Emilia. You are over five hundred years old. Act like it. And you." He spun around, arms clasped behind his back. Both Alaric and Emilia slammed to a stop before running into Kuroi. He tilted his chin up and narrowed his eyes. "You might be an ignorant human, but your village chose you as tribute for a reason. Attempt to seek that potential while you remain a guest in this temple."

Kuroi led them up a flight of stairs past the throne room and into a formal dining room. A massive ebony table sat in the middle of the floor, festooned with a cloth of gold table runner. There were two chairs on each end of the long table, but only one place was set, a glimmering molten gold charger beneath a matte black ceramic plate covered with a cloth of gold napkin. The flatware was also gold.

"There's, um," Alaric began then stopped and rubbed his arm. Candles gleamed in alcoves along the walls and had been laid on the table, giving the room an ethereal quality. It was very quiet, and no one else was in the room. The great hall in his village was nothing compared to this room, and yet, Alaric missed the raucous laughter and smell of spilled ale.

He glanced at Emilia, who grinned up at him. No help there. "Can Emilia stay with me? I don't want to eat alone." He sounded pathetic, but what could they expect? He was the only human in a temple full of supernatural beings, and only one of them seemed interested in being near him.

Kuroi braced himself before he answered. "Emilia may stay since I know she stuffed herself with shade pastries while the chef was busy yelling at you." He glanced at the small girl by Alaric's side, but she wasn't bothered that Kuroi had seen her theft. She put her hands behind her back and smiled up at the terrifying man. Alaric wouldn't have dared look at Kuroi that way or stolen food from the kitchen.

"Thank you," Alaric said and bowed.

Kuroi raised an eyebrow. "All this bowing is going to give us big heads. Please, sit. Your meal will be brought up presently."

Emilia dragged Alaric over to the table and shoved him into a plush, high-backed chair. He gazed down the long table, wondering if anyone ever sat at the other end. Maybe the Sun God ate somewhere else.

"Don't look so worried," Kuroi said before ducking out of the room to attend to his other duties. "I'm certain Shefu has found suitable food for you."

"Was that a joke?" Alaric asked Emilia when the door swung shut.

"I don't know. He's not normally very funny," she admitted, grabbing his knife and looking at her reflection in the shiny gold and picking between her teeth.

Alaric was glad he at least had one friend in the temple even if she was a five-hundred-year-old child.

A week and a half passed without Alaric catching a glimpse of the Sun God. He spent his days wandering around the temple with Emilia, reading in the library, which she hated, or lounging in the solarium, at which she excelled. She hadn't allowed him near the throne room or the main doors, besides bringing him to and from his room, keeping him corralled to her favorite places.

They snuck down to the kitchens in the early mornings when the sun peeked over the horizon to beg for fresh bread or sweets, and the kitchen staff supplied them readily. Shefu must have gotten a handle on human pastries because the staff were ready with tarts, croissants, and fluffy biscuits for Alaric while also giving Emilia shade-edible food. She liked to smell whatever Alaric got, inhaling the fresh aromas like a starving man in a barren desert.

"Shade food just isn't the same," she pouted as he sank his teeth into a buttery roll.

"It's not my fault you're dead," Alaric joked, elbowing her in the shoulder.

"It could be!" she yelled, tackling him out the kitchen door as the bakers cackled.

It got a little easier every day for Alaric to be in the temple as he got to know the shades and tried to talk to Shefu, who hip-checked him out of her kitchen if she caught him there, but it also became more difficult. He worried that his parents didn't know what happened to him, and since Ichigo was stabled at the foot of the mountain, they didn't have a horse returning without a rider either. It was as though Alaric and Ichigo had disappeared into nothingness, merely a memory that might fade.

On the third day, he asked Emilia if he could send his parents a message just to let them know he was okay, that he was alive. But she evaded the question and bothered him to take her swimming in the big indoor pool. If Emilia wasn't willing to talk about it, Alaric doubted asking Kuroi would do him any good.

The stern head of the temple flitted in and out of their days, ushering Alaric to the dining room in the evenings and watching with blank eyes when they moved from the solarium to the library for Emilia's daily reading torture. Alaric was sure Kuroi wanted to stay away from them, needing to tend to his own job, but something kept him coming back. Alaric knew it would be rude to ask, so he didn't. Kuroi wasn't just a servant. He was the towering beam that held up the household. Alaric wondered if the Sun God appreciated that.

It had almost been two weeks since the ceremony day when Kuroi burst into the library to find Alaric pouring over a scroll about an ancient war, Emilia nearly comatose in a chair nearby, a book draped across her lap like an errant cat.

"Return to your room immediately and dress for dinner," Kuroi said, back straight and lips a slim line. Emilia's book fell to the floor as she bounced to her feet, fully awake in an instant. Something in Kuroi's tone recharged her, and her eyes stared helplessly at Alaric. He had the feeling their vacation was over.

"The way I'm dressed isn't okay?" Alaric asked, stepping away from the scroll. Emilia's eyes widened, and Kuroi's posture stiffened. Alaric raised his hands. "Okay, okay. I can take a hint. What's going on?"

Kuroi cleared his throat and motioned for Emilia to leave. She scampered out of the library faster than Alaric had ever seen her move. When she was gone, Kuroi's shoulders fell a fraction of an inch, almost imperceptibly. He quirked a finger at Alaric, signaling him to follow. They left the library and headed for Alaric's room. Kuroi didn't speak until they were behind the door, and Alaric felt so nervous he thought his body might split in two. Emilia wasn't in his room.

"His most excellent highness has requested your presence for dinner," Kuroi said stiffly, and a shudder ran down Alaric's spine. He tried to fashion an excuse in his mind for why he couldn't go; a stomach pain, a headache, his leg had mysteriously fallen off. But he knew nothing would deter the god's iron will.

"What do I do, Kuroi?" he whispered, fingers twisting together. "I don't know what to do."

Kuroi walked up to Alaric and brushed nonexistent lint off his shoulder, and Alaric was violently reminded of his mother. Emilia put an extra thick layer of kohl around his eyes that morning, so he held back the tears that wanted desperately to fall. He stood up straighter and swallowed back his panic. Kuroi actually smiled at him and grasped his arms with strong hands. Alaric remembered that Kuroi was god-touched, infinitely stronger than him and yet his touch was light.

"I don't know what he wants from you," Kuroi admitted. It was as if the words had been forced from his lips, but he continued, voice an authoritative drawl. "I love my master, and I know him better than most. But in this...you are alone. I cannot help you."

"How am I supposed to talk to him? I spit at his feet that day." Alaric choked back a sob, and Kuroi's grip tightened. "I should be dead. I dishonored the Sun God in his temple. I looked at him. I *saw* him. But he didn't kill me." Alaric tugged at Kuroi's tunic, which was more substantial than Emilia's clothes. Kuroi was still alive, his tunic real and soft in Alaric's hands. Alaric clutched the man like a life raft. "He's the most beautiful person I've ever seen, but I'm afraid. Please tell me something. Anything."

Kuroi shoved Alaric backwards but held him so he didn't stumble, and Alaric thought he saw a light flash in the man's blank eyes. He said, "Alaric Shina, from Togarashi village, you are unbreakable."

Chapter Three

Alaric had never worn anything so fine as his dinner outfit. Kuroi chose it for him—a high-collared long-sleeve tunic in black velvet, chased with gold piping along the neck and cuffs, and simple black trousers. Kuroi told Alaric that the fabric from both garments came from a distant place, an island full of master textile artists, and Alaric believed him. The clothes appeared out of nowhere, definitely not from the trunk at the foot of Alaric's bed, and were laid on the bed, waiting for him. He felt unassailable in these clothes, untouchable. And yet, he knew if the Sun God wanted to touch him, he would.

Kuroi said, "Don't rub your eyes; the kohl is set from this morning. Your hair is fine, but we'll need to touch it up soon. If that's what you wish."

Alaric smiled at that, saying, "Yeah, I like my hair. No one else in the temple has red hair."

"Indeed," Kuroi said. "They do not."

After he dressed, Alaric found Emilia cowering outside his room, afraid for him. She stared at him, eyes wide, her mouth a small o-shape, and she grasped his hand as they walked to the dining room. Alaric was glad for the tiny comfort of someone holding his hand because Emilia wouldn't be allowed in the dining room tonight. Kuroi led them and shooed the girl away when they reached the door. He arched an eyebrow at Alaric but also smiled, teeth showing through his lips.

"You can do this," he whispered before running his hands across Alaric's shoulders, smoothing the fabric.

The door swung inward, and Alaric stepped through.

The dining room didn't look different, but Alaric felt like it had sunken thousands of feet underwater. The candles burned in the alcoves and across the table, and the table settings were the same.

A smartly dressed shade with thick brown hair and a pleasant face stood beside the door and gestured Alaric to his seat at the long table. The shade pulled out Alaric's chair, and he sat, heart pounding.

The matching chair down the table was empty.

The table was laden with food, and it smelled delicious. Shefu had gone all out for this dinner, covering the table with vegetable dishes and fruit, succulent whole trout and whitefish in the center, a caramelized rabbit saddle, and countless plates of cheese and bread. Alaric counted three different honeys just on his end of the table.

He dared touch nothing. The male shade stood beside his chair ready to serve, but the Sun God did not appear. Alaric held his head aloft and his hands in his lap, waiting. If there was one thing Alaric was good at, it was waiting.

Twenty minutes passed, and steam stopped rising from the dishes. Alaric knew there was some kind of godly power afoot that would keep the food hot, but Shefu was a stickler for presentation and punctuality. She couldn't be pleased that her master was late to his own dinner.

At half past, the door on the other end of the room finally slammed open, and Alaric stiffened in his chair, the shade beside him equally nervous. He felt tension wafting off the shade and hoped no one else could. He wanted to reach out and grasp the shade's hand, but he couldn't. The shade loosened up beside him as though he felt Alaric's wish for his comfort and straightened his back.

A harassed-looking female shade with dark hair in a severe bun marched up to the table on the Sun God's side of the room. Alaric had never seen her before, but she put out a dominant energy, making the shade on his side take a step back.

"His most glorious countenance," the female shade began, voice like darkened honey, "the God of the Sun, Governor of the Day, Keeper of the Eternal Light." She bowed her head and stepped backwards away from the table.

And the Sun God stepped through the door.

Alaric let out the breath he had been holding, and the shade beside him pretended not to notice. Not wanting to stare at the Sun God, Alaric peered at his shade attendant and thought his name might be Matthias. Poor man, forced to attend on a human who had no idea what to do or how to behave in front of a god. Why hadn't Kuroi explained anything? Why had he left Alaric to flounder alone?

Why was the Sun God so beautiful?

The Sun God wore the same barely-there clothing from the offering ceremony, the kilt hanging off his hips, daring anyone not to look at his toned torso or powerful thighs. Now that Alaric wasn't exhausted, he understood why the god had chosen his apparel: it was subtle but rich, elegant but simple, contradictory, and sure to put people off balance. He stalked up to the table, arms swinging, and glared down the length either internally criticizing the food or Alaric's appearance.

Alaric lifted his chin and stared right back. Whatever the god's arrogant nature, he seemed to appreciate poise and strength, and Alaric could fake both. He vowed not to be the first one to break the silence. The candles flickered, unmoved by the sentient actions in the dining room. Alaric wondered how the light reflected off his hair because it did dazzling things with the Sun God's unruly locks.

Both shades looked at each other, then at Alaric and the Sun God. They couldn't agree non-verbally on a course of action, so the female shade stepped to the Sun God's side and whispered in his ear. His eyes shifted ever so slightly toward her but tracked right back on Alaric after a moment.

42

His eyes glowed in the candlelight, and Alaric felt his heart leap in his chest. He really hoped the shade couldn't see the faint twitch in his trousers, but the man didn't budge.

Keep it together you idiot. This god wants you dead or at least broken. Don't listen to your dick.

The female shade pulled out the Sun God's chair and beckoned him to sit. And he did, surprising Alaric. Did the Sun God listen to this female shade? Why hadn't Alaric seen her when he and Emilia scouted the temple?

Once the Sun God was seated, as if on an unseen cue, both shades stepped forward and grabbed the golden napkins off Alaric's and the Sun God's plates and draped them dramatically in their laps. Alaric suppressed a "thank you," not knowing if it was appropriate, but his shade winked at him, acknowledging the sentiment.

Once the unveiling of the napkins was over, more shades filled the dining room. They hovered, grabbing dishes, and circling the table, offering the Sun God and Alaric items from each plate or tray. Alaric noticed that they brought the dishes to both of them, so the Sun God must be able to eat human food. He waved away almost everything, taking mostly vegetable dishes and fruit, all while watching what Alaric chose. Not wanting to upset Shefu, Alaric took a little of everything until his plate was full. The shades all smiled slightly in turn when he nodded at them to serve a portion, and he tried to appear cheery and positive.

Having served everything, the shades disappeared from the room, leaving only Alaric's and the Sun God's personal attendants.

Alaric waited for the Sun God to take the first bite, which took longer than he expected. He peered around the dish-laden table, looking for a sign that the god had started eating. Finally, his shade attendant gave him a small signal, one finger pointed down at his side, and Alaric breathed out, knowing he could eat.

They didn't speak as they ate, and the candles drooped lower across the table, wax dripping down their sides. Alaric tried to enjoy the feast because he knew it had been meticulously made for him. Alaric nibbled at the fish and rabbit, savoring each bite. After a while, he forgot that the Sun God was at the other end of the table and dug in with gusto, giving in to his appetite. This was the first time the chef had served anything close to meat, and Alaric realized he was starving for it. He finished off the rabbit on his plate, and his shade attendant moved forward swiftly, pulling the dish off the table to offer Alaric more. He murmured a thank you, grateful for his help.

When he had finished off the rabbit, Alaric heard a dark chuckle from the other end of the table. Alaric's shade stiffened beside him, then moved away into the shadows, hugging the dining room wall. Alaric looked around, wondering if he'd done something wrong.

"You're cleaner than most humans, I'll admit, and you've been taught how to use a fork," came a familiar, thick raspy voice, and Alaric's silverware clattered onto his plate. The voice made him feel less than he was, and Alaric fought the urge to cower under the table. Instead, he reached a shaking hand out to his wine glass, picked it up, brought it to his lips, and sipped.

The female shade also retreated against the far wall, and she stared up at the ceiling as though she weren't listening to her master.

Since the Sun God spoke first, Alaric felt obligated to respond, "We do cherish cleanliness in Togarashi. And forks." He took another sip of his wine and heard his shade attendant draw a hasty breath.

Alaric saw a white flash across the table—the Sun God's teeth, canines sharp and gleaming in the candlelight.

"Good to see a week of luxury didn't spoil you completely."

The Sun God picked up his wine glass, swirling the honey-colored liquid, but didn't continue. Was this an invitation to start a conversation? Alaric had been to enough dinner parties to know the basics, but would that work on a god?

"This is the best food I've ever eaten," he began, and he felt the Sun God's gaze fall on him again. "Shefu is marvelous."

It must have been a misstep because the female shade behind the Sun God shook her head a fraction of an inch.

The Sun God put down his wine glass gently, but Alaric saw the female shade tense behind him, and her eyes found his. There was pity there. But there was nothing she could do.

"You think I don't know the value of those who live and work here?" asked the Sun God, his voice low and dangerous.

Alaric panicked and didn't speak. What? That wasn't what he'd meant at all. He wished that he could sink into the chair's fabric—anything to get away from the Sun God's outrage.

"What did I tell you about answering me?" The Sun God had barely raised his voice, yet Alaric heard it across the long table. He knew he had to say something, anything. Spit out words. He was supposed to be good at this sort of thing.

"Forgive me," Alaric finally strained out, inclining his head to hide his fearful eyes. "I come from a humble village where it is customary to praise the cooking and the chef if we find the meal satisfying."

A string of seconds whirled by, and Alaric perceived his shade attendant behind him and the table in front of him. He couldn't focus on anything else and kept his head bowed, his hands clenched on the chair's armrests. He always fell back on politeness and couldn't believe that he'd tried a witty courtly comeback earlier. He was lucky the Sun God hadn't ripped out his throat with the dessert fork.

A chair pulled out down the table, and soft steps echoed in Alaric's ears. The Sun God was coming toward him. He kept the same obedient posture but pried his hands off the chair and put them in his lap. No need to further anger the Sun God by mangling the chair with his fingernails.

Alaric felt the warmth before the god was close to him, and his body suddenly yearned to lean toward the sensation like a flower bending toward sunlight, so he let his head fall to the side right when the Sun God stepped beside him. He rested his head against the god's body, and a vibrant energy flowed through him, enlivening his entire being. The pulsing golden glow vibrated into his arms and legs, enveloping him, and Alaric hummed, appreciating the muscled torso beneath his head. It was like spring itself was singing through him, sun falling upon newly opened flower buds, red petals ready to burst forth.

Perhaps startled, the god didn't break their bodily contact until Alaric looked up and met the god's eyes. He blinked for a few glorious seconds and drank in the dark orange irises, trying to memorize every golden fleck in their depths. Alaric thought he saw hundreds of years go by in the god's eyes...as well as someone who looked like him, grinning, with spiked crimson hair. He reached up one hand as though to touch the god's face, entranced. But the god's own hand slashed forward, seizing Alaric's wrist in a vise grip.

"How dare you?" seethed the god, and he grabbed Alaric by the hair with his other hand, ripping his head back.

Alaric felt hot breath on his throat through the high collar, but it didn't frighten him this time. He didn't resist the Sun God's grip on his wrist or in his hair. Instead, he reached his free hand up behind his head and caressed the god's fingers that held his hair. The god let go, and Alaric's head fell, but the god saved it from hitting the table by dragging Alaric to his feet, hand still grasping Alaric's wrist. The chair toppled behind them, but neither noticed. The god held Alaric's wrist and had also grabbed his waist, holding him up, their faces close to touching.

Alaric's eyes filled with tears as he searched the god's expression for compassion, for a sign of anything positive. But there was nothing, just infinite unseeable depths behind the mask.

"Please," he whispered, and that broke the god's attention. He dropped Alaric, who tumbled to the floor. His shade attendant stirred but stayed back with a hard scowl from the god.

"You will never touch me without my leave again," rasped the god. Alaric clutched his head, expecting a blow that didn't come. He lay on the floor long after the door on the opposite end of the room slammed, chest heaving. His shade attendant waited against the wall, wishing he could help the red-haired boy with the lovely almond-shaped eyes.

Another week passed, and Alaric ate in the dining room each evening with only Emilia for company. The Sun God was somewhere in the temple—Emilia let slip that he never left the premises—but he didn't seek Alaric out or cross his path unexpectedly, and Alaric was grateful.

He was a dervish of confusion, mind telling him to stay far away from the rage-prone god, but something else gnawed at Alaric's heart—an ache from when the Sun God's inner flame left his body. He hadn't asked anyone about that, what he'd felt when his skin connected with the Sun God's. The miraculous sensation of light trickled from his body slowly once he'd been led back to his room by Matthias after the disastrous dinner. He'd been right about his shade attendant's name, and the man was surprised Alaric knew it.

"I think that went pretty well," he'd joked when Matthias helped him take off the velvet tunic. Matthias tried to hold back a coughing fit, but Alaric ended up patting the shade's back, apologizing for his poorly timed humor. "If you see Emilia, can you tell her not to come tonight? I don't want her to see me like this."

A palm-shaped bruise had already started to form on Alaric's wrist, and he knew his face must look terrible.

Matthias nodded and opened his mouth as if to speak. Alaric waited, wondering what the attendant might say. The shade clutched his own hands and shuffled from one foot to the other, and Alaric patted his shoulder. "It's okay, Matthias. You're not supposed to talk to me, right?"

"No, sir, I can speak to whomever I want," answered Matthias, but he looked uncertain. "It's just…I never knew that humans could be so brave."

"Me? Brave?" Alaric laughed as he collapsed on his bed. "You need to meet some better humans."

"I haven't seen a human in two thousand years," Matthias admitted. "Perhaps they've changed." He paused and nodded, deciding something. "I'll be sure to tell Shefu that you enjoyed the meal even if the company wasn't what you expected."

Without another word, Matthias gave a deep bow and left Alaric to his thoughts.

"Matthias? He's all right, I guess," said Emilia as they walked to the servants' quarters. Alaric preferred spending time in places the Sun God was least likely to be, so the servant areas were high on the list.

"Don't be jealous," said Alaric, nudging Emilia with his hip. "I can have more than one friend."

"I'm not jealous," she said but wouldn't look at him. "*I could dye your hair.*"

"Moping doesn't look good on you, Em. I think Kuroi needed something for Matthias to do. Apparently, he was a master tanner and dye-smith when he was alive."

"I did interesting stuff when I was alive too," she mumbled. "Does this mean you won't be able to take me to the pool today?"

"Ha! I can still take you. I just can't get my hair wet."

"That's no fun," she pouted then continued on a new track. "I like your tattoo," she said, peeking at his clothed back. "But you can only see it when you've got no shirt on. Isn't the whole idea to show it off where other people can see it?"

"In my village, a tattoo is very personal because it has a lot of meaning. So, we don't strut around like peacocks," he teased, and Emilia rolled her eyes.

She said, "Your village has a lot of dumb rules."

"And this place doesn't?" Alaric asked, fighting laughter.

Emilia smacked his arm but didn't reply. She hated rules of any kind.

They reached Matthias's room, and Alaric batted Emilia's hand away from the doorknob, shaking his head at her as he knocked. "What did I tell you about that?"

"Something about how everyone deserves privacy?"

"See, I knew some of the lessons were getting through that thick skull."

Matthias opened the door, and he attempted to hide the worry that covered his features as he ushered them inside. Emilia didn't notice and leaped atop Matthias's bed. The shade must have been deep in thought because he didn't chastise Emilia.

"Something the matter?" Alaric asked. There was a small table with two chairs in the corner, and Alaric sat down next to the dyeing supplies. Matthias used the same flowers for the dye mixture that were switched out in Alaric's room each day: fire lilies from down the mountain. Though they didn't have a strong smell, the flowers were shocking red in color with dark garnet centers. Matthias said they didn't need to be cultivated; the lilies grew wherever the seeds landed.

"No, everything's fine," Matthias said, and Alaric wondered why he was lying, but he was glad Matthias had stopped calling him "sir." The shade stood beside him, ignoring the racket Emilia made. He pulled a comb from a little kit on the table, which also had scissors and a small brush. Matthias hummed as he parted Alaric's hair with the comb, checking his roots situation. "You have wonderful hair, Shina. The original color is just as nice as the red."

Alaric chuckled and felt his cheeks flush. "Thanks. I guess I never really thought about it."

"Matthias?" said Emilia from the bed. "Do you think Alaric's pretty?"

Both Alaric and Matthias choked and glared at her. She shrugged and said, "It's just a question."

"Impertinent child," muttered Matthias. He tapped Alaric's chin to have him face forward. The dye was already prepared, so Matthias circled Alaric as he worked, daubing the red mixture on Alaric's roots with a small paintbrush, covering most of his head. "I'll leave the ends. I think it will be a nice contrast to have the new color blend into the first dye."

Alaric nodded. Whatever the shade thought would look decent was good with him. "And, yes, Emilia," Matthias said, "Shina is a very good-looking human." Alaric snorted, and Matthias laughed. "That has to set for about half an hour, so don't mess it up."

"Do you think the *master* thinks Alaric's pretty?"

Matthias grabbed the bowl of dye mixture and left Alaric in the chair. He didn't answer Emilia.

Alaric had been meaning to bring something up with Matthias because he didn't think Emilia would know. She was a good everyday companion and kept him entertained with her antics, but Alaric doubted she knew much about the Sun God.

"Um, Matthias? Tell me if I'm being too familiar, okay? But does the Sun God even *like* men?"

"Like men?" Emilia asked loudly. "Like men for what? Oh, the sex."

"You. Are. Infuriating," Matthias said. "Don't make me kick you out. I'll send you down to the kitchens faster than you can blink." Matthias settled in the chair beside Alaric and sighed. "I knew you'd ask something like that eventually. As far as the master's preferences, I really can't say."

"I thought so," Alaric said, head hanging. "In most of the stories, the gods don't really care who their partners are, so long as they're, um, nice to look at."

"That is a safe assumption," said Matthias, mischievous. "I've only worked in the Temple of the Sun, but I can attest that most of the gods aren't, how should I word this...picky. However, love matches aren't unheard of. The Lord of the Underworld and his husband have been together since the dawn of time. Not that there haven't been rough patches in *that* marriage."

"That's good to know… that gods can fall in love," Alaric said and fiddled with his fingers.

"Alaric?" Emilia asked, and he was almost afraid to answer her. Emilia's mind moved a mile per second, and her questions sometimes hit like hammers. She scooted to the edge of the bed, face serious. "Do you like the master?"

Yes, questions like sledgehammers. Matthias sat still, eyes on the table. He hadn't chastised Emilia for *this* impertinent query.

"I don't really know him, Em," Alaric said.

"But he's handsome, right? And he smells nice, like oranges. And he's real muscle-y. Not as much as you, and he's shorter too, but that's not a big deal."

Since Emilia died before learning about love, she focused on a person's superficial characteristics. Alaric didn't blame her, but he wasn't sure how to explain relationships to her. Alaric had almost no experience when it came to love either, but he knew what it wasn't.

"It's not about how a person looks," he started, and Matthias raised his eyebrows. "There's a lot of other things to consider when deciding whether you like someone or not."

"Like if they're rich?"

Matthias nearly fell out of his chair as he belly-laughed, and Emilia looked insulted. "What's so funny? I'd be worried if I fell in love with a poor person. How would they take care of you?"

"Kid's got a point," said Alaric, and Matthias laughed harder, tears running down his face.

"All right, I think that's enough love talk," said Matthias when he overcame his laughing fit. "I need to take Shina down to the baths to wash his hair. Emilia, can you go help in the kitchens for an hour or so?"

"Are you punishing me for talking about sex?"

"No! By the heavens, girl, have you ever gone to the baths with Shina?"

"Ugh," she said and slumped off the bed and onto the floor like a puddle.

"Right then, off you go." Matthias poked Emilia's side with his foot until she slithered out of his room on her belly.

The temple baths were infrequently used, mainly because shades did not need to bathe. The god-touched were allowed to use them, and Alaric supposed that Oken, the unseen demigod, might enjoy a bath on occasion. There were three pools of varying temperature, but Alaric loved the hottest one best. Steam rose in roiling corkscrews from the water, which was clear blue. There were changing stalls along one wall, and one was stocked specifically for him. His towels were varying purple hues, and two robes, twins to his tribute robe, hung on ornate hooks behind the curtain. Emilia showed him the stall on his second day in the temple, and Alaric had forbidden her from entering the bath area if he was using it.

Alaric wore a loose-fitting tunic with a wide neck, so he could easily remove it with a head full of red dye. His trousers were also loose on his hips and easy to remove. He grabbed a towel and padded to the moderate temperature bath. Matthias said cold water was better for the dye, but Alaric despised the idea. They compromised by having Alaric wade into the moderate pool, then Matthias dumped colder water on his hair. Alaric worried about the dye in the bath, but Matthias assured him it was fine. When the unfortunate ritual was over, Alaric toweled off in the changing room, put on a robe and went to put his feet in the hot bath. Matthias knelt behind him and towel-dried his hair, checking the color.

"Looks good," Matthias said, running his fingers along the sides. "We'll probably have to do this every few weeks if you want to keep the color vibrant."

Alaric nodded and hummed, enjoying the feeling of Matthias's fingers on his scalp. Matthias froze when Alaric made the contented noise and moved away, sitting on the step that led down into the bath area from the changing rooms. He put his face in his hands and shuddered.

"Hey, are you okay?" Alaric asked and pulled his feet out of the water. He sat near Matthias on the step, and the shade didn't move. He resisted reaching out and touching Matthias though he felt that was what the shade might want.

"What you said to Emilia," Matthias said, "about considering what you want from a partner. That was very wise for someone your age. I wasn't so careful."

"Oh," said Alaric, unsure what else to say.

"And I wasn't that young, so I can't blame the fog of youth," he said and shifted next to Alaric. "That's how I died. People weren't so forgiving of certain proclivities then. My lover was caught with someone else, another man, and he agreed to trap his other lovers into revealing themselves. The last night we were together, he cried when they came for me, but it wasn't real. He didn't really care; otherwise, why would he have done that?"

"That's awful, Matthias. I'm so sorry it happened to you. Nobody deserves that."

Matthias sat up and rubbed his eyes, his jaw set in a small smile. "You might not know this, but most of the shades who work here have similar stories. Our 'tales of anguish and woe.' I think the master takes pity on luckless fools like us."

"You're not a fool," Alaric countered, thinking about what Matthias said. Taking in shades who'd been wronged was a very benevolent thing to do and might explain the servants' loyalties to the Sun God.

"That's nice of you to say, but you don't know me very well either." Matthias sighed and tried to change the subject. "So, what *do* you look for in a partner?"

"I always thought I'd end up with someone kind," Alaric said. The silence stretched between them, and Alaric shoved closer to Matthias and dropped his head onto the shade's shoulder. They sat like that for a while, watching the steam rise from the nearby pool.

Until a growl erupted from the entrance on the other side of the room.

Matthias shot to his feet as though he were on fire and bowed low, backing against the wall. Alaric stood too but situated himself between the shade and the approaching inferno. The Sun God burned brightly in his anger, skin ablaze with light, eyes fixated on the shade as he stalked around the bath toward them.

"Stop!" Alaric yelled and held out his hands. "It wasn't his fault; it was mine!"

When the god made to move around him, Alaric got in his way, blocking Matthias from the divine wrath. The Sun God glared at Alaric, as though possessed. His pupils were blown, and the golden flecks in his orange irises pulsed with energy.

The god huffed out a breath, eyes not leaving Alaric's, and snarled, "Out."

Matthias skittered away, and Alaric thought he heard a small sob. At least the shade was safe for now. Maybe he could calm the god down or at least direct the god's rage at himself. Alaric realized his hands were still up and almost touching the Sun God's chest, so he dropped them slowly.

"Nothing happened," he said, voice firm. "He was just helping me with my hair."

The god dimmed his brilliance, regulating his anger, and light danced across his palms before dissipating across his entire body.

"He knows his place," the Sun God rasped. "Or at least he did."

Alaric had had enough of the god's posturing. He'd just wanted a quiet moment with his friend, one of the only people in the temple who seemed to enjoy his company and was willing to speak to him for longer than a minute. He might not have known his role or *his place*, but Alaric would be damned if Matthias was punished for something he'd done.

"Don't lay one finger on him," Alaric said, "or I swear that I'll—"

"You'll WHAT?" the god asked, contemptuous. His skin began to glow again, but Alaric held his ground.

"I'm not afraid of you," he said, hoping he sounded more confident than he felt.

The god's eyes narrowed, and he moved forward, forcing Alaric one step back. "You should be," he said, and golden light crackled in his eyes.

"You can hurt me all you want but leave Matthias alone."

53

"Is that what you want? For me to hurt you?"

The god snapped his teeth, and Alaric lurched back. His shins hit the stone step and he fell, arms flailing. The Sun God bolted forward and caught Alaric right before his back hit the step, and Alaric was suddenly very conscious of the fact that he was naked under his robe. The Sun God's powerful hands dug into Alaric's back through the robe, and Alaric fought the urge to touch the god, though part of him was losing the fight. The most traitorous part.

"Do you crave pain?" the god asked, and he opened Alaric's robe across his chest, exposing the dangling gold chain. "Answer me."

"No," Alaric murmured. "That's not what I want."

"Are you sure?" the god asked, sculpted eyebrow arching. He grabbed Alaric by the chin and forced him to look into burning eyes. "Because you've courted pain at our every encounter." His hand dipped to the bar on Alaric's left nipple, and he flicked the cool metal, sending a shock wave through Alaric's nervous system. Alaric involuntarily arched his back, bringing the nipple back to the god's hand. He laughed, cruel but satisfied. "That's what I thought."

He scraped his hand down Alaric's chest, letting it catch on the gold chain for an ecstatic moment, before trailing it down Alaric's torso. He traced each of Alaric's abdominal muscles with a finger, scratching hard against the last one, then angled his hand behind Alaric's hip.

"You yearn to chase the pain with pleasure. I can help you with that."

The god took his hand away, and part of Alaric's brain screamed from the loss. He tipped his head back to stare at the ceiling, hyper-aware when the god's hand reappeared on his thigh, fingers inching up past the robe's hem. Alaric felt as though the god was throwing kindling onto an inner fire, one he hadn't been aware of until coming to the Temple of the Sun.

Alaric's hands gripped the stair as he waited for the god to do as he pleased. His cock had been slowly hardening since the god entered the bath's steaming air, and he didn't try to fight it this time. He moaned when the god's fingers dodged up under the robe and his thumb pressed into the thin skin of his inner thigh.

"Do you want me to touch you?" the god whispered, lips close to the shell of Alaric's ear. The god's warm breath on his ear sent a shiver through his body, and Alaric nodded.

"Is that a yes?" teased the god, licking his upper lip in anticipation.

"Yes," Alaric breathed out, and the god tore the robe fully open. He leaned closer to Alaric and grabbed the gold chain again, letting it glide through his fingers. The god's eyes became all pupil, the white and orange taken over by pure blackness, as he salivated over Alaric's body. He kept a light grip on the chain but also moved the other hand back up Alaric's exposed thigh.

"Please," said Alaric, closing his eyes. His cock throbbed fiercely, glistening, aching for a touch. The god grinned.

"If you wanted me to fuck you so badly, all you had to do was ask."

Alaric's eyes rolled back in his head as the god took hold of him.

"Oh, my gods!" came a startled voice from the bath's entrance.

Alaric's eyes slammed open, but with the god's hand wrapped around his dick, he didn't dare move. He felt fingers tighten pleasantly around the shaft then shook his head, clearing his touch-starved mind.

Someone else was there, and Alaric was splayed out like a feast day roast.

"You have got to be fucking kidding me," said the Sun God.

Chapter Four

A man with curly deep-green hair stood in the doorway, dark doe eyes wide in shock. Twin ram's horns sprouted from his head, and his light green cheeks were dotted with a sea of freckles. Shorter than the Sun God, the man was broader in the shoulders, his arms heavily scarred and muscled, and his ears were pierced multiple times. He wore a kilt similar to the Sun God's though it was the color of a forest floor shadow and slit past a powerful thigh. His bracers were dark green like the kilt and his jewelry golden like a honeycomb. Thin gossamer gold chains draped over his robust chest, and a hideous, twisted scar covered most of his left shoulder and arm.

Another god.

Alaric could feel his power from across the room. It was kin to the Sun God's but wildly dissimilar. This god gave off a serene energy, and he made the room smell of fresh grass and morning dew.

"Bashi!" exclaimed the other god in a tremulous voice. "I can see that you're busy, so I'll just go wait in the throne room until you're, uh, finished." He spun around, back ramrod straight.

But the Sun God yelled across the room, "What the fuck do you want?"

The other god's shoulders hunched, and he turned back around, cheeks ablaze with embarrassment. He started muttering to himself, eyes moving around the room in a constant circle, wanting to look anywhere but at the Sun God and the human whose legs were spread wider than a damn canyon.

"If you're not going to join me," the Sun God drawled, a demonic look in his eyes, his smile like a knife, "spit out what you came to say and get out."

The Sun God tugged on Alaric's gold chain like it was a leash, and Alaric groaned. The god's hand was still clasped indelicately around his cock. To Alaric's horror, his erection wasn't flagging. He thought extreme shame might have done the job, but that wasn't the case.

A shadow fell on the green god, and another man came through the door, much taller and slimmer. He had coal-black hair shot through with white strands and bright turquoise eyes. The large scar that covered half his face and went past his hairline did not detract from the man's good looks. Opposed to the green god, the other was stoic, his face giving away no emotion.

"That's a human," the taller man said.

"Thank you for stating the obvious, Zebra Head," barked the Sun God. "Of course, this is the time you choose to drag your sorry ass back here."

Alaric looked from the Sun God to the two men in the doorway. What the hell was happening?

"The human doesn't look very comfortable," the man the Sun God called Zebra Head continued as the green god spiraled out of existence next to him. "Is that what humans enjoy? Have we been doing it wrong, Bell?"

The green god threw up his hands and exclaimed, "You can't just say that!"

The Sun God grunted loudly and finally dropped Alaric's dick and the gold chest chain. Relief and disappointment flooded through Alaric, but he quickly closed his robe.

"Did I say you could cover up?" The Sun God asked, voice low and harsh. Alaric didn't pay him any attention. He slid across the stone step until his shoulder hit the tiled wall, getting as far away from the awkward conflict as possible.

"We're going to discuss your inability to *listen* later," the Sun God warned. Then he yelled, "Kuroi!" The black-eyed, god-touched man appeared next to the Sun God, expression blank. Alaric's eyes widened. Had Kuroi materialized out of thin air?

Kuroi took in the scene, and his mouth twitched. "Master Cypress. Oken. I was not told of your arrival."

"That's because they barged in instead of sending an envoy," the Sun God said, annoyed. "I can handle them. Take care of *that*."

The Sun God motioned behind them, and Kuroi saw Alaric cowering against the wall. Alaric couldn't imagine what was going through Kuroi's mind, but he showed no emotion as he took in Alaric's disheveled appearance and damp hair. He nodded to the Sun God and walked over to Alaric, staring at him until Alaric rose, clenching the robe closed, his fingers white.

"Leave the clothes. I will send Emilia for them later." Kuroi's voice was sharp, telling Alaric not to argue. He needed to get the human away from the unpredictable gods. Alaric nodded and bit his lower lip.

As he followed Kuroi out of the baths, the last thing he heard was the Sun God declaring, "This had better be good."

After assuring Alaric that Matthias would be fine, Kuroi took his leave. "As you can no doubt tell, there are a few messes that I need to clean up."

His clipped tone bit Alaric to the bone, but he resolved to check on Matthias later. He didn't trust the Sun God not to expel the poor shade from the temple or for Kuroi to stop his master from doing the expelling. Could anything stop the Sun God if he wanted to do something?

He thought about the god's rough hands mapping out his body and shivered when his cock perked back up.

"Damned hells!" Alaric swore and lay down on the bed. He just needed to take care of this, then he could try and think. Already slick, his cock responded happily to his touch, and Alaric bit back another curse. It almost hurt to touch himself.

Is that what you want? For me to hurt you?

He closed his eyes and grasped the blanket, imagining those blown-out eyes staring down at him hungrily. What would it be like when the god eventually got Alaric alone without interruptions? How would it feel to have the god's mouth on his, to taste his lips?

Do you crave pain?

Did it really matter what Alaric wanted or imagined? He would do whatever the god told him to do, just to feel what it was like, just to have those hands on him, fingers digging into his flesh, branding him with scars. To have that sunlight rush through his nerves, through his blood. Anything to get closer.

Do you want me to touch you?

Yes, that's what he wanted at the moment, more than anything. Now that he'd felt the god's desire, saw the way his eyes flared with ravenous yellow flames as he looked at Alaric's body. Had felt the god's hot breath on his skin. It wasn't a good idea. It was a terrible idea. He shouldn't be thinking that way, not about a god who was brutal force incarnate.

If you wanted me to fuck you so badly, all you had to do was ask.

Alaric felt heat pool in his belly, a writhing eddy that threatened to destroy him from within, and he arched his back, imagining the god's tongue tracing the outline of his ear, his teeth nibbling up his neck, hands trailing downward, forever downward.

Alaric bit down on his hand when he felt the release, and he heaved in dozens of breaths, eyes wide, legs shaking. That was the hardest he'd ever come. With just his hand and thoughts of a disdainful god's raspy voice.

Fuck, he thought. Why had that other god intruded?

"No one told me a human lived here now."

Khresh Bashima closed his eyes and counted slowly, taking deep breaths. *You don't want to kill him, you don't want to kill him,* the mantra flowed through his mind. But he did. He really did want to kill the demigod asshole.

"Don't bother making yourselves comfortable," he said, glaring at the Forest God. "This won't take long."

"I think I'll go to my room now, Bell," the demigod said. "Come for me when you leave."

Oken Cindras slipped out of the throne room via a hidden side door, and Bashima battled whether or not to kick him out of the temple for good. He had that thought every time the demigod returned, as if he didn't disappear for months on end, traipsing in as though it was *his* damn temple.

59

When the door closed behind Oken, the Forest God cleared his throat. Before he could speak, Bashima rolled his eyes and stalked to his throne, collapsing onto it in a huff. He pulled the black mask from his face and let it clatter to the ground. Rubbing his eyes, he tried to clear his mind and focus on the sun. The Forest God let him take a few moments to recenter, ever the respectful bastard.

"I'm sorry I came without sending word first, but…"

"Why're you here?" Bashima asked, voice tired but cutting.

"…but do you think it's a good idea to have a human here?"

Bashima glared at the Forest God, who stood in front of the throne, arms crossed on his chest, judgy, concerned look on his face. Bashima snorted. "Did I get on your ass about Oken when you started that nonsense?" he asked, flipping a hand, ending the subject.

"Yeah, you did, but that's beside the point." The Forest God took the hint from Bashima's glare and changed the subject. "You can ignore my letters, Bashi, but you haven't answered Vaultus yet."

"Did he send you? You're such a fucking lapdog."

"I came on my own—"

"That's just sad. Isn't that what you keep Oken around for?"

Ignoring Bashima's taunt, the Forest God said, "Whether you agree or not, the summit will be held at the Temple of the Sun this cycle." His voice was apologetic but firm. He was sympathetic, but Bashima didn't care. That was just the way damn Tengu was. He felt bad, but he never did anything about it.

The Forest God approached the throne, and Bashima let him. He was in no shape to spar after expending so much focusing energy in the baths. He hadn't overreacted like that in centuries.

"Vaultus knows I'll obey," Bashima said. "He doesn't need my answer."

"But he'd appreciate it…" The Forest God trailed off and sighed. He ruffled the back of his hair, sending leaves falling. "It's been a long time, Bashi…are you sure about, you know?"

"Didn't I say that it was none of your business?"

Bashima flashed a warning sneer, and light played across his shoulders and down his arms. The Forest God shook his head and shrugged, and Bashima looked away. "If it'll get you out of my temple, I promise I'll send Vaultus my official response today, fucking seal and everything."

"It's not like I expected you to invite me to dinner," the Forest God laughed, his earrings swinging. "Want me to check the greenhouse before I go?"

"Sure. And remember to take Zebra Head with you. He's a fucking nightmare."

The Forest God choked on a laugh and inclined his head. He left through the main throne room entrance, leaves fluttering in his wake.

"Messy asshole," Bashima mumbled.

Once the Forest God was gone, Kuroi appeared from behind the throne. "Would you like me to draft the response to the king?"

"That's fine. Just bring it to me when you're finished so I can affix the seal. Then I suppose we'll have to start making arrangements."

"Already begun, Master," Kuroi said, smiling. He paused before adding, "Shina is safe in his chamber though I doubt Master Cypress is a serious threat to him."

"Huh, you'd be wrong there. Tengu is one of the most dangerous people in the damn universe."

"And yet, you shouldn't have to worry for the safety of anyone in this temple, even a human. At least from that quarter."

Bashima didn't answer, and Kuroi changed tracts, "Matthias is...concerned that he will be banished."

"Fucking hells, I'm not banishing anyone. Tell Matthias to calm the fuck down."

"I shall though I might choose a more soothing delivery." Kuroi rubbed his mouth as though thinking how to state his next question. "Is there anything amiss? Matthias explained what happened, but he was more than a little hysterical."

"Everything's fine. It's not his fault that human has no fucking idea how to behave."

Kuroi chuckled. "He is rather..." Kuroi began, but he cut himself off when Bashima leveled a cautionary stare at him. "Leave the preparations to me,

Master. I'll return shortly with the king's letter." He retreated behind the throne.

Bashima sunk lower in his throne, trying not to think about red peppers or wide crimson eyes.

Chapter Five

"You saw Master Tengu? I'm so jealous!"

"Emilia, don't call him that; it's disrespectful," Matthias snapped, throwing up his hands. "And don't tell me 'Master says it all the time.' I'm very aware. The master can call him whatever he wants; you cannot."

The shade turned to Alaric and said, "'Tengu' is a childish nickname, so pay it no mind. Master Bell Cypress is the Forest God. He and our master are childhood friends, of a sort. You may of course, call him Cypress. Emilia will call him Master Cypress, which she full well knows."

"They're not friends," scoffed Emilia, ignoring Matthias's thinly veiled chastisement.

"It's like humans," Alaric said. "Use their family names and not given names? At least at first?"

Matthias nodded. "Yes. You may use their chosen names if given permission, or if they introduce themselves in that fashion. Since gods have no names upon birth, they bestow monikers on themselves later in life."

Alaric nodded. "That's so unusual. Parents don't name their children?"

"Nope," Emilia said, grinning. "Godly kids pick their own! Pretty neat, huh?"

They sat in the library, Alaric sipping a calming tea and recounting some of his misadventure in the baths. He left out the cripplingly embarrassing parts but told the two shades about the Forest God and the demigod who barged in on him and the Sun God.

"Oken is an acquired taste," laughed Matthias. "But he's polite and keeps to himself when he's here."

"What's his story?" asked Alaric. "Must be an interesting life, being a demigod."

Matthias and Emilia shared a quick look. Gauging how much to tell Alaric, maybe? He didn't mind if they kept Oken's story to themselves; Alaric was glad Matthias was still in the temple. Matthias told Alaric not to worry when he'd checked on him, that the Sun God was understanding and forgiving and magnanimous. Alaric wondered if he would ever meet this good-twin version of the god.

"Being a demigod isn't that great," Emilia said. "At least, I've never met one who looked happy."

"Straddling the human and god worlds isn't easy," Matthias admitted. "Oken's father is a god, and his mother was human."

"Was?" asked Alaric. Did every god-meets-human story end up with a sad ending?

"As far as the gossip goes, she's god-touched now. You can't have four demigod children and not become god-touched," Matthias said, raising his eyebrows. "More tea, Shina? Oken's father will be at the summit, so you might catch a glimpse of him."

"This summit's a big deal, huh?" Alaric asked, and Matthias and Emilia both nodded. The temple shades had been in an uproar all day, rushing around the temple as if the volcano activated. Alaric had seen the Sun God's personal shade, Tika, marching through the halls beside Kuroi, more shades in their wake, arms laden with scrolls.

"A God Summit happens every fifty years," explained Matthias. "They gather to discuss the state of the world and attempt to destroy each other emotionally."

Alaric spit out his tea, and Emilia thumped him on the back. He wiped his mouth with his sleeve and gaped at Matthias. *"What?"*

"Gods live forever, so they get bored easily," said Emilia.

"Exactly," agreed Matthias. "Most of the gods stay either in or near their personal temples, unless they're like Lady Pressa or Master Cabari. It's easy for them to control their power from anywhere, so you could find them all over the world in theory."

"They're the Goddess of Music and the Lightning God," Emilia whispered to Alaric.

"No matter their domains, the gods travel to the summit when they're summoned unless they have a very good reason not to attend."

Alaric frowned. "But you said the Sun God hasn't left the temple..."

The shades both looked at their hands. Finally, Matthias said, "The master is allowed to remain at the Temple of the Sun." He didn't elaborate, so Alaric let it go. The Sun God must have had a good reason for not wanting to leave.

"Is the Sun God's name Bashi?" Alaric asked, recalling something the Forest God had said. Emilia burst out laughing and Matthias shrunk down into his chair as though Alaric had slapped him. Alaric looked from one shade to the other, confused. "That's what the Forest God called him, so I assumed..."

"*Never* call the master that," chided Matthias. Alaric put his hands up in surrender.

"I think it's his nickname," Emilia said happily, and Matthias hissed at her. "What? You told Alaric not to say it, so it's fine. We don't call the master by his name, anyway."

"Can you tell me his preferred name? It's weird, not knowing, especially after the baths." Alaric's face burned scarlet, and Matthias pretended to have not heard him, but Emilia beamed. He put up his hands again and said, "It would be weird no matter what! I've been living here for weeks and still don't know his name."

Matthias put a hand over Emilia's eager mouth and said, "You can ask Kuroi. Emilia and I are just shades. We're not supposed to say or do anything that might compromise the master. And we wouldn't want to," he reminded Emilia.

"I get it," Alaric said, disappointed. Even something as simple as a name, and they couldn't tell him. "Are you sure I didn't mess things up for you, Matthias?"

The shade smiled, eyes crinkling. "I promise that nothing you do would mess things up for me."

"Weren't you worried that you'd be sent to the Locker?" asked Emilia, and Matthias shushed her.

"Shades who have done evil in life or in death..." Matthias started after seeing Alaric's confused expression. Matthias rubbed his hands together, sweat beading his forehead. "They're put in a kind of suspended animation. Solitary confinement. You're frozen but can perceive everything around you. Not that there's anything to see from what I've heard."

"Isn't that a little extreme?" Alaric almost yelled, standing up.

"Please don't be upset," said Matthias. "The master would never send me there. He was angry at my presumption—"

"You didn't do anything wrong!" Alaric did yell this time. "He was out of line!"

Emilia cowered in her chair, holding a book over her eyes.

Matthias stood and tried to quiet him, but Alaric was enraged. "Did he threaten you? Kuroi promised that nothing would happen!"

"And nothing did. I'm fine. I was just scared for a moment."

"But you *were* scared, and that means you had a reason. You shouldn't have to be scared! That's no way to treat someone who works so hard! Just because he hired you doesn't mean he owns you!"

Matthias didn't answer, his eyes fearful.

"Wait. He *owns* you?"

Matthias grabbed Alaric's shoulders and shook him hard, jolting Alaric out of his planned rant.

"It's not the same thing as what humans mean. Yes, we sign a contract with the master and vow loyalty. Yes, we live here and can't leave, but that's because outside the temple grounds, away from the mountain, we would cease to exist. We'd go straight back to the Underworld. At least here, we have jobs we can be proud of, and other shades covet these positions. We all choose to be here and stay here. Do you understand?"

Alaric slumped back in his chair and grabbed the sides of his head, bending over. "I think I might be sick. Is this all we have to look forward to when we die? Endless servitude?"

"That's not fair," said Emilia, and she bolted to her feet, eyes shining with tears. "Why are you being so mean?" She raced out of the library, face in her hands.

"I'm...I wasn't thinking. Matthias I'm so sorry. Seven hells, I just make a mess of everything."

Matthias knelt beside Alaric and said, "Emilia has been the happiest I've ever seen her these last few weeks. She's not just helping you; you're helping her. You're helping all of us. Although the other shades are certainly envious that Emilia and I have the illustrious duty of watching over you."

"Why? I'm just a human from a small village. I can't really help anyone. Or..."

Alaric thought about how stressed the shades were, how difficult the next month would be as they prepared for the summit. If they were harried now, he could only imagine how the temple's atmosphere would feel as the summit got closer.

He snapped his fingers. "Do you think it would be okay if I did something for everyone? You're all working yourselves to the bone, and it's just gonna get worse."

Matthias tilted his head. "What would you do?"

"Stress relief! I can't cook my way out of a kettle, so that's out, and I'd probably mess up shade food royally. I'm really strong and can lift a lot, but that's not very fun to watch. Oh! Does anyone have a harp or a lyre?"

"Hmmmmm," Matthias looked thoughtful. "The master is proficient with the large standing harp as well as the koto. I think Draiden might play a little."

"The guy from the offering ceremony?" asked Alaric. "He lives here?"

"Obviously," said Matthias, raising an eyebrow. "He's one of the god-touched."

"Could you ask him if I could borrow his instrument? A hand harp or lyre is best. I'm not that good, so I don't want something complicated."

"And what are you going to do with a harp?" asked Matthias, befuddled.

Alaric grinned, sharp teeth gleaming. "We just need to find a good time for me to put on a little concert."

Draiden lent Alaric the lyre with a wry look in his eye. He looked as exhausted as he had during the ceremony, and Alaric wondered why he was so sleep-deprived. Must have been a job with long hours.

Alaric wanted a few days to practice, so he mostly stayed in his room or the library where he wouldn't bother anyone. Emilia forgave him for hurting her feelings and joined him as he attempted song after song, trying to find the ones that worked best with the lyre.

"My voice isn't that great, but I guess it'll be fine," he said, tuning the lyre.

"I think you sound wonderful!" Emilia said, bouncing on his bed when he started playing again.

"Ha! Thanks. I'm no balladeer, but I do like singing and playing."

He strummed the strings back and forth, thinking about what song would work for his finale. He'd picked eight songs, hoping it would be enough. Matthias suggested that amount because the shades' dinner time wasn't long; there was too much to do. He would play four modern songs and four older ballads, things the shades might recognize. He wanted to try a song from his village as a finale, but he was having trouble remembering all the lyrics, which were in an ancient language. He thought he had a fairly good handle on the music at least.

"We haven't heard music in so long," sighed Emilia. "The master used to play sometimes, and his songs were really beautiful and also really sad. I hope you picked happy ones."

"Don't worry. Three of them are technically drinking songs, so they sound pretty happy."

Alaric made a huge mistake.

He sat in front of the shades' dining area on a tall stool, lyre gripped in talon-like hands, surrounded by sixty or so shades, the ones who could attend his concert. A few had to work through the night, so he'd promised to do a smaller set for them during the day. But now, sixty sets of eyes stared at him.

Most of them were smiling and waiting patiently for him to start, but he saw a few frowns and one outright scowl.

How had he thought this was a good idea?

He took a deep breath. He couldn't back out now.

Emilia waved enthusiastically from the front row and danced in her seat. Matthias sat next to her and smiled up at him. Shefu stood in the very back with Draiden, her arms crossed, a harassed look on her face. Draiden still looked tired, but he nodded at Alaric, sending him encouragement.

"Um, okay, hi everyone," he started, thankful he'd inherited his mother's loud voice. Everyone settled down and turned their full attention on Alaric. He gulped and laughed nervously. "I'm Alaric Shina, but you all know that. You've been working so hard, and I wanted to do something to contribute. It's not much, but I hope you enjoy it. So, here we go."

He strummed the lyre, focusing on it instead of the audience, and found his note. He launched into an upbeat song about a man trying to woo a woman at a wedding. It was funny and a bit lewd, but it was a good opener. Most of the shades moved along to his playing, and a few even started clapping together near the end. After the first song went well, Alaric felt confidence swell in his chest, and he tore into the rest of his set.

The shades liked the modern songs, but they really got into the older ones, especially the two raunchy ones. A group of them got up to dance and sing with him on the eighth song, and they roused most everyone else to do the same. As Alaric sang about a woman outsmarting her cheating lover and out-drinking him, the shades clapped and cheered and raised their mugs. It felt amazing.

When he finished the raucous song, he picked at the lyre strings, deciding to do the ninth song. The shades chatted with each other, still buzzing from the last one, so Alaric waited for them to calm down before starting the last.

"I know you all have a lot to do, so I'll only keep you for one more song."

There were a lot of groans, which disheartened him at first, then Alaric realized that the shades were sad that he was almost done. They looked up at him, expectant.

69

"You'll have to bear with me a bit, because it's a really old song from my village. I don't have a translation for the words, but we sing it every year during the autumn harvest festival. I hope you like it."

Before he began, Kuroi appeared at the back of the room and stood with Shefu and Draiden, who leaned over to whisper something to the black-eyed man. He wasn't sure why, but Alaric wanted to impress Kuroi. Maybe singing competently in another language would do the trick.

Alaric cleared his throat, licked his lips, and began.

No one from his village knew exactly what the words in their autumn song meant. They had been singing it for hundreds of years as they brought in the crops and stored food to see them through the winter. The melody was simple, mournful with an underlying layer of hope. Alaric hoped he was conveying it well.

No one in the audience spoke as he sang, and Alaric felt like he was floating, so he closed his eyes and let the song take hold. He went through the three verses slowly but slammed into the bridge with all the pent-up emotion from the last weeks. Missing his parents, wishing he was back in his village with his friends, wanting his normal life back. He poured every raw emotion he possessed into the words: his concern for Matthias and Emilia, the uncertainty of his life, his complicated feelings for the Sun God.

As he let the last note fade from his lips, Alaric opened his eyes. The shades let out a collective breath, sighing as one. Emilia and Matthias were stunned, mouths agape. Alaric tried to hide his panic. Had it been that bad? Had he ruined the entire night?

In the back of the room, Shefu hunched over on Draiden's shoulder, sobbing. The tired god-touched man stared at Alaric in open-eyed horror, one hand covering his mouth, looking more awake than anyone in the room. Kuroi's entire face had gone white, his black eyes unreadable, his mouth a thin line.

But Alaric's eyes were drawn instantly when he saw a flash of gold.

The Sun God stood behind Kuroi in the doorway, his face blank. Light played across his skin in a rainbow of sun colors. As though jolted from his seat, Alaric felt like he and the god were the only people in the room. The rows of dazed shades disappeared, and separate spotlights hit him and the Sun God, illuminating only them. The god's gaze pierced Alaric's heart, and he knew he'd done something horrible that he couldn't take back.

He knew he'd somehow hurt the Sun God.

Bashima didn't hear what Kuroi said at first. He saw Kuroi's mouth moving, but there was no sound, no sound in the entire room. He felt the human's essence like an unbreakable chain pulling him, trying to drag him off his feet. He wanted to crash into the human at full force, a meteor hitting an unsuspecting planet. Those damned eyes, wide and innocent, staring across the hall, looking at him, through him.

"Master!" Kuroi said in a loud whisper. The trance broke, and Bashima saw that the shades were turned toward him, eyes down, hands shaking. Dammit, he'd vowed never to make them afraid of him ever again. He mentally begged Kuroi for help, and that was all it took. His chief attendant blocked the room from view and led him away, but not before Bashima saw Shefu weeping and Draiden's heartbroken face.

Bashima went to the throne room, and Kuroi followed, not speaking, knowing not to. It was one of the things Bashima valued most in Kuroi: his innate ability to know what the god needed. He burst into the room and let out an anguished bellow, tearing the mask from his face and hurling it against the far wall. Small flames formed on his palms, and he hurled fire, breaking decorative vases and urns, reducing them to clay rubble. Every candle flared brightly, snuffing themselves out from the force. Bashima ripped the golden chest plate from around his neck and set it ablaze, the gold melting quickly. He wanted to tear everything off his body then burn himself to ash, but he was impervious to his heat and fire, so instead he screamed until his lungs ached. He collapsed onto his knees, fury ripping through his heart. His palms burned into the stone floor, smoking.

"Why?" he growled. "Why did I do this to myself, Kuroi?"

"Master?"

"Don't do that, you bastard," Bashima said, glaring at the black-eyed, inscrutable man. "You know exactly what I mean. You told me it was a bad idea, and here we are. Don't you want to gloat? I give you so few chances to do it." His voice sounded so bitter, and his words tasted like ashes.

Kuroi had kept his distance, so as not to be singed by the god's wrath, but now he walked closer. Bashima tried to send him a calming energy, so that the man would know the danger had passed, but it wasn't working. He was as far from calm as he'd been in centuries.

"We both know I never gloat," said Kuroi kindly, and Bashima laughed, but there was no humor in it. Kuroi crouched beside Bashima, hands resting on his knees. "What would you like me to do?"

"What you should do. Laugh your ass off."

"I will follow any order you give, Master, but I will not laugh at you for this."

"I'd deserve it," Bashima snapped. "I'm a massive idiot."

Kuroi's mouth jerked into a small smirk and he sighed. "I would never begrudge you for trying, Master. Seeing you this emotional...hasn't been easy for me either. And the boy..."

Bashima waited for Kuroi to continue, holding his breath. Kuroi had been against keeping the human at the temple, had campaigned for his immediate return to his village, perhaps after taking a forgetting potion for good measure.

Kuroi looked up through the skylight at the night sky, which was a clear, deep indigo and littered with stars. Bashima thought he might be searching the constellations for answers. Kuroi brought his gaze back to the Sun God and smiled sadly.

"The boy is exceptional."

"Ugh," muttered Bashima. He stood up and paced the room's perimeter, avoiding the broken pottery and melted candle wax.

"Master, if I may," said Kuroi quietly. "Why did you come to the throne room instead of back to your chambers? Perhaps if you search for that reason, inspiration will strike." He bowed his head and took his leave, off to contain the chaos that most likely had erupted in the shades' hall.

Why had he come to the throne room?

Because it was his temple, and he could go wherever the hells he wanted. Because it had great acoustics but none of the servants would hear him there.

Because there were plenty of things to smash but nothing irreplaceable. Because it was the room where he felt most connected to the sun, his place of power.

Because *his* room was close.

He paced faster, feeling his heart rate skyrocket.

Damned fucking human with his fake red hair and very real, massive garnet-colored eyes. The scar over his brow. Who smelled like hot spices and autumn apples. Unusual sharpened teeth that didn't match his nature. Ridiculously well-built body—what was his job, carrying heavy water jugs to and from his village all day and eating only meat?—that Bashima couldn't help but stare at. Even under the robe on the offering day, Bashima had sensed how strong the human was, that he was the kind of man other men would challenge for dominance just because of his physique.

And obviously his absolutely flawless dick.

But he wasn't just one of the most perfect human specimens that Bashima had ever seen. No, of course he also had to be more considerate than the fucking Forest God. Thoughtful. Kind. Optimistic. He might as well be covered in wildflowers and feeding baby deer from his hand.

Bashima watched how the human treated the shades and was astounded at every turn. He'd leapt in front of Bashima to protect Matthias without a thought. He'd offered himself up for punishment, all for someone he'd just met. Why? Then, without any sort of prompting, he'd organized a whole damn *event* for the shade servants because he noticed how hard they were working to prepare for the summit. And they enjoyed it!

And the constant smiling and laughing.

It was annoying. It was insufferable.

How the fuck could someone be that good? That...exceptional?

Bashima stopped pacing in the center of the room and looked at his throne. It was meant to be intimidating, the back reaching all the way to the ceiling, one great slab of tempered gold. The human had stood right here with his modest basket of peppers, had showed very little fear in a god's presence. Made himself known instead of bowing and scraping and fleeing the room the instant the god wasn't as benevolent as he'd expected.

The human was also a defiant, stubborn little shit. How long had it been since anyone stood their ground against him? Bashima knew the exact moment, but he pushed the thought far back in his mind.

The moon's glow filtered down from the skylight and illuminated the room.

But still Bashima didn't move.

Alaric told Matthias and Emilia that he could walk back to his room alone, and they hadn't questioned him. Drained after the performance, he didn't feel like talking. When the Sun God left the hall, the shades all clapped for Alaric, murmuring gratitude and praising his talent.

Shefu fled the room, but Draiden stood at the back, tears in his eyes. When Alaric tried to give Draiden back the lyre, the man shook his head and said, "It wasn't mine to begin with, and now, it's found a more suitable owner."

Perplexed by the night's events, Alaric clutched the lyre as he walked to his room. The halls were quiet, peaceful. They didn't know that Alaric had made another mistake somehow. He dragged a hand across the wall and tried to think. It had to be the song. Emilia said she'd never heard such a sad song but that it was beautiful, and Matthias hadn't said anything. He'd stood with Emilia, wringing his hands and trying not to look at Alaric.

What did the song mean? He had no idea what the lyrics meant, but it affected the three god-touched and the Sun God. Maybe they knew what the words meant and were so offended that they couldn't be in the same room as Alaric once they recovered from the shock.

Kuroi and the Sun God sure left in a hurry. Maybe the Sun God was right about Alaric. Maybe he did seek out ways to make the god angry whether he meant to or not. Maybe it was something subconscious. It didn't matter because he was still messing up. If he made enough errors, would he be sent home? How many chances would he get? Did he even want more chances?

When Alaric reached his door, he paused, resting his head on the warm wood. Did he want to go home? He couldn't give himself a definitive answer, and that scared him almost as much as the shattered look on the Sun God's face when Kuroi whisked him away from the concert.

The candles in the hall flickered as though a breeze had gone through.

Alaric breathed out, then a rough hand grabbed his arm and spun him around so quickly that he dropped the lyre. He didn't have time to make a sound as he was shoved against the door and powerful fingers pulled his face down. Eyes flashed like lit gunpowder, and the Sun God's lips pressed to Alaric's, tasting of smoke and dark honey. Forgetting that he shouldn't touch the god, Alaric grabbed the back of his neck and drew him closer, need and want flaring through his body like multiple lightning strikes.

The god stiffened for a moment before deepening the kiss, opening Alaric's mouth with an urgent tongue. He kissed as though he needed Alaric's breath to live, mouth savage and wild. His hands roamed from Alaric's face, down his neck, and to his chest, grasping Alaric's shirt and pressing him firmly against the door. Sliding a knee to part Alaric's legs so he could get closer. The god's thigh rubbed against Alaric, and Alaric groaned, hastening the god's searching lips and tongue.

Alaric reached for the door handle desperately. He needed to get the god in his room. In his bed. Nothing else mattered in that moment. When the god saw what Alaric was doing, he pulled away, and Alaric's lips followed, missing the god's mouth on his. But the god pushed him back, breathing heavily, and Alaric noticed that he wasn't wearing his mask or the gold chest piece.

His face was even more beautiful bare, with sharp cheekbones and a slightly upturned nose, though his eyes were narrowed and his mouth set in a skeptical frown. Alaric backed up against the door and bit his lower lip, unsure what to do now that the god wasn't kissing him.

The god's pupils blew black across his eyes, and he barreled into Alaric like a tidal wave, pushing them through the door and into Alaric's room. His lips were back on Alaric's, his hands in Alaric's hair, tugging lightly. Alaric tried to stretch away so he could remove his tunic, but he wasn't fast enough; the god tore his shirt off him with no effort. He wasted no time in sweeping Alaric's legs out from under him, so he fell on the bed, eyes wide.

Before the god's ferocious mouth could find his again, Alaric said, "Wait!"

The Sun God stopped instantly, the black receding in his eyes. "I want you," he rasped. "You want me." He sounded like a caged leopard, and Alaric's cock twitched in his trousers.

"I do, but...can you tell me your name?"

It must have been the last thing the god expected him to say because he raised an eyebrow. "My name? I don't have a name."

"Then, what you'd like me to call you?" Alaric ruffled the back of his hair, shy. "Even if it's just in my head. If you don't want me to use it out loud." Then the words wouldn't stop. "It's just, I've never done this before, I mean, I've kissed some girls and one boy but nothing else, and I'd like to know your name, and I'm a little nervous, and you're really beautiful, and I..."

The Sun God pinned Alaric down on the bed, wrists on either side of his head, straddling his hips. "Hells you never shut up, do you?" He dipped his head and breathed in deeply next to Alaric's neck, and Alaric yanked his hands free, grabbed the god's hips, and pulled them down to grind on his own. The god purred contentedly and whispered in the shell of Alaric's ear, "You may call me Bashima when we're together, alone."

The name suited the Sun God, Alaric thought. It sounded unyielding and free.

"Why are you still wearing pants?" the god—Bashima—whispered again, tracing his tongue down the outside of Alaric's ear. Heat bubbled inside Alaric, and he pushed off his pants and underwear as Bashima balanced on top of him. Alaric didn't mention that the god was still wearing his kilt, but he doubted that mattered. One of the god's golden thigh bands caressed the outside of Alaric's thigh, cool and smooth. Hells he was so hard.

"Since this is your first time, I'll go easy on you," Bashima said, grinning. With one hand he unclasped his kilt, and it slipped off the bed, pooling on the floor. He held out his other hand, and one of the glass bottles on Alaric's washing table flew into it. "This oil is made specifically for nights like this," he said, dousing his fingers in the thick substance. It smelled like the sea after a storm. "Now, I'm going to make you ready for me." His eyes gleamed, hungry, the black pupils spreading. "Do you want me to touch you?"

"Gods yes," Alaric said, squeezing the god's thighs, and Bashima laughed.

"This will be uncomfortable at first," Bashima warned, "but all pleasure begins with pain."

He leaned down and kissed Alaric's lips tenderly then coaxed his thighs apart. Alaric thought his heart might beat out of his chest. He couldn't believe that the actual Sun God was kissing him, was naked on top of him. Hells he hadn't even looked at the god's dick—what if it was huge?

Alaric felt pressure and held his breath as Bashima slid one oiled finger inside him, and while it felt unusual, it also felt right. Alaric couldn't believe he'd ever been attracted to anyone else; none of them could compare to the Sun God.

"Ready for two?" Bashima rasped into his mouth, and Alaric nodded, panting, trying not to tense up. Bashima had ignored his cock, but now he rubbed up against it, and the friction drove Alaric's head back onto the bed. Alaric grabbed the bed sheet for dear life. Bashima moved his two fingers, pushing further, stretching, and one hit something inside Alaric, sending pleasure shooting through his limbs.

"That feels amazing," he groaned, and Bashima smiled as though he knew a secret no one else did. He caressed the spot, and Alaric nearly choked. "More," he begged. "Please don't stop!"

Bashima slipped a third finger in, and Alaric's hips bucked, but Bashima's strong body kept him in place. "Oh, I don't plan on stopping. Not when you ask so sweetly."

He moved his fingers, grinding his hips up and down. "You're so tight," whispered Bashima. "Feels perfect."

When he gently pulled his fingers out, Alaric nearly yelped from the loss. He felt too empty. Bashima covered his protesting mouth with his lips and massaged Alaric's tongue with his own. Unable to keep his hands twisted in the sheets any longer, Alaric grabbed Bashima's lower back and rubbed down to his ass, cupping it, which made Bashima cry out lightly. Alaric smelled the sea again as Bashima rubbed oil along his length. "Patience isn't your thing, is it?" he asked, smirking.

"I want you inside me NOW," Alaric said, and Bashima's eyes went completely black, yellow light crackling around his head in a dazzling halo.

Bashima grabbed his dick, which Alaric noted was gorgeous and of a hopefully manageable size. It felt incredible and warm and hard, and Alaric thought the Sun God was holding himself back, but barely.

One hand wandered to the gold chain across Alaric's chest, fingers wrapping and unwrapping, and Bashima dipped his head and took one nipple in his mouth, tongue playing across the piercing. Alaric muffled a cry and wrapped his legs around the god, never wanting the feeling to leave him. Bashima put his face in the crook of Alaric's neck, and Alaric held onto him, raising his hips in rhythm with the god, accepting all of him.

Alaric dug his nails deep into Bashima's back when he hit that intense pleasure spot again, and Bashima, surprised, bit down hard on Alaric's shoulder, which sent him tumbling over the edge. Alaric was too late to warn the god. Bashima shuddered on top of him, letting out a massive moan, still latched onto Alaric's shoulder. Alaric's entire body went rigid, like lightning was coursing through his body, then he melted into the bed, spreadeagled, spent.

"Shit," said Bashima, face on Alaric's shoulder. "Are you all right?"

Alaric could barely mumble out, "I don't think I've ever been better."

Bashima stayed where he was, chest rising and falling with heavy breaths. Alaric wanted to reach out and touch Bashima's soft, untamed hair, but he couldn't get his arms to move.

"Except, I can't move."

"Fuck," said Bashima, and he eased away from Alaric, who missed the god's presence immediately. He whined in protest, but the god ignored him. He tried to lift his head, but it wouldn't listen. Bashima used a shred of Alaric's destroyed shirt to clean himself then he reached down and touched himself, his hand coming away covered in a shining gold substance.

"Even your cum is pretty?" asked Alaric, exasperated. "It's just not fair."

"Shut up, idiot," snapped Bashima. He muttered to himself, "Should be fine, just one time. At least he didn't eat it. Fuck, I'll have to ask fucking Tengu. Nightmare."

"What's wrong?" asked Alaric, noticing the god's semi-panicked state.

"Probably nothing," Bashima said but started pacing. Alaric admired the view, but it made him dizzy quickly.

"'Nothing' is why I can't move?" he asked, though his fingers and toes were obeying his commands.

"I didn't plan on you clawing up my back then coming all over me," Bashima mumbled. He stopped beside the bed and crossed his arms. "You look so good splayed out like that."

"You didn't answer the question, *Bashima*."

The god's eyes flashed dangerously.

"I'm sorry," Alaric huffed, "but you're scaring me a bit."

"Fine. Just a minute, I can't keep looking at you like that, or I might attack you." Bashima shifted Alaric on the bed, so his head was on a pillow then covered him with a blanket. "You feel really awake right now?"

"Yeah," said Alaric, eyes darting around the room. "And I think I can smell colors."

Bashima put his face in his hand and sighed. "Well, you'll be passed out in about five minutes. We—I—have to be more careful. I can't come inside you, otherwise you'll end up like this, and you might feel great right now, but the hangover's gonna be a bitch."

"Oh," said Alaric, fascinated. "That's pretty weird."

"It also loosens tongues, so think about what you say next," growled the god.

Alaric hummed to himself and looked at Bashima from the top of his head to his toes. He still wore the bracers on his arms and the thigh and ankle cuffs. Alaric grinned, showing all his teeth and said, "You look really good naked."

"So I've been told," said Bashima. He grabbed his flowy kilt off the ground and wrapped it around his hips, and Alaric pouted, making Bashima laugh. "This is actually kind of fun. I could ask you anything, and you'd answer truthfully."

Something changed in his face when he said that, a sadness flowing into his orange eyes, and Alaric tried to reach for his hand, but only his fingers wiggled.

"Don't be sad," he said.

"How could I be sad when you're such a gods-damned ray of fucking sunshine," Bashima joked. "Ugh, I'll stay here until you pass out and get you something for the headache tomorrow."

"Okay," said Alaric. "Would you mind rolling me onto my side? I hate sleeping on my back."

Bashima raised an eyebrow but got on the bed and pulled the blanket back. He blushed as he re-positioned Alaric so he was laying on his side, an arm under his head for support.

"Thank you," Alaric sighed. "Can you stay with me?"

"Idiot, I already said I would."

"No, in bed with me."

Bashima's cheeks blazed, and Alaric's eyes drooped closed. He was out.

Bashima could have left. The human would never know the difference. He stared at the redhead for a while, not really believing what happened, what he'd done. Not just accidentally poisoning the human but everything. Had he really shoved the human against his door and kissed him? That felt like both centuries and seconds ago, and Bashima replayed it in his mind, the redhead's stunned eyes, his ready lips tasting like spiced apples. That sinful body, pliant for his every touch.

Every god had fucked a human at least once, but this felt different to Bashima, unlike how the other gods talked about it. Maybe because this was only the second human he'd ever let near him...

The redhead sighed in his sleep, and Bashima's heart plummeted. He couldn't leave. He climbed up onto the bed and pushed the hair out of the human's face. He was lovelier than Bashima expected, full of trust that the god would take care of him after he passed out. The bite mark on his shoulder stood out like a brand, and Bashima flinched away, almost bolting from the room. But something drew him back. That invisible string he'd felt in the shades' hall perhaps?

The Togarashi harvest song floated through his head, and he rubbed his eyes.

Stop it, he thought, *don't torture yourself. Just go. This doesn't have to happen again. It could be just this once.*

Bashima lay down beside the redhead and inched closer, so his back was against Bashima's chest. He smelled so damn good, like sex and spices and the sea-scented oil. Bashima draped an arm over the redhead's side and hesitated before intertwining their fingers. An impressive tattoo was on the redhead's left shoulder: a delicate yet fierce dragon twisted across the shoulder blade in ebony ink, its face turned toward whoever might see it, claws drawn. The dragon's eyes burned red.

Chapter Six

The two weeks leading up to the summit should have been tense, but Alaric fell into an easy pattern of bliss. Since his performance for the shades, Bashima came to him each night, the hunger in his eyes intoxicating. Their encounters became more intense and acrobatic as Bashima put Alaric through every position in his sexual arsenal, sending Alaric over the edge every time with ease. But the god was more careful after their first night together, making sure to finish himself away from Alaric's body. Though Alaric longed to touch Bashima, the god made it very clear that the long-term effects would be dangerous. Alaric wondered if it had something to do with becoming god-touched, but he didn't want to ask and risk Bashima leaving his bed.

Each time, when Alaric lay spent and happily exhausted, Bashima cuddled up to him until Alaric fell asleep then slipped out of the room like a shadow. He was never there when Alaric woke in the morning. Alaric tried not to be upset; the god was busy with summit preparations as well as doing his regular duties, and he started joining Alaric for dinner each night. He was quiet and contemplative and didn't seem to mind that Alaric talked through their meals. Bashima offered short responses, grunts, and a lot of raised eyebrows, but Alaric found this endearing, loved watching the god's reactions to his stories.

Matthias and Tika remained in the dining room throughout their dinners, standing back against opposite walls, and Alaric thought he detected Tika holding back smiles more than once, especially when the Sun God grew agitated if Alaric's story went on for longer than ten minutes. Alaric shrugged off the god's temper snaps and continued his tales, which made the god shiver with pent-up feigned rage.

Bashima liked when Alaric complied, but what seemed to actually entice him was Alaric expressing exactly what he wanted or showing defiance. After a particularly long tale involving a runaway goat, a broom, and a sinkhole, Bashima let out a frustrated shout, called Alaric "Redheaded Idiot," yanked him out of his chair, and ordered him immediately to his bedroom. This incident left Tika giggling in the corner, tears rolling down her face as she tried to stay quiet, and Matthias blushing furiously.

Emilia beamed when they spent the mornings and afternoons together, poking the mouth-shaped bruises on Alaric's neck, and asking him hundreds of questions. They tried to stay out of the other shades' ways as they bustled about the temple, chatting together and making the final decorating preparations. Alaric was fascinated by how much needed to be done.

Rooms were prepared for each god and their partner, some with very specific needs. A massive temporary structure was built at the base of the mountain to house the gods' servants. Draiden was in charge of that project and went through a detailed explanation when Alaric found him resting in the library. There would be hundreds of shades who needed rooms and about thirty god-touched. Alaric asked how the shades could leave their temples, and Draiden muttered something about alchemy. He changed the subject and asked how Alaric's lyre practice was going, a knowing smile adorning his lips. When Alaric flushed scarlet, Draiden chuckled and patted him on the shoulder.

Shefu was in charge of all food preparation and had endless lists of dietary needs and restrictions. Since the concert, she was amiable and answered Alaric's timid questions about the summit. Before, she would have chased him out of the kitchens, but Emilia told him everyone loved his music, particularly the chef. She gave Alaric snacks and sweets when he came down to the kitchen and showed him the elaborate set-up that would transfer shade-edible food directly down the mountain to their dining area. Alaric didn't quite grasp the process, because it involved transportation alchemy, a magic that was difficult to learn and comprehend. He told Shefu that he would never be able to pull off a tenth of what she did, and the chef shooed him out with an armful of apple tarts.

Alaric and Bashima were having a late dinner five days before the summit began, and Bashima seemed quieter than he'd been since he and Alaric had started...whatever they were doing.

"You're really calm tonight," Alaric said, drawing the god's attention.

Bashima had been reading through a scroll, and his eyes flicked up. "I'm always calm."

Alaric suppressed a snort and said, "Okay, then you're calmer. Any reason?"

Bashima rolled up the scroll, and a shade appeared to take it. When he disappeared with the scroll, Tika stepped next to Bashima and whispered in his ear, probably reminding him that it was late and that he still had more work to get through.

"Yeah, yeah, I know," Bashima muttered, looking down the table at Alaric. Tika stepped back to the wall and winked at Alaric. Bashima cleared his throat and said, "I've ordered some things for you to wear at the summit. Don't get too excited; it's just some fancier shit than what you usually wear. Can't have you looking like you worship fucking *Tengu* or the Lightning God."

Alaric nearly spit out his soup. He coughed and slapped his chest, and Matthias came up beside him to see what was wrong. Alaric waved him away and nodded that he was okay. Regaining his composure, he gaped down the table at Bashima, dumbstruck. "You...you want me to go to the summit?"

"Since the gods are all a bunch of fucking gossips, it would cause a whole damn scene if you didn't make an appearance," said Bashima, rolling his eyes. "You won't have to do anything, just stand around while I have to greet everyone and all that stupid hosting shit. It'll be boring, so if you get tired of it, just tell Matthias. He'll be with you the entire time and can get you out of there." He paused and mumbled, "Not that I'll be that lucky."

Alaric sputtered, "Um..."

"You'll be fine. Some of the gods will try and talk to you, bunch of nosy dicks. I'll have Kuroi give you a copy of the guest list, and Matthias can walk you through it. But you're *my* guest," he growled, "so if anyone gets obnoxious, tell Matthias or Kuroi. They can handle it." Bashima looked at Alaric's stunned face and frowned. "What's wrong? You're making a weird face."

Alaric wasn't sure how to answer. He still didn't have a handle on Bashima, let alone trying to mingle with other gods. What was he supposed to do? What could he possibly say that would interest a god? "I didn't think you'd want me to be there..."

"Why not?" asked Bashima, sipping the last of his wine. "You're decent to look at, you smile all the damn time, and you'll pull focus off me."

Alaric felt heat rise to his face and worried that he'd sweat through his shirt right at the table. "Okay... So long as you and Matthias are there..."

"You're not happy," Bashima stated, eyes flashing.

"It's not that; it's just that I don't know a thing about your world. I don't want to look like an idiot in front of your friends."

"They're not my friends. Don't sweat it too hard." When Alaric didn't answer, Bashima sighed and said, "Fine. I'll ask one the assholes to come early to meet you. Then you'll know someone."

Alaric breathed out in relief. That was a great idea! If he saw at least one friendly face, that was all he'd need. And Matthias would be there too, and he knew all about the other gods. They could have a study session in the library; Emilia would love to hear about the gods too.

"Now that that's settled," said Bashima, sidling along the table and grabbing Alaric's chin, "don't make me carry you over my shoulder to your room."

"I didn't think I could make you do anything," Alaric joked and tried to slip a hand around Bashima's hip.

"Do I have to tie your hands?"

Alaric's eyes lit up, thinking about it. He bit his lower lip and said, "That could be fun!"

The Sun God's eyes sparkled, and he flung Alaric up onto his shoulder and dismissed the shades.

"The list isn't as long as I feared," said Matthias, "but there's still a lot of names you'll need to know. Maybe I should make a chart…"

Alaric sat in his favorite chair in the library, Matthias pouring over the summit guest list, Emilia reading a tawdry romance story and not paying attention. He had four days to learn as much as he could, and Matthias took it as a personal challenge to make sure Alaric was prepared. Emilia was less concerned. Her job during the summit was to stay out of the way while running messages.

"Just start at the beginning, and I'll do my best to memorize everything," Alaric said. "I know we can do this!"

"That's the spirit," said Emilia, turning another page.

"Put that down," said Matthias to the girl. "You should listen too."

"Fine," whined Emilia, throwing the book on the floor and crossing her arms. "I already know the important ones," she mumbled.

"It would be better if you knew all of them," Matthias said and shook his head. He sighed and handed Alaric the list. The list was indeed long, and each entry had a small painting next to it, so Alaric would be able to recognize them.

"These paintings are really detailed," he said, running a finger over one.

"Hmmm yes, one of Kuroi's specialties, alchemic art. All he has to do is picture the person in his mind, say the right incantation, and poof, there's a painting. First and most important are King Vaultus and his wife, the Goddess of Spring, Hastia Cypress. They're the only ones you'll have to bow to; everyone else merits a polite nod."

"I'll try my best not to bow to everyone," Alaric said, self-conscious. He'd been trying to break the habit, but it had proven difficult.

King Vaultus was impressive-looking with layered black hair and large dark eyes. His smile was massive, and he looked like he could take out anyone in a fight. His wife looked familiar, with shiny light-green hair, kind eyes, and pale green skin.

"Wait a second," Alaric said, "her name is Cypress, like the Forest God?"

86

Matthias nodded. "Yes, she's Master Cypress's mother, and she'll ask you to call her 'Hastia.' She's one of the nicest people I've ever met. King Vaultus is Master Cypress's stepfather. His real father is some minor volcano god who lives on the other side of the world. He's not invited to the summits."

Alaric wanted to ask a few questions about that, but Matthias moved on quickly.

"Oof, next is Master Cindras, Oken's father. He's the Fire God, most powerful of the four Elemental Gods. The less he notices you, the better. If you see him, be polite and don't speak unless he asks you a direct question. With any luck, he won't deign to notice you. I doubt he'll allow his...children's mother to attend the summit, so you might not see her. She'll probably be in the god-touched quarters down the mountain."

"That seems harsh," said Alaric.

Emilia had perked up when Matthias mentioned Oken, whom she was fascinated with. "Will Oken be at the summit?" she asked, trying not to sound too interested.

"I assume so," said Matthias, sighing. "He'll have to represent his siblings. None of Master Cindras's other children have as much base power; they're more like normal demigods. Oken inherited his father's fire abilities but also gained an ice ability from somewhere on his mother's family line. I don't think he's seen his father since the last summit, and from what I heard, it didn't end well."

"He's friends with the Forest God, right?" asked Alaric. "So, they'll probably stick by each other during the summit. Maybe Oken won't have to interact with his father."

"Whatever Master Cindras wants to do, he will," said Matthias, sensing that Alaric was about to pry, "and don't even think about stopping him. He'd kill you as soon as look at you."

"Don't worry, I won't put my foot in my mouth," said Alaric. "Or I'll try not to."

"If it makes you feel better, the big-time gods probably won't even notice you," said Emilia, patting Alaric's knee.

"You two are making me feel really great about myself."

"She's right," said Matthias, "and that would be the ideal outcome. Look, most of these gods will seem funny, or nice, or charming, but be on your guard. I'll be sure to steer you in the right direction during the events. Master Cabari is chaos incarnate, but he's a good person for you to meet. Mistress Vesper would be another option. She's the Air Goddess, an Elemental, and is sweet and vivacious."

He sat back in his chair and rubbed his eyes. "And Lord Veles is bringing his son, Jace, which will make things awkward with his husband. I swear, the gods try to smite my will to exist."

Alaric took a deep breath and paged through the list to find Cabari and Vesper so he could pick them out in the crowd. "At least there'll be a few safe options," Alaric said.

Matthias choked on his tea and said, "If this is the *only* thing you remember: the gods are not safe. None of them. Any one of them could take us out by snapping their fingers. Even Oken would have a difficult time standing against a god, and he has two Elemental powers. Stay focused, stay with me, and if anything happens to me, find the master immediately."

Alaric gulped, and Emilia twiddled her thumbs, not looking at either him or Matthias. This summit was turning out to be more perilous than Alaric first imagined.

Alaric was on his way back to his room to change for dinner when he heard a loud crash from the throne room. Startled, Alaric ran to the door and let himself in. It was evening, so Bashima should be finished with his work, so what was going on? Another crash greeted him when he stepped inside, a clay pot shattering next to the door.

"I don't remember saying you could bring your talking dildo with you!"

Bashima stood on his throne's dais, glaring down at someone Alaric had never seen before. Two someones. Alaric surveyed the room for damage. Kuroi would have to replace the pottery again, and the room's candles were burning high, but the flames weren't boiling the wax, so Alaric figured Bashima wasn't too mad.

"Sweetie," said a sugary voice, "you really need to calm down. It's not like I brought my entourage."

The voice belonged to an athletic woman in a black leather skirt and bodice, but that's where her normalcy faded. Her skin was bright blue, like a robin's egg, spotted with lavender and brown markings. Two short horns jutted from her head, which was covered with dark blue curls.

The man slouching next to her gave off a relaxed air as though nothing concerned him and never would. Even being called a dildo by the Sun God. He was tall and lanky, and his posture was so loose it looked like he had no skeleton. His baggy tunic and pants didn't help the image. His choppy brown hair fell almost to his shoulders, and his face and ears held copious piercings. Small wings jutted from his elbows and ankles and flapped lazily.

This must be the god that Bashima invited early for the summit, for Alaric to meet. Stepping gingerly around the broken clay pots, Alaric inched into the room and said, "Um, hello."

All three gods' heads turned, Bashima and the woman surprised, and the slim man just smirked. Alaric smiled nervously and waved at them.

"Ohhhh, Bashima," drawled the woman. "Now I see why you never want to leave your temple."

Both Alaric and Bashima flushed darker than wine, and the woman and man burst out laughing. They doubled over and slapped each other on the back, cackling. Alaric didn't think it was that funny, but who was he to argue with a god's sense of humor?

"These two morons will be joining us for dinner, apparently," growled Bashima, stepping off the dais. He marched up to the other gods and shoved them over. They fell, still laughing, onto their backs, not caring that Bashima pushed them.

Alaric crept closer until he was behind Bashima. The Sun God's shoulders trembled with anger, so Alaric moved past him and extended his hands down to the two gods. "Would you like some help?" he asked.

Bashima crossed his arms over his chest and blew air out his nose.

"And so chivalrous!" The woman grinned and grabbed one of Alaric's hands and pulled herself up until she pressed her entire body against his.

"What do you do all day, honey? Swim laps? Lift heavy objects? Eat like, ten chickens?" She drew a circle on his chest and winked up at him. Her eyes were completely black, like Kuroi's, but she had bright white irises. Alaric felt like he was staring into the night sky.

"Get off him, for fuck's sake," said Bashima.

"Get a sense of humor," said the woman, but she let Alaric go and stepped back, assessing him. "They grow humans this big now?"

Alaric looked down at the man and reached out again. "Uh, any help?"

"Nah, I can enjoy the view just as well from down here." He grinned up at Alaric and waggled his eyebrows.

"You two are such dicks. Get the fuck up," said Bashima. "This is Alora," he pointed at the woman, "And this waste of air is Garyn."

"Moon Goddess," said Alora with a devilish smile.

"Messenger of the Gods, protector of merchants and thieves," said Garyn as his four wings lifted his body from the floor.

When Bashima didn't introduce him, Alaric rubbed the back of his head and said, "Uh, I'm Alaric Shina, but you can call me Alaric if you'd like. Everyone does."

"Ugh," said Bashima, he grabbed Alaric's arm and led him toward the door. "Better keep up, morons. I'm hungry."

Alora and Garyn followed behind them, giggling. "Walking?" asked Alora. "How blasé."

"We don't need to *fly* to the dining room," Bashima snapped.

"Why don't we just shift there?" she asked, voice whiny.

Bashima scowled at her, and his eyes darted to Alaric.

"Oh," said Alora. "Afraid you might scramble his brains?"

"What?" asked Alaric.

Alora grabbed his bicep and squeezed. "Hold on, honey."

The world turned in on itself. Alaric felt all the air leave his lungs as invisible walls crushed his body. It felt as though he were falling while being pressed into a very thin pancake. When the world came spinning back into focus, Alaric saw the long dining room table, and it tilted like a boat tossed in a storm. He fell to his knees, chest heaving, and almost threw up. He burped and held it in, not wanting to embarrass Bashima.

Five shades were setting the table, looking on, horrified.

"What in all cursed hells is this?" Tika shouted as she marched over, "Matthias! Get in here!"

"Oh hi, Tika," said Alora. "Great to see you."

"What just happened?" Tika asked, and Matthias appeared at Alaric's side. The shade rubbed his back, confused, and Alaric coughed. He tasted blood in the back of his throat, warm and coppery. Tika's eyes widened. "Did you shift with him? Damned hells. One of you," she shouted at the shades, "bring me the shift tonic from the store cupboard, hurry!"

"Shina," said Matthias, "how do you feel?"

"Like I was hit with a really big boulder," Alaric croaked.

A brilliant light flashed at the head of the table, and Bashima vaulted over it with controlled flame bursts from his palms, knocking Alora off her feet. They fell in a heap against the wall, Bashima's hands wreathed in explosive fire. Alora kicked him off, her own hands flashing blue-white and dripping with something that sizzled on the floor.

"I thought I told you to relax, brother."

"What the fuck were you thinking?" Bashima screamed. "He's never shifted before! That could have killed him!"

"He's fine," she said, ire dripping with her words. "And now I know you're actually serious and not just parading a human around to piss everyone off."

Bashima snarled and ran at her again, but Garyn appeared between them and buffeted them both with wind strikes from his wings. Bashima flew back into the table, and Alora hit the wall with a thud. Both of them glowered at Garyn, who shrugged. "You're both being jerks," he said and went to sit at the table. "This looks great. Human food? Wild shit."

Alaric raised his hand and sputtered out, "I'm good. I'm okay."

The shade returned and handed an orange glass phial to Tika. She threw off the lid and jammed the phial into Alaric's mouth. He gagged, but Tika slammed his jaws closed so he had to swallow. It tasted like warm bile, but he stopped shaking, and the room stopped undulating. "Now I really am good," he said, and Matthias helped him up. "What's in that stuff?"

Bashima snorted and said, "You don't want to know." He glared at Alora, who brushed herself off and sashayed past the fuming Sun God, taking a place across from Garyn.

"Well?" she asked, "Aren't you going to sit and tell me all about yourself?"

Bashima didn't say anything, so Alaric shrugged and went to his usual seat. The Sun God eventually slumped in his own chair and poured half a bottle of wine into his glass.

Matthias poured Alaric a small glass and whispered, "Sip this. Only one glass. Remember what I said."

"So, Alaric," Alora purred, saying his name like it was a savory truffle. "Did you know Bashima and I are twins?"

"No ,we're fucking not," said Bashima as he drained his glass. He didn't wait for Tika; he dumped the rest of the wine into the glass then handed her the empty bottle.

"What he means is that we're not 'technically' twins," said Alora. "We were born on the same day, the same hour, same minute, down to the second."

"That's...nice," said Alaric. He recalled the dizziness he'd experienced a moment ago and gripped the table. "I didn't know the Sun God had a sibling, even just a coincidental one."

Garyn snorted into his drink and wiped wine off his chin.

"Makes sense that we're the Sun and Moon then, huh?" Alora smiled. "Aren't you eating?"

Alaric looked around and Tika caught his eye, nodding. "Sure," he said, and the shades appeared and begin a circuit around the table, offering everyone the assorted dishes. "Gods can eat human food then?" Bashima had eaten plenty of human food, but Alaric wasn't sure all gods could.

"Of course," Alora said and bit into a pear, thin line of juice running down her chin. "Though we also need hardier nourishment. So, do you have any siblings?"

Finally, an easy question. "No, it's just me. And my parents. I always wanted a brother or sister, but it wasn't meant to be, I guess." He shrugged and continued, "But the other kids in my village were like my siblings. We used to spend nights out in the fields during the summer, bunches of us. Probably to give our parents a break."

"How sweet," said Alora. "We gods don't get much of a childhood."

"That's too bad," said Alaric, trying to image Bashima as a child and failing. "Being a kid, no real responsibilities, that's an important part of life. You have to work most of it, and sleep takes up a lot of time, I suppose, so I've always been grateful for when we could go fishing or play games."

Garyn looked at Alaric as though he were an angel. "I don't know how humans do it," he said and tore a chunk out of a chicken leg with his teeth. "You're born, live a little life, get drunk a lot, I assume, then die. But you're way more optimistic than most immortals I know."

Alaric laughed and rubbed the back of his head. "When you put it that way, it doesn't sound like much, but I like to enjoy the little things. The big things are important too, of course, keeping the world peaceful and being a good person, but we're all just a collection of memories wrapped in a body. In the end, I doubt I'll be thinking about how the cosmos are doing. I'll be happy to remember how my mom's pies taste."

All three gods stared at Alaric like he had three heads, but Tika smirked against the wall. She was once human, so maybe she knew what Alaric meant. Maybe she had a tiny memory that kept her going.

"Sorry," he said. "I've been told I talk too much."

"I think you're absolutely charming," said Alora.

They fell into easy conversation, at least Alaric, Alora, and Garyn did. While the two gods smattered him with questions and delighted in his answers, Bashima sat and watched, sipping his wine, eyes narrowed.

When the shades came to collect the plates, the candles were low. Garyn and Alora stretched their arms and cracked their necks, praising the food and Alaric's company.

"It's nice to meet new people," said Alaric, eyes bright. "Never in my craziest dreams did I think I'd ever be talking to gods. Are you all this good-looking?"

"Matthias," said Bashima sharply. The shade came forward beside Alaric's chair, expression blank. The Sun God looked at Alaric, but he wasn't sure what direction Bashima was trying to convey. "Take him to his room. I need to speak with Alora."

Alaric blinked and opened his mouth but closed it quickly with another look from Bashima. "Thank you for joining us for dinner," he said to Alora and Garyn. "Have a pleasant night." He let Matthias lead him from the dining room, wondering if he'd said something wrong.

"You're going to have to be very careful," said Alora as she poured herself and Garyn more wine. The winged god raised an eyebrow but didn't contribute his opinion.

"Fuck you," said Bashima, leaning back in the chair. He looked up at the ceiling, wishing he hadn't asked Alora to come. He didn't like how well the human got along with her or with her brainless tag-along. Not that he was surprised. The human got along annoyingly well with everyone.

"No thanks," she said and smiled. "I'm serious. Who else knows?"

"Knows what?" Bashima swirled the wine in his glass and couldn't meet Alora's eyes.

"That you actually like him. Hells, does *he* even know that you actually like him?"

"I'm fucking him twelve ways to Sunday; isn't that enough?"

Garyn downed his wine, sucked on his teeth, and stood up. "That's my cue to go to bed," he said and saluted both of them. Tika stepped forward and whispered to him. Garyn winked at her, saluted Bashima again, and disappeared.

"I hope you sent him to my usual room, Tika." The shade smiled at Alora and moved back against the wall. The Moon Goddess refocused on Bashima. "Is this going to be a problem?"

"Gods dammit you sound like Tengu. Can't you mind your own business for once?"

"Not when every god and their gossip-sniffing god-touched are going to be crawling all over this temple. Niall is going to lose his mind over this, and you're acting like a jealous little bitch when it's just me and Garyn."

"I'm not jealous. And Niall will be too busy pissing in Veles's demon spawn's nectar to notice anything I do."

"I know that it would raise too many eyebrows if he didn't make an appearance, but is Alaric ready for something like this? Are you?" Alora asked.

Bashima didn't answer right away. He had no doubt the redhead would navigate the poisonous party events well, and Matthias would be at his side, and Kuroi would also be watching. As for himself...

"It was going to happen sooner or later," Bashima said and downed his wine. "Vaultus wasn't going to let me be a social pariah forever."

"What's a couple thousand years between friends and family?" Alora asked. "Just think about what I said. And if this is something that you really want."

Alaric sat on his bed and waited. He waited for the candle to drip its last wax, snuffing itself out. He watched the thin coil of smoke rise to the ceiling and dissipate. When his eyes got used to the dark, he lay down and clutched a pillow to his chest.

The bed felt cold.

It was the first time he'd fallen asleep alone in a while.

Chapter Seven

Between Bashima working during sunlight hours and all the summit preparations, Alaric only saw the Sun God at dinner, but Alora and Garyn were with them, so he couldn't get Bashima alone. The visiting gods were jovial and easy to talk to, but Alaric could only think of his empty bed and that Bashima would hardly look at him. Alaric knew the Sun God was watching him, but he avoided Alaric's direct gaze. It was infuriating. He wanted to pull Bashima aside and ask him what was wrong, but the upcoming event must have been getting to the Sun God. Alaric didn't want to add his insecurities to the mix.

Matthias told him not to worry, to focus on memorizing the guest list and making sure his new clothes fit properly.

"I couldn't care less about clothes right now," Alaric said as Matthias and one of the textile-master shades prepared his outfits for the next few days. He felt like a doll, costume changes for the greeting ceremony, for the informal luncheons, for each nights' dinners. He had a different ensemble for every event. He secretly planned to avoid as many changes as he could.

Would Bashima be expected to put on this kind of show? The Sun God had various versions of his traditional garb, but Alaric knew he also had pants and shirts made of cotton so soft they felt like melting butter.

"Well, at least it's one thing you can control," Matthias said, distracted.

"I'm sorry," Alaric said and hung his head. "I'm being a mopey drip, aren't I?"

"When even Emilia stays away to do her chores, I'd say you're not acting like your usual positive self." Matthias touched his shoulder and gave him a small smile. "This was always going to be tough. You have to get through three days of nonsense. Then...things can go back to how they were."

The other shade finished organizing and ducked out of the room, and Alaric sat down hard on the bed. "Did I chase her away with my great attitude too?"

"I'm sure the master is just busy," said Matthias, an edge to his voice.

"He's probably mad that Alora keeps flirting with me," Alaric groaned. "It's not like I'm asking her to do that."

"Ha, the master is eons old. He may be prone to jealousy, but he knows you're not encouraging her. He's definitely on edge because she's here though. She used to come to the temple a lot, for visits, to cheer up the master, but she hadn't been here in a while."

"She seems unpredictable."

"Her kidnapping you via shifting clued you onto that?" Matthias smirked at him and sat down on the bed next to him. "Remember how the master reacted to what she did."

Alaric did. Bashima had been furious and protective.

Matthias continued, "Keep that in your heart during the summit because he won't have much time for you."

"I know," Alaric said. "Doesn't make it less hurtful."

"Let's finish your hair," Matthias suggested. He pulled Alaric up from the bed even though he tried to go limp. "Don't act like Emilia. Come on."

"I don't know, Em. Do you really think it looks okay?"

Emilia stood behind Alaric as he checked his hairstyle in the silver mirror.

"You look amazing!" she said and did a twirl on her toes. "It's fun to try new styles!"

Emilia arrived at his room with special clay that would make his hair stay in place and proceeded to twist it into elaborate braids and spikes. Two small chunks of hair in the front stood up like horns. He kind of liked it.

"You look like a dragon," she said, in awe of her styling prowess.

"Great," he said and laughed. "At least I'll look like I belong here. Sort of."

"Who said you don't belong?" Kuroi stood at his door, dour look on his face, a small box in his hand.

Emilia ran over to him and pointed at Alaric. "Doesn't he look good?" she asked, excited.

"Indeed. Emilia, it's almost time for the guests to arrive. Go to your assigned position and listen to your section leader." Emilia saluted Kuroi and bolted from the room. He sighed, tired. "Hopefully she doesn't run anyone over on her way there."

Kuroi stared at Alaric, something odd in his eyes. He shook his head and beckoned Alaric over. "You look adequate," he said, dusting off Alaric's shoulders and straightening his jacket. "The dark green was an excellent choice."

"It's not too showy?" asked Alaric, unsure.

"The master chose it, so he must have some idea of how he'd like you to look."

"Uh, yeah," said Alaric, uncertainty flooding his body.

"None of that now," said Kuroi. "Take advantage of your height. Most of the gods aren't as tall as you, and that hair gives you even more height and presence. Stand up tall and remember where you come from."

Kuroi opened the small box, hinging the lid so Alaric could see. Inside was a delicate white gold pin shaped into a swirling dragon, superimposed over an unfamiliar yet graceful symbol. Kuroi took the pin out of the box and affixed it to Alaric's jacket.

"Togarashi, the celestial dragon, he of the unbreakable will." He traced the symbol with a finger. "And the sigil of the Sun God. Let no one here forget who you are, including the master."

Alaric fought back tears. It was an incomparable gift. "Thank you," he managed to say.

"It's my pleasure," said Kuroi. "Now, let's make sure you don't miss your debut."

Bashima stood in front of the temple's main doors, thinking how the summit was a huge mistake and that he should send everyone home. Canceled. Everything should be canceled. But he couldn't do that. Not with the King of the Gods on his way up the mountain, a parade of gods behind him.

It had been a very long time since he'd seen Vaultus, since he'd seen most of them. He wasn't looking forward to greeting any of them or letting them into his home. But the staff were ready, the shades full of excited anticipation, the three god-touched ready to show off their considerable talents. The entire event was designed like a well-built machine, and there wasn't a lot Bashima had to do besides socialize and not lose his temper. Two things at which he did not excel.

And where was that idiot human? Kuroi went to collect him centuries ago. Bashima didn't want to think about the redhead, lest it show on his face in front of the other gods. Alora was right about one thing: if the other gods sensed the human was anything more than a passing fancy, some of them would take advantage. The redhead would be in danger.

So, Bashima had to control himself, keep his face a mask.

For the greeting ceremony, he wore his full godly regalia: golden breastplate covering a chain mail shirt made of tiny golden links; an armor-covered battle skirt, also gold, which hit him mid-thigh; shimmering sandals that laced up his calves to his knees; his usual bracers; earrings gleaming from both ears. He'd traded his formal mask for a bare face and was crowned with a thick golden band that sent sunlight flickering across the temple.

He imagined the golden chain that ran across the redhead's chest and shook his head, forcing the image away.

Banish him from your thoughts, he chastised himself.

"Master," Kuroi said behind him. "It's almost time. Shina is here."

Bashima grunted his assent and tried not to turn, but something caught his eye. The human's damned hair. Artfully braided around his head, showing off his entire face, which was set in determination. They'd traced his upper lids in thick black kohl, making his lashes stand out more, making his eyes look wider. They'd also pierced his left ear, and a golden chain hung from the top helix down to the lobe, connected to two golden cuff earrings. Bashima made a mistake on the high-necked dark green suit because the redhead looked too good. How was he supposed to look away? How was he going to focus on the other gods?

Then he saw the pin. Kuroi's work, for sure, damn the man to the seven hells. The dragon leaped regally on the human's upper chest near his collarbone, combined with the sign of the Sun God. Marking him as Bashima's.

Mine, he wanted to hiss. He wanted to drag the human back through the temple, get to the closest private corner, and tear the suit from his body into shreds. He would take the human's essence out through his mouth with the depth of his kiss and mark his lips and skin with bites so everyone would know who he belonged to. *Mine.* All of him, his body, his mind, his soul. He needed to claim him somehow, so the greedy gods wouldn't steal him away. The very thought filled Bashima with rage. *Mine.*

Then the redhead smiled at him. Bashima returned a savage grin and turned to face the doors. "Let them come," he said, and Kuroi raised his arm, signaling the doors to open.

Nerves threatened to break Alaric to pieces, but once he saw Bashima, his mind cleared, and his hands stopped shaking. The Sun God stood tall and haughty in front of the main doors, glorious black cape cascading down his back and a golden crown that sparkled with inner sunlight. Bashima needed him to be strong for the ceremony, so he would be. He couldn't give off the same commanding air as the god, but he could stand straight and smile at the oncoming challenge.

When Kuroi announced him and Bashima turned his head a fraction at their approach, Alaric was nearly floored by his expression: proud, noble, fierce, but a flash of need. The need cycled into feral want, and Alaric felt an invisible pull in his chest and nearly fell into the god's whirlpool eyes. Instead, he plastered a triumphant smile on his face, sharp teeth showing. The Sun God's grin spread across his face, and his eyes flashed red and gold.

"Let them come," said Bashima, voice deep and commanding.

Alaric wanted to grab the god's hand and interlace their fingers, but he held back. That wasn't why he was there, one step behind the Sun God.

The doors swung open on Kuroi's signal and sunlight blazed over them, illuminating Bashima in a dazzling spotlight. Alaric fought shielding his eyes; he wanted to see every inch of the god in his splendor.

There was plenty in front of him to grab his attention as well.

Standing in front of the doors were two gods, resplendent in their finery, and next to them was a slim, severe-looking man with an aquiline nose and piercing eyes. He stepped forward and handed Kuroi an iridescent, glittering scroll.

Kuroi nodded to the man and said, "His majesty, King Vaultus and her majesty, Queen Hastia."

Alaric was shocked by how big King Vaultus was; the god towered over everyone, easily over seven feet tall. His smile was easy and radiant, and he moved in to greet Bashima.

"My boy! You look splendid!" He laid a large hand on Bashima's shoulder, who offered a small smirk in return.

"King Vaultus, I am most honored to welcome you and Queen Hastia to the Temple of the Sun."

"It's been too long," Queen Hastia said, giving Bashima a knowing glance.

"I apologize for my long absence," laughed Bashima—*he genuinely laughed?*—taking the queen's offered hand. "If I'd known you'd miss me so much, I would have left the temple long ago."

It was the queen's turn to laugh, a light and airy sound that made Alaric think of a gentle stream.

"Liar," Hastia said. "But I'll forgive you. My son, on the other hand…"

Bashima snorted, which made the king and queen both chortle.

Kuroi stepped forward and inclined his head to the king and queen. "May I also present the Sun God's most honored guest?" He gestured Alaric forward, and Alaric kept the sweat at bay somehow, taking measured breaths. Kuroi's eyes glittered with approval at Alaric's demeanor, and he said, "Alaric Shina of Togarashi Village."

Alaric bowed at his waist and waited for the king to speak.

"You may rise," boomed the king, chuckling. "My, you're a fine-looking man. I hope young Bashima is being an accommodating host."

Alaric sensed Bashima tense beside him.

Young Bashima? How old was the king that he could call the Sun God young?

Alaric rose from his bow and grinned, "He is, your majesty."

"Charming," said the queen, extending her hand for Alaric to kiss. "Quite charming indeed." She shared a glance with her husband.

Kuroi and the severe man stood next to each other, and Kuroi said, "The throne room is prepared for the greeting reception, your majesties."

A Temple of the Sun shade appeared at Kuroi's side, and the severe man gestured for his godly charges to follow. The shade led them down the main hall to the throne room where they would socialize and eat a light lunch until the first meeting.

After the king and queen, the greeting ceremony became easier for Alaric. He could tell that Bashima was getting irritated, but the other gods didn't seem to notice. Each stepped in front of Bashima, and either a god-touched or shade attendant presented their scroll. Then, Kuroi introduced Alaric—who remembered not to bow now that the king and queen had passed. Finally, a shade would appear to lead the gods into the temple. Pretty straightforward.

The Elemental Gods came directly after the royal couple, and Alaric had to admit the Fire God, Cindras, was terrifying. The god was broad-shouldered as a bull, almost as tall as King Vaultus, with muscular arms thicker than columns. Ruddy skin dotted with darker red freckles made the man resemble an actual flame. His cold turquoise eyes barely registered Alaric, for which he was grateful. Matthias would be ecstatic.

The Water Goddess, Rizu, was tall and imperious; Vesper, the Air Goddess had friendly blue eyes, and she giggled at Bashima, teasing him like a younger brother, which Bashima accepted with little agitation; Daisuke filled out the group as the Earth God, whose black hair was done in elaborate braids. He stared at Alaric but made no comment, preferring to get past Bashima as quickly as possible.

Veles, God of the Dead and Lord of the Underworld, was less physically impressive than Alaric expected, but his eyes were hypnotizing. And bloodshot. The god looked infinitely more tired than Draiden. His long black hair fell around his shoulders, beard thick and braided, and his dark gray skin seemed to wither in the sunlight. He greeted Bashima as though he were a former student who had escaped numerous punishments. Bashima showed him deference, which couldn't be said for Veles's husband.

Niall was the exact opposite of the God of the Dead: blond, boisterous, loud, upbeat, with shining rose-colored skin. He announced himself as the Voice of the Gods before Kuroi could introduce him and shook Alaric's hand so hard that his arm strained in the socket.

"Stop that," said Veles. "We're holding up the line."

Niall beamed and continued shaking Alaric's hand. "A human! How splendid! You must tell me all about your life as a human!"

"You really mustn't," Veles droned, eyeing Alaric, and dragged his husband away. In their wake came a handsome, sullen younger man with a shock of messy mint green hair and bags under his eyes. It had to be Jace, Veles's demigod son. He followed his father without a word, nodding at Alaric and Bashima as he passed.

Alaric thought he heard Bashima mutter under his breath, "Weird," but couldn't be sure. Kuroi carried on as though Jace hadn't ignored the protocol, and Alaric wondered if Emilia was right: were any demigods happy?

The rest of the procession went off with few hiccoughs, though Alora and Garyn held up the line to fawn over Alaric and try to enrage Bashima. Alaric was impressed that Bashima didn't explode, though his face turned an extraordinary shade of red when Alora tried to hug him.

Cypress, the bright-eyed Forest God also stopped to speak longer with Bashima, quiet Oken at his side. Oken didn't look much like his father besides the eyes, and he didn't share the older god's jagged features or personality. Oken asked Alaric if he was having fun in a deadpan voice, and Alaric wasn't sure how to answer. Oken's advice was to wear comfortable shoes because Alaric would be standing for a very long time. That made Alaric laugh, and Cypress apologized. Alaric assured them both that it was fine, that he could

103

use the humor. Oken asked why his advice was funny, but Cypress led him away down the hall, still apologizing.

"They're an interesting pair," Alaric said to Kuroi, who had walked up beside him when there was a break in the line after Cypress. Kuroi merely smiled and moved to whisper something to Bashima, who nodded. They didn't have many gods left to greet.

There was one other oddity in the ceremony.

Kuroi introduced him as Chronas, God of Time and Lord of Order, and like most of the male gods, he was fairly tall and classically handsome with shimmering white skin, though his mouth had a cruel tilt, and his voice sent chills running through Alaric's body. Matthias hadn't mentioned anything particular about the god, just that he was on the do-not-engage list, but he made Alaric more skittish than the Fire God.

At least Cindras didn't hide that he was a bully; Alaric could read the Fire God. Chronas's smile didn't reach his cold gray eyes. Alaric felt as though he were being flayed from his skin to his bones when the god looked him up and down. Alaric could tell that Bashima disliked him, but the Sun God didn't treat Chronas differently than Cindras. Just another god that annoyed him.

Alaric noted that he should ask Matthias more about Chronas and stay as far away as he could.

When the last god entered and the doors closed, Kuroi stepped to Bashima's side immediately.

"We have the luncheon prepared in the throne room and will clear everything before the first session."

"Marvelous," groaned Bashima. "Are you tired?" he asked Alaric.

"Nope, I'm fine," Alaric answered and followed Bashima and Kuroi down the hall. Bashima grunted in response.

"Remember not to eat anything Matthias doesn't bring you," said Kuroi. "If the gods offer you something, politely decline. They know you can't eat manna-based food, but some of them might try it as a poorly-timed joke. If they're adamant that you try something, Matthias will step in and offer apologies then steer you away."

"Okay," said Alaric though he'd already heard this speech.

"Tika will be watching too," said Bashima, eyes ahead and darting with yellow energy. "If any of them try something, she'll be on them quick."

"Really, I'll be fine," Alaric said. "Don't worry."

"Ha, I'm not worried."

They entered the throne room to find it teeming with gods circulating, laughing, touching arms, eyeing one another. Alaric felt like he'd been dropped into a sea of sharks, but he knew what to do. He was ready. Matthias appeared at the door and nodded at Alaric, stepping directly behind him. Tika was at Bashima's side. Kuroi assured them that he would be available if necessary but that he was needed elsewhere in the temple.

Bashima's hand twitched toward Alaric's, but the Sun God took off into the room before Alaric could react. The Sun God entered the room like he was the King of the Gods and not Vaultus, and Alaric marveled at his poise and composure.

"Stop looking at his ass and get in there," whispered Matthias, and Alaric choked on the breath he'd been holding. "Find someone you recognize, Cypress or Alora to start."

It was easy to find them both. Cypress stood awkwardly, hunched over, Alora clapping him on the back and congratulating him for something. They both wore formal versions of their usual garb, and Alaric thought they had stepped out of a painting.

Alora caught sight of him and yelled, "Alaric! Come mingle with us!"

Cypress flushed as Alaric approached, which was fair. He saw Alaric completely naked not long ago. Alora tapped one of the spikes near Alaric's forehead. "Trying to copy me, honey?" She giggled and Cypress muttered under his breath.

"I'd make a poor copy," Alaric said, "especially when the inspiration was in the same room."

"Bashima really doesn't deserve you," she said and tickled his chin. "He's a complete gremlin. I have no idea how you put up with him."

"I'm sure the sex helps," said Oken, appearing at Cypress's side as if from nowhere.

"Oken!" Cypress exclaimed after spitting out most of his drink. A shade came up, grabbed Cypress's empty glass, and thrust a new drink in his hand then wiped the floor, all in about five seconds. Alaric reminded himself to congratulate the staff later.

"Was that one of the things I'm not supposed to mention, Bell?" Oken sighed. "I'll add it to the list, but it's getting too long to remember everything."

Alora snorted and nearly fell over. "You are a damn treasure," she said, wheezing. "I'm getting Garyn; he needs to hear this." She rushed away to find the Messenger of the Gods.

"Thank the seven hells," said Cypress. "She's exhausting. She's been here a few days, right?" he asked Alaric.

"Yeah, Bashima invited her, so I could meet another god before the summit. I don't think *our* first meeting counts." Alaric rubbed the back of his neck and grimaced.

"It made me quite uncomfortable as well," said Oken, sipping his drink.

Cypress put his face in his hands, and Oken wrapped an arm around him.

"Sorry about that," Alaric said, blushing. "We can have a fresh start now." He held out his hand to the demigod and said, "Alaric Shina, delighted to meet you."

Oken tilted his head and took Alaric's hand. "I was under the impression that humans were quite prudish, but you seem to enjoy the tactile experience as much as any god."

"I guess I do like hugs and stuff," admitted Alaric, laughing when Oken didn't drop his hand. Cypress reached out and disengaged their hands.

"So," said Cypress, "I'm guessing they gave you the rushed course on god politics? You looked really good at the greeting ceremony. Kuroi is a ball buster."

"You guessed right," Alaric said. "I spent about a week memorizing everyone's face. And a lot of them aren't even here."

Cypress nodded before saying, "They're either at one of the other two summits—there have to be three with how spaced out we all are now—or they ignored the summons. We're allowed to skip a summit once in four hundred years."

"Three summits?" said Alaric, surprised.

"Yeah. One here, one far across the ocean to the west, and one to the far south. This is the main one, so most of the major gods are here."

"Wow! Across the ocean? I never even dreamed of leaving my village," said Alaric, amazed. What kinds of gods lived across the ocean? Or down south? A thought hit him. "Um, are Bashima's parents..."

"Oh! Don't worry. You won't be subjected to that," assured Cypress, and Oken stared off at something or someone, not listening anymore. Cypress leaned in. "Bashima's mother is the Goddess of Youth, and his father is a minor earth god. They'll be at the southern summit since Rocky is here representing the Earth Elementals."

"Rocky?" asked Alaric.

"Oh, sorry—Daisuke. Rocky is his nickname, ever since he became the Earth Elemental."

"He wasn't always the Earth God?" asked Alaric, confused.

Before Cypress could answer, Oken said, still staring off into the distance, "Bashima wasn't the first Sun God. But I think he's much better from what I've heard."

Both Alaric and Cypress stared at Oken, mouths open. Oken finally refocused on them. "What?"

The Lightning God chose that moment to burst into the throne room, sending an electrical current across the halls, ruffling the numerous banners and making everyone's hair stand on end for a moment. Kuroi was at his heels, furious.

"No need to introduce me, Kuroi," shouted the Lightning God. "Everyone here already knows Raijin Cabari."

The god was shorter than most of the others with a slim, yet toned physique and wild dark hair zigzagged with golden highlights. A golden hoop nose ring caught the light, showing off the rest of his face. There was chaos in his golden eyes and feral grin.

He locked on Alaric, and the grin got wider.

"Except for that beautiful bastard!" Cabari blasted through the crowd of gods, angry curses in his wake, and landed in front of Alaric, his nose to his chest. "Well, you're a big fucker, aren't you? I didn't know Bashima fancied climbing trees."

A shade materialized next to Cabari with a drink, and he backed away from Alaric, beaming. "Bashima always has the best shades! Thank you!" Cabari raised a glass to the poor shade, who bowed shortly then fled.

"Cabari," warned Cypress, "everyone is staring."

"Really?" asked the Lightning God, looking around. "Good!"

Alaric couldn't help but laugh at the loud god. He nearly doubled over, trying to control it.

"At least someone appreciates me," said Cabari. "What's your name, future boyfriend?"

"Don't let Bashima hear you say that," warned Oken in his monotone voice.

"Oh, precious Bashi knows I'm just kidding," said the Lightning God, flipping a hand and guzzling his drink. The little shade came again with another then disappeared. Cabari said, "Keep them coming!"

"I'm Alaric Shina, from Togarashi."

He saw Bashima out of the corner of his eye, talking with King Vaultus as though he hadn't seen the Lightning God cause a stir. But Alaric saw the light playing over Bashima's skin. He wasn't pleased.

"Really?" asked Cabari, and Cypress shook his head slightly. Cabari looked back at Alaric. "Well, they certainly put something in the water in Togarashi, huh?"

"I'm pretty big for my village," Alaric said. "But my dad is taller."

"Seven hells," said Cabari, eyes glittering. He gulped his drink again and held out the glass for a new one. Alaric felt bad for the shade in charge of Cabari, but she looked pleased to be busy when she appeared and disappeared again.

"Hey, Cypress," said Cabari, "what's the deal with the summit this year? Same old boring crap, or is Bashima pulling out the stops?"

"This isn't going to turn into a giant orgy like three hundred years ago," said Cypress, rolling his eyes, and Alaric choked on his own drink.

Cabari looked Alaric over and stuck out his lower lip. "What a shame."

Alora and Garyn barreled over, tackling Cabari in hugs, and they brought demigod Jace in tow. He looked even more bored than Oken, which was an achievement.

Cypress was called away by his mother, and he grabbed Oken's hand, patted Alaric on the shoulder in apology, and fled the rambunctious group. Alaric didn't mind. It was nice to be around people who were bubbly and trying to have fun.

"Cabari," said Alora, slyly smiling, "Do you remember Jace from my party about five years ago?"

"Only five years?" asked Alaric, astonished.

"I've only been allowed to participate in god events very recently," said Jace, his voice low but pleasing. He wore a scarf draped over his shoulders and exuded a confident but carefree attitude.

"I've gotten used to hearing triple digits, sorry, man," Alaric said and smiled, eyes crinkling.

Jace raised a brow and the other gods laughed.

"How old are you, Alaric?" asked Garyn. "I kept meaning to ask, but it never came up."

"I'm twenty," said Alaric and blushed. Twenty years was like a heartbeat to the gods.

"Not bad," said Jace. "I'm only three hundred. My stepsister Nim is about one hundred and seventy. She's too young to come to things like this."

"Wow, Bashima likes them YOUNG!" said Cabari, slapping Alaric on the back. "Coincidentally, so do I," he added and smirked at Jace, who looked like he would rather die.

Kuroi told Alaric that the summit was three days long, but all the work was done on day two. The first day was mainly for socializing, letting the gods reacquaint themselves with one another, introducing new faces. The second day was all business, and Kuroi warned Alaric that he would only see Bashima at lunch and dinner. The third day was meant for drinking. And farewells of course. But mainly drinking.

Alaric had a chance to relax a bit after the luncheon on the first day after Matthias tore him away from the riotous group of younger gods. The gods had their own private meeting until dinner, so Alaric was free to walk the temple and get his bearings. He didn't want to bother Shefu and the kitchen staff or get in Kuroi's way, so he went to the library and read for a couple hours with Matthias. Emilia popped her head in to say hi, then had to leave when a harassed-looking shade came looking for her.

Matthias helped Alaric change for dinner into a similar suit from the morning. This one was blue so dark it was almost black, and twin embroidered dragons chased each other on the collar. Alaric hadn't noticed the detail before and wondered why Bashima suggested it. He'd obviously seen Alaric's tattoo, having been at the right angle numerous times, but he'd never asked about it. Alaric ran a finger over the gold thread. Bashima paid more attention than he thought.

The dragons turned out to be an excellent conversation starter at dinner.

Alaric was seated at the foot of the table, facing King Vaultus, which he thought was a mistake. Kuroi explained that the queen refused to sit anywhere but next to the king, so her expected place went to the host's partner. Alaric gulped at the word "partner," but Kuroi was too busy to notice. Bashima sat at Vaultus's right, as the host.

To Alaric's right was a rotund god who introduced himself as, "Shokomotsu, but please call me Mo." He was the God of Food and Wine and enjoyed every part of dinner. When Matthias brought Alaric's dishes, Mo showed interest, asking what was in each dish, nodding whenever Alaric explained something he enjoyed. "Cheese, Shina! Cheese and seafood! I can't get enough. Right Hachi?"

The god to Alaric's left looked mortified that anyone had spoken to him and lowered his head to the table, shaking. He was very beautiful with delicate features, violet skin, pointed ears, and deep violet hair that hid his eyes.

"Mo, why are you asking me that right now?" His voice quavered.

"Hey, are you okay?" Alaric asked, concerned.

"He's all right," said the god next to him, who sported styled white hair and oddly shaped, blue-black eyes. His smile was infectious. "We met at the greeting, of course, but I'm Desh, God of Peace. This gorgeous god is Hachi Raphe, God of War."

Desh wrapped an arm around Raphe, who melted into him and accepted an offered fruit skewer.

Alaric thought it should be the other way around; Desh was massive and imposing, and wouldn't that make a better God of War?

Mo must have read his mind because he nudged Alaric and said, "You might not think it to look at him, but Hachi is one of the fiercest warriors I've ever met. Though his main job is making sure you humans don't kill each other off in massive wars."

"Please stop praising me, Mo," begged Raphe. Alaric thought he might be more comfortable hiding under the table, but Desh had a good hold on him.

"It's okay to be nervous at stuff like this," said Alaric, hoping to cheer the War God up. "I was beside myself this morning."

"You're just saying that to be nice," moaned Raphe. "I can tell; you're just like Teigen. You can't help but be positive."

Desh pointed his thumb at himself and said, "Teigen is me. Teigen Desh. He's not used to calling me by my last name."

"That's fine," laughed Mo, chucking Alaric on the shoulder. "I can't help but call Hachi by his first name either. We used to train together," Mo said to Alaric. "You're pretty solid. I'll bet you could take a few hits in the sparring ring."

"I'm pretty sure you'd destroy me," laughed Alaric. "Me being human and all."

"That's true, but you *look* like you could wrestle a god!" Mo took down his goblet of ale in one go and looked down the table for a moment. "You know, you remind me of an old friend. A really good friend. He was from Togarashi."

"Really?" asked Alaric.

"Yes, your dragons reminded me. That's where you're from too," said Mo, looking at Alaric's collar. "Dain Bodo was his name. He was a master builder, an architect way beyond his time. Proficient in alchemy, which is probably what gave his work such *presence*. He designed and oversaw the building of this temple."

Alaric's mouth dropped open. A human designed the Temple of the Sun? That sounded familiar.

"I know, right?" Mo asked, reading Alaric's mind again. "Who'd have thought a human could make something like this! Either way, he was a great man, someone who stood up for himself and for others. He didn't care what anyone thought. That's why I knew he'd be a good match for our young Sun God. He wouldn't take any of Bashima's shit." Mo laughed, then his face fell slightly, perhaps lost in memory. "Dain and Bashima became great friends."

Alaric felt like a weight was pressed to his midsection. He looked down the table at Bashima, who was chatting happily with Queen Hastia and King Vaultus. Bashima once had another human friend? From the same village as Alaric?

Mo grabbed fresh ale from his assigned shade and slugged back a gulp. "You actually remind me of him," he said, looking Alaric over closely. "It's probably just the hair, but I can tell you're of the same spirit. How could you not be? In order to stay here! Do you ever go outside?"

Alaric was thrown by Mo's statements and swallowed back the bile rising in his throat.

As though sensing his distress, Matthias came to his side. "Master Shina? Do you need anything?" Alaric looked at him and shook his head. Matthias moved away but raised an eyebrow.

"Could you bring me more wine, please, Matthias? And let Shefu know everything is wonderful?" Alaric asked, the only thing he could think of on the spot. Mentioning Shefu was code for "all is not well but I can hold my own."

He sensed that Mo, Raphe, and Desh were watching him or listening intently, and Alaric remembered what Matthias drilled into him: none of the gods were "safe."

"Of course, Master Shina," said Matthias.

Alaric turned back to Mo, forced a smile with all his teeth, and said, "We haven't *needed* to go outside."

Mo dissolved into laughter and clapped Alaric on the back. Raphe glanced at him out of the corner of his eye, thoughtful, and Desh turned to the Forest God to start a new conversation.

"You won't be bothered," said Matthias when they entered the baths. "Each god has a temporary bath in their suite, and this area is closed off to them. But just in case, I'll be here, and I've stationed four other shades around the room."

Alaric was exhausted. Dinner went on long into the night, and Mo peppered Alaric with stories while Desh tried to get Raphe to engage in conversations. Alaric made many attempts to talk with the War God, who didn't seem to mind. He even smiled at Alaric a few times and answered questions about his job. All he really wanted to talk about was Desh. Once Alaric found a subject that interested him, Raphe wouldn't shut up. So Alaric learned all about Desh and how he was the literal sun, but "please don't tell Bashima I said that, because he's scary."

Now, he watched the steam rise off the bath and was grateful for quiet. Matthias helped him out of his dinner clothes and into one of his purple robes before he got into the bath. The four guard-shades all averted their gazes when he disrobed and slipped into the pool. It was molten hot, just how he liked it, and Alaric swam along the edge before diving under the hot water. When he came up, Matthias handed him his favorite soap so he could clean the clay from his hair.

"That didn't go too badly, did it?" Alaric asked, submerging himself up to his nose, peeking out like a crocodile.

Matthias smiled and put the soap aside, crouching by the bath. "For how long you had to be on stage, I'd say it went spectacularly." The shade's brow creased, and he continued. "But what did Mo say to you? I could tell something was off."

Alaric thought about how to answer. He wanted to know more about the other mysterious human who was part of Bashima's life. Where was he? If he wasn't alive, what happened to him? But Alaric knew Matthias probably couldn't give him the answers. He was bound to protect Bashima, which Alaric wanted to respect. He didn't want to put Matthias in an awkward position where he had to choose the Sun God even if he wanted to answer Alaric's questions.

"I just panicked a bit," Alaric said. Not exactly a lie. Just not the whole truth. "The gods are intimidating. But I really liked Raphe, and Mo was funny. At least they didn't ignore me because I'm a human."

"Yes, Kuroi sat them near you for that very reason. Although maybe Mistress Alora and Master Garyn would have been better choices? Or dare I say, Master Cabari?"

Alaric snorted into the water, sending bubbles spraying. "He's definitely unique, but he's one of the more genuine gods I met, besides the Forest God. I doubt Cypress could tell a lie if his life depended on it."

"You're not wrong. Also, just between us, but the master requested that you be seated nowhere near Alora or Cabari. They're known for...how do I put this..."

"Instigating orgies?" Alaric asked then laughed hysterically when Matthias almost pitched headfirst into the pool.

"That's one way to put it," said Matthias. "Can you imagine Master Raphe starting an orgy?"

"Who's starting an orgy?" came a gruff voice from the baths entrance. Matthias sprang to attention. Bashima emerged through the steam, dressed only in soft linen trousers slung low on his hips. His hair exploded around his head in an uncontrolled cloud, golden crown gone.

"Leave us," he said, and the four shades along the perimeter rushed out, heads inclined.

Matthias walked over slowly and said, "Master, all is well."

Bashima nodded and said, "You won't be needed for the rest of the night. Go sleep."

Matthias gave Alaric a quick look, went through the entrance, and left Alaric alone with the Sun God. It had been days since they'd been alone together, and though Alaric wanted to launch himself out of the bath and plaster his lips to the Sun God's mouth, he recalled how anxious he'd been, worried that he'd made a wrong step with Alora and Garyn or that he'd make a fool of himself during the summit. He swam away from the Sun God and did a lazy lap around the pool.

"I cast a blocking charm," said the Sun God. "So even if one of those pervert assholes wanted to, they couldn't spy on this room."

Alaric kept swimming and said, "Oh."

"Not coming out?" asked Bashima after Alaric had swum a second length in the large bath.

"I don't think so, no," Alaric said. He knew he sounded petulant, but he couldn't let the Sun God get away with ignoring him for days. Even if he wasn't in Alaric's bed, he could at least have acknowledged him while Alora and Garyn visited. Was the god really so easily riled by jealousy?

"Are you going to make me woo you?" Bashima asked, a casual sneer on his face.

Alaric didn't stop swimming, his face growing warm. The Sun God didn't like to be kept waiting.

Let him know what it feels like to be ignored, Alaric thought.

Bashima stood at the pool's edge, watching Alaric swim, so Alaric didn't stop. He somersaulted underwater when he reached one end and made his way to the other end, hoping Bashima was enjoying the view because he wasn't giving way first. He'd earned the right to pout a bit.

When he surfaced on the third lap, Bashima was nowhere in sight. Alaric tread water in the deep end of the bath and flipped his hair out of his eyes, then made his way to the shallow end in a smooth side stroke.

"You even look perfect when you're swimming," came Bashima's low voice. He shed his trousers and slid into the pool, not even wincing at the heat. He swam toward Alaric, his face a storm cloud. "But you're pissing me off."

Alaric snorted and swam to sit on the underwater ledge near the stairs that led out of the bath. He spun around and sat, swinging his legs in the water. Seated, most of his chest came out of the water, and the steamy air caressed him, his gold chest chain gleaming.

"Silent treatment too, huh?" asked Bashima. He went underwater in a flip and came up, water spraying off his riotous hair. Alaric wanted to run his fingers through that hair but held back, biting his lower lip.

Bashima's speed in the water was enthralling. He was in Alaric's space, hands on the ledge behind Alaric, face inches away. Alaric breathed in and out and raised an eyebrow.

"I just wanted to wash my hair," he said and ran a hand through it, dripping hot water. "I wasn't expecting you." *So I don't know what you're expecting,* was what he wanted to add but didn't.

"Well, I'm here," Bashima growled, not backing away.

"And what are you going to do about it?" snapped Alaric. He hadn't meant to say anything, but the hurt from the last few days bit harder than expected.

"Oh, you're mad," said Bashima, eyes shining. He parted Alaric's knees as he moved forward, and Alaric let him but didn't answer. "What would make it better?" He was standing now, and a hand dipped toward the water, playing on its surface.

Alaric tried to control his breathing and stared the god down. "You figure it out," he said and narrowed his eyes.

Bashima loved nothing better than a challenge. He grinned, teeth showing. "Seeing you talking with any other god makes my blood boil," he said, dipping his hand into the water. It dragged down Alaric's chest and caught on his golden chain, but Alaric held Bashima's gaze. "I heard what Cabari said to you, and I almost flew across the room to wring his scrawny neck."

The hand dipped again and traced Alaric's abs, and yet he remained still.

"I couldn't help but watch you all day with your stupid red hair and ridiculous smile."

The hand went lower, sliding along Alaric's inner thigh before surfacing again.

"I was thinking about what I was going to do to you tonight, all through dinner, wanting you..." Bashima's hand drew up Alaric's length, gripping lightly as it went, fingers teasing.

And Alaric gave up the fight. He pushed his hips forward, locking them with Bashima's, wrapped his arms around his neck, and kissed the god like he'd never tasted those lips before. Their hands were in each other's hair, scraping through wet tangles, then went searching over each other's backs and chests as they kissed. Bashima's tongue forced its way into Alaric's mouth, and he moaned with longing, feeling his hardness against Bashima's hip.

The Sun God broke their kiss and hoisted Alaric out of the bath, so he was sitting on the edge. He knelt on the underwater ledge and swallowed Alaric's length whole, bobbing up and down, tongue worshiping every inch.

Alaric bent forward and dug his hands into Bashima's hair, saying, "Don't stop; don't you dare stop." Which was of course when Bashima stopped. Alaric whimpered, but Bashima stepped out of the water, pushed Alaric down lightly, and straddled his hips, grinding against Alaric. He forced their lips together as Alaric opened his legs further, letting Bashima closer.

Faster than Alaric thought possible, Bashima had him up and pressed against the wall, grinding into him. He grabbed Alaric's arms and spun him around so Alaric was facing the wall, and Alaric marveled at the god's strength. He pushed his hips back, searching for the Sun God, but Bashima whispered in his ear, "You were ready to kick me out of the baths a minute ago. Be patient."

Alaric let out a whine that he wasn't proud of, but the empty feeling had returned now that Bashima was so close. So tantalizingly near. Bashima snapped his fingers and a phial of oil appeared in his hand.

"Hold onto that bar above your head," Bashima ordered, and Alaric complied. He pressed his forehead against the tile, waiting, and spread his legs at Bashima's touch.

Two oiled fingers slid into him, and Alaric bucked backwards, pulling the fingers deeper. Bashima hissed and pressed him harder against the wall.

"Not until you're ready."

He nudged the two fingers around, searching for Alaric's sweet spot. When he pressed it, Alaric moaned again and felt his legs shake.

"Almost," Bashima whispered, inserting one more finger, and reached around Alaric's hip to stroke him.

"Now!" Alaric snarled, and Bashima grabbed Alaric's hip, withdrew his wet fingers, and slid himself inside Alaric's waiting warmth. He thrust up twice, slowly, easing himself into the motion, and Alaric held onto the bar above him, though he wanted to reach around the god's waist and push his hips harder.

Sweat dripped off both of them from the steam, and a drop from his forehead hit Alaric's lips, salty. Alaric held on, edging closer to oblivion with every thrust Bashima gave him, filling him completely. Bashima increased his speed and rifled a hand through Alaric's wet hair, leaning his forehead against Alaric's back.

The Sun God bit and licked Alaric's shoulder and rasped, "Gods...you are a dragon, *my* dragon, and I'm going to fuck you until you see stars."

After that, Alaric didn't remember what happened.

The human was an irritant, but he drew Bashima in so easily. All the redhead had to do was show interest. Hells, he could even show blatant disregard and ignore the Sun God, and Bashima wanted to bed him, to bend the human to his will, to hear him scream his name. Having him up against the wall, prone, willing, and impatient, drove Bashima crazy. He wanted to touch every inch of the human's body, to possess every part fully, so he ran his hands into wet red hair and smelled sage and citrus, two of his favorite scents, so he inhaled deeply, losing himself inside the redhead's willing body. When he opened his eyes, the dragon tattoo stared at him, mouth wide, teeth sharp, an invitation and a challenge. He bit the tattoo hard, daring the dragon to bite back, then he licked the reddening skin.

When he told the redhead just what he planned to do to him that night, something changed. The human let go of the bar with one hand and reached to draw Bashima in and hold him in place. Bashima laughed quietly and drew away, pulling out. He was close, gods the redhead could make him come so fast.

"I know you want it," he whispered in the redhead's ear, licking the edge where the golden earring chain hung. "But you can't have it."

The human somehow heaved himself away from the wall, spun Bashima around, and pinned him against the wall by his neck. Bashima wasn't prepared, so he didn't react fast enough. But his dick did. He released all over the redhead's torso, gold running down his body.

Shit, Bashima thought, shocked.

The redhead's pupils were narrow pinpoints in his eyes, red irises taking over until there was no white left. He reached a finger and ran it down the god's torso, collecting Bashima's godly release, then he sucked his finger dry.

"NO!" Bashima screamed, putting his palms against the tile, releasing a controlled explosion that fractured the wall and hurled him and the redhead into the waiting pool. Underwater, Bashima watched the all-too-human body spasm, his eyes rolling back into his head. He grabbed the redhead around the waist and breached the water's surface, yelling, "Matthias!"

Chapter Eight

Alaric dreamed of drowning. He stepped off a verdant cliff's edge and fell toward crystal blue water, arms out as if he expected to fly. Air rushed by his face and ruffled his hair, smelling faintly of brine and fresh linens. He smiled, rushing headlong to greet the water. When he hit the surface, Alaric let himself sink, bubbles rising from his mouth and nose. The water was empty around him, and he couldn't see the bottom, just a pit of darkening blue fading into black.

Should I take a breath? Alaric wondered, holding his hands in front of his eyes, watching them float like jellyfish.

The water pressed in on him, but it wasn't like shifting. It felt like the water had been waiting to embrace him for centuries, enveloping him in warmth, holding him like a mother. He drifted lower, watching the surface recede, clearing his mind of everything he'd experienced the last few months.

Had he ever gone to the mountain, to the temple? In the water, he didn't think so. It was just a daydream wrapped in a nightmare. The water was better. It felt normal and safe and all-encompassing like a sweater his mother made, or perhaps he'd never had a mother. He couldn't recall her face, her voice, the way she moved. Had she been kind, or short, or loud? What of his father? Did the vast outline of his father fit into the dream? Did he read to Alaric when he fell asleep or toss him into piles of leaves in the autumn?

It all faded away as he fell, and he closed his eyes, thinking he should inhale the water so that it was part of him fully. Let it wash through him, consume him.

The water was like being welcomed home.

A shadow flashed across Alaric's closed eyes. Curious what could bother him at this depth, Alaric opened his eyes and peered into the darkening water. He was so close to release he could feel it in his core, but what else could be here with him? The shadow passed behind him, and Alaric whirled slowly, arresting his fall. Something brushed his shoulder. He rotated in the water, searching.

A great beast spiraled through the water, graceful and powerful, four legs tucked against its long, slim body, which was covered with shining ruby and gold scales. Thick whiskers protruded from its nose and moved with the water, and sharp teeth peeked out through its smiling lips. As it neared Alaric, the dragon undulated, dipping below Alaric. Looking down, he watched the dragon rise, and it twisted its immense body, spiraling around Alaric, who looked on in wonder.

A dragon! A real dragon! But what was it doing here, in Alaric's dream?

He tried to speak, but the water choked him, and Alaric grabbed his throat in fear and thrashed his legs. What was he doing? He couldn't breathe the cold water. As though sensing his distress, the dragon swam faster, forming a figure eight with Alaric in the center, and somehow, Alaric started rising. All around him turned completely dark, but he felt the dragon helping him breach the surface.

They exploded from the surface, and Alaric took a choking breath, spitting out black water, before realizing that he and the dragon were floating high above an endless sea. The dragon flew without wings, aloft as if by magic. It moved close to Alaric, face hovering so they were almost nose to nose.

"How...how am I flying?" Alaric asked.

The dragon smiled, which was quite fearsome, but Alaric felt no danger. Why would the dragon save him from drowning only to devour him in the open air?

The dragon flew in lazy circles around Alaric, smile never wavering.

UNBREAKABLE

"This is called cloud dancing," it rumbled, bass voice ancient and knowing. "An art of the dragons. I wouldn't recommend attempting it outside your dreams." The dragon winked.

So, dragons had a sense of humor, thought Alaric.

"Why am I here? What's going on?"

"You chose not to die," the dragon said simply. "Most noble of you."

"Well, that's good," said Alaric, shocked. "I'm not ready to die!"

"Indeed," said the dragon, reminding Alaric of Kuroi. He had the eyebrows for the comparison too, a thick crown of bone above his eyes.

When the dragon didn't elaborate on Alaric's current situation, Alaric cleared his throat and asked, "What now?"

"Now? That's a silly question. You choose to wake up."

Voices surrounded him, and his head felt weighed down, his body sore everywhere, but the bed beneath him was familiar, and fire lilies on the table drew his eye.

"At least he seems unharmed," said a nervous voice. "His breathing is back to normal."

"You call that normal?" A rough voice in a harsh whisper.

"It's the best you can hope for in this situation, Bashi." The nervous voice became irritated and accusatory. "What the hells were you thinking?"

"I told you! It came out of nowhere," grumbled the harsh voice. "He moved so damned fast..."

"We can think up an excuse for him to skip tomorrow's events."

Nervous voice belonged to the Forest God, Alaric realized. Bell Cypress. The Forest God was in his room...

"I can handle those assholes."

The harsh voice was definitely Bashima. What were they talking about? Missing the events? Alaric turned his head and saw an unusual scene.

Bashima leaned against the door, arms crossed, face a wildfire. He wore the soft trousers from the baths, and his hair floated around his head like an aura. Cypress faced away from Alaric, but the Forest God seemed tired and worried, his hands shaking. He was also dressed for sleep, a short-sleeved tunic that fit tightly and trousers like Bashima's.

Alaric blinked a few times to make sure he was seeing reality then flexed his fingers and coughed. Both gods swung around, eyes wide, and Matthias swooped in front of them and grabbed Alaric's hand. Where had Matthias been hiding?

"Shina!" Matthias exclaimed and squeezed his hand.

"I know you're worried," said Cypress, pulling Matthias away, "but let me examine him."

Cypress sat on the bed and looked down at Alaric, perplexed. He held Alaric's wrist for a few moments then bent to check his eyes. Alaric let him, head still heavy and voice lost in his throat.

"His heartbeat and eyes are back to normal. But I've never seen a recovery this fast." Cypress turned to Bashima. "And you're sure there was only the one other time?"

"Of course I'm sure," said Bashima, offended. "I know where I put my dick, *Tengu.*"

Cypress ignored Bashima's verbal jab and turned back to Alaric. "Shina, can you hear me?" Alaric nodded. "And can you move your fingers and toes?" Alaric wiggled, hoping everything was functioning. Cypress nodded. "But you can't speak?"

Alaric opened his mouth and tried to force out words, but nothing happened. He mimed writing and looked around the room.

Cypress leaned back, surprised. "Um, Matthias? Does he have anything to write on in here?"

Matthias went to Alaric's small desk and rifled through the top drawer, grabbing a piece of thick paper, pen, and ink pot. He helped Alaric sit up, put pillows behind his back to prop him up, and placed his breakfast tray in his lap. Alaric dipped the pen and wrote in a flourish: "What happened? Why can't I go to the events?"

"Well, uh...you...um," Cypress started, flushing and rubbing through his green hair.

"You ate some of my fucking cum like a damn animal," said Bashima, cutting through the tension.

"Bashi!"

"What? Eating cum's just fine, but he looked fucking feral when he did it."

Alaric's eyes widened in surprise, and he scribbled: "I DID WHAT?"

Matthias looked away, Cypress looked skittish enough to bolt from the room, and Bashima's light played over his skin, dark reds and oranges.

"What do you remember?" asked Cypress. "That's the best place to start."

Alaric blushed immediately and glanced at Bashima then down at his paper.

"Don't be so squeamish; he knows what we were doing, you idiot," said Bashima shaking his head and rolling his eyes.

Alaric thought about what he last recalled from the baths, and he told his interested body to settle down, trying not to focus on thick steam, the feel of Bashima behind him, biting his shoulder. Alaric's mouth filled with saliva, and he moved his legs closer together.

"Seven hells," muttered Bashima and walked back to the door and leaned back. "Stop sending out that energy or I'm going to jump you."

"You can feel him, Bashi?" asked Cypress, putting a hand on his chin. He started muttering under his breath.

"That's nothing new. Ever since that first night we fucked I could. Isn't that normal for something like this?"

"I'd have to...look into that," said Cypress. "Well, Shina? Anything coming back to you?"

Alaric thought again about Bashima biting him on the shoulder, on his tattoo, and he snapped his fingers and wrote: "Bashima said something about a dragon, then nothing." He almost wrote that he'd seen a dragon in his vivid dream but decided to keep that to himself. That was his.

"Yeah," said Bashima, "that tracks. That's when he grabbed me and his eyes went all weird."

"I'll see what I can find out," said Cypress. He stretched his back and rubbed the burn scar on his right arm. "Until then, take it easy,Shina. I'm sure you feel wrecked."

Bashima snorted and mumbled under his breath.

Alaric reached out and grasped the Forest God's pant leg, pointing at his paper: "But why can't I go to the events?"

Cypress read Alaric's note and chewed on the inside of his cheek. "I suppose...since you're awake now and feel okay..."

"Is that a good idea, Master?" interjected Matthias, always looking out for Alaric's welfare.

But Alaric didn't need a protector, and he wrote: "I want to go. I feel fine!"

Matthias raised an eyebrow and read what Alaric had written, a sigh echoing in his voice.

"At this rate of recovery, his voice will probably be fine by tomorrow, but if he doesn't feel well, he should rest," said Cypress. "And don't push it," he added, pointing at Alaric. "Pay attention to your body tomorrow, and if one *eyelash* feels off, go to bed."

He went to the door and Bashima moved out of his way. "Can I talk to you for a second?" the Forest God asked him quietly.

Bashima looked from Cypress to Alaric, his eyes contracted. "Matthias, stay with him tonight just to be sure he's fine. Come get me if anything changes. And you." Bashima marched to the bed and got in Alaric's face.

Alaric didn't think the Sun God was expecting a kiss, not with the murderous expression on his face, so he leaned back on the pillows.

Bashima said, "Don't fucking move from this bed until morning. If I find out you put one toe out of this bed, and Matthias *will* tell me if you do, there will be consequences. And not the kind of consequences you enjoy."

Bashima turned and stalked past a shell-shocked Cypress who waved at Alaric then followed the Sun God, shutting the door.

Matthias sat back down on Alaric's bed and gave him a disapproving look.

Alaric wrote: "What? I really do feel okay! Besides the overall body pain and that I can't talk..."

"I don't think it's a good idea to go to the events tomorrow," Matthias said. "The second day is supposed to be the toughest even if you're not going to the sessions. The gods will be tense and on edge, and we'll all be able to feel it."

"I promise," Alaric scribbled, "if I feel bad, I'll tell you."

"Good, because I don't feel like getting yelled at by the master for you being a stubborn ass."

They stayed quiet for a while before Alaric wrote: "I wish I remembered what happened. This feels so weird, like I did something really bad."

"You didn't do anything wrong," said Matthias, trying to comfort him. "The master isn't angry with you; he was just scared. Try to get some sleep. I'll be right here if you need me."

Alaric nodded and handed Matthias the tray. Matthias helped him move the pillows around so he could lie down. Bashima had been scared? He closed his eyes as Matthias blew the candles out and hoped he would dream of dragons.

"Do you really think it's a good idea for him to move around tomorrow?" Bashima asked, remembering how the redhead seized in his arms as he'd carried him to his room. He pushed the thought away and shoved his hands in his trouser pockets.

"That's really up to him," said Tengu as they walked back to the main bedroom wing. "But I'll watch him too if that makes you feel better."

"It's whatever. He'll do what he wants anyway."

"Sounds like you."

Bashima didn't answer and stared straight ahead as they walked. Tengu liked walking, said it made the world seem wider; shifting was easy, but you missed the scenery.

"You really like him, don't you?"

"He's a human," Bashima said, avoiding the question. He didn't want to think about that.

"They are fragile," said Tengu, contemplative. "But Shina is really resilient. There's no way he should have bounced back so fast."

"So you keep telling me. Isn't that a good thing?"

Bashima didn't know as much about god-touched as the Forest God, which he'd never admit, but he'd been the first person Bashima thought of when the idiot human went wild.

126

"I guess we'll see," said Tengu. "It's interesting that you can feel him though. From what Oken has said about his mother, she couldn't sense Cindras until she completed the god-touched ceremony. It nearly killed her apparently. It's amazing that having four demigod children didn't kill her..."

Tengu didn't talk much about Oken, probably because he knew Bashima didn't fully approve of whatever the fuck their relationship was, so Bashima listened. He owed damn Tengu that at least.

"I...I need to tell you something," the Forest God started, eyes lowered.

"Spit it out. You're not exactly the world's best secret keeper. But if it's some weird sex thing you and Zebra Head do, I'm not interested."

Tengu laughed and shook his head. "No, it's not that. I...you've shielded this part of the temple, right?"

Raising an eyebrow, Bashima said, "Of course. I don't need those assholes listening in on me, and I certainly don't need fucking Cindras barreling in here trying to get at Oken."

"Thanks for that, for letting Oken stay here."

"Fuck, he's barely ever here."

"Yeah, but he appreciates it." Tengu took a deep breath as if steeling himself. "Okay, don't laugh at me, but I think I have a soul bond with Oken."

Bashima stopped in his tracks, stunned. "What? That shit's a fucking fairy tale."

"I knew that's what you'd say. I wish it wasn't real," Tengu sighed. "But I can *feel* it. I don't know if Oken can feel it, I'm a little afraid to ask him, and he's part human, so maybe it doesn't work the same way. But...something's there."

"And what does it feel like?" Bashima asked, curious despite his skepticism.

"Like our hands are connected with invisible, unbreakable strings," said Tengu, his eyes shining, a small, sad smile on his lips. "Like if something were to happen to him, I'd die."

Bashima's voice caught in this throat. What the hell was Tengu talking about? Soul bonds were myths, pure and simple. There was no way that's what was happening. Maybe they had some weird demigod or god-touched thing going on, but no way they had a damned *soul bond*. Although the Forest God was one of the most studied in god-touched lore, in godly relationships in general.

"Why are you telling me this?" he asked, cautious. It was dangerous to talk too long with the Forest God. He got under Bashima's skin and liked to hibernate there.

"Because I needed to tell someone," Tengu said. "And I know you won't say anything."

"You're such a dick, Tengu." He started walking again. "But thanks for sharing, I guess."

They were to Oken's door when Tengu cleared his throat and said, "You know; now that I've met him properly, Shina matches the description of a minor celebrity in the forest near your mountain."

"How's that?" scoffed Bashima.

"The last time I was here, Oken and I passed through the forest, checking the growth, you know, normal Forest God stuff, and the birds would NOT stop chattering at me about this guy who rescued a little boy from the river."

"Huh?"

"They were freaking out, you know how birds get, and told me the story. Apparently, this red-haired mystery man heard the boy scream, jumped into the river without hesitation, pulled the kid out, then raced out of the forest like a monster was after him. Left behind a single red pepper," Tengu said, thoughtful. "Oh, and his shoes for some reason."

"Ugh, why did you have to tell me that?" Bashima asked, rubbing his face. "He's already too damn perfect; now, he's a fucking hero too?"

"I just thought it was interesting, is all." Tengu smiled, patted Bashima's arm, and let himself in Oken's room, leaving Bashima staring at the closed door.

Alaric's voice returned by the morning, and his body wasn't sore at all. He felt better than he had in a while actually. He found Matthias asleep in the desk chair, snoring, and the shade helped him get ready for the day, going over the schedule.

"You're only expected at lunch and dinner," he said, looking through Alaric's outfits. "It's the most formal day for the gods, but you don't have to look so severe."

He pulled out the morning outfit and showed Alaric. The tunic and jacket fabric was smooth and buttery, light cream in color, and skimmed Alaric's skin like flowing water. He stepped back, remembering the sea in his dream. Matthias frowned. "Don't you like it?"

"It's not that," said Alaric, holding up his hands to grab the tunic. "Just nerves again, I guess."

"At least you've met the gods and know what to expect," said Matthias. "They'll be so preoccupied with their agendas today they shouldn't make trouble. Once you're dressed, Emilia will be along to do your hair again. The braids and spikes make you stand out, not that you don't already."

The lunch went as well as Alaric hoped. He didn't feel fatigued, and no new gods spoke to him. Cabari jetted toward him the instant he walked in, but he was amiable and funny, poking fun at other gods in the throne room. Alaric jokingly told him off for being mean, but that only made the Lightning God jest harder.

"I'm only mean to the ones who deserve it," Cabari said, winking. "I'm sure good old Kuroi told you who to avoid. Just glad I made the cut!"

The others were more subdued than Cabari, reflecting on their agendas for the day. Even Alora and Garyn had a seriousness about them. Alaric found himself mainly with Oken and Jace, who weren't allowed in the godly deliberations.

"It would be a huge bore, anyway," said Jace, watching his father across the room. The Lord of the Underworld looked like he'd rather still be in bed, but his husband dragged him around the room to talk with different social clumps, animated and loud.

"Your stepfather seems agreeable," said Alaric. "He seems to get along with everyone."

"Everyone but me," Jace deadpanned.

"Oh, I'm sorry," said Alaric, mortified. "That must be..."

"It's fine," Jace said and shrugged. "I'd be pissed if my husband cheated on me with a human woman and got her pregnant too." He sipped his drink as though what he said was the most normal thing.

Alaric glanced at Oken, who didn't seem bothered.

Jace continued, "Not like Niall can talk though. He got back at Veles by cheating on him. And that's how I got a sister."

"I have a sister," Oken contributed.

"Hm," said Jace.

They both sipped their drinks, and Alaric stared at the dessert table, trying not to melt into the ground in embarrassment. He offered to show Jace around the temple while the gods were in session, and Oken perked up, saying he would join them, like he didn't know every inch of the place.

As they were leaving, Oken mentioned that he should tell Cypress where he was going, and Jace agreed that he should let his father know as well. They left Alaric by the door, who nodded to various gods who came and went from the throne room. Mo gave him a familiar knock on the shoulder, grinning, with Raphe in tow, who actually smiled a little.

Then Alaric heard a cold chuckle. The God of Time was in the doorway, looking Alaric over like he was a hank of meat at a butcher's counter. The god's blue-white hair was loose around his shoulders, a jet-black circlet holding it back from his face. He wore all white including pearlescent wrist cuffs and earrings. His smile was thin and cat-like, and his eyes shone with some secret mirth.

"I'd heard a rumor that Bashima was keeping a human again, but this is too perfect," said the god, voice oily. He cocked one brow. "His taste certainly hasn't changed."

Alaric expected Matthias to step forward, but before the shade could intervene, King Vaultus appeared at the Time God's shoulder and grasped it with a massive hand.

"Chronas," he boomed, "leave the young man alone. It's time to begin the session."

"As you wish, your majesty," Chronas said. His slash of a smile never faltered as Vaultus led him away. Alaric got the sense that he'd intended to say more. A lot more.

Oken and Jace made their way to him where Alaric was still shaken from the Time God's words.

"What did Chronas want?" Oken asked. "I didn't think he liked humans."

"That guy creeps me out," Jace admitted. "He's always watching people and smiling like he's the only real person in the room and we're all just ants crawling around a hill he wants to smash."

"Maybe it's because we're part human," Oken suggested. "He makes a lot of comments about demigods at the summits."

"It doesn't matter what he said," Alaric said. "Let's go check out the library."

Emilia surprised Alaric by hurrying out of the library when he entered with the two demigods. He caught her by the tunic and said, "What're you up to, Em?" He knew she'd been hiding or slacking off, so he pretended to be stern.

"Oh, it's just you," she said, wiping her brow. "I just needed a second, okay? I'm not used to running around so much." She saw Oken and Jace and made a small o-shape with her mouth. "Hello, Oken," she said and looked at her feet, suddenly shy.

"Hello?" Oken tilted his head, unsure who Emilia was.

Matthias came into the library and sighed heavily. "Emilia, get back to work. You can goof around with Alaric after the summit."

"Whatever, Matthias," Emilia sassed back, hands on her hips. "You just have to follow Alaric around. I have to run all over the temple all day!" She stormed out, nose in the air, and Jace laughed.

"I like her," he said and walked into the library, looking at the rows of books and scrolls. "So, Shina, this your main hiding spot?"

"Yeah, you could say that," Alaric said. "It's quiet in here, and I won't bother anyone."

"It is quite nice," said Oken. "I don't have a hiding spot here. I just go to Bell's temple."

"How's *that* going?" Jace asked, eyeing Oken.

"Quite well," said Oken, and he smiled. Alaric hadn't seen him smile yet, and it made him look more angelic. "I wasn't going to come to the summit, but Bell thought it might be good for me to be around other gods for a change."

"Beats hanging out with shades all day," Jace said, then looked at Matthias. "No offense. Shades who work in temples are different from Underworld shades."

"Really?" asked Alaric.

"They're content with their lot in death, I suppose," Jace said. "They just don't have these kinds of jobs. It's much more menial. Or they're stuck in the Locker. Wouldn't wish that hell on anyone."

Alaric glanced at Matthias, whose face was blank. That meant he was trying not to show any emotion. Alaric doubted Oken or Jace would notice.

"You two are part human, right?" Alaric asked. "So, do you ever interact with them? Or is it strictly a gods-only situation?"

"I used to see my mother and grandparents quite often," Jace said. "But there isn't much point interacting with humans. They live such short lives compared to us that it's better not to get too attached."

Alaric blanched but mentally shook it off. He couldn't worry about that right now. "That makes sense. It would be tough to make friends only to outlive them."

Jace looked at Alaric as though realizing what he'd said. He cleared his throat and said, "Exactly. But that doesn't mean gods don't mix with humans. Obviously." He indicated himself and Oken.

"I spent most of my childhood with my mother," Oken said. "After she had me, my father made her god-touched, so we had a lot of time together." He looked wistful, pensive.

"Are you okay?" Alaric asked though Jace shook his head, warning him away from the subject.

"I suppose so," Oken said. "I haven't seen my mother in a very long time. Not since she gave me the scar. Even though we still lived in the same temple for a time." Seeing Alaric's mortified face, Oken went on, "It wasn't entirely her fault. God-touched can get unpredictable when the ceremony is first completed. She lost control and burned the side of my face when her ability manifested."

"That's awful," was all Alaric could think to say.

"She's here for the summit. Down the mountain of course. My father couldn't bear to have her in the temple with him. Not like he can get rid of her anyway."

"That's messed up," Jace said. "I'm glad my mom turned down Veles on becoming god-touched. She would have been miserable in the Underworld."

"Do you think you'll go see her?" Alaric asked, and Oken looked at him as though he'd transformed into a goose. "Since she's right there? I guess I'd want to see my mother if she was so close by."

Oken's face remained blank, but Alaric could tell the gears were turning in his head. Had he seriously not thought about visiting his mother while she was here?

"I doubt she'd want to see me," Oken admitted.

"A mother not want to see her kid?" Alaric asked, astounded. "I'm sure she'd be happy to see you."

Jace watched like they were putting on a play, eyes bouncing from one to the other. After a few moments, Oken stirred, looking like he'd made up his mind.

"Maybe I will go see her."

Bashima remembered why he hated the summits as he listened to each god drone on and on about their work and how great they were at it. He couldn't stand most of them. Some were passable—the God of War was at least entertaining in his misery—but Bashima tried not to tune anyone out. Vaultus was paying particular attention to him, making sure Bashima was engaged.

Cabari finished a self-satisfied soliloquy about his production numbers; then it was Bashima's turn. The Sun God was great at his job, and he knew it. Vaultus knew it. He shouldn't have to talk himself up in a room full of minor gods. And yet here he was.

"The sun is still in the sky, it still rises, it still sets," he said, then fell silent. The other gods waited, watching him. Some of them shared knowing glances.

Vaultus let out a booming laugh from his seat. "You haven't changed one bit, Bashima! Succinct as ever. Though we haven't seen you at a summit in some time, it's good to know that you've stayed diligent and haven't turned to sloth."

A small cough arose from midway down the table. Chronas, the asshole God of Time, leaned over the table, fingers steepled in front of his face.

"I hate to speak ill of our illustrious host, but wasn't there an, how should I say this, oversight with that *unplanned* eclipse?"

All the gods' heads turned toward Bashima, who couldn't believe Chronas dared mention the eclipse.

"That was two thousand years ago," Bashima growled, fists clenched under the table. He should have known Chronas would be the one to say something. Most of the other gods were either afraid of Bashima's temper, couldn't be bothered, or claimed to be his friends and weren't fazed by it.

Alora chimed in, "That was partly my fault too—"

But Chronas cut her off. "It's just disheartening to see you in the same position you were back then. Here I was thinking you'd grown out of that phase."

So that's how it's gonna be, Bashima thought and sneered, "What can I say; he's a great fuck."

Everyone at the table stirred. Most turned their heads to Chronas.

"Maybe if you spent less time on distractions and more time on your given duties, these little slip-ups wouldn't happen," Chronas said. He looked pained as though he was worried about Bashima's welfare, but the Sun God saw right through his ruse. Chronas continued, "It's up to you, I suppose. Not all of us are lucky enough to have time to cavort with humans."

"Isn't *time* your literal job?" Bashima barked back, and half the table tried to hold in their laughter. Things were finally getting interesting for them, Bashima realized. This was the shit gods came to the summit to see.

"And then you flaunt the human—"

"Be very careful of what you say next, Chronas," rumbled Cindras, flames dancing in his red hair. His face could melt diamonds.

"As though I'd besmirch your choice of concubine, Fire God," assured Chronas. "She comes from a proud royal lineage, a princess of the highest order." He looked back at Bashima, sly smile on his putrid face. "Can Bashima say the same, or is his human some common village trash he picked up on the side of the road?"

Bashima nearly launched himself at the Time God, but Vaultus's voice erupted from the head of the table before he could move. "That's enough! We're not here to discuss such matters. It's unbecoming of us as gods to squabble like this. I chose Bashima long ago to be the new Sun God, and I am more than satisfied with his work. Let's move on."

Chronas bowed his head to Vaultus, but he smirked at Bashima, knowing he'd hit a nerve.

Don't let that asshole throw you off, Bashima thought. *That's his whole game. He's still jealous after all this time...*

Bashima hadn't given Chronas much thought over the centuries. He knew the Time God lobbied to be the new Sun God after Vaultus imprisoned the first, but he'd accepted the role as Time God readily. Bashima should have remembered that gods had all the time in the world to hold and develop personal grudges. Sometimes, there were things you just couldn't let go...

Well, fuck the God of Time and Lord of Order and whatever other titles he felt like bestowing on himself. Bashima was the Sun God, and Vaultus never doubted him.

Dinner was a shorter and quieter affair on the second day, and Alaric was glad for it. He'd spent the afternoon showing Jace and Oken around the temple, which was equally diverting and awkward. When Alaric mentioned that his horse was stabled at the foot of the mountain, Oken asked if they could go see her.

"Well, I don't know if I'm supposed to..." Alaric said, biting his lower lip. He had freedom to wander the temple but had yet to ask if he could go outside. He'd forgotten about it, if he was honest with himself, with all the distractions inside.

Alaric felt a familiar pang in his heart for his family when he thought of going outside. He'd been gone for three months, and he was certain they'd given him up for lost. Maybe the Sun God would let him visit, or perhaps his parents could make the short journey to the mountain. He vowed to ask Bashima when the summit was over, when things quieted down.

Jace, understanding what was going on, suggested going to the conservatory and greenhouse. "I heard that Cypress designed them. Is that true, Oken?"

Alaric silently thanked Jace as Oken lit up, talking about Cypress and how talented he was. Oken really had it bad for the Forest God.

After a quick dinner, where even Mo and Desh, the God of Peace, were subdued, Alaric finally felt tired. Luckily, it was a normal weariness, not like his entire body wanted to shut down. Bashima appeared moody at dinner, speaking only with Vaultus and Hastia, so Alaric didn't bother him after. Tika came to his room to check on him and sent the Sun God's regards. Alaric tried not to be disappointed as Matthias helped him get undressed.

"We can wash your hair in here tonight," Matthias suggested gently. "Emilia asked to see you. Would you like me to fetch her?"

"Of course, I'd love to see her," Alaric said though he ached to be in bed.

Once he was in his night clothes, Matthias reappeared in his room, holding Emilia by the hand and a deep basin under his arm. Emilia looked exhausted from running messages, her eyes barely open, but she was ecstatic to see Alaric.

"Your day had to be better than mine," she whined, sitting on his bed while Matthias washed Alaric's hair. "My feet hurt so much! And you got to spend time with Oken." Her cheeks went pink when she mentioned the demigod, and Matthias laughed.

"I think he's taken, Emilia," said the shade, smiling.

"I can still look at him," she said, pouting. "What's he like, Alaric?"

"He's definitely interesting," Alaric said and smiled. "He's easy to be around even though he says a lot of awkward things. I think he's a little sad."

"It was kind of you to speak to him about his mother," said Matthias. "We tend to skirt the subject because, well, he told you what happened."

"Oh, how he got his scar?" asked Emilia, picking at her nails. "Moms can be mean."

"Yeah," said Alaric, thinking of the large scar on Oken's face. Alaric had no history with that kind of thing. He felt lucky that his parents were loving and supportive. Sure, they had arguments, but nothing like the things Oken was dealing with. "But they can also be really kind and loving."

"Mine was," Emilia said. "Before she drowned me."

Alaric sat up, spraying water everywhere, and Matthias squawked, getting drenched. "What?" Alaric said, astonished.

"That's how I died," Emilia said as though it were the most natural thing in the world. "There was a plague, and she didn't want me to die that way. At least, that's what Lord Veles said when I arrived in the Underworld."

"Does Veles greet every shade?" Alaric asked, hair dripping. Matthias muttered under his breath, toweling Alaric's hair.

"He doesn't," Matthias said, tone flat. "He would never rest if that were the case. His god-touched handle most of the day-to-day greetings. But he does greet certain new shades. It's very disorienting when you first arrive in the Underworld. Most shades know how they died, which can be very traumatizing if it was a violent death, so Veles usually greets them."

"Oh," Alaric said. Knowing how his friends died made Alaric think about inevitability. "That makes sense. When I die, I hope it's peaceful."

Emilia snorted. "You're not going to die. That would be stupid."

Alaric and Matthias laughed. "Well, it's not like I plan on going anytime soon!" Alaric said. "But I am mortal, so it's not like I can avoid it forever."

Emilia jumped off the bed and slammed into Alaric, hugging him fiercely. "I forbid it! You can't die because I said so!"

"I'll try my hardest, Em," he said, hugging her back. He looked up at Matthias, who returned to toweling Alaric's hair, expression thoughtful. "At least tomorrow's the last day of the summit," Alaric said. "Then things can get back to normal."

The last day of the summit dawned with Alaric feeling wonderful. Soon, the other gods would leave, and the heavy tension running through the temple would lift. It felt like thunderheads settled over the temple the last two days, and Alaric was ready for them to move on.

The final luncheon was served in the conservatory, which was festooned with floating lanterns lit with soft candlelight. Small red and gold butterflies danced in the air, one of Kuroi's alchemy spells, and the fountains were on full display with lotus-blossom lights drifting across the water. Cypress received many compliments for the flowers and plants, which made him blush. Alaric overheard one god whisper that they didn't know Bashima *had* a soft side after taking in the room's warm glow.

Most everyone was in better spirits than the day before, now that their chief business was done. Alora, Garyn, and Cabari swarmed Alaric when he came in, faces bright and already a little tipsy.

"Bashima is a demon," said Cabari, "but he has the best booze."

"Oh, be nice," Alora scolded. "He's behaved himself the whole summit even when Chronas tried to bait him about—" Garyn elbowed her in the side, and she nearly spilled her drink. "—his dining room," she finished and shoved Garyn back.

Alaric laughed and said, "You gods get into the strangest arguments."

"Yup," said Garyn, and all three of them sipped their drinks.

"So," said Cabari. "What did you think of this debacle, Alaric? Was it everything you dreamed of? Beautiful gods, delicious food, plentiful wine..." He spied something across the room that caught his attention and grinned wickedly. "Demigods who ignore your innate sexual magnetism."

Alaric followed the Lightning God's gaze and saw Jace leaning against the wall, uninterested in the tediousness around him.

"Daddy issues, here I come," Cabari said, and he made right for poor Jace.

"Remember how much you owe me if he seals the deal," Alora said to Garyn.

"Wow, I hope you guys don't bet on me," said Alaric.

Alora answered much too quickly, "Of course not, sweetie." She reached up and patted his cheek hard.

When Cypress walked up, Alaric was grateful. He didn't want to think about the wagers Alora and Garyn might have made about him.

"Hey, Cypress. Oken told me that you designed the conservatory. It's really something."

The Forest God smiled and said, "Bashi isn't the best at decorating, and he has no patience for plants."

"Or anything he has to take care of," joked Alora.

"Is Oken coming?" Alaric asked, looking around for the demigod.

Cabari leaned aggressively into Jace's space by the wall; the demigod was at least paying attention to the Lightning God, but he didn't look enthusiastic about his company. Alaric admitted that Jace never looked enthusiastic, so it was hard to tell how Cabari was faring.

"He's actually visiting his mother down the mountain," Cypress said, eyes shining. "He said you gave him the idea."

Both Alora and Garyn looked shocked, mouths slightly open.

"Oh!" said Alaric. "I wasn't sure that he would. I didn't mean to pry, he just sort of told me what was going on and that she was here, and I thought about how much I miss my own mother, and…"

Cypress held up his hands and shook them back and forth, "Oh, no, it's okay! It's better than okay! I'm just happy that he talked about it with someone. He talks to me about it, but he's never shown interest in reaching out, and I didn't want to make him think he was a bad person that he didn't see her. Not that I thought he was a bad person for not seeing her."

"Are you seeing this?" Garyn asked Alora.

"Yeah," she answered. "It's uncanny."

"They both got so sweaty, and they're talking so fast."

Cypress calmed down and said, "I wanted to thank you for talking to him and see how you were doing. These things are stressful for gods; they're killers on anyone even part human. We gods put out a lot of…energy."

"I'm good," Alaric said, knowing what Cypress was asking so as not to alert Alora and Garyn that anything off had occurred. He rubbed the back of his head. "Kuroi and Matthias made me study everything backwards and forwards, so I felt really prepared. It's a lot, but nothing I can't handle." He finished with a big grin he hoped looked genuine. He had been prepared, and his body felt fine, but Mo's comments from the first night and the unsettling run-in with Chronas were eating at him.

"I'm just glad it's almost over," Alora yawned. "It's a pain having to stay awake all night with the moon AND have to do this stuff during the day.

Bashima's gotta be feeling it too, trying to split his attention between the sun and the sessions."

Alaric winced.

And then I made him worry about something so dumb, he thought. He'd been trying so hard not to add to Bashima's burden.

"Don't worry, honey," Alora said and pet his arm. "He'll be back to his usual charming self in no time."

"Yeah, charming like a piranha," muttered Garyn.

The gods came away from their final session full of vigor and chattering excitedly. As they made their way toward the dining room, Alaric ran with Matthias to his room to change. He'd be wearing his favorite outfit that night: a wine-colored suit that was the twin to the green one from the first day. This one had his (apparently) signature dragons embroidered along the jacket cuffs in gold thread. Matthias affixed his dragon pin, and they were ready to go.

"I'll bet the shades are ready for this to be over too, huh?" Alaric asked Matthias on their way out of his room.

"They do enjoy a challenge. Most everyone likes being busy, unlike Emilia," Matthias said and shook his head. "But yes, it's been a taxing few days. The shades stationed below are particularly tired. The god-touched can be pushy and rude."

"Was that severe-looking guy from the first day King Vaultus's god-touched?" Alaric asked, remembering the hawk nose and dour expression.

"Savos? Yes, but he's never a problem. He and Kuroi get along famously. Probably because they're both anal perfectionists." Matthias smiled and said, "Savos stayed in the temple because King Vaultus has many needs. As a king does," he finished quickly, as though he'd said too much.

Alaric heard loud steps approaching, and both he and Matthias turned around to see who it was. Emilia came tearing around the corner, coming from the main doors, out of breath and red-faced. Tears streamed down her cheeks. When she saw them, she skidded to a stop, grabbing Alaric's hand and pulling.

"Please! Help him! Please!"

"Breathe for a second. What's wrong?" Alaric asked.

"He's hurting Oken! That big scary Fire God!"

Alaric and Matthias looked at each other, and Matthias didn't like what he saw in Alaric's face, because he said, "No, Shina, let's go find someone else."

Alaric shook his head and said, "Go get Cypress and Bashima. It's my fault Oken was alone, and you can shift to them."

"Remember what the master said!"

"There's no time. Emilia, take me there." He spun on his heel, Emilia pulling on his hand, leaving Matthias cursing by his door. She led Alaric down the hall from his room and past the throne room toward the main doors, but Alaric didn't need her to lead for long, because hot flames lit the entire main entrance hall. Alaric was blown back a few steps from the heat, and he shielded Emilia, turning his back.

"Get away from here," he shouted to Emilia, her terrified face looking up at him, pleading. "Go find Kuroi and get him here fast." She dashed away, looking back once before rounding the hall corner.

The flames died down when Emilia was gone, and Alaric saw the Fire God looming over Oken near the main doors. The demigod was pressed against the wall, fierce expression set on his face, fire dancing in one palm, snowflakes in the other.

What in the hells am I doing?

Alaric strode forward down the hall and yelled, "Hey! Back off!"

Angry turquoise eyes flashed over to Alaric, and the Fire God's hair and shoulders erupted in flashing flames. His ruddy skin turned black and crackled with shining fissures like cooling magma. The heat was more intense than Bashima put out, Alaric realized, though he doubted he'd seen the full extent of the Sun God's power.

"Stay out of this, human," the Fire God rumbled, and Oken looked afraid. He put a hand up, telling Alaric to stop. Cindras lashed out, knocking Oken down. "And you, stay down. You're coming home with me. This sorry phase has gone on long enough."

Alaric skittered around the distracted Fire God and went to Oken's side. "You okay? Can you get up?"

"What did I just say?" roared the Fire God. He grabbed Alaric by the collar and lifted him off the ground, Alaric scrabbling at his hands, which were singing his collar.

Yup, this was a terrible idea.

"You think I care that you're Bashima's concubine? He can always find another human willing to be his bed warmer, so don't test me, *boy*."

"Oken!"

Alaric looked down the hall and saw Cypress approaching, and he looked terrifying. Green energy bolts radiated off his entire body, and green vines emerged from his hands. His eyes turned solidly white and crackled with rage. His hair sprang up around his head, snapping around his face.

"Put him down."

Alaric didn't recognize the voice that came from Cypress. It felt ancient and frightening and serious as death.

"Oh, good. The other person I wanted to see," said the Fire God, unmoved by Cypress's new form. He threw Alaric down near Oken, driving the breath from Alaric's lungs. Oken crawled over to him, golden blood dripping from his forehead.

"Bell's too angry," Oken said, fearful. "He can't control himself like this!"

"It's okay," Alaric said, trying to sit up. "I sent Matthias to get Bashima."

"I'm afraid that won't be enough either," warned Oken. "My father is one of the strongest gods, and he's older than Bashima. With King Vaultus in his condition, I don't think he could hold back my father either."

What about the king?

Alaric thought he'd heard Oken correctly, but there wasn't time to worry about that. Cindras stood like a column to meet Cypress, who launched himself at the waiting wall of fire. Cindras lurched back when the Forest God hit him, but he soon had Cypress by the throat. The Forest God's vines wrapped around the other god's arm and torso, tearing at his clothes and skin, but the flames were too hot, and the vines couldn't get purchase. He snarled and flailed in Cindras's grasp, but the Fire God squeezed his throat, causing the vines to snap back into Cypress's fingers.

"And you think you're good enough for my son?" Cindras rumbled, slamming Cypress against the wall. Cypress shrieked, a sound so piercing that Oken covered Alaric's ears. When the scream ceased, Oken dragged Alaric away from the brawl and covered him with his slim body.

"What the hell does he want?" Alaric shouted in Oken's ear.

"He wants me to come back home," said Oken. "I'm his prized possession, and he's been trying to get me back for a while. But he's never dared make a move while I was here or in the Temple of the Forest. I think he's gone mad."

"Seven hells," said Alaric, watching the Fire God pummel his flaming fists against Cypress, whose green lightning was fading.

"Gods can't be killed," said Oken, "but that doesn't mean they can't hurt each other."

The Fire God hurled Cypress back down the hall, and the Forest God fell in a heap, the last of his green light flickering around his body. Oken stood to try and get past his father, flames shooting from his left side.

"Leave Bell alone," he said coldly and advanced on his father.

Before Oken or the Fire God could attack each other, a laugh echoed down the hall.

"Perfect. I've wanted to kick your ass for the last five thousand years."

Bashima strode into the hall, power billowing off him like smoke. His palms were down, fingers clenching into claws. Stopping near Cypress, he said, "Tengu, you good?"

Cypress stirred at his feet, and Bashima rolled his eyes. "I told you this would happen eventually. Oh well. Oken, grab that red-haired idiot and get over here. Take your boyfriend and go to the dining hall. I'll deal with dear old dad." His smile was predatory.

The Fire God let them pass, Alaric's arm draped across Oken's shoulder. When they got to Bashima and the fallen Cypress, Alaric said, "I can help get him up, Oken." They grabbed the Forest God's arms and lifted him. He groaned, his clothes and hair steaming from the Fire God's hits. Alaric looked at Bashima and started, "I—"

"If you even think about saying 'I'm sorry,' I'll kick your ass right along with this fucker." Bashima moved into a fighting stance and said, "Now go. This is gonna get ugly." He smiled again, his eyes flickering gold and red.

Of course, the human had to get involved. After Bashima specifically told him not to get wrapped up in the other gods' bullshit. Not that Bashima was surprised. The human was shit at following orders. And of course, it had to be fucking Cindras, the only one whose raw power matched King Vaultus or Bashima.

The other god stood tall as a damn mountain, flames blazing off his body in torrents. The way Tengu looked, Cindras got a lot of hits in probably because the moronic Forest God charged him with no plan. Tengu had a lot of power, but he hadn't gotten the hang of it when he was mad yet. And if he was right about having a soul bond with Oken…seeing the demigod hurt probably drove Tengu over the edge.

Oken hadn't looked much better than the Forest God though his eyes were alert, and the human looked half-singed but not too hurt.

Fucking humans.

"So, you thought you'd take a chunk outta your kid, huh? Real big god, Cindras. And in my house too."

"Maybe if you'd kept your nose out of my affairs, this wouldn't be necessary," said the Fire God, pompous and hulking. "Oken belongs to me."

"He doesn't belong to anyone," Bashima scoffed, "let alone a loser like you." Small flames played across Bashima's palms but didn't draw Cindras's attention. Since they were both fire-types, Bashima wasn't sure how a fight between them would play out, but he'd been aching to try.

"Don't think I'm going to hold back just because you're the summit host, child."

"Wouldn't dream of it."

Cindras hurled a flaming fist at Bashima's head, and he easily dodged the blow, swinging around to the Fire God's left side and bombarding him with small blasts from his palms. The air smelled like ash as the two gods tried to hit each other with their powers and their fists.

Bashima was faster, but Cindras still moved quicker than expected, turning to meet Bashima's redirected blows each time. Bashima used a blast to flip over the Fire God's head, finally landing a blow on his back. But Cindras recovered fast and flew toward Bashima like a flaming battering ram. The Sun God sidestepped at the last moment, sending Cindras skidding across the hall. The massive god spun around, yelling in frustration, and charged Bashima again.

If there was one thing Bashima knew how to do, it was irritate people. He moved around Cindras, firing off flames and light blasts as he went, pesky as a horsefly. The Fire God expended his power in one large attack after the other, trying to knock Bashima out of the air. Bashima did another flip, and the Fire God thought he had him, but Bashima changed course mid-air with another blast and hit the floor, shooting out his leg. He swept the Fire God off his feet and flipped onto the god's chest, grabbing his throat with one hand. He threw his other hand back and let off a massive explosion that shook the hall and sent him and the Fire God shooting toward the main doors. At the last moment, Bashima let go, and the main doors opened, expelling the Fire God flat-backed onto the front landing.

Breathing hard, body covered in soot and armor littered with burn marks, Bashima stood at his temple's main doors and glared down at the Fire God, whose own flames had gone out.

"You all think I'm a fucking joke just because I don't leave my temple," Bashima said. "You think I'm some damaged recluse, but I hear things. If I find out you were responsible for burning Cypress's forest, I will spend the rest of eternity making your existence miserable."

There were a lot more things he wanted to say to the Fire God, but most of them would get him in bigger trouble with Vaultus than he was already in. At least he had a good excuse for beating another god senseless at a supposedly peaceful conference.

"Thanks for coming to the summit," Bashima said and spat outside the entrance.

The main doors closed with great force as he turned and walked away.

Chapter Nine

The gods were astir that Bashima forcibly ejected Cindras from his temple. Once the Sun God explained what happened to Vaultus and Hastia, the Goddess of Spring showered thanks on both Bashima and Alaric, who was overwhelmed with the attention. Vaultus saw the two battered gods, demigod, and human and accepted Bashima's explanation, though he wasn't happy.

An invitation to the summit meant safety, and he didn't like getting embroiled in family drama. But the Fire God had not only attacked Oken, who lived in the temple, but also Alaric, who was a helpless human. Alaric was somewhat offended by being called helpless, but he figured it was a fair assessment. The Fire God had tossed him around like a dried leaf.

It was decided that Oken and Cypress would remain another night at the temple, enough time for Cypress to recover though he would be a mess for about a week, according to Tansey, the Medical Goddess. She wasn't happy healing so many injuries, especially Cypress. She made her displeasure known by tutting around the room, spitting reproachful comments. She couldn't do much for Alaric because he was human.

"Messing with the human body isn't worth the pain you'd have to endure to recover," she explained. "My power drains stamina, and humans are too fragile. You can take a simple healing potion. Not as good as me, but it will do the job."

Alaric understood, and he was the least hurt of the group. "It's just a few scrapes," he said and asked if there was anything he could do to help her.

"I like this one," she said, laughing, then she patted his cheek and moved on to Oken.

Since the dining room was turned into a make-shift field hospital, dinner was canceled; every god would be served in their rooms. Alora, Garyn, and Cabari gave Alaric ovations as they left, and Jace was with them. He smirked at Alaric before Cabari threw an arm across the demigod's shoulder and pulled him out of the room.

Alora must have won the bet, Alaric thought.

Once the shades were dismissed—including Tika and Matthias, who had to debrief with Kuroi—the only ones in the room with the Medical Goddess were Oken, Cypress, Vaultus, Hastia, Bashima, and Alaric. Hastia fussed over her son, who was stretched out on one of the smaller tables until they could move him. He looked up at her, dazed and covered in burns. Nothing as bad as his arm, according to the Medical Goddess, but nothing to ignore either. Oken held Cypress's hand and murmured encouragement.

Bashima and Alaric sat apart from the others, Bashima's mouth set in a scowl as he watched them crowd around Cypress. What was he thinking? Who was he watching?

Alaric thought about what Oken said about the king and observed Vaultus closer. He still looked magnificent to Alaric, but now that he was really paying attention, the king's posture had fallen, and his hair fell down across his face, smile less radiant. Had he let his guard down once the other gods left the room?

Bashima was angry with him, of that Alaric was sure. He hadn't said a word since entering the dining room, just thrown the occasional glare in Alaric's direction. The Sun God's knuckles were singed, and Alaric tentatively reached out and touched one hand. Bashima didn't move away, but he didn't acknowledge Alaric either.

"Do these need bandages?" Alaric asked, voice soft.

"No," said Bashima, moving his hand away. "Burns don't affect me the same as other gods." He glanced at Alaric. "Or idiot humans."

"I know you're mad," Alaric said, but he raised his head, sure that what he'd done was right. "But I could never forgive myself if a friend was in danger and I did nothing."

"Even if it gets your ass killed?" Bashima's voice was rough, but there was concern in the question.

"Isn't that when it really matters?" Alaric asked. "I don't expect anyone to do the same for me, but if I'm given the chance to make even the smallest difference, I'll take it every time."

"Fuck," was all Bashima said.

Alaric didn't have godly powers. He was *just* a human, but if the few seconds he gave deflecting the Fire God's attention aided in the victory, he was happy to give those few seconds. And he wasn't going to let Bashima make him feel bad about the decision.

Bashima huffed then laid his hand palm-up on his knee. Surprised, Alaric stared at the hand, unsure what to do. Bashima snapped, "It's a hand not a damn spider."

Smiling, Alaric interlaced his fingers with the Sun God's, and everyone else in the room disappeared.

Once all the gods were gone, Alaric felt the storm clouds move off the temple. Alora, Garyn, and Cabari wanted a breakdown of what happened with the Fire God, but Bashima tried to chase them off, yelling, "It's none of your damn business; get out of my house!" They'd all laughed and made their good-byes though they hinted at future visits.

"Now that Bashima is tolerable again," teased Alora, which made the Sun God stalk away in a huff. "Really," Alora whispered to Alaric, "he's so much better."

Cabari raced away when he saw Jace trailing behind his father and slung an arm around the demigod's shoulder. Jace didn't remove the arm, but the look Veles gave the Lightning God could have burned straight through the world.

148

King Vaultus and Queen Hastia were the last to leave, later in the afternoon. Cypress was still recovering, but they needed to return to their temple. Hastia wrapped Alaric in a warm hug and kissed his cheek. He happily returned the hug, though it made him think of his mother.

The king had more than a hug for him, saying, "Not just any human would confront the Fire God with no hesitation. I commend your bravery; you most likely saved Oken and my stepson from days, if not weeks, of recovery. But take care not to act so rashly in the future. You have the heart of a lion, but even a lion must know his limitations."

Bashima grumbled at that, making Vaultus laugh.

"And you, Bashima, my boy! It was wonderful to see you looking so well. I think I know the reason for this sudden change, so make sure you keep it close." The king winked, took his wife's arm, and made his way down the steps to where they could shift down the mountain.

"Glad that's over," Bashima said and raised his arm, which signaled the doors to shut. As they closed slowly, Alaric looked across the valley, wistful. Seeing the open blue sky and smelling the mountain air rejuvenated his yearning to walk outside the temple. Maybe Bashima would allow him to visit Ichigo at the stable. That was at least technically part of the temple.

"I gave Matthias the day off," Bashima said as they walked down the hall toward the throne room. "Do you think you can manage one day without breaking something?"

Alaric laughed and ruffled his hair, which was loose and braid-free. He said, "I'm sure I can manage."

Bashima looked at him askance, "Good." When they reached the throne room, Bashima turned and said, "I have to recharge today, so you might not see me until much later."

"I don't mind," Alaric said, cheery. "The summit was a lot to manage. I'm drained and I hardly did anything."

Bashima raised an eyebrow but set free a small smile. "I'll see you later."

Alaric felt weightless for a moment, lost in the Sun God's smile. When he came to, Bashima had closed the throne room doors, and Alaric was in the hallway, looking stupefied.

Wow, he thought. *I've got it bad.*

His taste certainly hasn't changed...

The Time God's words came back and punched Alaric in the stomach, almost doubling him over.

Stop being an idiot, he thought.

Alaric had a romantic past, limited but still there, so Bashima probably had one too. He was eons old, for godsake; he'd probably had countless lovers. The idea of Bashima kissing anyone else sent a jealous wave through Alaric's body, and he became very aware that the Sun God was on the other side of the door, sitting on his throne, meditating. Alaric smelled cinnamon and burnt sugar, and he started salivating.

Alaric smacked himself in the face. That knocked him out of his possessive trance, and he rubbed his cheek. What was wrong with him? He needed to go somewhere and relax. Alaric went to the library first and tried to read, but the only books that caught his attention were romances. It was like his brain had malfunctioned and only chose the love stories. Emilia would certainly approve.

Giving up, he went down to the kitchens to see how the shades were doing. They greeted him warmly, and Shefu only tried to shoo him away once. When she saw his face fall, she let him stay and shoved a few biscuits in his hands.

"If you're going to sit here, at least make yourself useful and try this new recipe."

Alaric let himself float mindlessly as he sat and ate the buttery biscuits, which also had some sort of cheese mixed in. He devoured them and gave Shefu a rave review, then sat and watched the shades work.

Emilia was nowhere in sight, so she must have merited a day off as well. She deserved it after alerting Alaric and Matthias to Oken's plight. She'd gotten a commendation from the king and queen, which Alaric knew would go straight to her head.

After a while, Alaric needed to move around, so he said good-bye to the shades and Shefu and went back upstairs. He could go to the baths, but that made his libido awaken and remind him that the Sun God was currently sitting in the throne room. Nope. Not the baths.

Matthias had shown him the temple gym, which Alaric had been using to keep up his strength. It was full of odd machines that Matthias demonstrated, but Alaric preferred using the free weights. They were like nothing he'd ever seen in his village. There, he'd do his chores, help in the fields, and go hiking around the forest to stay in shape. Matthias teased him for the human world's lack of innovation, but it didn't bother Alaric. He was glad to discover and learn new things. The gym didn't feel right either. He needed to burn off his nervous energy, but lifting weights would probably get his blood boiling.

So, Alaric chose the conservatory. He could hide in a cozy corner on a stone bench and listen to the tranquil fountains, surrounded by plants and the butterflies that still flew about. But the conservatory was occupied.

Oken sat next to the main fountain, watching the lotus blossoms float along the surface. His hand dipped into and out of the water, and he let it drip down his hand, observing its path. Alaric felt like he'd stepped into an artist's grotto, like Oken was waiting to be painted. He was achingly lovely and seeing him sitting alone made Alaric want to give him a hug.

Oken heard him by the entrance and turned, eyes sad. "Hello, Shina. Needed a quiet place too?"

"Yeah, I guess," said Alaric. "Mind if I sit with you?"

Oken shrugged and went back to looking at the fountain. Now that the other gods were gone, the koi fish that usually swam there were back. Matthias mentioned that the gods enjoyed pranks, so having live animals around was too tempting. Alaric had no idea what kind of prank a god would pull with a koi, and he hadn't asked, fearing the answer. The fish swam in lazy laps around the fountain, bobbing to the surface when Oken dipped his hand in the water.

"How's Cypress doing?" Alaric asked, the silence overwhelming him.

"He's well," said Oken though his voice was low. "It could have been much worse. Bashima got there before my father could damage him too deeply."

"I'm glad he did," said Alaric, remembering Oken advancing on his father with no fear.

"It's a complicated situation," Oken offered. "Bashima was kind enough to give me a place here when I escaped my father's temple. Bell thought it was best since he would have looked for me in the Temple of the Forest first." He stopped talking.

"You don't have to talk about it if you don't want to," said Alaric, "but I can listen if you need someone to listen."

Oken finally looked at him, and tears shone in his eyes. "No one ever wants to talk about it," he said. "Except Bell, obviously, but he's the only one. It's not like what my father was doing was a big secret."

"Um, what exactly was he doing?" asked Alaric, confused.

"Trying to make a 'perfect' demigod," Oken said. "The gods mainly marry or partner with other gods, you know; then their children are full gods. My father wasn't interested in that. A god partner would be too close to his equal, and he wanted to fuse godly abilities, make something new."

"Seems strange," said Alaric, thoughtful.

"I suppose," Oken said. "Gods only have one ability though they can morph that power into different techniques. If a demigod child manifests, they also have only one power if any at all. But me…" He ignited one palm, and the other froze over with blue ice. "I have two. I'm something new."

The fire crept up Oken's arm, but the ice stayed in place and sparkled.

"I'm still having trouble with the fire," Oken admitted, forcing the flames back to his hand. "I wasn't using it at all, but when my father came for me, I knew the ice wouldn't help. It's not strong enough. I thought, maybe if I showed him I could use fire, that he would leave me alone."

"And the ice is from your mother?" Alaric asked. He brought his feet up onto the bench and rested his arms on his knees, putting his chin on his arms.

"She's a princess from a kingdom in the west, or at least she was," said Oken. "Her family boasted power from an ancient alchemic spell, or curse if that's how you want to look at it. The ice ability was in her bloodline, but she didn't exhibit the power outright. My grandparents sold her to my father for an exorbitant price, or so I'm told."

"Sold?" asked Alaric, shocked. That archaic practice was long gone from his village. He couldn't imagine his parents selling him into marriage.

"She wasn't a first born, so it wasn't unusual back then to make those kinds of deals. Especially if the Fire God came to your kingdom with a sizable offer. So, my father took her as his lover, just to have children. It was hard on her; she had a frail disposition, but I think she actually loved him. Or told herself she did."

"He...didn't even marry her?" Alaric asked, somber.

"He doesn't care about that," Oken said, scornful. "He was obsessed with getting his heart's desire. My three siblings didn't fit the bill. No one even knows where my oldest brother is, my oldest sister fawns over my father and takes care of him, and my other sister hates him."

Oken paused and looked at his reflection in the fountain. "Once I was born, he took pity on my mother, maybe because she'd finally 'done her duty' by him. They performed the god-touched ceremony, and everything seemed fine. But she started to develop her ice ability, and one day she lost control." He touched his scar. "Nothing can remove it. No one is sure why except that since it was made by a god-touched ability, it can't be removed. That's Bell's theory. Something to do with the ceremony and branding."

"Branding?" Alaric thought of his tattoo. It hurt, getting the dragon inked on his shoulder, but he expected branding hurt more.

"Standard for the ceremony," Oken said. "First, the human drinks a potion prepared with the god's blood, there's an incantation, then the god puts their seal on the person. It's nothing big, about the size of a coin, usually on the shoulder. Then, the god and human are bonded forever."

"Forever?"

"That's why it's so rare," explained Oken. "The god is responsible for their god-touched. Connections vary, of course. My mother and father's connection is heightened because of their relationship. Whereas a lot of the other god-touched were friends of the god. Whatever being a friend to a god means."

"Like Savos is to King Vaultus, I suppose," said Alaric. He wondered how Bashima was connected to Kuroi, Draiden, and Shefu.

"Savos is the king's chief caretaker," said Oken. "I doubt Vaultus could have gone to the last few summits without him."

Alaric swallowed. He had a feeling this was a tightly kept secret and that he shouldn't press the demigod about it. He could drop it. He could let it go.

He asked, "You said something about that before. Is there something wrong with the king?"

"I wasn't alive when it happened, but it's gotten worse these last few hundred years from what Bell says." Oken looked across the conservatory. "He sustained some kind of injury fighting the first Sun God. Apparently, that Sun God went insane and threatened to unmake humanity. He planned on making a centuries-long eclipse that would wipe out most life on the planet, start fresh."

Alaric paled as Oken spoke. "Why would someone do that?"

"No one really knows," Oken said. "His followers disappeared when Vaultus defeated him. He was put into forced hibernation and thrown into the Locker. Been there for tens of thousands of years."

"Then, Bashima became the new Sun God..." Alaric said.

"Exactly. Vaultus needed someone young and strong, so he chose Bashima, who was one of the strongest fire-type gods."

"I guess I'm glad he didn't choose your father," said Alaric.

"Unlikely. Vaultus doesn't like my father."

Alaric snorted and laughed. Oken tilted his head and said, "Was that funny? It's the truth."

"Oken, you're very funny even when you don't mean to be," said Alaric.

"Thank you? Most of the gods think I'm weird."

"There's nothing wrong with being weird," said Alaric, shaking Oken's shoulder. "I'm weird."

"Being human doesn't automatically make you weird, Shina."

"Besides," Alaric said, "normal people are boring. And you're definitely not boring." He wondered something about Vaultus, though. "If King Vaultus doesn't like your father, why didn't he step in after what he did to your mother? And to you?"

"He's not supposed to meddle in the other gods' personal affairs too much," Oken said. "I don't blame the king. I was able to get away from my father with Bell's help, but there's no way he could have gotten into the Temple of Fire without someone telling him how."

"And you think the king did that?"

"Most definitely." Oken suddenly stood, alert. "Bell needs me. Would you like to see him? I'm sure he would enjoy that."

"Whoa, you can tell he needs you from here?"

"Of course," said Oken. "Would you like to come and visit him?"

"Sure! I'd like to see how he's doing. Shina!" yelled Cypress, pulling the duvet up over his chest, cheeks flushed.

"Oops! Sorry, Cypress," said Alaric, giggling. He hadn't seen anything, but Cypress had been getting out of bed.

"What did you need, Bell?" asked Oken, ignoring the embarrassed god and human.

"Oh, I was just going to get some tea…"

"You're not supposed to walk that far until tomorrow," scolded Oken. "I can call for some tea." Oken went to the side of the bed and pulled a long, braided cord, which must have been a signal to the kitchens. He spoke loudly and clearly, "Tea, green, hot with lemon."

"I know, but I wanted to stretch my legs," said Cypress, guilty.

"You can stretch your legs just fine in here," Oken said.

The demigod was right. Oken's chambers were spacious, spreading from the entryway to the bedroom and beyond. They were sparsely decorated, done in the usual Temple of the Sun gold tones but with a few contrasting accents. Oken apparently liked the color blue. A magnificent landscape dominated the wall across from the bed, giving the perspective of staring through tall, imposing mountains at a secluded beach. It gave the illusion that the water was moving, the waves coming in from afar. Alaric could almost hear the waves crashing on the shoreline and smell the salt in the air.

"That's stunning," he said.

"Kuroi made that for me when I first arrived," said Oken, smiling. "A sort of welcome present I suppose."

"He's so talented," said Alaric, in awe.

"He was an artist as a human," Oken said. Cypress cleared his throat, getting Oken's attention. He gave an almost imperceptible head shake. Alaric wondered what that was about but didn't push. He could always ask Kuroi about his talent. And how he'd become one of Bashima's god-touched.

Getting the hint that Cypress wanted to be alone with Oken, Alaric said, "I'll leave you two alone. I can read until Bashima's finished meditating."

"Oh good, he's regenerating," said Cypress, letting the duvet fall. His upper body was riddled with bruises and healing burns, and Alaric winced. The Forest God looked down and grimaced. "It looks worse than it feels honestly. Say, I never got to thank you for helping Oken."

"It was nothing," Alaric said, holding up his hands. "I barely did anything, really."

"You sell yourself too short, Shina," said Oken, smiling. "I thank you as well."

Alaric felt color rising in his face, and he tried to hide a smile.

"It takes someone very weird to stand up to my father," Oken said, and Alaric burst out laughing, confusing Cypress.

Outside Oken's room, Alaric said goodbye and asked if he would see them before they left for the Temple of the Forest.

"I'll make sure we see each other before we go," assured Oken.

"Thank you! I've never been to this part of the temple," Alaric said, looking around "So thanks for the extended tour. I can add this to the itinerary for the next one I give," he joked.

Oken turned serious, "That wouldn't be a good idea. I don't mind people seeing my room, but Bashima's is right down the hall, and he wouldn't be happy at all."

It felt like an icicle drove through Alaric's head. Bashima's room? Oken gave him a puzzled look, and Alaric said, "Oh, no! I was just joking! I'd never show someone else's space!"

"Sorry," said Oken, "I have a hard time telling when someone is joking."

"That's okay! It wasn't very funny anyway," Alaric said. "I'll try to work on my delivery."

"Okay, feel free to keep trying your humor on me," Oken said. "Goodbye, Shina."

Chapter Ten

Alaric waved as Oken shut the door. He turned to leave but felt weighted to the spot. Right down the hall. Bashima's room. It called to him like a mesmerizing siren. He slowly turned the other way and looked down the candlelit hallway, which was like every hallway in the temple. He would never have known he was that close to Bashima's secret space.

He should definitely go to the library. Yes. That's what he should do.

But Bashima was in the throne room and would be for a few more hours. Preoccupied with refocusing his power.

That's right, you idiot, Alaric thought. *Remember that he's much more powerful than you.*

And he probably wouldn't like if someone went snooping around his room. How would Alaric feel if Bashima did that to him?

But Alaric's room in the temple wasn't really *his* room. He slept there. He ate breakfast there while chatting with Matthias, and Emilia did his hair there. But he hadn't chosen it. He'd been put there. Bashima could enter Alaric's room whenever he pleased, permission be damned, because it wasn't really Alaric's room.

His taste certainly hasn't changed...

If Bashima could have secrets, then so could Alaric.

157

He didn't pause once he'd made up his mind. There was only one other door besides Oken's in the hall, so Bashima's chambers were immense. They were probably ostentatious too, befitting the Sun God's flashy power.

Alaric almost knocked on the door then stopped himself. He was way past asking for permission. If the door was locked, he'd leave it alone. There was no way around a lock.

It wasn't locked.

The door handle turned too easily in Alaric's hand. He took a deep breath and stepped inside and was instantly taken aback. The rooms were large, of course, but the design was simple, elegant, even subdued. The sun colors still dominated, but they were muted and soft, like a sunset on an autumn evening. The furniture in the sitting room was made of polished ebony wood with curved edges and comfortable-looking orange cushions. A well-used desk sat in one corner, overflowing with used candles and sketches that were quite good—mostly plants and figure drawings. None of the people had faces, but the figures moved fluidly, well-muscled and graceful.

The air was permeated with scents of sage and citrus fruit, and Alaric breathed deeply, feeling engulfed in everything Bashima.

He moved deeper into the chambers and saw a magnificent standing harp, golden, with glistening strings. Sheet music littered the ground as though Bashima had just been seated at the instrument, figuring out a difficult progression. There was also a koto covered in delicate floral etchings, and Alaric remembered that Bashima was proficient in both instruments.

The bedroom was as surprising as the rest of the rooms. It was commanded by a large bed covered in luxurious black, silky bedding and a small heap of black and orange pillows. There wasn't much else besides a massive ebony wardrobe, ornately carved with Bashima's signature sunbursts, a large bookcase next to the bed with hundreds of books, and his washing table.

What the room lacked in furniture, it made up with art. While not overly crowded, oil paintings and watercolor scrolls covered the walls, making Alaric's jaw drop. Each piece fit well with the others, an intricate art puzzle. Most of the pieces were abstract with bold colors on a black background, but interspersed with those paintings were obviously Kuroi's. Landscapes so lifelike that they took Alaric's breath away. One piece depicted the mountain at sunset—golds, reds, purples, all coming together in a piece that sang to Alaric.

Feeling guilty for intruding on this beautiful space, Alaric felt short of breath. If Bashima found out he'd been in this room, had seen this art, which seemed like pieces of the Sun God put on display, he might not forgive Alaric.

What was he doing? How could he do this to Bashima? Hyperventilating, Alaric gasped for air and stumbled to the bed, sinking onto the plush mattress. Telling himself to calm down, Alaric focused on the bedside table, which housed four books, all with bookmarks at varying spaces. Two were fiction and two nonfiction, and Alaric smiled. Bashima *would* read multiple things at once.

Two paintings sat propped on the bedside table, much smaller and of greater detail than the works on the walls. They were the most lifelike works Alaric had seen yet. More of Kuroi's doing. Looking closer, Alaric had to smile. One depicted four people, three of them familiar: Kuroi at the center, eyes normal and dark brown, huge grin on his face that looked alien; Shefu on the left, still large for a woman but not as tall as she was now, her hair loose around her shoulders; Draiden with sandy brown hair instead of pure white and mischievous eyes that held no exhaustion. The other person in the middle was unfamiliar, but he struck Alaric straight to the core.

Alaric stood up abruptly and stared at the painting. Then he looked at the second, which was mostly hidden behind the books. The man in both images was striking. Tall, broad-shouldered, muscular, ruggedly handsome with a jaw that could cut glass. Laughing maroon eyes and dark red hair spiked forward like a challenge. A smile to die for as though he knew all your secrets before anyone else did. Freckles strewn across his nose.

Alaric realized this is what he might look like in ten or fifteen years.

His taste certainly hasn't changed...

Realization and panic rose in Alaric's blood. Oh gods...

Alaric didn't mean anything to Bashima. He was nothing but a stand-in for the man with the laughing eyes and the devastating smile. A man that would turn heads no matter where he went. Whose three friends lived and worked in the Temple of the Sun. The god-touched...Who hadn't told Alaric what was happening. Who led him along like a lamb to slaughter. Had any of it been real? Was it some twisted game they played? Why? Why had they treated him with any sort of kindness?

Had Matthias known? Surely not Emilia. She had too big a mouth and was probably too young to have known the man in the paintings. It was like he was laughing at Alaric, as though he was in on the secret game.

The architect. Mo's good friend. He who made friends with gods like it was easy. The one Mo introduced to Bashima to build his temple, who wouldn't be intimidated by the Sun God's quick temper. Who would stand up to him and laugh at his tantrums. The architect from Togarashi.

It was all some sick joke.

"What the fuck are you doing in here?"

The voice hit Alaric like a hammer. It couldn't be. He should still be in the throne room. It was too early. Alaric turned around, aware that he probably looked terrible. Bashima stood in the doorway, anger flowing off him like steam.

"I asked you a question." He was quiet, which scared Alaric more than if he'd yelled. This was Bashima shocked and hurt. And so angry.

"I...I didn't mean..." Alaric started, lost for words while the image of the red-haired man tumbled through his mind, mixed with Chronas's cutting words and what they really meant.

You aren't special. You're just a lesser version of this other man. And everyone knows it. Every god knows that Bashima was with this man. Felt for this man. Loved this man.

"I think you definitely meant to sneak into my room," Bashima said, accusing.

How dare the Sun God act innocent? When the dots were starting to connect. When he'd used Alaric as a stand-in, made him feel like he meant something. Alaric realized something with horror. What if he hadn't been the first?

"Why do I look like this man?" Alaric asked, hoping to hear a reasonable answer but not expecting it.

"What?"

The question threw the Sun God off. Good. "This man," said Alaric, grabbing the small painting and brandishing it in front of him. "In the painting. I look like him."

"Put that down," hissed Bashima, and light played across his skin, moving in roiling ripples.

"Is this what gets you off?" Alaric shouted. "Fucking people who look like this? Is that what happens to all the missing tributes? Do you...do you kidnap them and use them up and throw them away when they're no good anymore?"

"What the fuck are you talking about?" Bashima moved a little closer, so Alaric backed against the bed.

"Tributes go missing from the Temple of the Sun. Every ten years or so. Just last year, a guy from the village closest to us, he vanished, never came back. Now me." Alaric's voice quavered. "I'm *missing!* My parents have no idea where I am!"

"I have no fucking clue what you're talking about," Bashima said, voice low and even, but the colors flashing in his eyes told a different story. Alaric knew those eyes. Or he thought he did.

"Then who is this man? Why am I here? What do you want from me?" Alaric yelled.

"Put the painting DOWN."

"No! Not until you explain this!"

Alaric's fingers curled around the painting, nails scratching the paint, and Bashima exploded. He tackled Alaric to the bed and wrenched the painting from his hand, hissing, cradling the canvas when he stood up and moved away. He looked down at the man, then at Alaric on the bed, breathing hard, rage growing in his orange eyes. It might have been hate.

"He was the love of my fucking life; that's who he is! He's the only person who's ever loved me!"

Alaric felt a massive emotional burst radiate from the Sun God: sorrow, pain, regret, fury, guilt. It hit Alaric like a punch straight to the jaw. Bashima was telling the truth. The Sun God stood, crouched over as though the painting were something to cherish and be ashamed of, something to hide behind a pile of books and only catch a glimpse of on occasion but still close to where he slept. Where he dreamed.

An image forced its way into Alaric's mind: that man standing beyond the temple doors, sun fading behind the horizon, his back turned to who was watching him, wind tugging at his shirt and hair. The man turned slowly, as if answering a summons, and the sun hit his eyes perfectly, illuminating them in shining crimson, his mouth curled into a content smile, emitting absolute happiness.

That was how Bashima saw the man. He was light. He was perfection. And he was gone.

Alaric stammered, getting off the bed slowly, hands up. "I'm so sorry, Bashima, I didn't know. I thought..."

Bashima was done hearing Alaric say he was sorry. He put the painting face down on the bedside table and glared at Alaric as though seeing him clearly for the first time.

"He was the sun to me, and you're *nothing*. You will always be *nothing*."

The Sun God moved with incredible speed. He grabbed Alaric and spun him around, jamming him face-first into the bookcase so his cheek was right against the volumes, his arm twisted behind his back. Alaric didn't bother to fight. He braced himself for whatever the god dealt him.

Bashima shoved his hand down Alaric's pants and palmed his ass, fingers constricting. "This is all you're good for," the Sun God hissed, voice crackling with rage. Alaric tried to wrench free, but Bashima shoved him against the shelf again, knocking the breath from his lungs. Then the hand on his ass moved to his dick and squeezed hard, painful. He whispered in Alaric's ear, "These are the only parts of you that interest me."

Alaric let out a sob that echoed across the room, ringing in his ears, and he was ashamed that he'd felt anything for the Sun God. Ashamed that he'd ever let the god touch him. Their quiet moments together rushed through his mind, the voracious kisses and burning desire, but so did the times where Bashima had hurt him, taunted him, made him feel lesser.

Alaric let the tears run down his cheeks. He sunk down and Bashima let him fall, crumpling to the ground. He didn't make another sound. He wouldn't let the Sun God have any more of his pained cries.

He felt the Sun God behind him, felt the white-hot fury drain from him. What was left was disgust. His voice was gravel, "Get out of my sight."

Alaric collected himself before speaking. He couldn't let his voice quaver. Not meeting the god's eyes, he said. "Where would you have me go?"

"Anywhere but here," the Sun God said. He put an invisible force behind what he said next, "GET OUT."

This was the voice that had asked Alaric why he wasn't on his knees the first time they met. Then, Alaric was unable to resist. The voice was commanding and absolute and all-encompassing. Now, he felt it, the weight behind it, but he also felt that he could push back if he wanted.

He could be commanded no more.

He stood slowly, composing himself, and stood to his full height, puffing out his chest. The tear tracks on his cheeks stood out like scars, and the god's face faltered for a moment before resetting to cold indifference.

Let him keep his painting. See how close it let him get. See how it felt to worship a memory and nothing else. Let him stay stuck on a man that was gone, trapped in his temple. That's what the Sun God deserved. Alaric owed him nothing.

He spun on his heel and walked slowly from the room, leaving the Sun God fuming silently.

Once he left the Sun God's chambers, Alaric lost his composure. He sagged against the wall for a moment, trembling. He couldn't stay there long, or the Sun God would find him drooling in a stupor. No. This was his chance. The god commanded him to get out, and he would. He was finally free.

He stepped away from the wall and hurried down the hall. Oken stuck his head out his door, looking concerned. When he saw Alaric, he said, "Shina, what's wrong?"

Alaric shook his head. He was done with gods and demigods and god-touched and the whole lot of them. They'd tricked him into thinking he had a chance of belonging with them, and he'd risked his life. He'd risked enraging a powerful god to help the demigod in front of him. He could have died. And for what?

A loud, cascading scream rent the temple, coming from the Sun God's chambers. The walls and floor shook, putting Alaric off his stride, and candles on the walls sputtered in their sconces then burst into full flame, melting the wax. Oken's eyes widened, and Cypress shouted from inside the room, but Alaric kept going. He couldn't stop now. Even though the Sun God's anguish called to him.

Alaric found the strength to run.

He didn't stop for anything. He didn't go to his room to collect his new belongings or his pack. He would get home with just the clothes on his back or nothing at all. He could practically feel his parents' arms around him, telling him that everything would be fine. Showering him in love. Real love.

He ran past the conservatory, the baths, the library, past the entrance to the downstairs kitchens. Frightened shades stepped aside to let him pass. A few called his name, fear in their voices. He couldn't stop to assure them that everything was fine. It wasn't their fault that they worked for a monster. He thought fleetingly of Emilia and Matthias and held in another sob. He couldn't think of them, or he would stay.

He turned the corner at the throne room, remembering how Bashima stalked around him that first day, how the god played with him like a predator played with a meal. That was the true Sun God, not the one Alaric made up in his mind. Not the god who took in wayward demigods or recruited shades who were victims of terrible hate crimes. Not the god who worried over him or got angry when he attempted to thwart the Fire God by himself. Not the god who opened his burned hand, offering it to take.

None of that was real.

He was almost at the main doors when Kuroi appeared in front of them, a concerned expression instead of his usual stoic features. The temple shook again, tossing Alaric to the floor. Kuroi held his balance, barely. When the building settled, Alaric stood up, breathing hard, glaring at Kuroi. Had he known the entire time? Had he been laughing with his two god-touched friends about how foolish Alaric was?

"He told me to leave," Alaric growled. "So I'm leaving. Let me out."

Kuroi's eyes widened, and the temple shook again. Alaric wondered how many temper quakes the building could take before it fell, but he couldn't muster the energy to care. Kuroi's black eyes showed no emotion, and Alaric pictured the dark brown eyes of the man who was the *real* Kuroi, posing with his friends in a captured painted scene.

"Kuroi, open the doors!"

"I can't!" Kuroi shouted. He looked up as though hearing a far-off voice. "It's not what he actually wants!"

"Bullshit! He told me to get out. He used that voice thing on me again."

Kuroi's mouth dropped open, and he said, "And you...you fought it off?"

"I know exactly what he meant. I felt it in my bones. Just because I can ignore it now doesn't mean anything."

A rumble went through the foundation, not quite as strong as the other blasts.

"He must be tiring himself out, throwing these tantrums. You better go check on him," Alaric snarled, and Kuroi looked hurt and a little afraid.

He put up one hand, conciliatory, and said, "Please rethink this. I must obey him. I can't help you."

"Yes, you can!" Alaric yelled. "You could if you wanted to, if you tried hard enough. But I'm just a stupid, worthless human, right? I don't deserve your help. I'm not *him*."

Kuroi's face fell, eyebrows contracting across his brow. "Oh hells, did you..."

"Yeah, I found out your big secret," Alaric said, and a sob broke from him. "What the hells is wrong with you people? Do you do this for fun? I'm guessing it worked really well on me, the simple human. I'm glad to have been of some use."

"Shina, it's not what you think."

"And what do I think?" he screamed. "Tell me what I think! You've all been really great at that so far." He took a breath and looked at the doors, determined.

When he reached Kuroi, the god-touched man reached out and brushed his shoulder. Alaric froze, remembering Kuroi giving him the dragon pin before the summit, how he'd made the paintings for the guest list for Alaric to memorize, his stunned face when Alaric sang the Togarashi harvest song. All of the soulful paintings in Oken's and Bashima's rooms. Could the man who made that art be spiteful and malicious?

"Kuroi," Alaric begged. "Please, just let me go."

"I...I can't," he said and smiled. "Do you remind me of my friend? Yes, you're so much like him. It's been like watching his ghost wander the temple these last months." His breath caught in his throat, and Alaric stifled his tears. He had to leave. He had to get away, but the man held him in place. "But know this—you aren't him. And that's not a bad thing. You are miles away from him. You're the man he wished to be but never got the chance."

Alaric swallowed hard. They were just lovely words meant to keep him there.

He had to see the sky.

He stood in front of the doors and said, "Let me out."

After a pause, the main doors swung slowly open, and Alaric let out a huge breath. The temple listened to him. He felt a new power surge through his body, lighting pathways he never knew existed. He heard a rumbling laughter in his head and saw a flash of a smile. A maroon eye winking in the setting sun.

He turned to Kuroi, who stood, stunned, next to him. Kuroi said, voice faltering, "You...the doors..."

"I'll be at the stable," Alaric said. "Seeing to my horse before I go." He looked out at the sky spread vast before him and took a step. Then he paused and dropped his shoulders. "I'll wait. But I won't wait long."

Bashima surveyed the wreckage of his room and couldn't remember destroying it. Luckily, he'd spared the art. Kuroi would never forgive him if he'd ruined the paintings. The bookshelf lay in broken timbers along with the wardrobe, which was torn in half. The books might be recoverable, his clothes, less so. His bed was a shambles, pillows in feathery shreds, though the frame looked intact. The windows broken, but that was an easy fix. He shuddered to think what the rest of his chambers looked like.

He checked the sun to be sure he hadn't lost complete control. It was stable in the sky, so he hadn't neglected his duty, and it was almost time for it to set anyway. However, he'd unleashed terror on the temple. Hells, the shades were probably shitting themselves. Fuck. He put his face in his hands. What had he done?

"Bashi!" came a familiar shout from his chambers entryway.

"I'm in here," he muttered and sat down hard on the bed, which sagged under his weight.

The Forest God limped into his bedroom, eyes wide and unsure. For once, Zebra Head wasn't trailing him like a trained spaniel. Tengu looked awful, the huge cut above his eye especially ugly, and he favored his left leg as he shuffled in. His mouth gaped as he took in Bashima's bedroom.

"What the hells happened?" The Forest God asked. "One minute I was enjoying some tea, the next second I was knocked out of bed by an earthquake. I half-thought the volcano was erupting."

He glared at Bashima as if he already knew part of the answer, which Bashima hated him for. Tengu always knew when Bashima fucked things up royally. When Bashima didn't answer, he said, "Oken saw Shina running away like he'd been set on fire." Tengu paused. "Did you set Shina on fire?"

"What? Fuck, no I didn't," Bashima said. What he'd done and said was much worse. "The human was in my room, snooping around."

"How the hells did you know? Weren't you in deep meditation?" Tengu asked, rubbing his burn scar.

"I...I felt that he was in distress," Bashima admitted. He shuffled his feet on the floor as the Forest God stared at him. Bashima finally glared up at him after a few minutes of silence. "What?"

"I didn't say anything," Tengu spit out, crossing his arms. "So, what did you do?"

"Why'd you say it like that?" Bashima asked. "He's the one who broke in."

"Which means you were an asshole," Tengu said and sighed. "It must have been pretty bad to make you freak out like that."

Bashima looked away, preferring not to recall what he'd said to the human. The painting still sat face-down on the bedside table. Fucking Tengu saw him looking at it and inhaled sharply. "Oh," he said. "Are you okay?"

It was the last thing Bashima expected the Forest God to say, and he looked up, eyes pleading.

"I...I don't know. I don't think so." He looked at his hands and remembered that he'd barely held back from blasting the redhead, had imagined flesh curling from the heat of his flames. "I think I fucked up."

"I think you did more than fuck up," came an annoyed voice from the doorway. Kuroi stood there, looking over the room, shaking his head in disgust.

The Forest God glanced from Bashima to Kuroi and put his hands up. "I think I'll go back to Oken's room and rest. Could you let us know if there are going to be any more disruptions?"

Both Bashima and Kuroi gave him searing looks, so the Forest God made his exit.

Bashima could feel how vexed Kuroi was. It radiated from him through their god-touched bond, which meant that Kuroi wasn't attempting to control it. He let his emotions hit Bashima full on.

"You can stop now," Bashima said. "I know how you feel."

"What happened?" Kuroi asked, voice icy.

"I found him in here, got mad."

"That can't be it," Kuroi said and turned the painting back over. "He saw this? And the one of us four together?"

Bashima nodded and shrugged. "He came in here uninvited and accused me of kidnapping tributes."

"Well, he was correct on one count of kidnapping," Kuroi bit out, slamming the painting back on the table. "I warned you this would happen."

"You picked a great time to use your 'I told you so,'" said Bashima.

Kuroi wasn't impressed with his attitude. "You need to apologize. Immediately. I don't care what you said to him. I'm sure it was atrocious. Don't think for a second that I've forgotten *anything* you used to say to Dain, how you were before he agreed to be with you."

Bashima flinched away from Kuroi's disappointment. It felt like small daggers in his skin. "It's too late. He's gone. I felt the doors let him out. Dain let him out." He paused and gathered himself. "I used Compulsion on him."

"Oh, I'm aware," Kuroi seethed. "But he wasn't affected. He left the temple of his own volition."

"What?" Bashima asked, shocked. The human had thrown off his Compulsion?

"That's beside the point." Kuroi looked him in the eyes, those black endless pits staring through Bashima. "He has left the temple. But I don't think he truly wants to go."

"Let him go," Bashima said, resigned. "He doesn't belong here. With me."

Kuroi raised a bushy eyebrow. "Do you care for him?" he asked, voice soft.

"No," said Bashima. "I don't know. He's just a human."

"Then why are you so concerned that he might leave? You shook the entire temple, multiple times," Kuroi said.

Bashima thought of the human's sharp-toothed grin and how his hair looked in the candlelight. How his lips tasted after they'd grappled together in bed, salty and spicy. He said, "Maybe I'm just a lonely asshole who doesn't want to lose his bed filler." He slumped down on his bed, head bent.

"Master Bashima," said Kuroi, sighing. "We both know he's more than that." He picked his next words carefully. "Would my friend want you to be alone forever, pining for his memory? Draiden, Shefu, and I. We stayed so you wouldn't be alone, but we can't replace him. I think two thousand years has proven that." He stopped and sat next to the god. "Shina can't replace Dain either. But you could be throwing away something gods so rarely get. Something new."

Bashima's shoulders shook. He didn't know what to do. He didn't know how to move forward. He had been content in his temple, ruling the sun and

169

ignoring the world. Then, the world crashed into his throne room carrying a basket of peppers.

"I have nothing to offer him," Bashima said. "Not when I still love...someone else."

Kuroi sighed and stood. He didn't have time for godly inaction. "Then you have a choice: give Shina whatever you have to give and see if he accepts it. Or let him go. He's down at the stables. But I doubt he'll be there for long."

The head of his household strode from the room without looking back, his judgment thick in the air.

The sun moved differently and felt more distinct outside the temple.

Bashima wasn't in the throne room's locus of power, but being outside the walls made everything seem wider and more important. The horizon was consuming the sun, and Bashima realized sunset was probably his deadline. To do and say what, he wasn't sure. Could anything he said change the outcome? He doubted it. People were slow to forgive and even slower to forget.

But he had to try.

He stood on the edge of the mountain path and looked down, eyes finding the small stable they'd constructed for the horse. The temple was fully able and prepared to offer temporary care to the horses tributes used to drop off annual offerings, but a permanent structure hadn't been needed in two thousand years.

No, Bashima thought. *It's not the time to think about him, even though you're so close...Dain...*

Being outside was suffocating. The air threatened to close around him, snuffing out his courage. Bashima couldn't let the world do that to him. He was a god of the highest order, the ruler of the sun itself. No matter how much his panicked mind shrieked at him to go back inside the temple, Bashima found strength to master it. He closed his eyes and shifted down the mountain.

The stable smelled pleasant, like hay and oiled leather. A small cart sat outside the stable, nothing inside. So, he hadn't even stopped to collect his things before he'd gone. He was that motivated to leave. The Sun God almost turned around to shift back to the temple, but then he heard it. Laughter like bells.

Shina wasn't graceful, but his movements had purpose, no motion wasted. He lifted the bags of feed, one arm up then down, repeating the motion, his bare back glistening from the effort. His powerful shoulders gleamed in the fading light, illuminated dust motes drifting through the air like fireflies. The dragon tattoo stared at Bashima, knowing, challenging.

A roan horse stood in the only occupied stall, nodding her head along with whatever Shina had been saying. She shook her head and snorted, and Shina laughed again. He was content, Bashima realized. Content to be in the stable, talking to his horse and lifting those bags. Babbling to the animal when he should be babbling to Bashima.

Kuroi's voice played in his head: "You're jealous of a horse now?"

"Shina," Bashima said, and the redhead's shoulders tensed. He put the bags down and turned toward the Sun God. He looked as different outside the temple as the sun had. He had wrapped a strip of cloth around his head to keep sweaty hair out of his eyes — those huge, gorgeous eyes, lashes long and curled. But there was a hardness to Shina's face that hadn't been there that morning. His unfailing innocence was gone.

Bashima expected Shina to say something back, so he stood awkwardly waiting for the redhead to speak, but he was motionless, looking through the Sun God. So Bashima walked over to the horse, who tossed her head and whickered, nibbling on his hair. He rubbed her nose, and she nuzzled his head.

Shina snorted, "Traitor."

Bashima looked over at him but saw the same coarsened expression. The redhead picked the feed bags back up and moved them against the wall, dusted off his hands, and said, "She's a terrible judge of character." He leaned against the wall and crossed his arms, observing Bashima from a distance.

"I'm..." Bashima started. "I..."

"There's a story they tell in my village when we're kids," Shina said, and Bashima was grateful. He never excelled at conversation, and he felt a rush of relief when the redhead launched into a story.

"I totally forgot about it. It's not something we focus on much outside of the nursery. As far as I know, we're the only village with this story, which

171

makes sense, because it makes us feel important. All we have to do to remember that we're blessed is tell the story of the Sun God and the Architect."

Bashima's skin went cold. He had no idea anyone still spoke of that.

Shina went on, "Supposedly, the Sun God was temperamental and capricious, and no one could hold onto his heart. No god, no human, no one. 'The Sun God does not love.'"

The last part was a recitation, part of the actual story, no doubt.

"But he needed a home that would match his magnificence. He searched high and low for an inspired architect, someone who could build something that had never been attempted. It took a while because the Sun God was fastidious, and no architect, god or human, could see his vision. Until a man from Togarashi sought him out and suggested building his temple from the remnants of a mighty volcano, the most powerful force in the world. Inspired by the Sun God's indomitable spirit, the architect designed and constructed the most unique and beautiful temple of the gods, mighty enough to eclipse the king's own temple."

Shina paused, seeing how Bashima was reacting perhaps. When the Sun God didn't respond, he continued, "With his architectural marvel complete, the architect declared his undying love for the Sun God, and all was as it should be. But the architect wasn't a god; he was mortal, and he died young. The Sun God shut himself in his temple and never came out. He allowed people inside once a year to offer tributes and bestowed good fortune on all those who came before him."

Bashima looked at Shina, the setting sun igniting his red hair like flames, red eyes glistening. But he wasn't crying. His face was set but not in sadness. It was pity.

"The story leaves out a few things, but I'd say it's pretty accurate," Shina said with a tired laugh. He touched the gold chain on his chest, and Bashima felt a pang in his heart. "This chain symbolizes the connection between the Sun God and Togarashi. I guess I never thought about what that actually meant."

"I'm sorry," Bashima blurted.

"For what?" Shina asked. "For loving someone? Why should you be sorry about that?"

172

"I'm sorry for what I said to you."

"It's not like you were wrong," Shina said and looked away. "I'm nowhere near as special as that man. He was a genius and obviously talented with alchemy, right? To have made the temple?"

"Yes, but—"

"How could I be upset about that? That you loved someone so much you fell apart for two thousand years? That's a romance epic, something people like me dream about, a story we get to hear but never live."

Bashima stepped forward, but Shina's hand shot up, warding him off.

"Please, don't touch me," he said, and Bashima's heart shattered. He hadn't realized it was whole enough to break, and yet here he was, standing in a stable with a village boy, actually feeling bad for something he'd done.

"I...I won't touch you unless you want me to," Bashima said, voice low. "I was wrong to say those things to you. What I said...I don't believe that. You're not nothing."

"Bashima—"

"You can't help but shine," Bashima said, cutting Shina off. "Especially when you try not to. Every god at the summit knew it, could feel it. And I could sense them feeding off you, drawn to you. It drove me crazy."

Shina stared at him, stunned and unsure. Bashima started to move forward again but stopped himself. He would respect Shina's space since he'd violated it so completely earlier. What he'd said and done flooded back to him: pushing Shina against the bookcase, twisting his arm until it hurt, shoving his hand...it horrified him. Shina had every right to run from him. He deserved to be abandoned.

"Dain Bodo," Bashima said, shaking. "That was his name. His talent was extraordinary, and he was magnificent. He was bombastic and courageous and singular. But you're..." He wasn't sure exactly what he wanted to say.

Shina started as an amusement, someone who looked so much like Dain that it startled Bashima the first time they'd locked eyes. Bashima only meant to toy with the boy in the throne room then send him on his way. But he'd been so feisty, so defiant. He dared to stand up to a god. Bashima lost himself in that moment, fueled by centuries-long pain and anger, and he'd let it boil over. Then the human fainted. Bashima saw how fatigued and injured the human was, inner thighs scraped raw from riding, and called the healer shade. And gave him a room.

Kuroi was against it from the start, but the human intrigued the Sun God.

"He was never afraid of me," Bashima finally said. "Not like you were, that first day. But then you shook the fear off, quicker than anyone I've ever met. Most men would be drooling messes if I showed a single thread of my power. But not you. You stood there and took it. Why did you do that?" His last question came out in a pained voice, pleading for an answer.

Shina looked like he'd rather do anything than answer, but he said, "My father taught me to stand up to bullies. That not enough people do." He paused and smiled as though recalling a long-ago memory. "He said that if you could stand up, then you should. If someone thought they could break you, then you had to become unbreakable."

"Unbreakable?" Bashima asked. "You kept saying that." When Shina looked at him, confused, Bashima continued, "That first night after you passed out. You kept muttering it under your breath: 'unbreakable.'"

Shina watched Bashima as though wary of a predator. He stood straight-backed against the wall, but his body tensed, ready for flight. Bashima suddenly knew what he wanted to say.

"You're better than he was. In a lot of ways. Dain could take the world in his hand and own it with his forceful personality." Bashima paused, fiddling with his fingers. "But he didn't have your goodness. Or that really annoying positivity." Bashima chuckled, but Shina wasn't laughing. The Sun God looked the human in the eye and said, "Dain only thought he was unbreakable. But you *are*."

A tear trailed down Shina's cheek, and Bashima wanted to rush forward and wipe it away. He'd already caused the redhead so much pain, and now, he'd done it again. He was terrible at this. All he could do was hurt people.

Shina bit his bottom lip, and Bashima had to hold himself back. All he wanted to do was take that lip in his mouth and drink deep. The redhead's eyes flashed to Bashima, and the Sun God thought he saw something flare in Shina's eyes like a heartbeat.

Shina sighed and said, "I can't be what you want me to be."

"I don't want you to be anything," Bashima said quickly.

"I've got to be something," the redhead said, annoyed.

"You know what I mean," Bashima answered, his own impatience and attraction flaring. Why was the human so damn attractive like this? *Calm down,* he thought. *This is no time to let your dick do the talking.*

"Obviously I don't," Shina said. "You came all the way down the mountain. Why? To say all these *nice* things? How can I believe them? When you told me I was worthless half an hour ago. Why do you want me here?"

"I..." Bashima started, but he wasn't sure if his reasons were good enough. Did he have any right to try and make Shina stay? "I don't know, all right?"

"*Do* you want me here?"

"Yes," Bashima answered almost before Shina finished his question.

"But you still love him?"

"I do," Bashima admitted.

They stared at each other, neither moving an inch. Bashima knew he still loved Dain, and he couldn't change that. He wouldn't lie to Shina, just to get him to stay, but he wanted so badly for him to stay. He didn't know what he was feeling, but he didn't want Shina to go. Bashima's blood screamed for the human, ordering him to grab the redhead and take him right there in the stable.

Shina moved first. He walked to a pile of baled hay. His tunic was draped across the top, and he shook it out before slipping it over his head. He brushed the excess hay off the shirt and bit the inside of his cheek. Did he intend to leave?

Bashima couldn't bear the thought of watching Shina riding away on his horse, not looking back, so he said, "Will you come back up to the temple?"

"I..." Shina started. He clenched his jaw, and his whole body shivered. "I will. I just need a minute. Alone."

Bashima read Shina's intention: Go back to the temple. Leave me alone. I'll come when I'm good and ready. So, the Sun God left the stable.

Once outside, he watched the sun sink below the horizon. The ground swallowed the sun whole.

If I stay in his orbit, what will happen?

Alaric walked up the mountain path back to the temple though he wasn't sure why. Bashima apologized and spoke truthfully as far as Alaric could tell. The Sun God felt bad for what he'd done, of that Alaric was certain, but he was less sure the god knew why he felt bad or why he should. Could gods feel that kind of remorse? Had Bashima only said what he thought Alaric wanted to hear? Then why say it at all? If he really thought Alaric was nothing, why come after him?

He left the temple for you, his mind whispered.

He shifted down the mountain, Alaric spat back at himself, *not exactly some epic journey.*

But still, it was a nice gesture.

He said your name…

Was it the first time the Sun God had called him by his actual name? Had it taken that long? Was that something he should hold onto as evidence that the god cared? A name was so simple, and yet, it held so much weight. Alaric remembered when the god told him his name or what passed for his name. It could be used as a talisman, a symbol of closeness. Or it could be a cudgel, designed to make Alaric feel special but more like a weapon against his good sense.

Don't latch onto something that inconsequential, he admonished himself.

Alaric wanted so many things. He wanted to go home, to see his parents and tell them what happened, to share his wild adventure with them. He also wanted to keep it secret, something that only he held. He felt like shouting to Matthias and Emilia that he wasn't leaving, that it was going to be okay. He was their friend and wouldn't leave them, but he also ached to leave. To turn and ride into the forest, to wind his way along the river until he spotted the fields outside his village.

More than anything, he desired to make the Sun God his own, to claim Bashima from the ghost who haunted the temple, who held so much power over the god. He wanted to grab Bashima and kiss him and spin him around and take him and hear him moan at his touch, to become one like they hadn't yet.

He also wanted to stay as far away from the Sun God as he could. He felt the god's hot hand slipping down his pants and saying he was only worth as far as his ass and his dick could take him.

He thought he was unbreakable, but it's you who is...

Alaric wanted to scream into the twilight, to unleash everything he was feeling into the night sky. He stopped in his slow wandering up the path and looked at the approaching temple. What did this place have for him? Did it want him there? Had he embraced what it meant if he stayed? Could he be content to always be the human off to the side, the man in the shadows watching the Sun God shine?

You can't help but shine...

He kept going. What did it matter? Bashima admitted his continuing feelings for the architect but he wanted Alaric to stay. He'd laid his heart bare and said kind things. He hadn't pushed. Hadn't gone too far, hadn't begged. And yet, Alaric felt the distress in the god's heart like a man drowning.

Alaric remembered falling in clear blue water, wanting to breath in and become one with the depths. Was that what he was doing if he went back to the temple? Was he embracing the water?

Somehow, he didn't think so. His body would have screamed at him to jump onto Ichigo's back and flee. The damn horse liked the Sun God, and she didn't like many people. No accounting for taste.

When Alaric reached the main doors, he stopped again and breathed in a few long, deep breaths. If he went in, it meant he accepted the Sun God's apology and explanation.

No, whispered a low voice in his mind. *It means that you're willing to try.*

He clenched his fists at his sides and glared at the doors, the creation of his long-dead rival. Alaric didn't know if he could win the Sun God's heart. But he was willing to try.

He didn't have to speak. The doors opened for him.

He went right to his room, seeing no one on the way down the main hall and past the throne room. The temple seemed no worse for wear from Bashima's tantrums. New candles were in the alcoves, and the dust had been swept away as though nothing happened. Alaric wasn't sure if he should be relieved or angry. Shouldn't there be evidence that the Sun God unleashed his rage against Alaric? Had it been against him? Or was it just the god's pain releasing in a torrential storm?

Alaric thought he heard a contented humming and looked around, seeing no one.

His room was as he'd left it. The bed made, his desk neat and organized by Matthias, his washing table stocked with new oils. The wine-colored suit, the one he thought was ruined by the Fire God, hung on the door of his small wardrobe, repaired and brushed. His dragon pin sat in its box on the bedside table, reminding him that he was both himself and also that he belonged to the Sun God. He closed the box lid and shoved it in the secret drawer with the silvery mirror. Fresh fire lilies mocked him from the vase on the table.

Every day. Fresh flowers.

His stomach rumbled. Escaping was hungry work, but he didn't want to go to the dining room to see if Shefu laid the table. He didn't feel like journeying to the kitchen. He didn't want to go anywhere. Instead, he curled up on the bed, hugging a pillow. He fell asleep though the sun was newly set.

In what felt like seconds and an eternity, a knock came on his door. Alaric froze. What if it was the Sun God? He couldn't take that. Not yet. He didn't want to see Bashima's beautiful face yet. If he did, he might forgive and pull the god into his room. That would only make things hurt more.

"Shina?" A soft, familiar voice. Alaric leaped from the bed and pulled the door open. Matthias stood on the other side, eyes red and worried. The shade trembled, and his eyes fell, ashamed. "I must apologize for my behavior. I kept things from you, and that is unforgivable. Even if I owe the Sun God, you are my charge, and I owe you as well. I'm so sorry." He crumpled into a bow, and Alaric pulled him into a hug.

178

"It's not your fault," Alaric said, and the shade hugged him back, shuddering. They stood like that for a while, just holding each other, neither saying a word. Finally, Alaric dragged the shade into his room and closed the door. "It's me who should be apologizing. I almost left without saying goodbye."

"I wouldn't have blamed you if you'd run away," Matthias said, wiping his eyes. "I told Emilia she couldn't come yet. I thought that might overwhelm you."

"I'll talk to her tomorrow," Alaric said and sat on his bed. Matthias stood by the door, wringing his hands. Alaric sighed and said, "Seven hells, just sit by me."

The shade moved quickly and sat on the bed next to Alaric, still guilty.

"I know that part of what happened today is my fault," Alaric said. "I went into his room. I went into his space and broke that trust. I came to some very wrong conclusions and accused him of something awful."

"What did you say?"

"That he'd been kidnapping tributes to…use and throw away." Matthias's shocked face said everything. "It didn't come out of nowhere. There are stories of tributes not coming back from the Temple of the Sun. A village near mine lost their tribute last year."

"That's terrible!" Matthias said. "So, your parents think that you're…"

"I'm not sure what they think," Alaric said and put his face in his hands. "If you'd let me send a letter. Even one sentence to let them know I was okay."

Matthias blushed, ashamed. "Do you still wish to do so? I'm sure the master would let you now."

Alaric shook his head. "This isn't something you write down in a letter. It's too strange. I want to tell them in person, so they know I'm serious, that I haven't gone mad."

Matthias nodded. "Do you want to ask me anything? I'll answer best I can."

Alaric thought about his conversation with Bashima, what they'd said and left unsaid. Something still gnawed at Alaric, but maybe he had missed something.

"When...Dain died," he started, and Matthias swallowed hard. Alaric went on, "Why didn't Bashima go get his shade? It wouldn't have been the same, but they would have been together."

Matthias bit his lip, trying to find the words perhaps. He said, "Not every shade makes it to the Underworld. Sometimes they get lost or stuck and become adrift. As far as I know, Master Bashima asked Lord Veles to return Dain's shade to him, but Dain never arrived. It's not common, but it does happen. He didn't end up in the Locker either. The master went to the Time God's temple and Master Chronas went through the hibernating shades with him. Dain wasn't there."

"So, he's just lost?" Alaric asked, appalled. "Forever?"

Matthias wouldn't meet his eyes. "Yes."

Alaric felt like a weight was pressed on his heart. "So Bashima has spent two thousand years not knowing what happened."

"Yes," Matthias said. "The master used to be...difficult. He hired shades based on what happened to us in death because he felt pity for us, but he was a terror. He demanded excellence and wasn't shy about airing his displeasure at our performance. Then Dain came and tamed him. Or made him softer. I don't think the master can really be tamed. After Dain died, the master became easier to deal with. He forgave mistakes and helped new shades get used to their positions. Emilia followed him around for a week when she first arrived, and he never complained."

"This Dain sounds like an amazing person," Alaric said, in awe. He changed Bashima's personality with pure willpower.

"Shina, no one is perfect," Matthias said and patted his arm. "The master and Dain would get into huge arguments. They could destroy a room in an instant. It was terrifying if you were caught in a room with them. Neither would back down or give way."

Alaric felt guilty for having caused Matthias or any of the other shades distress. He and Bashima might not have fought a lot, but their last encounter must have frightened everyone especially if they were used to a more benevolent Sun God. "I'm sorry, Matthias," Alaric said. "If anyone was afraid because of me."

Matthias grabbed Alaric's shoulders and shook him. "No one here is afraid of you or anything you've done. You're nothing like Dain. You're gentle and kind and forgiving. You protected me from the master when you hardly knew me, when you didn't even know why he was angry. Somehow, you threw yourself into danger. Please don't think that any of us shades blame you for what's happened these last few months. If anything, you've made our lives brighter."

Alaric hugged Matthias again, drawing the shade closer, and he sobbed into the man's shoulder, letting loose all he'd been holding back since leaving Bashima's room. Matthias patted his back, embrace tight. He let Alaric cry all over him, never flinching away.

"I'm so tired," Alaric admitted, letting the stress from the day melt off his body.

"Would you like to sleep?" Matthias asked, and Alaric nodded.

"Can you stay with me?" Alaric asked, drawing away from the shade.

"Always," Matthias said. He moved to sit in Alaric's desk chair, but Alaric grabbed his hand.

"Can you...lay next to me?" Alaric asked, and Matthias's eyes widened. "Only if you're okay with that," Alaric said. "I just don't want to be alone."

Matthias smiled sadly and nodded. Alaric lay down on the bed on his side, and Matthias lay down beside him, facing him, not touching but there.

Alaric took a shuddering breath and said, "Thank you." Then he passed out.

Shina went down to the stables in the late afternoon every day. He saddled Ichigo, led her into the fading sun, then swung up onto her back, and rode across the valley. They started at a trot then gradually accelerated to a full gallop, stretching Ichigo's legs from weeks of low activity. At first, the horse hadn't wanted to run. She was content to be in her stable or walk casually around outside, tail swishing. Bashima could tell the horse was annoyed with Shina as she shook her head and stamped her hooves at his commands, but all it took was a whisper in the horse's ear and a pat on the neck to get her going.

Shina was an excellent horseman. He sat tall and steady in the saddle, thighs engaged, his heels down in the stirrups. His entire being shone like a star when he rode, moving with Ichigo, red hair billowing behind him, wearing a determined smile. There was no urgency to the gallop; man and horse simply wanted to run, to see how fast they could go.

Bashima had never been more attracted to Shina than the first time he saw the redhead take off across the valley on the horse. Something about Shina taking control and leading Ichigo through her paces drew Bashima like he was on a hook.

If Shina perceived Bashima watching him from the stable or more commonly on the path, he gave no notice, and Bashima made sure to shift away before horse and rider returned to the stable.

They dined together each night, Shina keeping polite conversation going though he told no enthusiastic stories. He asked after the Forest God and Oken, who left the temple the day after Bashima's meltdown. They'd made it back to the Temple of the Forest but would return as soon as they could. Shina seemed pleased with that. He actually enjoyed Tengu's and Zebra Head's company.

Before they'd gone, the Forest God visited Bashima once more, helping him fix his room. Bashima hadn't wanted to bother the shades with cleaning when he was capable of fixing his own mess, but he couldn't keep Tengu away.

"He came back?" Tengu asked as they vanished the broken bookcase and wardrobe. They'd salvaged as many books and clothes as they could, but Bashima destroyed a lot of his possessions.

"Yeah," Bashima said, voice curt. "The temple let him back in."

Tengu nodded, clearing away the broken glass from the windows and putting up a barrier spell by snapping his fingers.

"Sorry," he said. "It's a little sloppy, but it'll do for now. Until you can get someone in to do the tougher repairs." He rubbed his scar absentmindedly, surveying the room. "At least you kept most of the damage in here. From the way the temple was shaking, I thought you were blowing everything up."

"Mmm," Bashima muttered, trying not to remember.

"Is it true that he threw off your Compulsion?"

"Apparently," Bashima said and flipped through a book of poetry that wasn't too singed.

"Never heard of a human doing that," Tengu said softly.

"Yeah, well, I told you he was a stubborn ass," Bashima snapped. Fucking Tengu always had to pick the scab until blood was everywhere. Bashima didn't know how Shina ignored his command. He was just glad the redhead did.

"So, now what?"

"Fuck, what do you want me to say? I have no idea. He came back, but what am I supposed to say to him? I did the whole telling the truth thing, but I don't think that was the best idea."

"The truth is usually a good idea, Bashi," Tengu said. "You should be able to replace the books and clothes easily enough. I have doubles of some of these." He indicated the pile of burned books at his feet. "And your tailor shades are incredible." He paused for a moment and looked at the two small paintings on the miraculously intact bedside table. "Just give Shina some space. Let him work out what he wants on his own."

"I'm not the best at waiting," Bashima admitted, sulky.

"If anyone knows that, I do," the Forest God said, laughing. "But please try. It'll be good for you to practice patience."

"Whatever."

Almost two weeks passed, and Bashima left Shina alone. After dinner each night, they stood and said good night, and Bashima saw Matthias, standing against the wall with one palm up in a stopping signal. Matthias took his responsibilities to Shina's welfare farther than expected, and while it vexed Bashima to see that upraised hand every night, he was also thankful the redhead had someone watching over him.

On the first night of the third week, Bashima could take no more. Seeing Shina riding that day had been difficult. The redhead went on his usual circuit, but this time he'd stopped in the center of the valley and stared off into the dark forest as though he'd seen something in the trees. Ichigo stamped her hooves, eager to return to the stable, yet Shina held her in place, looking into the distance.

183

Bashima had felt pain sear through the valley, unhappiness coming off Shina in waves. Bashima couldn't stand it, had needed to shift away rather than be consumed by the redhead's emotions. It was happening more often now, Bashima feeling Shina's distress. He kept it at bay when they ate dinner together, but anguish followed Shina like a shadow.

Kuroi didn't say much, just went about his duties, raising his eyebrow whenever Bashima mentioned that Shina hadn't spoken to him or still hadn't acknowledged anything Bashima said at the stable.

"What do you expect him to say?" Kuroi asked, exasperated. "Perhaps you should make the next move?"

"I did!" Bashima said. "I told him I wanted him to stay!"

"And he did," said Kuroi, shaking his head. "You gave him time to reconcile his decision. What comes next is up to you. He's waiting for you."

"But I don't know what to say," Bashima said. "Gods are used to being worshiped, not having to chase after people."

"You think I don't know that?" Kuroi asked, but he softened when Bashima looked hurt. "Don't say what you think Shina wants you to say. Say what *you* want to say. Show him something of yourself that he hasn't seen."

"I always say what I want to say; that's why I'm in this mess," Bashima whined.

Kuroi stalked away, muttering something about obstinate gods.

So, that night at dinner, after Bashima experienced Shina's anguished emotional cry in the valley, Bashima decided what he would do.

"I need something to change, Matthias," Alaric said, sighing. He changed out of his riding clothes and into something more comfortable for dinner. "Every day I go through the same routine: get up, hide in the library with Emilia, go for my ride with Ichigo, have dinner with Bashima, who says nothing, then back to my room. I don't know how much more I can take."

Matthias nodded, taking Alaric's jacket for cleaning. "Would you like to go to the baths after dinner? Relax a little? That reminds me; it's almost time to dye your hair again."

Alaric took a thick chunk of hair and rubbed it between his fingers. "It's gotten so long."

"We could cut it if you'd like," Matthias suggested. "Back to the original length."

"No," Alaric sighed. "I like it longer. I can actually put it up."

He twisted his hair into a bun and secured it with a string of black leather. Some of it came free and fell around Alaric's face, but he didn't mind. He thought it made him look carefree. He didn't want Bashima to think he was suffering from their lack of contact. He didn't want to think about it himself.

The Sun God had been nearly silent since his confessions in the stable, either unwilling or unable to say more. And he'd been watching Alaric ride. He'd seen Bashima one day on the mountain path, blond hair tossed by the wind, but the god hadn't come to the stable to meet him. He stayed away. Alaric knew that was partially for him. He'd told the god not to touch him, so Bashima kept his distance. So now Alaric looked for the god every afternoon when he came back from his ride.

"Well," he said to Matthias, "let's go."

When they entered the dining room, however, the table was bare. Confused, Alaric looked at Matthias, but he shook his head, equally puzzled. "Did I mistake the time?" Alaric asked.

"Master Shina?" came a voice from the other side of the room. Tika, Bashima's personal aide, strode forward, knowing smile on her lips. "The Sun God would like to extend an invitation to enjoy dinner in the conservatory tonight."

Alaric's eyes popped and his mouth fell open. "What?"

Tika's smile got bigger. "He thought you might like to try something new." She stood with her arms behind her back, waiting for his answer.

Alaric glanced at Matthias, who shrugged. It was up to him; the shade would follow.

"Okay," Alaric said, suspicious but curious. "Lead the way, Tika."

The conservatory was filled with serene light; candles floating in the air and along the stone paths. Matthias drew in a breath, impressed, and Alaric chuckled.

185

"What?" asked Matthias. "This is above and beyond what we did for the summit."

Matthias was right. Fireflies danced within the plants and twinkled like small suns. The fountains were on and filled with lighted lotus blossoms, water cascading in a pleasing sound. It made Alaric feel a calmness that had eluded him for weeks.

They made their way to the center, to the main fountain, and next to it was a small table set for two. Bashima stood next to the table, trying not to look terrified and partially succeeding. He fidgeted, hands behind his back, and his eyes darted all over the room. He was dressed almost casually in an open-collared black shirt and soft black trousers, and Alaric was blown away by the simple styling, which only showcased how beautiful the god was. Alaric felt under-dressed and nearly grabbed at his messy bun, but Bashima didn't seem bothered. His orange eyes flared in the candlelight when he finally settled his gaze on Alaric, and Alaric held his breath, waiting.

Bashima swallowed and cleared his throat. "I thought we could have dinner here tonight." His voice was so unsure, not at all like the Sun God Alaric knew. Bashima said so low that Alaric almost missed it, "And I was sick of sitting so far away from you."

Matthias nudged Alaric with his foot, and Alaric breathed out, then blushed.

Well, Alaric thought, *this was a change.*

Alaric walked toward the table, and Tika went past him to stand behind Bashima's chair. Matthias stationed himself behind Alaric's. They pulled the chairs out in unison to let the god and the man sit together. Before Bashima could say anything, Alaric noticed shining lights from the fountain.

"Seven hells! Are the koi glowing?"

Bashima snorted, "Don't worry; it's just a simple alchemy charm. It won't hurt them and will wear off by tomorrow morning." Alaric's face must have been startled because the god went on, "It's too much isn't it?"

"It's certainly different," Alaric said and laughed. When he did, Bashima's face softened as though he hadn't heard Alaric laugh in centuries.

186

"I asked Shefu if she could make your favorites," Bashima said, confidence returning, proud that he knew to make the dinner about Alaric.

Not wanting the god to get too cocky, Alaric said, "I'll be sure to thank her later." Bashima's mouth became a straight line, lips almost disappearing, and Alaric giggled.

Shades brought course after course of Alaric's favorites including the caramelized rabbit that he'd loved from early after his arrival. Bashima stuck with his usual vegetarian choices, letting Alaric take the meat and fish. He watched Alaric eat and talk in avid fascination, and Alaric liked being so close to the god while they ate. It felt like they were existing in the same space instead of just being at the same table, disconnected.

Bashima asked, "Are you enjoying riding?" He didn't mention that he'd been overlooking Alaric's jaunts across the valley, but Alaric decided not to tease him.

"Yes," Alaric said, "it's almost like flying when I let Ichigo have her head and run. And the valley is perfect now, so open. It's my favorite time of year. The trees are changing colors..." He'd almost mentioned that autumn was upon them, then cut himself off. No need to bring that up when they were having a nice evening.

Bashima sidestepped the subject also and asked how Ichigo liked her exercise.

"She hated me at first, but we have an understanding," Alaric said. "She doesn't buck me off, and I give her apples and sugar cubes."

"You're going to spoil her," Bashima said, smirking.

"She deserves it," Alaric said.

The evening wound down, and Alaric didn't want it to end. They'd stayed in the conservatory for two hours, much longer than their dinners had been lately.

"This was really nice, Bashima," Alaric said as the shades cleared away the dishes, leaving the table empty. "Thank you."

Bashima looked panicked. He pursed his lips and went pale, holding something back. Then he said, nerves back full force, "Would...would you like to hear me play the harp?"

187

Taken aback, Alaric frowned and tilted his head.

Bashima went red, and said, "It's fine if you don't."

"I'd really like that," Alaric said though he was unsure. What was the god planning? Having him go to his room where the harp stood? Was it a proposition?

Bashima's eyes widened. He hadn't expected Alaric to say yes. Flustered, he snapped his fingers, and the standing harp appeared in a small alcove off the center of the conservatory. It sparkled in the candlelight, fireflies swooping around it. The Sun God was certainly great at dramatics. A small stool appeared with the harp, and Bashima stood, hands trembling. It took him a moment to make sure the strings were intact from the shifting, then he sat and leaned forward, not looking at Alaric. He closed his eyes and let go a deep sigh, bringing his normally destructive hands to the strings.

Alaric expected the Sun God to be good, but he was amazing. Bashima's fingers flew over the strings, making the instrument a part of himself, rolling from a simple melody into complex harmonies, his hands moving in blurs. Alaric never heard anyone play so well, had never seen the speed and grace the god put on display. He flowed from one song to another, not stopping. It might have been disorienting, but Bashima made the songs fit together as though they were meant to join all along.

Transfixed, Alaric sat and listened. Who else had heard Bashima play? He thought of the god's lost love and pushed it away. No, this moment was for him. What did it matter that the man most likely heard Bashima play many times? Bashima meant this performance for Alaric.

The Sun God let the last note fade from the strings, and Alaric stood and clapped, excited.

"I've never heard anything like that," he said, in awe. Both Matthias and Tika looked at Bashima as though they'd never seen him before but were happy with what they saw.

"Tika? Matthias?" Bashima asked, not taking his eyes from the harp. "Could you please give me a moment with Shina?"

Tika bowed her head and left, and Alaric saw a tear running down her cheek. Matthias came up to Alaric, asking if it was okay for him to leave. Alaric nodded. The shade also sported red eyes, but he wouldn't leave the room if Alaric protested.

When the shades were gone, Alaric heard the water trickling from the fountains, peaceful. He still wasn't sure this was a good idea. What was the god planning? But he wanted to know more than he wanted to run.

"Bashima..."

The Sun God bent toward the harp again and started playing, much slower this time. Alaric's stomach fell, and he sat down hard as Bashima played the harvest song from Togarashi. He leaned into the harp as though wishing he could disappear into the strings, and light played over his skin, illuminating his face and hands. The harp wept, chords melancholy and hopeful at the same time, calling for an end to autumn and the coming of winter. Alaric could feel the song, what it actually meant, like Bashima was mentally sending him the translation.

A man, knowing it would be his last harvest, for a long and difficult winter was approaching, gathered the crops with his family and friends. He celebrated with them in the great hall, all the while knowing what needed to be done. When he'd wished his grown sons a good night and hugged his grandchildren, the man went to his home and kissed his wife, telling her how she made his life better just by accepting his hand in marriage and staying with him though things had never been easy. When his wife was asleep, the man ventured out into the night, frost already growing thick on the ground. He walked out of his village with nothing in his hands or on his back and greeted the winter like an old friend.

Bashima's hands stopped, and the strings hummed, missing his touch. Was this how Alaric made the Sun God feel when he sang the song? It must have been a horrible shock to hear something he never expected to hear again. And from someone who looked so much like his lost love.

The Sun God broke away from the harp, tears streaming down his face, but he made no sounds. Lips quavering, Bashima finally looked at him, and Alaric felt a wave of pain hit him, but not just pain, a plea for help. Since the god would never ask, Alaric stood and raced to his side, enveloping him in a fierce hug. That broke something in the Sun God, and he choked back sobs, hands grabbing Alaric's back, pulling him in. The stool came out from under Bashima, and they knelt by the harp, leaning into each other. Bashima's face buried into Alaric's shoulder, his whole body shaking. Alaric ran a hand through the god's cloud-like hair and let him cry.

Alaric held Bashima's hand, leading him to his chambers. The god stopped crying, but he was dazed, and he'd grabbed Alaric's hand and hadn't let go. When they got to the god's room, Alaric ignored the panic rising in his chest. He hadn't been near the room since he sneaked in and found the painting of Dain. Bashima felt him pause and hung his head, letting Alaric's hand fall, like he was waking up.

"I'll be okay," he said and opened his bedroom door.

"Are you sure?" Alaric asked. "Tell me the truth."

The Sun God's shoulders quaked, and he shook his head. He looked up at Alaric, eyes puffy. "Will you stay with me? Just...until I fall asleep?" Alaric nodded, and Bashima went inside.

Alaric followed him, body tense and alert. The Sun God wandered, slightly off-kilter, into the bedroom and collapsed on the bed, which had been repaired and had new pillows and bedding. Bashima didn't move, but it would be uncomfortable to sleep as he was. Alaric gently removed Bashima's shirt, pulling his arms free with care. His bare chest called to Alaric, but he told his body to settle down. He realized they hadn't touched in three weeks and bit his lip.

Alaric pulled back the silky duvet and folded Bashima under it. The god snuggled under it and hid his face, fluffy hair peeking out the top. The two paintings sat on the bedside table, the portrait mostly hidden by books. Alaric wanted to flee the room. It wasn't fair for Bashima to ask him to stay.

"Shina?" Came a quiet voice from the bed. Alaric turned away from the paintings, ready to leave the room. Bashima's hand emerged, and he brushed Alaric's hand with his fingers. "I'll always miss him, but you make the days bearable. I don't feel like I'm being crushed by the world when I'm with you." Tears slid down the god's perfect eyelashes. He closed his eyes and was asleep.

Alaric could leave. The god wouldn't know the difference. He'd only asked for Alaric to stay until he fell asleep. Bashima looked achingly young as he slept, completely trusting that Alaric would take care of him.

He couldn't leave.

Alaric stripped off his tunic and climbed onto the bed but stayed on top of the duvet. He curled up near Bashima, making sure they weren't touching, staring at the slow rise and fall of the god's back as he breathed. Alaric shoved the tears he wanted to unleash far inside and waited for sleep to take him.

Chapter Eleven

Bashima dreamed he was flying. This was nothing new; he could fly in reality as well as in his dreams, and he often dreamed of flying. But this time, instead of soaring through clouds, getting as close to the sun as he dared, Bashima floated over an immense sea that churned below him, dark and foreboding. The sky was clear and bright, but the water below thrashed, warning him to stay in the air.

And beside Bashima flew a familiar figure, one who definitely could never fly.

"Dain?" Bashima asked, dreading what he'd hear.

"For the last time, Khresh, no. Stop trying to persuade me."

Oh, so it was *that* conversation. Bashima knew his lines well. He said, "You promised me you'd at least think about it."

"And I did, and the answer is still no." Dain floated next to Bashima, stern expression set. His eyes showed annoyance but also affection. "You've known how I felt about this since the first time we met. Alchemists have been playing around with eternal life for centuries, but it doesn't interest me."

"But," Bashima said, hating the pleading tone of his voice, "then we would be together forever. Don't you want that?"

"I love you, Khresh," Dain said and smiled sadly. "But I can't stay tied to you forever. Not like that. It would kill me. Has it done any favors for that poor girl the Fire God turned?"

In the dream, Bashima couldn't answer. His past self knew that Cindras was a tyrant who most likely treated his god-touched concubine as he treated everyone else. And in the present, after seeing the Fire God abuse his son, his supposed only treasure, Bashima doubted that the woman was any better for becoming essentially immortal.

"You're never silent, so I'll take that as my answer," Dain said. "I will be with you as long as I'm able, but when it's my time, I will go gladly to the Underworld. I wasn't meant to wile away the centuries on this earth. I shall live as I please and do with my life what I will."

"I don't want to lose you," Bashima whispered.

"As though you could ever lose me," Dain laughed, a great booming sound that echoed across the dreamscape. "Even when I'm gone, you'll always remember me."

"What if that isn't enough for me?"

Dain didn't answer right away. They flew in silence as the sea roared beneath them. "I'm going away for my next project soon, but it shouldn't take long. We can talk more when I return."

The dream flashed Bashima and Dain's conversation forward in time though they remained flying together over the water. Disoriented, Bashima's control slipped, but Dain grabbed his shoulder, keeping him aloft.

"Don't worry, Khresh," Dain said, a light cough dulling his voice. "It's nothing. A little cold I caught in the province to the north. The Emperor really enjoyed my take on water gardens by the way."

Another flash, and Bashima tried to fight it, but the dream carried him forward.

Dain was racked with heaving coughs, his brow covered in sweat, face pale and drawn. He'd lost so much weight in only a few months, and though his large frame remained robust, his muscles were eating themselves, fading away. His eyes hadn't lost their sparkling conviction, but he was losing the fight that nature unleashed upon him.

"I assume from your face that I've looked better."

"Shut the hells up, Dain. A healer is coming from the north where they're dealing with whatever this disease is."

"Ha! My little cold has become a monster!" Dain laughed at his own humor, then doubled over in another coughing fit. "The healer may come, but there's nothing they can do for me. Don't argue with me. Aren't you tired of arguing?"

"I'd argue with you for eternity if it meant you'd stay," Bashima said, fighting anger. If only the hulking human listened to him. If only he'd gone through with the god-touched ceremony like Bashima wanted, then Dain would have been immune to the disease that was draining his life away.

"For a while longer then, my heart. I'll stay a while longer."

The waves crashed below, and Bashima listened to the sound cascading in his head. He saw an empty bed and a lyre that made no sound. He gave the lyre to Draiden, unable to bear the weight of seeing it next to his harp.

"But you didn't," Bashima said, staring down at the tumultuous waves. "You left me alone."

"Things aren't so bad without me, are they, Khresh?"

This was different. Dain never spoke in Bashima's dreams unless it was to repeat their centuries-old conversations. Bashima had them firmly in place in his mind: every interaction, every fight, every moment they were together. He looked at Dain, surprised.

"Dain?"

"You've got my three best friends, right? They went along with your crazy scheme when I wouldn't and have lived long lives. Maybe not the most fulfilling?" He gazed at Bashima, whose face reddened. "That's what I thought. Well, at least they're able to use their gifts though not in the way they intended."

Bashima remembered the four young humans, all alchemists, all incredibly talented. Kuroi's art was second to none, Shefu created culinary masterpieces, and Draiden's poetry was gaining fame across the world. All had bright futures, and Dain was their leader, the shining star of the architectural world. Did his three friends regret the choice they made, living in obscurity with a Sun God whose attitude was shitty sometimes? Bashima grimaced, okay most of the time. Did they ever wonder what could have been?

"Hmm don't tell me you're only thinking about this now," Dain said. "I've been gone for two thousand years."

Bashima tried to fly away from Dain, but the dream wouldn't let him. The red-haired ghost remained by his side. "You've never avoided me before," Dain said. "Are you feeling guilty about something?"

"I need to wake up," Bashima muttered.

"Maybe what you need is to have an honest conversation with yourself, *God of the Sun.*"

"Ugh, why are you doing this? Leave me alone."

"But I thought you wanted me with you always," the man laughed, eyes shining in mirth.

"Not to torment me although you did a pretty good job of that when you were alive," Bashima snapped and stopped flying forward. He hovered over the sea and thought about plummeting down. Letting the water take him. Would it be so bad?

"I seem to be doing an excellent job of tormenting you even though I'm dead."

"Why didn't you just listen to me?" Bashima shouted. "Then I wouldn't be stuck here talking to myself. You're just a fiction of my mind trying to shame me. I am the Sun God! I feel no shame!"

Dain didn't answer, but he raised a brow. Dain was the man who yelled back, who didn't give way. This dream-Dain was patient, waiting for Bashima to come to his own conclusions.

"You were my anchor," Bashima said. "It's no wonder I drifted."

"Anchor?" asked Dain, amused. "If anything, I was a kite, always flying off on some adventure or another. I loved you with all my heart, but I was always going to escape you. One way or another."

"Maybe I shouldn't have given you the choice," Bashima growled, not believing it. There was no way he would have forced Dain to do anything. Dain would have hated Bashima for it, which the Sun God couldn't have handled.

"You certainly tried!" Dain laughed then was silent, floating next to Bashima. "It's almost time to wake," he said, voice calm. "Is there anything else you need to tell me?"

Now that it was time, Bashima didn't want to wake up. Dain was here, talking to him, and though he knew it wasn't real, all he wanted was to stay in the air for a while longer.

"There are so many things I would tell you if it was really you," Bashima admitted. He tried not to think of the melancholy song from Togarashi or how Shina held him after he played the harp. It felt wrong to even think the redhead's name in his dreams.

The Dain in his dream smiled and began to fade, "I know."

Then he was gone, and Bashima felt a looming presence behind him. He turned his head and saw brilliant flaming eyes and smoke billowing from between razor sharp teeth.

Bashima jolted awake, a scream dying in his throat. What the hells had that been? One moment Dain was there and the next…Bashima didn't want to linger on it. Whatever that monster was didn't matter in the waking world. Dreams were what your mind wanted to shove down your throat without warning.

Bashima hadn't dreamed of Dain for a while, his sleep untroubled by the loud voice or playful eyes, daring him to talk back or tackle him into bed. The man always managed to find his way back and replay whatever overwrought memory Bashima's mind dredged up.

His head and eyes ached, staring up at the familiar ceiling that still had a few scorch marks in the corners. He'd take care of that later. At least his bed was back to normal. Except it wasn't. His duvet was weighted down on one side and HOLY HELLS.

Shina lay beside him, sleeping on his side, facing Bashima. Eyes closed, lips slightly open, drool tendril trailing from the corner of his mouth. Breathing slow and even and unconcerned. Naked from the waist up, his chest chain rising and falling as he breathed. Some of his red hair had come loose from the bun and framed his face where freckles formed from his recent time spent outside.

The weight of his presence could send the entire bedroom collapsing into the volcano.

Bashima vaguely remembered asking Shina to stay with him last night and wanted to slap himself. How was *that* giving the redhead space? When the night was supposed to be about him? Bashima hadn't intended to lose his composure after playing the haunting Togarashi song, but playing it was different from hearing Shina sing it. It made him remember all the times he played the song for Dain, teasing the man that the saddest song in creation was used for celebrations.

"Not the way you play it," Dain's lost voice whispered in his ear.

Shit. This was the exact opposite of what he'd planned. Bashima wanted to reach over and tuck the loose strands of hair behind Shina's ear or drape his arm across his body and hug him tightly. He yearned to crumble against Shina's chest, rest his head beneath the redhead's chin. Trace his spine with a finger, find the small of his back, discover his life by touching every inch of his skin.

Don't touch me...

He wouldn't, not unless Shina wanted him to. The redhead swept over him like an ocean wave last night, but that was his choice, that driving force within him that made him move to help people before he even knew he was doing it. No plan, just action.

Bashima wanted to believe Dain had been that sort of man as well though it wasn't fair to either man to compare them. Dain had been brave to look the Sun God in the face and tell him no, not just once but many times. He would have put his life on the line for his three closest friends without question. But what about strangers? Would Dain have thrown himself in the Fire God's way to help a person he'd just met? Or protected a shade? Or dashed into a river to save someone he'd probably never see again?

Bashima wanted to believe it, but Dain was never in put those positions. He didn't concern himself with things or people that didn't matter to him. The only shade he knew by name was Tika, and that was because she was the Sun

God's shadow. Shina probably knew almost every shade's name in the temple at least those he'd met and talked to.

Shina mumbled something unintelligible, and Bashima wished he'd speak again, wanting to hear a voice that wasn't Dain's or his own.

Want, want, want. That's all he was good for, giving in to his own desires. Had he done anything that was just for Shina, ever? Given a gift that wasn't for a specific purpose? He felt that he knew both everything and nothing about the man sleeping beside him. When was he born? Who were his family? What was his life before the temple? Bashima recalled the redhead telling stories through their dinners, and this made a rough sketch of his life, but it wasn't a completed piece. He should be painting in the past parts of Shina and not just those in the present that he shared with Bashima.

Just because Dain didn't enjoy talking about his family or his life before he became a renowned architect didn't mean Shina was the same. The effort was Bashima's to make.

The sun was rising; Bashima needed to get to the throne room, but he didn't want to wake Shina. Light peered through the windows and fell on the redhead's sleeping form, bathing his face in both light and shadow. Bashima clenched a fist in the bed sheets, fighting back his urge to kiss the man. He slipped from the bed and pulled the service cord next to his bed, calling down to the kitchen for breakfast, asking for human food as well. If the shade on the other end of the summons was shocked, Bashima would never know, but he imagined the voices in the kitchen getting higher-pitched.

He went to the sitting room where the clothes he and Tengu salvaged sat in folded piles. Ever since Shina came to the temple, Bashima wore clothes instead of walking the temple naked. He enjoyed clothes and how they felt on his body. He chose the supplest silks and soft cottons, wanting his body draped in comfort. Shina hadn't mentioned that Bashima no longer stalked around in his formal godly attire, but he'd caught enough hungry, appreciative glances to know that his fashion choices were sound. He pulled on simple black trousers and a black tunic and admired himself in the mirror. He didn't look too bad for someone who'd had a breakdown the night before.

"Where am I?" came a confused yelp from the bedroom, and Bashima poked his head inside. Shina sat up on the bed, bleary eyes wide, hair messy. He looked adorable. He spotted Bashima and fell back on the pillows. "Seven hells, you scared me."

"I'm sorry," Bashima said, remaining in the doorway. "Would you prefer that I left?"

"You're fine. I just woke up and had no idea where I was or how I got there," Shina said. He sounded annoyed, and Bashima's temper flared. Had it been that bad to sleep in the Sun God's bed? The redhead looked over at him, saw him fuming, and grinned, shark's teeth on full display. "Your bed is really cozy."

"I'm aware," Bashima said and snorted. He walked into the room, bare feet padding silently. "I wasn't sure when you'd wake up, so I asked the kitchen to bring up breakfast."

"What?" Shina asked and blushed. He searched the floor beside the bed for something. Bashima saw his shirt at the foot of the bed. He laughed then picked it up and showed the redhead. "This what you're looking for?"

"Hurry, give it to me!" Shina was even cuter when he panicked, eyes giant with apprehension.

"And if I don't?"

"Oh, come on! This is so embarrassing. The shade could be here any minute." Shina dove under the duvet and hid, a lump that could in no way be mistaken for anything but a person.

"You know, you're not very inconspicuous...in my bed."

"Shut up," he whined from beneath the blanket. "I know that they know that we...you know. But it's the principle of the thing! And to be fair, you never stayed in my room until the morning." His voice trailed away, and Bashima felt another guilty pang in his chest. Would the ridiculous guilt ever end?

"If you would rather, I can have them serve you in your room."

Shina made a noncommittal sound, so Bashima shrugged. He placed the shirt on the bed. When Bashima went to the sitting room again, a shade appeared with two covered trays. She beamed and looked around, probably searching for Shina.

"On the table, please," he said and sat, giving no explanation. The shade didn't stop grinning, and she didn't leave. Bashima asked, "Was there something else?"

"Kuroi would like you to know that Matthias has been informed where Master Shina is and will be on his way presently." Bashima hadn't known her smile could get bigger, but it did, and then she spun on the spot and disappeared back to the kitchens.

Hells.

He opened the cover on his breakfast and glanced at the bedroom, waiting to see if Shina would come out. It was like watching for a rare, beautiful bird to emerge from its nest. After a few moments, a head full of messy red hair peeked around the door.

"Did she just say Matthias was on his way?"

"Yup," Bashima said, sipping black tea the shade brought with his meal. "It's too late. Now everyone will know."

Shina narrowed his eyes. "Good to know your sense of humor is so sharp this early in the morning."

"The sun may rise on its own, but you've got to wake up pretty quickly to keeps its ass on task," Bashima said, holding back laughter.

"You're getting way too much enjoyment out of this."

Shina walked into the sitting room, drawn to the lovely aromas coming from his breakfast tray. He edged closer to the table, wary of the Sun God, so Bashima ignored him and drank his tea, pretending to read a scroll that was on the table.

Shina finally reached the table and sat down, knees facing out, in case he had to make a hasty retreat. Bashima glanced over when Shina lifted his tray, and his stomach let out a hungry gurgle. Shina turned bright red and looked up to find Bashima fighting a laugh.

"Don't you dare laugh. I'm always really hungry in the morning."

"Noted," Bashima said, regaining his composure.

Shina and Dain definitely had one thing in common: they ate meat with reckless abandon. Along with toast and fruit, the kitchen shades piled his plate high with bacon and sausages, which the redhead tore through like he might die of starvation at any moment. For some reason, it really turned Bashima on though he wouldn't touch meat if his life depended on it, and he licked his lower lip, watching Shina inhale his bacon. He crossed one leg over the other, holding back his very interested dick.

As though sensing his thoughts, Shina looked up, the red in his irises shining. "What?" he asked, wiping his mouth quickly with a napkin.

Oh nothing, Bashima thought. *I was only imagining hand-feeding you, that's all. While we were both naked...*

There came a loud knock at the door, and Bashima yelled, "You may enter."

Matthias walked into the sitting room, uncertain what he'd find. Bashima suspected the shade was irritated with him, but there was nothing to do for it now. Shina slept in his bed, but at least nothing happened.

"Morning, Matthias," Shina said, waving, having lost his shyness upon being fed. "Shefu went all out on the sausages today, so crispy."

Matthias's mouth twitched, but that was all the emotion he gave. "I trust last evening's dinner was...successful?"

Bashima averted his eyes. He was already feeling like shit about what happened, then Matthias had to come in being all judgmental. He pursed his lips and looked out the window instead of at the shade.

"It was great," Shina said and popped a grape into his mouth. "But I think Bashima needs to work, so let's go to my room and get ready for the day." He raised both brows at Bashima, then rose and walked out towards the door.

Matthias gave Bashima a small nod, but his demeanor said, "I'm watching you." Then he left as well.

They started to have dinner in Bashima's room when Alaric returned from his daily rides. Bashima still hadn't descended from the mountain path when Alaric took Ichigo across the valley, but Alaric knew he was there. Not every day, but he'd spy the shining blond hair and smile. Maybe one day he'd be brave enough to come all the way down. So, Alaric made the next move and suggested having dinner in Bashima's room. He was measuring how far

Bashima would let him go, how far he could stake his claim in the temple. And Bashima let him.

Under the watchful eyes of Tika and a very terse Matthias, Alaric and Bashima ate dinner and conversed easily. Alaric shared new stories, and Bashima listened though he almost boiled over a few times when Alaric teased him with stories that had multiple endings.

"But that wasn't the last of it," he'd say, and Bashima would groan. Once, he even put his forehead on the table while Tika giggled and Matthias glared, Alaric continuing his story.

Bashima ventured questions about Alaric's life, his parents, things he enjoyed. Alaric was more than happy to answer. He'd chance a question for Bashima occasionally, just to see if that was pushing too far. He stayed away from any potential landmines, kept to the usual courting questions: who are your parents, where did you grow up, friends, all those details.

The first time Bashima talked about his parents he'd rolled his eyes about a hundred times.

"Ugh, my old man and the hag live to the south now; he's no one important, but she's the Goddess of Youth. People worship the shit out of her, so she's really full of herself. I have no idea why she's with my dad, but she flirted with him so hard they ended up married."

Alaric giggled while he was drinking, and white wine dribbled down his chin, making Bashima laugh out loud. He hadn't heard the god laugh that hard in...maybe ever. It wasn't what people would call an attractive laugh, too loud and a smidgen maniacal, but it was all Alaric wanted to hear.

"I'm serious!" Bashima said. "I think he's still shocked about it."

Alaric's parents knew they would marry when they were very young. He was a councilman's son, and she was from the village's most ancient and respected family. Not an arranged marriage, but close. They'd actually liked each other, which made the match easy.

"My teeth came from my mom," Alaric said, bearing his fangs and pointing at them. "And my eyes, so she says. But it must be far down in her family line because she doesn't have red eyes and neither did my grandmother. Apparently, it used to be more common."

Bashima's gaze intensified when Alaric talked about himself, drew attention to himself. It made Alaric shy, so he would change the subject; feeling like the Sun God was focusing all of his power on him was intimidating.

He decided on a bold invitation one night: "Would you ever come riding with me?"

Bashima looked at Alaric as though he were an unusual archaeological find. "What?"

"Well, I've seen you sometimes, you know, watching me come back from my ride with Ichigo. I thought maybe you might like to join me sometime."

Bashima's eyes widened in panic. "I don't have a horse," he mumbled and put all his attention on his dinner.

"You're a god," Alaric said. Bashima hadn't said no. "Can't you get one?"

"I'll think about it," Bashima muttered, and Alaric felt satisfaction coursing through his body.

Alaric bid Bashima good night after every dinner, not repeating their chaste sleepover from the conservatory date. Bashima looked disappointed when Alaric rose to leave, but he didn't press. He stood and watched Alaric leave with Matthias, who Alaric admitted looked a little frightening when they left.

"Matthias," Alaric had joked, "You don't have to scare him."

"Yes, I do, Matthias said. "Maybe if he's afraid of me, he'll continue to be a gentleman."

Alaric snorted and patted the shade on the shoulder. "What would I do without you?" That made Matthias smile.

"Hold on, Em," Alaric said, and Emilia clung to the saddle in front of her. She was equally terrified and exhilarated, seated atop Ichigo with Alaric. Kuroi performed a special charm, which allowed shades to leave the temple for a short time. They used the same alchemy during the summit when shade attendants were needed for the work at the base of the mountain. It wouldn't last forever, but it was enough for Emilia to enjoy a quick ride.

Emilia was able to go outside the temple for the first time since she started working there. Alaric started them at a slow walk, and Emilia gave a small whoop. Ichigo wasn't bothered; Emilia didn't weigh much. Alaric got them up to a trot and a canter as they crossed the valley. He didn't dare try a gallop with an inexperienced rider.

Emilia turned to look back at him a few times, her smile immense, eyes gleaming with joy. He wondered again about the lives of the shades and how unfair it was. They'd gotten so little time in the world, then worked for the rest of eternity. They were still capable of experiences like riding a horse for the first time or making new friends, of finding contentment.

"Alaric?" asked Emilia on their way back to the stable. "I'm really happy you didn't leave."

Alaric smiled at the back of her head and leaned down to rest his chin on her hair. "Me too. I'm really sorry that I almost left without saying good-bye."

"You've said that about a million times," said Emilia, shaking her head and dislodging his chin.

"I mean it, one million times."

"Do you think you'll leave eventually though?" Emilia asked, voice small.

Alaric didn't know how to answer her. He didn't know what Bashima actually wanted, besides company so he wouldn't be lonely. Bashima liked him, wanted him around, was attracted to him, but the god held back. Alaric wasn't sure that he could push through the barrier Bashima had around his heart.

"I don't know, Em, but it won't be for a while."

Satisfied, she quieted.

Almost to the stable, they heard a loud whinny from behind them, which startled horse and riders.

"Whoa, Ichigo!" said Alaric, squeezing her side with his legs to steady himself and grabbing onto Emilia. "Steady."

"What's that?" asked Emilia, pointing across the valley.

A gorgeous black horse approached from the forest, mane thick and lustrous, with a white blaze running down its forehead to its nose. It loped easily toward them, neck high and proud, coat shining. Alaric had never seen a more magnificent horse.

"Fucking finally," came a gruff voice from the stable. Bashima stood against the wall, arms crossed, agitated set to his shoulders. "Thought he'd never show up."

"Um," said Alaric as Ichigo sidestepped around, watching the other horse approach with great interest. "Ichigo, keep it together, girl."

"That might be impossible," Bashima said, a manic gleam in his eye. "He's a stallion and also extremely attractive."

Alaric rolled his eyes at the god and walked Ichigo toward him, aiming a kick in Bashima's direction that he easily dodged. He needed to get Ichigo settled before the stallion arrived. Even with a brush-down and fresh oats, Ichigo wouldn't stop looking at the stable entrance.

"Yeah, I know girl. Bunch of show-offs."

He patted her nose and went back outside. Emilia stood next to Bashima, ogling the stallion. Up close, he blazed with vitality and power, and Bashima had a hand on his nose, rubbing.

"Yoru, you're very late." Bashima looked at Alaric and said, "This is Yoru, my guest."

"I'm sorry, but what?" Alaric asked.

Bashima glanced at Alaric as though he were willfully not understanding him. Alaric looked from the horse to the god to Emilia and back. The horse dipped his mighty head to sniff at Emilia, who hooted with glee and patted his nose. The horse proceeded to grab Emilia's tunic and flung her up onto his back.

"It's okay," laughed Bashima, seeing Alaric's face as he lunged to grab Emilia down. He put out his hand to stop Alaric but quickly put it down at his side. "He's the smartest horse on the planet. He won't hurt her."

"All right," Alaric said, still nervous. The horse looked powerful but also calm. He let Emilia tug on his mane and ears, not moving an inch. When Alaric approached cautiously, the horse turned his head and put his nose in Alaric's hands. "He's gorgeous."

"As if I'd get an ugly horse," Bashima scoffed. "Not that he's mine. Yoru is his own horse. He's just offering his assistance to the gods. But if he likes it here, he might stay for a while."

Yoru shook his head and snorted, delighting Emilia. "Can we keep him, please?" she begged.

"Ha! You don't keep a horse like Yoru," said Bashima. "He keeps you."

"That sounds ominous," laughed Alaric.

"Once he's settled in, we can go for a ride," Bashima said in a quiet voice.

Alaric watched Emilia try to figure out how to dismount, and when Yoru didn't help her, Bashima went over and reached up. She put out her arms and wrapped them around the Sun God as he pulled her down gently, setting her on her feet.

"That would be great," Alaric said, holding in his rapidly expanding emotions and...other rapidly expanding things. He spun around and ran into the stable to calm himself down.

That night at dinner, Alaric couldn't keep his mind off how Bashima looked with Emilia. The exasperated yet indulgent smirk, how he hadn't hesitated to help her down from the horse, the kindness in his voice when he spoke to her. Alaric never thought about how Bashima would be with kids. It made his heart flutter when he pictured Emilia's face, happy to be outside and trying something new and how she was willing to throw herself into the god's arms. She trusted him completely.

Alaric's mind wandered to the little boy he rescued from the river on the offering ceremony day and wondered if he was okay.

Alaric must have been staring off into space, because Bashima said something, then looked amused on the other side of the table.

"Hmmm, what? Sorry," Alaric sputtered and took another bite of his dinner.

"I asked what the hells you were looking at," Bashima said, gruff but smiling.

"Just thinking..."

"That's dangerous," the Sun God teased.

"Just that you were so nice to Emilia today. I don't think I've ever seen her that happy. I thought she'd be terrified, but she hopped on Ichigo no problem.

206

Then that monster stallion launched her onto his back…" Alaric paused. "It was great to see her have fun."

"You two don't have fun messing around all day?"

"Hey! I got her to read! She hated it at first and now she won't stop. I'm afraid to tell her it's time to leave the library most days."

Bashima rolled his eyes. "You're way too soft."

"Better than being cranky most of the time," he said and grinned, pointing his fork at the god.

Bashima made a face, disbelieving. "I'll have you know that I'm only cranky about half of the time."

Alaric giggled, and his mind went back to the boy from the river. How he'd clung to Alaric until his mother found them on the path. Even then, the little guy hadn't wanted to let go. Alaric had been in a hurry, of course, because he was worried about being late for the offering ceremony.

Ugh, he thought, recalling that day and how anxious he'd been, how intimidating it was. The way the Sun God—Bashima—looked at him, like he was an insignificant insect. A chore he needed to check off a list.

And now…Bashima sat across from him, relaxed, funny, warm. Alaric wasn't sure how far he could trust the god, not with a temper as explosive as his, but Bashima went a long way to make him comfortable since that day in his bedroom. Alaric's heart ached, remembering what he'd accused the god of.

"So," Alaric said, fidgeting with his hands, "there's been something I've been meaning to say to you. I just didn't know how. It's probably not the right time, but would there ever be a right time to say something like this? I don't know, but I've felt terrible since I said it and…" He looked up at Bashima, whose face was concerned and possibly a little afraid. "I'm really sorry about the things I accused you of that…that day."

Alaric's mouth felt dry, and Bashima didn't say anything, so he spit it out, "I should never have thought you'd do something like kidnap tributes. It was very wrong of me, and I'm sorry."

He saw Tika and Matthias exchange glances, their faces drawn. Maybe it was a mistake to bring that up. He probably should have kept his mouth shut and let them have a nice dinner. He put his face in his hands and said, "And I'm sorry for bringing it up. I'll just be quiet now."

"Thank you," Bashima said, eyes down, "for apologizing, but you really didn't have to...I know you didn't mean it."

"I was just so mad," Alaric said, "and hurt, and I don't know, every emotion there is?"

"I do feel bad, you know," Bashima went on, "that tributes don't make it home. Maybe there's a way we could offer protection. I'll ask Vaultus about it— see if any other gods have issues."

"It's not your fault," Alaric said. "Anything can happen out in the world, you know? People get lost, or an animal could attack them—some people drown." He thought about the boy in the river again, how cold the water had been.

"Especially without you around to save them," Bashima said.

"What?" Alaric asked, shocked. Had Bashima known this whole time? "How did you find out about that?" He blushed, not wanting the attention.

"Tengu told me. He's a slut for forest creatures. They tell him everything. Especially birds, the gossipy fuckers."

"There were a lot of birds around when it happened," Alaric said, chin in his hand, thinking back to the riverbank.

"And that's why you were late to the offering," Bashima said.

Alaric looked up, and there was something different in the god's eyes. Admiration perhaps? But he also looked ready to leap across the small table and push himself onto Alaric's lap.

Alaric cleared his throat and flushed even harder. "Yes."

"I'm really glad you were."

Alaric felt the god's presence across the table, his voice low and husky, his need and desire naked on his face, in the way he held his body. It seeped out of his every pore, bombarding Alaric's senses until his mouth watered. He needed to do something before he also leaped from his seat and attacked the god.

"Can you make the harp play on its own?" Alaric asked, an idea forming.

Bashima, surprised by the question, said, "Yeah, but it doesn't sound great. A spell is never as good as the real thing when it comes to music."

"Would you like to dance with me?"

The Sun God went pale. "You want to dance?"

His anxiety made Alaric smile, and he said, "What's wrong? Did I finally find something you're not good at?"

"I'm a fucking amazing dancer," fumed Bashima standing up and throwing his napkin on his plate. "I'll dance with you right now. I'll dance with you so hard you'll forget ever dancing with anyone else."

Alaric grinned, enjoying that he knew how to stoke the god's competitive side. He stood up too and said, "Okay." Which only made the god panic more.

Bashima looked around the room, eyes seeking Tika, who offered no help. Matthias looked deadly on his side of the room, eyebrows an angry line.

"Just play something," Alaric said, laughing. As though sensing another challenge, Bashima narrowed his eyes and snapped his fingers, and the massive harp sprang to life, the strings plucking out a jaunty tune. Tika tried to hold back a giggle, and she gave the Sun God a hand signal, pressing her palm down toward the ground. Bashima reddened but he snapped his fingers again, and the song was slower. More romantic.

"Could you two give us a minute?" Alaric asked, and Bashima looked from him to the two shades like he wanted them to leave but also desperately wanted them to stay. Alaric liked having the upper hand for once. Both shades gave a small bow and left though Matthias looked mutinous. He didn't think enough time had passed for extended alone time, but it wasn't up to him.

When the door closed, Alaric went to Bashima and placed one of the god's hands on his waist and held the other, putting his own hand on Bashima's shoulder. They hadn't touched each other since the night Bashima played the Togarashi harvest song, and goosebumps appeared over Alaric's body. He was glad he'd worn long sleeves so Bashima wouldn't see. He waited for Bashima to lead him.

"You have no idea what you're doing to me right now," Bashima mumbled. His hand flexed on Alaric's waist.

"Oh, I have a pretty good idea," Alaric said, smiling.

With that, Bashima pushed lightly on Alaric's waist, and they moved slowly across the floor, the harp cuing them to their next moves. The Sun God was, unsurprisingly, an excellent dancer. His hold was light but firm, head up and proud, shoulders back but not stiff. He turned Alaric around the room easily, eyes never wavering. They blazed at Alaric with such intensity like the god needed to prove something once and for all.

"I'll bet we look really good, dancing," Alaric said.

"Fucking right we do," said Bashima, pushing and spinning Alaric in a simple turn. When Alaric came back, Bashima smiled. "You're not so bad yourself, Red."

"It might have been the first thing my mother taught me," Alaric said, laughing. "'No son of mine won't be able to dance!'"

"You shouldn't mention things like that," Bashima growled playfully. "Thinking about you dancing with anyone else might push me over the edge."

"If it makes you feel better," Alaric teased, "none of them were as good as you."

"That's obvious. I *am* a god. Although Tengu isn't very graceful, so don't judge all gods by my superior abilities."

Alaric laughed and nearly tripped over a rug as he misstepped. Bashima reacted fast and pulled Alaric in so they were chest to chest, hips pressed together. Bashima didn't move. His lips pressed together in a surprised, thin line and his pupils dilated. His hand tightened on Alaric's hand and at the small of his back. But he still didn't move in.

So, Alaric closed the distance between them.

As he leaned in, Alaric closed his eyes, and Bashima's lips met his. The god's grip on his back strengthened, but he let Alaric lead, his lips parting slightly. The kiss was soft like the god was kissing a rose and didn't want to damage the petals, and he sighed into Alaric's mouth. Alaric dropped Bashima's hand and wrapped his arms around the god, pushing a hand slowly through his hair, rubbing his temple. Bashima's hair was damp from their dance and probably nervousness, and Alaric delighted in its softness. Bashima cupped the back of Alaric's head and Alaric tilted his chin in that direction, pulling Bashima's face in closer.

It was different from the god's hungry, desperate kisses; he was patient and attentive, answering Alaric's searching tongue with tentative touches. He didn't fear Alaric's sharp teeth either though he never had. Kissing Alaric might be dangerous, but Bashima was accepting and careful, navigating through their kiss with ease.

It really wasn't fair how good he was at everything.

Alaric released Bashima from the kiss and backed away, leaving the god looking abandoned. He was done teasing. He pulled off his tunic and threw it on the floor then walked forward and grabbed Bashima by the shirt, pulling him into another kiss, this one more urgent. The god responded with zeal, running his fingers through Alaric's hair and breathing harder. Alaric broke the kiss, pushed Bashima back, and pulled at his shirt, tugging it off over his head. Bashima's hair fluffed out, making Alaric smile.

Before he could initiate the next kiss, Bashima asked, "Are you sure?"

Alaric nodded and said, "Yes."

"Just tell me what you want," Bashima whispered.

"You." Alaric reached out for Bashima's hand and said, "Come on."

Bashima hesitated for only a moment before taking Alaric's hand and letting him lead them to the bedroom. Upon seeing the bed, something jolted the god, and he said, "We still have to be careful. I don't want to hurt you."

"I know," Alaric said.

He pulled Bashima down onto the bed, and this time his was the hungry kiss, the kind that could drain a person's soul. He felt Bashima harden almost instantly, then warmth stirred in his body. Bashima, sensing Alaric's arousal, reached down and pulled off his trousers. His eyes asked if he could do the same for Alaric, who nodded. Then they were kissing again, and Alaric lost himself in the feeling of Bashima touching him. He heard the god's fingers snap, smelled the salt of sea air, and ground his hips into Bashima's, rubbing against the god's thigh, which made Bashima shudder.

Since it had been so long since they'd been together, Bashima went slowly. Alaric felt every touch and arched his back, wanting more, wanting to be filled. He was a terribly impatient lover, but Bashima settled him back with deeper kisses, whispering encouragement to him. Alaric touched and stroked himself as Bashima rested his forehead against Bashima's shoulder.

"Oh hells," Bashima said, "I might not last long. You feel so good."

Alaric bit down lightly on Bashima's shoulder and rocked his hips up.

"I really won't last if you keep doing that." Bashima started with gentle thrusts and pushed Alaric lightly back down on the bed, looking down at him. "You're so beautiful."

Alaric wrapped his legs around Bashima and reached up to catch his lips, grabbing his neck. Bashima went faster, his tongue searching Alaric's mouth for something, maybe forgiveness, maybe relief.

Alaric answered, sucking on Bashima's tongue and nipping his lower lip. Bashima grasped Alaric's hands with his and leaned forward, pushing Alaric's arms back as he chased his release. He rested his forehead against Alaric's and stared at him, eyes pleading and blown to full black. Bashima hit the pleasure point, and Alaric's back arched again, so Bashima kept going, angling to hit the spot again and again.

Alaric could so easily lose himself in these moments with Bashima. When they were together, it felt like floating, like flying, as though they were keeping each other aloft. He worried that Bashima might fly away without him, hand open, but Alaric unable to follow. As Bashima watched him now, intent on him, Alaric felt a tear fall down his cheek. Bashima reached down and kissed it away, and Alaric pulled their foreheads together, breathing with the god.

Alaric closed his eyes and breathed out, "I'm close." His body tightened, and the Sun God's breath was hot on Alaric's mouth.

"Hells, seeing your fucked-out face is gonna be the end of me," Bashima said. He pulled himself out slowly, trying to control his breathing. He laid on his back next to Alaric and stroked himself, eyes wide and famished. Alaric intertwined his fingers with Bashima's free hand, and the god smiled, gripping tightly. It didn't take long for him to finish, gorgeous gold cum sliding through his fingers and onto his abs and chest. He rose and grabbed his trousers from the floor and wiped himself down, keeping it away from Alaric.

"Hmm," he said, turning his attention to Alaric. "You're a mess." He bent over and licked Alaric's abdomen clean, satisfaction on his face. Alaric ruffled the god's hair.

"Oh, sure, it's fine if you do it," Alaric joked.

"You're damn right it is," Bashima said and fell back, purring. "I warned you it would be fast."

Alaric attempted a shrug, but he was spent, at least for the moment. "I have faith you'll be ready to go again tonight."

"Oh, definitely," Bashima said, rolling on top of him. He set his arms on Alaric's chest and rested his chin on top, looking at Alaric like he was a long-lost treasure. "Are you okay?"

"Yes," Alaric said and smiled down at the god. "Better than okay."

Bashima reached up and pecked him on the lips, then lay his head on Alaric's chest.

After their third round of love-making, where Bashima made Alaric come so hard he thought he blacked out, Bashima pulled him under the covers and nestled himself behind Alaric, kissing between his shoulders and tracing his tattoo.

"Even your tattoo has red eyes."

"Hmm, yup. The artist did that on a whim. He couldn't say why—inspired or something."

"A dragon suits you. Proud, strong, wise."

"You'll give me an inflated ego if you keep that up."

"Never. There's room for only one ego in this bed," Bashima said in mock sternness. He sounded tired but in a contented way.

"Did I tell you that in my village, most people don't show their tattoos?" Alaric asked. "That's because you're not supposed to pick a design until you're ready. Until you've received some kind of sign. I still don't know what my mother's or father's tattoos are. Only they know." He stopped, thinking about how to explain. "The only person besides the artist who's seen mine is the healer, who made sure it didn't get infected. The healers keep records of the tattoos, showing the village history and all that. She said no one had chosen a dragon in hundreds of years."

"So why did you choose it?" Bashima asked, sleep gone from his voice.

"I had a dream," Alaric said, "that I was flying with hundreds of dragons. Every color you could imagine, flying in a giant spiral together, perfect unison, like they could read each other's thoughts. They didn't mind that I was there, some human interloper. They just kept flying." He smiled and nuzzled back into the Sun God. "That's why."

Bashima didn't say anything. He kissed along Alaric's neck and shoulders, his nose sending warm breaths down Alaric's spine. In Bashima's arms, Alaric fell asleep and dreamed of nothing.

Chapter Twelve

Matthias stared at the closed door, wondering if he made the right choice by leaving. Master Bashima seemed calm if a little nervous, but Matthias knew that could change in an instant. What if he took offense to something Shina did or said and flew into another rage?

He'd almost choked when Shina brought up the tribute's accusation, but the Sun God took it well, had even brought up talking to the king about tribute safety. Which threw Matthias for a loop. Concern for humans? If Matthias couldn't be sure who the Sun God was anymore, how could Bashima be trusted with Shina?

Tika stood beside him, stoic as ever. She tapped him on the shoulder and said, "I know what you're thinking."

"I doubt that very much," Matthias said, trying to keep the vitriol from his voice.

"Master Bashima is a god, and Shina can do as he wishes. We have no say in the matter." Her voice was stern but kind. Tika had been with the Sun God longer than the other shades. Hand-picked by Bashima to be his personal attendant, she wielded authority almost equal to Kuroi, but she rarely used that power.

Matthias sighed. There was concern in her eyes, and he knew what she was thinking: *don't get too attached, that's not our job.*

"I wish he wouldn't give his heart away so easily," Matthias said.

215

"I believe that is one of Shina's greatest strengths. He isn't one for half measures. Much like Dain."

"He's nothing like Dain," Matthias spat back.

That man never thought twice about leaving the master to carouse with his friends, hadn't acknowledged any of the shades during his time in the temple unless he needed something, was loud and abrasive and almost as scary as the Sun God in his temper.

"Do you believe Master Bashima would be drawn to Shina if he wasn't like Dain? They might not be the same, but they both have warrior spirits. That ability to stand fast in a storm. Otherwise, they'd stand no chance against the Sun God."

Matthias had to agree with her. Shina showed remarkable resilience and the ability to forgive. Matthias wished he had that level of empathy and compassion, but the Sun God treated Shina too poorly in the past for Matthias to move on quickly.

"I owe the master a great deal," he said. "I remember arriving at the Underworld, being so afraid and not quite recalling what happened to me. Lord Veles flagged me for Master Bashima immediately, and it was the best thing anyone has done for me."

Matthias paused, thinking of Lord Veles's tired but compassionate eyes then of the Sun God's mighty presence on his first day of work. "At least, it was the best thing until Shina. He's...special."

Tika smiled and said, "And you're not the only one who knows that. You're not the one who sees Master Bashima fret over these dinners. If he's doing the right thing. Worried he'll say the wrong thing. He's ashamed of what he did to Shina, and gods aren't used to feeling shame. This entire situation is new for him, which gods don't deal with well, as you know."

Matthias wondered if Tika knew what transpired in the Sun God's chambers that day because Shina hadn't gone into details. Had the Sun God confided in her?

Tika looked at the closed door then turned to go. "I've known the master for my entire death, and I've never seen him like this, so unsure of himself, and maybe that's a good thing."

"Maybe," Matthias echoed.

"Get some rest," Tika said. "They won't be needing us again tonight."

"I know," Matthias answered and reluctantly left alongside her.

Bashima woke before the sun rose and was elated to find Shina next to him. Some part of him doubted the redhead would stay—that kernel in his soul that always expected to be left behind. Shina nestled against the Sun God, breathing easily, hair draped over his eyes. This time, Bashima reached out and tucked the hair behind Shina's ear, and the redhead smiled in his sleep and murmured something Bashima couldn't hear.

Tracing the line of his jaw, Bashima propped himself up on his elbow to see as much of the redhead's face as he could. Even closed, his eyes and long lashes dominated his face, giving him an ageless innocent quality that Bashima couldn't resist. He wanted to touch each freckle on Shina's nose and cheeks.

"Are you watching me sleep like a weird stalker?" came a sleepy voice, and Bashima snorted. Shina opened his eyes and smiled, then pulled away and turned over so he was facing the god. He scooted back in, intertwining their legs, and Bashima ran his fingers down Shina's arm, causing goosebumps to rise.

Bashima felt himself getting excited, and Shina giggled, which was way too adorable.

"Good morning to you too."

He reached up and fluttered his lips against Bashima's, who leaned in and deepened the kiss, pressing himself closer and wrapping his arm around Shina's waist, letting his hand trail down to the small of his back. The redhead sighed into Bashima's mouth, spinning his mind into a small frenzy, and he pushed Shina back and rolled on top of him.

Shina broke their kiss, grinning, and said, "You're so heavy."

"You're heavier than me, idiot," Bashima said. Shina wiggled his hips and waggled his eyebrows, and Bashima winced. "You should not be attractive when you make that face."

"And yet here you are, finding it irresistible."

217

"Shut up or I'm gonna flip you over and show you how irresistible you are," Bashima growled, and Alaric's eyes flashed.

"Oh, I thought you were going to do that anyway." The redhead batted his eyelashes and pressed his hips up. That was all the invitation Bashima needed. In an instant, he flipped the redhead onto his side and slotted himself right up against Shina's back.

Bashima ran his hand down Shina's perfect side, fingers dipping at his waist and rising at the slight swell of his hip. Shina made a pleased purring sound, for once not impatient. He let Bashima touch every inch of him and didn't interrupt, his skin smooth and pliant under the god's fingertips. Bashima roved his leg and foot up and down Shina's calves and thighs, marveling at the taut muscles.

"You are absolutely perfect," he said. Gods, it didn't take much from the redhead to get Bashima going. Just him lying on his side, poised to accept the god fully, made Bashima want to burst.

He willed himself to have a little self-control and breathed deeply before sliding his fingers inside the willing warmth of Shina's body. After last night, the redhead didn't need much preparation, and Bashima held onto Shina's chest with one arm and guided himself inside with a quick, hard thrust that made Shina gasp. He was used to Bashima going slower to start, but he didn't pull away. Bashima grinned and held on as the redhead ground his hips back, working in harmony with Bashima's movements. Shina's fists clenched the bed sheets as the god thrust home again and again.

He cried out, "Harder, deeper, don't stop!"

Bashima obeyed, railing Shina like both their lives depended on it. He dug his fingers into Shina's hip and the redhead grabbed that hand, pressing down harder. He then grasped his own swelling dick and stroked it, breathing hard, taking Bashima's full force and length. But Bashima didn't want Shina to finish that way. After one last plunge of his hips, he pulled out and tore the covers off the bed, grabbing Shina's leg and opening him up so his chest faced the ceiling, back flat against the bed. The redhead looked up at him in surprise.

"I want you, Red. I'm going to taste *all* of you." He fell upon Shina's beautiful cock like a starving man, sucking, licking, humming around it.

Shina's hips bucked up automatically and he put his hands in Bashima's hair and held on for dear life as he groaned in pleasure. He kept going, relentless, loving the tension that roiled through Shina's body.

"I'm coming," Shina said, fingers digging into Bashima's scalp like claws. The god felt Shina's entire body shake then hot sweetness filled his mouth. He waited for Shina to be spent then rocked back on his heels and swallowed, wiping his mouth with a wolfish grin.

"Damned hells you taste so good," he said and slithered up Shina's body. He'd take care of himself in a moment. First, he wanted to see the redhead's sex-dazed eyes. He nearly jumped from the bed: Shina's eyes were almost pure crimson, and his breathing was short and rapid, like the night he'd overpowered Bashima in the baths.

Bashima froze, hoping the spell would pass. He wanted to comfort Shina, but he wasn't sure what talking to him or touching him would do. After a few minutes with neither of them moving, Shina's eyes slowly returned to normal, and his breathing settled. When he focused on Bashima on top of him, he flew from the bed, knocking the god over the other side and onto the floor.

"Holy hells! I'm so sorry! Are you okay? I don't know what just happened, but it felt really weird and then I saw your face and had this urge to bite you, so I tried to get away. I didn't want to hurt you, I'm sorry!"

Bashima groaned from the floor, and Shina's face appeared above him from the bed, peering down at him.

"That's not exactly how I thought that would go," Bashima said. His erection had fled in a damned hurry, probably when he'd seen Shina's blown-out eyes. "Don't worry about me. Are you okay?"

"I mean, my ass is really sore, but that's nothing new."

Bashima snorted and sat up. He said, "That's the second time you've blacked out like that."

"I'm sorry. I don't understand why. I liked everything you were doing. A lot. So why would I want to bite you?"

"Who the hells knows," Bashima said, standing and rubbing a hand through his hair. "You pack a punch for a human."

Shina's face reddened prettily, and Bashima leaned down, grabbed his face, and planted a deep kiss on his lips. He pulled away and walked naked out of the room, saying "Even fucking Tengu had no idea, and he's the closest thing to an expert on that stuff who lives near here. I guess we could ask Maida. She's a fertility goddess."

"Fertility?" Shina sounded panicked. He jumped off the bed, pulled on his trousers and followed Bashima to the sitting room. The sun peeked through the windows, and Bashima stared at it, pondering what to do.

What set the redhead off like that?

"Yeah," Bashima said, "she's into all kinds of kinky sex stuff. Probably the best person to ask. And she's not a fucking gossip, so that's a plus."

"Do you think something's wrong?"

Bashima turned and Shina looked horrified with himself. He gazed down at his hands, which trembled.

"Wrong with me?"

"Fuck no. I said you're perfect and I don't lie." Bashima said as he crossed the room and grabbed Shina's face again, making the redhead look him in the eyes. "There's nothing wrong with you. Probably just some obscure reaction. If anything, it's my fault for being careless."

Shina's bottom lip wobbled, and he said, "But what if I hurt you?"

"Did you miss the fact that I'm a god? You can't hurt me. You can annoy the shit outta me though."

"I don't want to be a burden."

"Has anything I've said made you think that?" Bashima flinched, recalling some of the things he'd said to Shina in anger.

"No, but it's scary, not knowing what's going on with your own body."

Bashima held Shina by the shoulders and said, "Well, I like your body."

The redhead loosed his magical laugh and hugged Bashima. Then Shina cleared his throat and said, "You're still very naked."

It really, really wasn't fair how good Bashima looked on a horse. The god sat on the black stallion, tall, haughty, and altogether much too handsome. The wind tossed his blond hair, giving him a rakish air, and the horse stood as though he were a god himself. Bashima said he didn't need a saddle, that it would be criminal to put one on Yoru. The horse would never let Bashima fall, but the god was also adept enough to keep his ass in place, thank you very much.

"So long as you think you can," Alaric joked. "I'd fall right off."

"You just grip with your thighs," Bashima said, gesturing at his legs. "It's not that difficult."

Yoru nodded and whinnied, causing Ichigo to dance in place, huffing. The stallion side-stepped over to them and nudged Ichigo, who snapped at him.

Bashima cackled. "Good to see your horse is as hard to get as you, Red."

"She's a lady," Alaric said and patted Ichigo's neck.

"All right, Yoru, enough flirting," said Bashima, and the stallion took off at a fast canter.

Ichigo, not intending to be shown up, pursued them, making Alaric grip the reins from the sudden movement. Then, he leaned forward slightly, settling into the canter that became a gallop. He had no idea how Bashima was staying on Yoru besides god's magic and Yoru's supposed control, but they looked magnificent, Bashima dressed all in black, feet bare, leaned forward to streamline their ride.

Alaric urged Ichigo on, and she gladly found new speed. They rode across the valley, Ichigo finally catching up with Yoru. Once they were level with each other, Bashima glanced over at Alaric and smirked. Alaric could already hear him: "See, I told you I was a great rider."

Alaric would make it his personal mission to find something the god wasn't good at, besides social gatherings and long conversations. He signaled Ichigo to branch off to the left, surprising Bashima. Ichigo tore off toward the forest, Alaric laughing on her back, Bashima cursing up a storm behind them. It didn't take long for Yoru to catch them, but it was exhilarating to see Bashima's competitive face, bottom lip stuck out a little, eyes narrowed.

Alaric urged Ichigo to cut in front of Yoru, who tossed his head, enjoying himself. As they turned to head back toward the temple, Ichigo flagged a bit, and Alaric thought he saw something in the forest, a shadow crossing a clearing in the trees. He tried to focus on it, but whatever it was had gone. Probably just a stag watching them.

Bashima noticed Alaric and Ichigo slow down and matched pace, saying instructions for Yoru.

"What is it?" Bashima asked, looking towards the woods.

Alaric shook his head, "Nothing. Just a deer maybe."

"Or fucking Tengu wandering around," Bashima said, rolling his eyes. "I swear he can get lost in his own damn forest."

"Ha! This isn't Cypress's realm though, right?"

"Technically every forest is his realm, but he lives farther south about fifty miles or so. He's always going on about root systems and shit like that, how he can feel every forest. That's how he got that burn on his arm."

"I..." Alaric paused.

"'S all right," Bashima said. "He'd tell you the story if you asked. Not a big secret. He was visiting Zebra Head here when the asshole still lived here more than half the year. The forest surrounding the valley alerted him that *his* forest was burning close to his temple. Tengu shifted there, which was a huge mistake. It's too far for one shift, even for older gods, so he got there and was too tired. Collapsed before he could try anything."

"Wow...but he's alive."

"Of course. He wouldn't have died, but the recovery would have been a bitch if he'd gone much further. Years probably. Oken told me why the moron shifted out of nowhere, so we went after him. Got there in time for Oken to use his ice power and stop the blaze before it consumed the temple. The forest though...it took ages for Tengu to get over that. There's mostly young trees surrounding his temple now."

"Did you find out what started it?"

Bashima made a strange face, and light played over his skin, but he shook his head. "Nothing conclusive. No humans were in the area, so they didn't set it. Could have been a lightning strike, I suppose."

Alaric wanted to say, *but that's not what you think,* but he held back. This was something Bashima needed to keep to himself, at least for now. He said, "At least you saved what you could."

"Yeah, making it even more fucking difficult to get rid of Tengu whenever he shows up. He's so grateful all the time; it's disgusting."

"Yeah, how dare he be grateful?"

Bashima glanced at him and raised an eyebrow. "Don't make me kick your sarcastic ass all the way back up the mountain."

"Don't threaten me with a good time," Alaric joked, and Ichigo snorted, taking off again. Alaric could have sworn that Yoru actually laughed as Bashima told the horse to hurry up.

They arrived at the foot of the mountain and led the horses in a walk to the stable. They dismounted, Alaric gawking at Bashima's ass in his tight riding leggings. They were made of soft leather and were perfect for touching. Alaric walked Ichigo past the god and ran his hand over Bashima's ass. The god spun and grabbed his hand, grinning.

"Watch your hands, Red."

"I couldn't help myself," Alaric said. "Watching you ride," said Alaric, wetting his lips, "and those pants…just so manly."

"Don't call me manly," Bashima said, pouting. "If anything, I'm godly."

"Fine, I'll be manly, you be godly," Alaric said, laughing.

"Did I tell you that you look fucking amazing on a horse?" Bashima asked, eyes flashing.

"No, but it's nice to hear," Alaric answered, heat forming in his gut.

Alaric had put his hair in a low ponytail, tied with the leather strap, and his hair rested over his shoulder. Bashima reached up and tugged lightly on the tail, bringing Alaric's face closer to his.

"Your hair is getting long," Bashima whispered. "I like it." He tugged again, bringing Alaric's lips to his. "What do you say we skip dinner?"

Chapter Thirteen

Bashima could tell Matthias was unhappy with the current situation, but there wasn't much he could do. Besides showering the damn redhead with affection, which he wasn't going to do in front of anyone. Except the damn redhead, obviously.

The shade stood in the sitting room during their dinners, attempting to keep his face neutral, but Bashima could feel the intensity coming off Matthias like a belligerent cloud. Shina hadn't mentioned it. He saw Matthias as an older brother, or something similar, and was very attached to him. He would have to account for Shina's feelings on the matter. Bashima was thinking about how the redhead might feel about a lot of things lately, which was exhausting.

Tika wasn't concerned or she would have traded Matthias out with another shade. It shouldn't have bothered Bashima, but after another week of coiled tension, he was ready to snap.

"You're quieter than usual," Shina said, bright eyes inquisitive.

"Eh? Oh, it's nothing to worry about," Bashima said.

The shades had already been dismissed, but Bashima wasn't sure how to approach the subject. All the new situations and emotions associated with Shina were overwhelming, and he wanted to solve this problem on his own without having to involve the redhead. His mother would say something about finally showing maturity. Hag.

"Okay," Shina said, though Bashima doubted he would let it go. Shina was getting too good at reading the Sun God's moods, which could make things onerous. Now that the redhead was in his bed, it was going to be damn difficult to get him out of it. Not that Bashima wanted Shina out of his bed. If they could stay in Bashima's room all day and night, the god would have made it so. But Shina made it harder for Bashima to concentrate on anything else once the sun went down.

"Do you need me to stay in my room tonight?" Shina asked. Bashima looked up at him in surprise. Was he reading the god's mind now?

"What?" Bashima asked, taking a quick drink of his wine.

"You seem preoccupied with something. You don't want to say what it is. So, do you need some alone time to figure it out?" The redhead's expression was curious and concerned, and Bashima could sense no annoyance or hurt from him.

"Would you mind?" he asked carefully. "It's not that I don't want you here," he added.

"I'm not worried about that," Shina said. "I need to grab a quick soak anyway. The ride today was really dusty." He flipped his hair behind his shoulder.

"Talking about baths is just going to make me follow you outta here," Bashima said, smirking.

Shina laughed and stood up. He came around the small table and kissed the god slowly.

"That doesn't help either," Bashima said, pouting.

"Do what you need to do," Shina smiled. "You know where I'll be."

Matthias re-entered the sitting room, looking worried. When he didn't see Shina, he paused, posture pristine, and asked, "You have need of me, Master?"

The shade's tone was reasonable and polite, but Bashima knew Matthias was harboring resentment. Bashima stood by the window, looking up at a full moon, trying to figure out how best to approach the shade where neither of them would lose their tempers.

"No, Matthias, but Shina does."

"Master?" Surprised by the answer, Matthias flushed.

"He needs you around. You're basically his best friend. But things have been tense with you."

Bashima perched on the window ledge, trying to hold back the intimidating stance his instincts wanted him to take. Matthias wasn't an enemy. In fact, Bashima could destroy him if he pleased, which the shade definitely knew. And yet, he was still putting on the protective attitude.

Matthias didn't say anything, but he looked both embarrassed and stubborn.

"Well?" Bashima, asked, irritation rising.

"I don't know how to respond, Master."

"And I don't know how to carry on this kind of conversation, but it's necessary." Bashima crossed his arms and leveled with the shade. "Shina cares about you, so I've let the attitude slide. However, I won't overlook it forever."

"I will do whatever you or Shina ask of me, Master," the shade said, words stiff.

"But you're angry," Bashima said.

Matthias stood still, lips pursed, eyes cool. Bashima made a keep-it-moving gesture, twirling his hand, which jolted Matthias.

"I am angry with the situation, Master."

"That's a great political answer, Matthias, but it won't work on me. You've worked here for what? Over two thousand years?"

"And I'm very grateful to be here—"

"That's not what you're here to discuss," Bashima said, terse. "I know you're grateful. Every damn shade who works here is grateful. I try not to take that for granted."

Matthias interrupted him, "You are an excellent master, sir. You treat shades with far more courtesy and genuine care than I know other shades experience."

"But you can't get past what I did to your friend."

Bashima must have hit the bulls-eye, because Matthias fell silent, but his gaze was mutinous. The Sun God marveled at the depths of attachment Shina brought out in people. Matthias was showing open displeasure with his god to defend a human he'd known for so short a time. Bashima recalled how Shina's head had rested on Matthias's shoulder in the baths. How insular they'd looked together. The seeming closeness that sparked Bashima's jealousy.

"Ah, because you love him." It was so obvious, now that Bashima thought about it.

"Of course," said Matthias, instantly. "Shina is everything that is good in this world. I would lay down my life a second time for him if he needed me to."

"Is this going to be a problem?" Bashima asked, keeping a lid on his resentment. He couldn't let himself be jealous of a shade. Matthias was dead and couldn't do anything about his feelings if he wanted to.

"A problem?" Confused, Matthias tilted his head a bit, finally showing some emotion. "Isn't that what I'm supposed to do for him? Protect him? From everything and every..."

"And everyone?" Bashima asked.

They stared at each other for a moment, neither moving. Matthias's eyebrows contracted, giving him a recalcitrant expression that reminded Bashima of Shina. His rebelliousness had rubbed off on the shade.

Matthias cleared his throat and said, "I know my duty is to you, Master, but you also charged me with watching over Shina. I believe I can do both. It is just...difficult at the moment." He swallowed once, thinking, and went on, "You asked if I love him. I do, but I'm not *in* love with him if that's your concern. I don't want to see him hurt."

Bashima flinched internally, knowing exactly what the shade meant and that he had every reason to be wary of the Sun God. Dain's friends had encouraged him not to begin a relationship with a god, that it was too unpredictable and dangerous to pursue. Bashima's tentative first years with the three god-touched, them heartbroken but for some reason willing to stay with him though they hadn't approved of him being with Dain. The god-touched respected Bashima and served him, but he would be fooling himself to think they cared about him.

Here was a shade who died horrifically, who was just as sheltered as Bashima for the last two thousand years, allowing himself to attach to a human.

Letting himself care about someone else when all he was assigned to do was watch the human and make sure he didn't get in the way. Matthias didn't have to care. He didn't have to love Shina.

"I can't say that I'll never hurt him again," Bashima said. It felt odd speaking with a shade this openly, but if it would smooth things over and make Shina happy, then he'd do it. "Because that's how these things go. But I don't plan on hurting him. I don't want to hurt him."

"May I speak plainly?" Matthias asked.

Bashima was loathe to give the shade permission, but he nodded.

"You may not want to cause him pain, but you also can't help it. Not when you can't give your whole heart to him as he's obviously given his to you." Matthias bowed his head and sighed. "I will attend to my attitude, Master. It's not right of me to condemn you for how you feel. And Shina is happy."

He took something from his tunic and held it out to Bashima. "Kuroi asked me to give this to you," he said.

Pained by what Matthias said, knowing the shade was right, Bashima took the proffered scroll and said, "You may go."

Matthias bowed his head and turned to go, leaving Bashima with a message from Maida, the Fertility Goddess.

He unrolled the scroll and read:

Greetings Sun God. I hadn't thought to ever get a personal message from you, and on such an intriguing topic no less. Congratulations on the new lover by the way. It's been too long for you.

As you know, gods and demigods often exhibit eye color changes during arousal or dire circumstances, usually when stressed or angry. But I've never heard of it happening to a human. You mentioned that your god-touched has a similar condition, but that his eyes are black all the time. This is also uncommon, but not unusual, and his eyes don't change, they are always black. So, whatever is happening with the human is a different phenomenon.

If it is occurring because he consumed some of your bodily fluids, that would also be unprecedented in a human. A human can become god-touched from prolonged exposure to bodily fluids like semen or blood, but this takes longer than two exposures unless the ceremony is carried out directly after. Which I assume you haven't done.

The excessive strength could be attributed to the after-effects of the god-touched ceremony, but once again, that doesn't pertain to your human. Are you sure he doesn't have demigod lineage? Some of these older villages hide plenty of secret godly connections from the past, and it could stay dormant for centuries. It's very rare, but it could happen.

One other option: have you considered that you are soul-bonded? I know what you'll think of that. Soul bonds aren't real, blah, blah, blah. But just because you've never seen one, doesn't mean it's not real. All kinds of uncanny things can supposedly happen with a soul bond.

Do write again if you have any more questions, especially if they're about this intriguing new lover you've found. Remember to always pull out.

Maida, Goddess of Fertility

"Matthias? I didn't expect to see you until morning. Is something up?"

Alaric was in his room, attempting to braid his wet hair to little avail. The strands wouldn't stay put.

"I hadn't planned on stopping by, but, oh for hells sake, sit down and let me do that," Matthias said.

Alaric's eyes widened, but he sat on the stool near his bed, and Matthias came up behind him and finger-combed his hair into three bunches. He braided Alaric's hair into a neat queue, saying, "Why did you want to braid it anyway?"

"Lazy," Alaric said, grinning. "Something different. My hair hasn't been this long before."

"And growing at an exponential rate," Matthias grumbled. "We'll have to do your roots again soon."

"Matthias," Alaric prompted. "Late night visit? What's going on?"

The shade sighed and sat on the bed, facing Alaric. His eyes were serious and a little damp. He said, "I need to apologize for the way I've been acting. It's rude and inconsiderate and not at all what you deserve."

"Oh, Matthias, it's okay," Alaric said, patting the shade's knee. "I know you're just looking out for me. It's nice to have someone who's on my side."

"And I am," Matthias said. "But I've been a bit of an ass since you decided to stay at the temple. It's none of my business who you want to be with or who you spend time with." He bowed his head.

"Did Bashima say something to you?" The Sun God's miles-away behavior at dinner suddenly made sense.

"He did, but don't be cross with him," Matthias said, eyes pleading. "He wasn't unkind. He didn't reprimand me. He said that you need me. I can't give you my full attention if I'm angry with the Sun God on your behalf."

"He did seem preoccupied at dinner," Alaric said and took a deep breath. "So long as he didn't yell at you, I guess, but he made you feel bad."

"I did that to myself. He was very honest with me."

"Still, I wish he'd trusted me enough to say something. I could have helped."

Matthias laughed, "It's amazing that he kept his head at all." The shade leaned forward and said, "I think you've been very good for him. So long as you're happy, my opinion has no say in the matter."

"I think I'm happy," Alaric said, touching the braid that went down his back between his shoulder blades. "I think...I love him, Matthias."

The shade's eyes popped for a moment before he got them back under control.

Alaric said, "I know what you're thinking. I'm stupid to fall for a god. It's pretty much the dumbest thing a human can do, right? And I know he still loves Dain, but he's gone." He paused and bit his lip. "Do you think a person or a god can love more than one person in their lifetime?"

"I'm not the best person to ask," Matthias admitted. "I don't think I've ever really loved anyone, let alone multiple people. But gods are eternal where most other life is fleeting. So, yes, I think it's possible to love more than one person."

Alaric nodded, wanting to believe the shade. He couldn't believe he'd said it. Putting it into words, even if it was with his friend and not Bashima, made it real. Made it dangerous. He knew Bashima liked him and liked spending time with him, but love might be too much to expect.

Dain had been his sun. How could Alaric possibly measure up to that?

They'd had a slow day and a slow night, yet Bashima felt exhausted. He lay in bed with Shina, both of them reading, Bashima sitting up against a mound of pillows, Shina on his stomach with a book. Bashima looked over the scroll for the hundredth time, unable to focus. He couldn't blame the redhead for that. Shina had been quiet all day too and wasn't conscious of the fact that him reading made the god amorous. Bashima didn't want to pull Shina from the book though, with which he seemed to be enthralled.

Cracking his neck, the Sun God tossed the scroll on his bedside table and yawned. After stretching, he saw Shina watching him from the corner of his eye, assessing. Maybe the book wasn't that interesting after all. He smiled and said, "How's the book, Red?"

Shina flushed, the red racing across his cheeks and nose. "It's good," he said. "I'm just distracted."

"Way you were staring at it, I thought you might fall into it nose-first."

Shina sat up, the blanket falling off his shoulder. He was wearing a sleeveless sleep shirt that showed off his arms, and Bashima reached out and stroked a finger down Shina's bicep.

"Bashima," he said, serious.

"Yeah?" Such gorgeous arms...Bashima wanted to nibble on them.

"I love you."

"Uh huh..." Bashima reeled himself back in, focusing on Shina's face. His eyes were wide and bold, very sure of himself. Oh shit. Had he really said it?

"I love you."

Yes. Yes, he'd said it, and all Bashima could say was, "Shut up."

Seeing the redhead annoyed was quite something. He was usually flustered and couldn't say what he actually meant, muttering to himself, but he was more than annoyed now.

"Did you even hear me?"

"Yes, I did, and you don't love me," Bashima sat up straighter and stared at Shina. What the hells was the redhead thinking? What did he know about love?

231

"You can't tell me how I feel," Shina said, appalled.

"You bet your sweet ass I can," Bashima said. "I'm the only person you've been with. Hells, I'm one of the few people you've even kissed."

"What does that have to do with anything?" Shina asked, crossing his arms.

"How the hells are you supposed to know you're in love if you've only had sex with one person?" Bashima asked, panicking. The redhead wasn't going to back down. He had that gleam in his red eyes. He would dig his heels in and not budge. Dammit, why did Bashima think that was sexy?

"This isn't how I thought you'd react," Shina said, eyes narrowing. "I thought you'd say, 'obviously you love me because I'm a god, the most amazing god who ever walked the earth.'"

"That is *not* what I sound like," Bashima said. He got out of bed and stormed away, out to the sitting room. Not that running away would solve anything because Shina followed right on his heels.

"Don't walk away from me," Shina said, eyes ablaze. "And don't you dare shift out of this room."

Dammit, that was exactly what Bashima planned to do. "I wasn't going to," he said, sulky.

"So much for never lying," said Shina, hands on his hips. He looked really good mad...could Bashima possibly fix this with a quick seduction?

Shina pointed at him. "Stop looking at my dick." He pointed to his eyes. "Why are you acting this way? You don't have to say it back, you know. I just wanted to say it to you, so I did."

"That's bullshit," Bashima said, walking toward him. "When someone says...that...they're expecting the other person to say it back!"

"Well, I'm not sorry I said it!"

"Well, I'm not either!"

They both stopped yelling, breathing hard, glaring at each other.

"Look," Bashima started, but Shina cut him off. He held up his hands, calling a truce.

"I know I'm just a human, and you think I'm an idiot, but it's how I feel. I'm not going to take it back or pretend that I didn't say it."

"Shit, I don't think you're an idiot." Bashima ran a hand through his hair. "I don't care that you're a human either, obviously."

"Then what?" Shina asked. Bashima didn't know how to answer because he wasn't sure how he felt. Dain knocked on the inside of his head, proclaiming that he was the only one the Sun God could ever love and that anyone who tried to supplant him was a fool. But that wasn't really Dain, Bashima knew. It was just his own fucking mind, torturing him.

"Have you actually thought about this?" Bashima finally asked, making Shina roll his eyes. "It's a valid question," Bashima growled. "Humans tend to act rashly about things like this."

"Why? Because we live shorter lives? Yeah, that did enter into my thoughts, *Bashima*." Shina fumed and started to pace. "Maybe I want to spend my life with you."

Bashima flinched away from the redhead, who angled toward him. Shina stopped and pulled back, biting his lower lip, which sent Bashima hurtling toward him. He grabbed Shina and pressed his lips onto the surprised redhead's. At first, Shina kissed back, melting slowly against Bashima, but after a few moments, he pushed the god gently away.

Seduction was off the table. Bashima sighed and said, "That's a lot to put on yourself."

"Not if I get to spend my time with you," Shina said. "Even if you're one of the most difficult people I've ever met."

"I've got all the time in the world," Bashima said, ignoring Shina's joke. "You don't."

"That's what you're worried about? Time?" asked Shina, incredulous. He zoned out for a moment. He snapped his attention back to Bashima, who didn't like what he saw glistening in those huge eyes. "Isn't there a way to fix that?"

"Huh?"

Shina looked like he'd been hit with the greatest idea of all time, and Bashima paled, knowing where his mind had gone. The only solution he could come to.

"You could make me god-touched."

Bashima pulled away, frowning and shaking his head. This escalated too quickly. Dain came roaring back into his head, proclaiming that he would never do the ritual, that eternal life held no fascination for him. Saying he'd only be gone for a few weeks. He'd be back and they could plan a holiday together.

What if Dain had agreed? They'd still be together. Bashima wouldn't be standing with another stubborn human, but one who was willing to go through with the ritual had suggested it himself with no prompting from Bashima. And Bashima was horrified.

"That's out of the question."

Affronted, Alaric blew a huge breath out through his nose. "Why? Wouldn't that solve the early death problem?"

Bashima hissed. "The fact that you think it's a shortcut means you have no idea what being god-touched is. You'd be *tied* to me forever. Wherever I went, you'd HAVE to go. The ritual is binding and eternal."

"Isn't that the point? And aren't god-touched mortal?"

"Sure, the bond breaks if you die, but that's not the issue. You're willing to give up your humanity for me? Why don't you ask Kuroi if that's such a great idea? Or Shefu? Or Draiden? Or how about Oken's mother? Cindras treats her like a piece of luggage."

"You wouldn't treat me like that," Shina said.

"There's no way you can know that," Bashima said, putting his face in his hands. He couldn't believe they were having this conversation. All he'd wanted to do was read a bit, maybe have some sex, and sleep. He'd gotten to do one of those things, the one that least interested him. What was he going to do?

"What, you think you would?"

"I wouldn't mean to, gods!" Bashima stalked to the window, not wanting to look at Shina anymore. He could feel the rage growing inside his chest, and red and orange light shimmered over his skin. He made fists with his hands and tried to calm down. He took deep breaths and imagined he was somewhere relaxing.

"What if this is what I want?" Shina asked, defiant.

"Well, it's not what I want!" Bashima shouted as he spun around, his palms smoking. Shina took a step back but then stood his ground. His face was set.

Bashima's hands stopped shaking, and the light drifted from his skin. He said, "You should go home."

"Home?" asked Shina, confused.

"To your village, to your parents. I've kept you here too long." Bashima's heart slammed in his chest. Was that what he wanted? Or was it some last-ditch effort to save the redhead from himself? He was young. So young. He didn't understand what eternity meant. It was a vague concept he'd heard about but couldn't comprehend. Humans were like fireworks, burning brightly but gone in an instant, while the gods lived as forever-burning stars.

A god and a human could never be together.

Shina kept his distance, but Bashima could feel his confusion and indecision from the other side of the room. Shina wanted to walk toward the god but held himself back, but it was taking everything he had. Then, the feeling was gone as though Shina had slammed a door.

"Do you want me to come back?" Shina asked.

"It's not that simple," Bashima said, looking at him askance.

"It's not that hard, either," Shina countered. "It's a yes or no."

"Yes! All right!" Bashima yelled, energy crackling over his arms. "Fuck! You're so irritating."

"You're not winning any popularity contests either," Shina said. "Why should I go back to my village? Why now?"

Bashima bit the inside of his cheek. He imagined Dain standing next to Shina. They were very alike especially when they put their minds to something. Both knew who they were and what they wanted. Bashima just didn't want to see it in Shina. Why couldn't he choose easy people?

"If this is something you think you want, you need to take some time and make sure it's the right thing for you. Don't think about me. Go see your parents. Hear what they have to say. What if you get back there and realize you almost made the biggest mistake of your life?"

"I'm sorry to ask this, but I have to," Shina said. "Is this about Dain?"

Bashima's heart rate picked up, hammering, making him want to lash out or run or both. Instead, he said, "Dain wasn't interested in eternal life. He refused my offer."

"So, you would have done it for him but not for me?"

"I was wrong to ask him, you idiot. Don't you get it?" Bashima stalked back to Shina and grabbed his arms. "It needs to be completely your choice. Whether we do the ceremony or not, even if you just stay with me as a human, it needs to be your choice, after you've thought through all your options. I couldn't give that to Dain, and I won't deny it to you."

"You're right," said Shina, pulling away. "I don't understand. But I'll go. You're right that I should see my parents and explain...everything."

Bashima felt like he might cry, like a small part of him had been severed. But gods shouldn't cry.

"Let's go to bed," Shina said. "Talk about this more tomorrow when we're both not so..." He didn't finish his thought, just walked back into the bedroom, hand dragging through his hair.

Alaric slept fitfully, his dreams a swirling chaos of indiscriminate visions and colors. There was a constant roaring sound as though he were surrounded by a roiling sea, and he thought he caught a glimpse of the red and gold dragon, but it disappeared as fast as it appeared. Underneath the din of rushing water, someone whispered to him, mocking.

He doesn't love you. He can't love you. You're nothing but a cheap copy. A replacement for something truly precious.

Alaric jolted awake and sat up in bed, sweat covering his body. He breathed rapidly, trying to shake the dream and that hideous voice. Was it his own voice? It hadn't sounded like the Sun God, which was at least comforting. Their fight was intense but not vicious. Bashima had been evasive, not confrontational. He'd followed Alaric to bed without question, and they'd fallen asleep curled up together but drifted apart in the night.

Though still close to each other—Alaric could reach out and touch Bashima—Alaric felt a distance between them like a wide chasm. Alaric hadn't expected the god to reciprocate his declaration though there was a bit of hope in his heart, and he wouldn't ask Bashima if he loved him. He didn't want to be that weak though he wanted to know the answer. Bashima hadn't said he loved Alaric back...but he hadn't denied his feelings either. Then why did Alaric feel a tightness in his chest, like his breath was caught?

He told you to go home, Alaric's mind said, *so that's what you should do.*

Bashima admitted that he wanted Alaric to come back. This wasn't banishment. Not goodbye. Just farewell until I see you again. So why did it feel permanent?

Alaric bit his lower lip and gazed at the sleeping god. Bashima had fallen asleep the instant his head hit the pillows and hadn't stirred except to move closer to Alaric, his chest against Alaric's back, arm around his waist. Now, with the morning arriving lazily, he looked serene. Only in sleep did the Sun God achieve a peaceful countenance, which Alaric loved. No one had seen this Bashima for centuries. Alaric should be happy to experience it, but he wanted more than Bashima's sleeping calm like the eye of a hurricane. He wanted everything. He wouldn't be content with second place.

Alaric pulled his knees up to his chest and rested his chin on his knees. Maybe leaving and getting perspective would help. He could talk to his parents and decide what to do. Though he knew he would return to the temple, the ache of separation was already hitting him.

"I want to be with you all the time," he said quietly. "Not just sometimes or when it's convenient." He sighed. That wasn't fair to Bashima even if it was how Alaric felt sometimes.

You're with him basically all the time, he thought. *He makes as much time for you as he can.*

Alaric rose from the bed, trying not to disturb the Sun God. He'd go to his room and pack some things for the trip.

Not everything, he told himself. *I'll be back.*

He needed to talk to Matthias and Emilia and let them know he was leaving for a while. Then he would confer with Kuroi as to the fastest route back to his village. Maybe there was a shortcut through the forest he didn't know about.

Bashima stirred and mumbled, "Where you go?"

"Just to my room," Alaric said.

He leaned across the bed and kissed the Sun God, who muttered, "'Kay," and rolled over.

Kuroi hid his surprise better than Matthias or Emilia, who dissolved into varying levels of tears. After assuring them of his planned return, they settled down, but Emilia made Alaric swear on his life that he would come back. He'd gladly done so, promising they would see each other again.

They helped Alaric pack, and though he didn't need the extra hands, he was thankful for the company. He filled the pack he'd come with: two sets of clothes for the trip and toiletries. He took his purple robe, the one his mother painstakingly made for him. He wanted to give it back to her, so she had something to hold onto when he left again.

Now, he stood in front of Kuroi, who looked nonplussed. Kuroi said, "The route you took to the mountain is the most direct, and I wouldn't suggest leaving the path if you can help it. Following the river is the best idea." He had a stack of scrolls in his hands but called a shade to take them. "What brought this excursion on?" He didn't ask, but his tone implied: did the Sun God do something again?

"Bashima and I had a...um...a discussion last night," Alaric said, ruffling his hair with a hand. "And he thought I should go visit my parents. To get perspective. Or something."

Kuroi raised an eyebrow.

"Okay, we had a fight," Alaric admitted. "Don't worry. He won't blow anything up, I think, but he was pretty steamed at me."

"Indeed," said Kuroi.

"Fine, we argued about whether I should become god-touched or not. Jeez, you really know how to twist a guy's arm."

Kuroi's eyes widened. "Did the master suggest this to you?" His tone was icy, dangerous.

"No, it was me," Alaric said, sheepish. "I might have told him something and he got all mad and the only thing I could think of to solve the problem was becoming god-touched."

Kuroi's anger diffused, and he crossed his arms. "Why would becoming god-touched solve your problem?"

Alaric grimaced, thinking maybe he had been an idiot for suggesting it. He said, "You know...almost eternal life or whatever..."

"Eternal life, whether it's forever or close to forever, rarely solves anything," Kuroi scolded. "You know that Shefu, Draiden, and I are god-touched. We made the choice after months of deliberation and weighing every option. Right before he died, Dain made us promise to watch over the Sun God although I doubt he had becoming tied to Bashima forever in mind."

"So then why did you do it?" Alaric asked. If it was such a terrible thing, why had all three of them agreed to it? And why had Bashima gone through with the ceremony?

"You'd have to ask the others why they made the choice. Of course, we knew our alchemic gifts would probably increase exponentially, so that was a plus, but we also knew we had to remain with Master Bashima. A gift and a curse.

"We were also older than you, in our forties, so we figured the most interesting parts of our human lives were over. None of us planned on marrying, so there were no lovers left behind. But what made me decide?" Kuroi paused, looking at Alaric. "This may be painful to hear."

"That's okay," Alaric said. "I'd like to know."

"I realized Bashima hadn't been faking his affection for Dain, who was my best friend."

Alaric shivered but kept his eyes on Kuroi. He could get through one story especially if Kuroi trusted him enough to share. Even if it caused his heart to skip.

"We all assumed Dain was just a passing fancy to the Sun God as most humans are treated by the gods. The higher beings enjoy playing their games and don't care who they hurt along the way. But when Dain fell ill, Master Bashima never left his side. He didn't sleep for days. We feared for the sun, but he kept control. Such is his power. He couldn't keep control on his emotions, however. The instant Dain died, Master Bashima fell into a mourning so deep we thought he might not recover."

"That's…a lot," Alaric whispered.

"When he returned from the Underworld without Dain's shade…that's when we knew how in love the Sun God had been. There was an accidental eclipse. Mistress Alora helped put everything right, but it was a near thing. When a god loses control like that, it can have devastating consequences. So, I decided if there was anything I could do to help my best friend's love, I would. Gradually, Master Bashima came back, irascible personality intact, but he was quieter. He didn't order us around or yell at the shades for making mistakes. He let us run the temple how we wanted though we knew his preferences and tried to make him as happy as he could be without Dain."

"All three of you," said Alaric. "That's incredible. What you did for him, what you gave up."

"It hasn't been the easiest two thousand years," said Kuroi, smiling, "Though these last months have certainly been interesting."

Alaric winced. "Sorry to be such a bother." He hated thinking he caused uproar in their lives.

"You have nothing to apologize for," Kuroi said. "You might not realize it, but you've made Master Bashima very happy. He needed a partner who could spar with him. And the fact that you come from Togarashi and have Dain's stubbornness…fate certainly has a sense of humor."

"I always thought the idea of fate was romantic, but now it seems like fate is an unstable jerk."

"Fate may play a role in our lives, but it's not all-controlling or all-encompassing," Kuroi said. "All of us have made countless choices that brought us to this moment. The fact that you walked back up the path from the stable that day…I don't think fate could have made you do that."

Alaric nodded, thinking on what Kuroi told him. Maybe becoming god-touched wasn't the best idea. He hadn't thought about what it would mean, not just for himself but for Bashima too.

"Will you be returning to us?" Kuroi asked, voice soft.

"I plan to," Alaric said, smiling. "If I don't, I owe Emilia one life."

Kuroi laughed, something Alaric had never heard. It lingered on the air as though the world missed the sound, echoing through the hall. Alaric felt the temple hum around him.

"We don't want to let Emilia down," Kuroi agreed. "When will you leave?"

"Not until tomorrow," Alaric said. "I wanted to talk to everyone first and..."

"Make sure Master Bashima knows you're coming back?" Kuroi suggested.

"Yeah," Alaric said. "Something like that."

The next morning, Shina stood by the stable, Ichigo hitched to the small cart that held his pack, simple provisions, and nothing else. He was flushed from the morning's activities. It took a long time to leave the kitchens as each shade hugged him and ordered him to come back from his village. Shefu stuffed his hands with food, trying not to cry, and they'd packed him a basket. Draiden was there, emerged from his records-keeping chamber, and patted the redhead on the shoulder, saying he hoped to see him again. Shina thanked him for his patience on the first day they met—which Bashima hadn't heard of until then—and the god-touched man smirked knowingly.

It seemed like every shade who lived in the temple was out and about that morning and in places they normally weren't. They wanted to either shake Shina's hand, hug him, or shyly nod at him. Bashima wondered if the redhead would ever get to walk out the main doors.

But he did.

Kuroi walked with Bashima and Shina down to the stable, arms behind his back, keeping some distance behind them. Shina chattered about his plans, who he would see, what he would bring back from his village, how long he'd be gone. Bashima didn't say much. He grunted whenever Shina paused, which didn't throw the redhead off his stride in the least.

Bashima didn't like this one bit. He didn't like seeing the cart attached to Ichigo—Yoru wasn't crazy about it either, stamping his feet and snorting in the stable—and he didn't like the small pack in the back. He didn't like that Shina seemed so carefree about the whole thing as though he was leaving on vacation. Bashima tried not to think about Dain leaving on his last trip, making similar promises.

Kuroi didn't speak. He stayed off to the side while Shina prepared Ichigo to go. The mare tossed her head and keened, looking back at the stable. Even the horses were pissed about the situation, so why wasn't Shina concerned?

Shina rubbed Ichigo's nose, telling her they'd be back and not to worry. It was all a mistake. Bashima wanted to yell at Shina not to go. He wanted to grab the redhead and shift him back to the temple and put him in his room and lock the door.

Don't be an asshole, he told himself. *You're the one who told him to leave. Twice. It's not his fault that he finally listened.*

His distress must have shown on his face because Shina smiled and came over, his hair in a loose ponytail that draped across his shoulder. Bashima reached for the tail and let it run through his fingers like a red wave.

Shina took something from his pocket and held it out to the Sun God, a small box. He said, "I want you to hold onto this for me. Give it to me when I come back."

Bashima opened the box, and a gleaming dragon pin stared back at him, his own godly symbol emblazoned with the majestic beast. Kuroi's gift. His hand shook, so he closed the box with a click and put it behind his back.

"I suppose you should go," he mumbled. "It's a long journey."

"Not that long," Shina said, rubbing his arm, unsure what to do. They stood, awkward, waiting for each other to make the next move. Kuroi cleared his throat behind them, and Shina started to speak then stopped, suddenly without words.

"You wouldn't stop blathering all the way down the mountain; now, you're tongue-tied?" Bashima said, growling. That broke the redhead's stupor, and he laughed.

"I will be back," Shina said, eyes filled with mirth, all awkwardness gone. He was both the naive boy who'd spit at a god's feet and a man choosing his own way. Bashima bit the inside of his cheek, and Shina said, "Don't worry."

"I'm not worried," Bashima spit back, crossing his arms.

"Well, then don't wait up for me." Shina winked at him, grinning. Bashima looked away. The redhead's smile was too tempting. Bashima might make him stay.

Shina stepped closer and cupped Bashima's face, making the god meet his eyes.

"I'm coming back," he said, enunciating each word. Then he bent forward and caught the god's lips with his own. Before Bashima could wrap his arms around the redhead, Shina pulled away, determined expression on his face. He looked so much like Dain that Bashima took a step back, but then his silly sharp-toothed grin returned, and it was all Shina.

"I won't say goodbye, because that's not what this is," he said and looked behind Bashima at Kuroi. "Make sure he doesn't burn the place down while I'm gone."

Light flew across Bashima's skin, affronted that Shina thought he couldn't control himself.

Kuroi said, "Not on my watch, Master Shina."

He would ride Ichigo for the first few miles, getting far into the forest before stopping for the night, so Shina mounted up and patted the horse's neck. She reached around and nibbled his leg with affection, then shook her head. They were ready to go. Shina turned in the saddle and waved at them, face shining with potential.

Bashima didn't move until the cart was past the treeline, then he stumbled and nearly fell. Kuroi was at his side in an instant though he didn't try to touch the god. But he was there.

"This is ridiculous," Bashima said, clutching his chest. "He said he's coming back, so he will."

"Indeed," said Kuroi, standing tall beside Bashima.

"I know what you're thinking, Kuroi," said Bashima, huffing. "I can sense another smug remark coming."

"Master Bashima, it's almost as if you know me," Kuroi said, smiling. "It's been a long time since I had to convince you to go into that dining room for your first dinner with him."

"Yeah, that turned out really well," Bashima said, chuckling. He turned toward the mountain, grasped Kuroi's arm, and shifted them to the top. From the temple's summit, Bashima could see much more of the forest that claimed Shina. He imagined the redhead riding down the path, heading to the river, following it to his village. To his home. When faced with his home, would he be able to turn back?

"Kuroi," he said, and the god-touched man stopped. He'd been turned toward the temple, most likely thinking of the list of items that needed attending to. Bashima needed to talk to someone, and Kuroi knew him best. Had known Dain best.

"Shina…his face. It's replacing Dain's in my dreams."

He stopped and surveyed the valley, imaging riding across it with Shina at full speed, the intense joy that made him almost forget that Dain ever existed. "How did I let this happen? He was supposed to be an amusement. That's it. How would Dain feel that I let someone usurp his place? I've betrayed him."

"You knew Dain better than that," said Kuroi, frustrated but understanding. "Caring for someone else doesn't diminish the love you felt for him. In fact, it makes your world better, makes *our* world better. Just look what Shina has done for this temple. For you. You're *outside*, Bashima."

He touched Bashima on the shoulder and squeezed. "Dain wouldn't hold your feelings against you for all the lifetimes of this world."

"I'm afraid, Kuroi," Bashima admitted. He had to tell someone. "I loved Dain more than anything, and his death nearly destroyed me. But this…if Shina doesn't come back…it feels like I might die."

The Forest God's words about soul bonds and Maida's suggestion echoed in his mind, and a warm wind blew across the mountain, rustling the Sun God's hair and carrying his dread across the valley.

You didn't make a huge mistake, Alaric told himself. Then why did he feel so awful? He put on a brave face when leaving, wanting nothing more than to bury the Sun God in never-ending kisses. He needed to go though. His parents waited long enough. His village might be holding out hope for his return.

He settled Ichigo into a steady walk, not wanting to tire her. They would stop for the night around the same place from their journey to the mountain, then finish the trip the next day. He imagined how wonderful it would be to see his parents, but Bashima always found his way back into Alaric's thoughts, orange eyes pleading for him not to leave. It felt like a thin cord connected them, and now they were stretching that cord, testing its limits.

Ichigo neighed and tossed her head.

"I know, girl. I'm sorry. I'll make sure you come back with me. Mother probably bought a new horse already, so she won't need you to help anymore."

Ichigo snorted as if any horse could ever replace her. Alaric sighed and patted her neck. He said, "We'll only be gone a few days, a week at most. Once they know I'm safe, it will be okay. I can always visit them. It's not that long a journey."

The forest was quiet around them, only the occasional rustling from the underbrush or birds chirping. Alaric didn't mind. It was peaceful—how he imagined Cypress's temple might be. He smiled, thinking he would meet the Forest God and Oken again, looking forward to seeing them and hearing more colorful commentary from the demigod. He chuckled and looked ahead on the path.

"Yup, Ichigo. It won't take too long. Then I can go back to him."

Alaric heard a sharp crack, Ichigo crying out in panic, then everything went black.

Chapter Fourteen

A briny breeze floated in off a nearby sea, and Alaric thought of Bashima and smiled. He could almost taste the salt on his lips, sand beneath his feet, seabirds calling in the distance. Was he already back? Had they gone to a beach and fallen asleep as the waves crashed against the shore?

"This was a great idea," he murmured and tried to reach out, thinking Bashima was beside him. But his arm wouldn't move. Something cut into his wrist, restraining him. Alaric's eyes opened in alarm.

He heard waves breaking upon something, but he couldn't see them. He couldn't see anything. He was blindfolded, and his arms, legs, and chest were immobilized. He tried to move, thrashing around, but he couldn't budge an inch. He tried to control his breathing, but his heart beat a terrified rhythm in his chest, making him anxious.

What was going on?

He had been on Ichigo's back, heading to his village. There was a strange sound, then Ichigo panicked, then nothing. He wanted to yell out, but something stopped him. He didn't want to alert whoever tied him up. How could he get out of the restraints? Whatever tied him down felt cold and sturdy on his wrists and ankles when he flexed.

And the smell. He was near a sea or ocean; no fresh water smelled like that. There was no ocean near Bashima's temple or his village.

It was going to be okay. This was obviously a mistake. Maybe he'd been caught in a hunter's snare, and they'd found him and overreacted. There were plenty of paranoid loners living in the forest. No there weren't. Maybe a person could come across a hermit in the woods, but those people kept to themselves. They didn't catch unsuspecting men on well-trod paths and tie them up…

He didn't hear anyone approaching, but a cold finger traced its way down his bare torso, and Alaric jumped, yelping.

"Oh, good you're awake. You've been out for quite some time."

That voice. It sounded welcoming but chilly, like a party host greeting his guests, wanting them to leave as soon as possible. Alaric's eyes roved underneath the blindfold, but he saw only darkness.

His taste hasn't changed…

"Chronas," Alaric said, trying to keep his voice steady.

"Splendid!" The god clapped his hands, happy Alaric came to the right conclusion. "I was afraid we'd have to go through a long-winded introduction."

"What's going on?" Alaric asked, putting weight behind his question. He was in big trouble. A god had him trapped without sight, and Alaric had no idea why. Why did the gods do anything?

"I wanted to have a little chat and make you an offer of sorts," Chronas said, nonchalant. He'd moved across the room, so Alaric's head went automatically toward the sound, disoriented.

"About what?" Alaric asked. He needed to keep the god talking; of that he was certain. This had to be some kind of prank. According to Matthias, the gods were always coming up with elaborate schemes, messing around with humans. And with each other.

Oh shit, he thought. *This is about Bashima.*

Why else would the God of Time kidnap him? Chronas didn't care about random humans. He was trying to get the Sun God's attention by taking something that belonged to him. But why? Matthias's reminder that no god was safe reverberated through Alaric's mind.

Chronas chuckled, and it felt like being doused with freezing water. He said, "You are a remarkable specimen, I must admit."

He was at Alaric's side again, like a flash, running his hands over Alaric's cheek and chin. It felt like spiders trickling across his face, and Alaric flinched away. Chronas clicked his tongue. "You might as well get used to my touch, human."

"You don't know what you're doing," Alaric warned though he knew a threat was pointless. He had no chance against a god. Keep him talking. Keep him talking. "Bashima will find out I didn't make it to my village. He'll come for me."

"That's what I'm counting on," said the Time God, scoffing. "However, you seem to be under the impression that he'll come because he cares about you."

Alaric swallowed hard.

He doesn't know anything about you, he told himself. *He doesn't know anything about Bashima. He's trying to get under your skin.*

"You have no idea what you're talking about," Alaric said, voice hard.

"I've known the Sun God much longer than you," Chronas said, then he put on a whiny high-pitched voice, "'Bashima, Bashima'…disgusting. It's all you said in your unconscious state. Pathetic. It's almost like you believe he loves you."

Alaric didn't respond, but he felt goosebumps and a red flush creep across his skin.

"Oh. You do. That's adorable," said Chronas.

The blindfold was ripped from Alaric's eyes, and bright white light assaulted him, making him blink rapidly. Where was the god?

"You might not know this," Chronas said, and Alaric searched for him, turning his head, looking around. The voice came from out of his eye line, and he cursed. The god was playing with him. Chronas went on, "but gods have ways of inflicting permanent damage on each other. Each of us wields incredible power, and we're capable of terrible things. Pain beyond imagining, injuries that even *we* can't recover from. Of course, we'd still be alive, but what a way to live. Debilitated, crippled, forever staring into the void of existence and not being able to act."

He paused, and Alaric heard him moving closer. "It's truly awful what we can do to each other. Just ask the *former* Sun God."

Chronas was upon him, leaning over him, gray eyes a storm. The Time God was terrifying in his beauty: cheekbones sharp, nose inches from Alaric's face, eyes empty. Bright blue light came from his palm, and an elegant dagger emerged from it, materializing from his skin. He twirled it in his hand, and Alaric knew there was no escape. The god didn't mean for him to leave at least not intact.

Moving faster than Alaric could perceive, the god drew the dagger's point down Alaric's arm, searing into the bicep. Alaric lurched but held back a shout. The dagger burned with blue flames, savoring his blood, which reddened the blade. The dagger sucked up Alaric's blood, changing back to pure blue.

Alaric's breathing increased in speed, and he glared at the god. "He might not love me, but he will come."

"Are you hard of hearing? Or just stupid?" Chronas asked, spinning the dagger in his hand. "I hope he does come. He deserves the beating I'm going to give him. Maybe he'll be so injured that the sun itself will fall from the sky. Can you imagine?"

Could that happen? Kuroi talked about the accidental eclipse when Dain died, so Alaric knew Bashima lost control once. What if Bashima came after Alaric and the Time God surprised him? Was it possible that the Time God could defeat the Sun God?

"You have such pretty eyes," Chronas said. He lingered over Alaric, and the dagger tipped toward Alaric's face, tip landing on his cheek right below his eye. It burned. "Should I remove one of them and send it to the Sun God? Entice him a little? He'd be in such a rage that I dared touch one of his possessions. He'd come barreling in here without thinking. A shame, really. And all for you, a lowly human."

Chronas pulled the blade away and shrugged. "I suppose it would give you some infamy, the human who helped bring down the Sun God."

"Stop," Alaric said, unwilling to imagine Bashima hurt because of him. If there was a way to stop that from happening, he had to do it. He wouldn't be the one to end the Sun God. He didn't mean enough for that. "What do you want?"

"You can be reasoned with," Chronas said. "Excellent. That saves me a lot of time and energy."

He pushed on whatever Alaric was tied to, a table of some kind, and Alaric was whipped up into a standing position. Reeling from the sudden movement, Alaric held in a gasp. His head fell forward, but the Time God pushed it back, pressing on his forehead. "It's very simple. You pledge yourself to me, and I leave the Sun God alone. He'll be annoyed, of course, but he'll get over it. And he'll be safe." The god's smile could cut glass.

Alaric knew where this was going, and his body shrieked against it, telling him not to go through with it, no matter what. But his mind was clear. What was his life compared to Bashima's? He controlled the sun. What would happen to the world if he lost that control even for a moment? What would happen to Alaric's parents? Or the people at the Temple of the Sun? No, Alaric couldn't put them at risk. If all it took was him giving up his future, he'd do it every time.

"What do you need me to do?" he asked, resigned.

The god snapped his fingers, and the cuffs binding Alaric to the table released, and he fell to the floor on his hands and knees. He gritted his teeth and looked up at the god, glaring, eyes aflame.

"There's so much fight in you," Chronas said. "I'm going to enjoy breaking you of that."

Someone came into the bright room, either a shade or a god-touched, expression blank, eyes empty. He shuffled over to the Time God, holding a steaming goblet. Chronas took the goblet, and the servant disappeared, shifting away. He held up the goblet to his nose and sniffed, savoring.

"I'm sure you know what this is," the god said, sneering. "I'm told it tastes awful for the human, but it smells divine." He held the goblet out to Alaric, eyebrow arched. "Let's see how far you're willing to go for your god."

Alaric thought about making Chronas promise not to involve Bashima after he'd taken the potion, but that was ridiculous; the god would break his word as soon as blink. Alaric could ask for a million promises, and it might not make a difference, but he had to try.

"Swear that you won't hurt Bashima."

The Time God shrugged, saying, "I swear not to hurt the Sun God."

Alaric took the goblet and drained it, trying not to choke. The liquid was thick and unpleasant, smelling metallic and tasting vile. It was bright gold in color and shined in the white light, the god's blood mixed with whatever else made the god-touched potion. Alaric's eyes watered, but he held in the tears. He needed to do this. Bashima would be safe, and Alaric would still be alive. Not the outcome he wanted, but he would try and make the Sun God understand.

When he finished the potion, Alaric gagged and lowered his head to the floor, trying to keep it down. His entire body shuddered, filling with power as the god's blood flowed through him, but it was borrowed power and felt alien in his skin and blood, pounding at his nerves. It was infinitely worse than what he'd experienced consuming Bashima's cum. This felt like he might be ripped apart from the inside out.

The whole time Alaric's body writhed, the Time God laughed.

Once Alaric collapsed onto his stomach, the energy coursing through him making him feel equally powerful and powerless, Chronas knelt beside him.

The god said, "Hurts, doesn't it? I sure hope so. But you're not done yet." He straddled Alaric, crouching over his hips and Alaric heard the dagger's flames roar to life. The branding. He braced himself for the dagger to pierce his skin, but the god instead reached out and ran his hand over Alaric's shoulder, across his tattoo.

Please, no, Alaric thought.

"You really are such a fool," the god said, laughing. "Nice tattoo. You think you're a dragon, boy from Togarashi? Let's see if you can handle a little fire."

The dagger's point touched Alaric's shoulder, and he bit his lip, drawing blood. The god pressed down slightly, and Alaric saw smoke from the corner of his eye.

"My sword would be quicker, and much less painful for you, but let's make this last."

Alaric held in the scream until he smelled his skin burning.

Bashima snapped awake.

"KUROI!" he yelled, vaulting from bed. His back felt like it was burning, which normally wouldn't cause him pain, yet it cut straight through his body, doubling him over on the floor. He reached over his shoulders, trying to see what caused the agonizing sensation, and let out a string of curses. There was nothing. His skin felt normal, yet the pain continued, raking up and down his back as though he were being whipped.

"FUCK! KUROI!"

"Master Bashima!" Kuroi ran into the bedroom, eyes wide, "What's happening?"

"Don't...know...hurts...my back," Bashima bit out, curling up into a fetal position. "What...is...it?"

Kuroi raced to his side and looked, saying, "There's nothing on your back!"

As suddenly as it began, the pain vanished, leaving behind a phantom burning. Bashima breathed hard and jumped to his feet. Kuroi's shocked expression would have been amusing if the feeling hadn't been there like something was flaying the skin off his back—hungry fire.

"I've never felt anything like that," Bashima said, panting. "I've overheated before, but that was nothing compared to this."

"Would you like me to get the healer?" Kuroi asked, concern radiating off him. He wasn't regulating his emotions, so Bashima felt every inch of his fear and anxiety. He felt it...just like he could feel...

"Shina."

"Master? He's not here, remember? He left early this morning."

"No, something's wrong with Shina. The way it cut off just now. It was like the pain disappeared completely, like he blacked out."

"You're not making sense, Master," Kuroi said, touching his shoulder. Bashima flinched away. Kuroi put his barrier back up, and even though he knew the man was trying to be helpful, Bashima needed Kuroi to listen.

"I need to find him. I can shift my way to his village. It's close enough so you wouldn't have to go with me. I need to make sure he's okay."

"Is that necessary?" Kuroi asked. "I know you share a connection with him, but it was just a dream, a nightmare."

"Since when does a nightmare keep going when you wake up?" Bashima shouted, and Kuroi took a step back. "I'm sorry, but I wasn't dreaming. This is real. Kuroi, listen to me. Send for Tengu."

"Master Cypress?" Kuroi looked dazed as though worried Bashima had gone insane.

"I know how I sound, but I'm not wrong," Bashima said. He went to his new wardrobe and pulled out his battle armor, something he hadn't needed in thousands of years. Kuroi sputtered behind him. Bashima's eyes flashed, and he said, "Kuroi! Go!"

Before Kuroi could shift away, Draiden appeared in the sitting room and called for Bashima, frightened. "Master Bashima! Something just arrived for you. The message shifted right into my study, priority." He sounded like he might be sick.

Draiden stumbled into the bedroom, face pale, clutching something in his shaking hands. Bashima didn't want to look at it. There was no way Shina already reached his village; this couldn't be good news. Kuroi stepped forward and grabbed the maroon-stained rolled parchment, and when he opened it, something fell out and hit the floor. All three of them stared down at the shredded purple cloth, which was covered in blood and wrapped around a length of red hair.

"Read it," Bashima said, voice like thunder. Draiden and Kuroi looked at each other before Kuroi read:

Greetings, Bashima, God of the Sun, Keeper of the Day, and whatever other honorifics you prefer. I cordially invite you to my new temple for your inaugural visit. Really, I can't believe you've never been here. It's a shame. It's quite stunning. Nothing to compare to your palace in the sky but I'm sure you'll enjoy your stay. Why, just this morning, I invited a young guest to stay, whom you may know. He really is delightful, full of sparkling conversation and wit. But, oh, so fragile, the silly thing, cut himself on the way here. He was asking for you so ardently, I couldn't refuse. Won't you please make haste so we might partake in some of his sterling anecdotes?

Most sincerely, Chronas, God of Time, Lord of Order

"Master Bashima," Draiden said, but Kuroi grasped the man's arm and squeezed.

Bashima had almost forgotten they were in the room. His power roiled over his skin in a dazzling haze of color, illuminating the two god-touched men who stood motionless in front of him. He wanted to release the power and obliterate everything in sight, to bring the temple down around him. He felt a shriek filling his lungs. With one yell, he could rip the temple from the mountain and send them all crashing down to the valley.

Draiden's eyes pleaded with Bashima, and Kuroi whispered something, filling the room with his calming energy, letting it seep into Bashima's mind through their bond. Bashima didn't want to feel calm. He wanted everything to be over, and he sent that emotion back to Kuroi whose limitless eyes filled with tears from the force of Bashima's fear.

I know, came a thought from Kuroi, *but then how can you save him?*

Bashima hit his knees, choking back the screams, and Kuroi and Draiden knelt beside him, released from his perilous rage.

"Draiden," Kuroi said. "Send for Master Cypress immediately. Alert everyone. No one is close enough to assist swiftly, but King Vaultus needs to know what's happened. This is a breach of godly boundaries of the highest order. Tell none of the shades what has happened, but Shefu will have felt this surge. Go to her after you send the messages. The gods can mobilize."

"I'm going now," Bashima rasped, throat sore.

"Master, at least wait for the Forest God," Kuroi pleaded as Draiden spun on the spot and shifted away. "You'll need help against Chronas."

"I won't need any help to knock that asshole into the fucking sun."

"Don't lose control," Kuroi warned, but he could tell that the Sun God was already pulling away from him, "Bashima, listen to me. Khresh!"

Bashima's attention flashed to the god-touched man, and his anger flared. Kuroi dared speak that name.

"Chronas is a trickster," Kuroi said. "This could be a ruse to lure you away from the temple. It could be a sick game meant to make you act against him. Think."

"I am thinking, Kuroi," Bashima said, voice low. "Whatever I felt earlier, Chronas was doing something to Shina. It felt like he was being whipped within an inch of his life. I'm going. *Now*."

Kuroi's face fell, but he nodded. "I'll assist with your armor," he said. "Approach with caution. We will send help as soon as we can." Bashima nodded and allowed Kuroi to help him into his armor.

Kuroi was right, of course. That fucking prick Time God could be planning anything just to piss Bashima off. But this wasn't the usual game the gods played. Chronas meant to get an instant reaction with the letter and what it contained. Every moment Bashima blinked before shifting, the length of red hair fell to the ground before his eyes, and he fought to breathe. Shina's blood drenching the purple fabric.

He made himself slow down and not shift too far at once. He'd do Shina no good showing up exhausted from a stupid mistake, but he was coming for the redhead. He hoped Shina knew he would come for him.

I didn't say enough to him before he left, Bashima thought on his final shift. *I should have made him take an escort.*

Not that it would have helped against a renegade god.

Bashima only had a vague idea why the Time God would harbor enough poisonous resentment to act so rashly. Why antagonize the Sun God? Because Chronas wanted his job? That didn't seem like a good enough reason to Bashima, but he knew how petty gods could be especially if they felt slighted and had centuries to fixate on it.

At the summit, Chronas accused Bashima of ignoring his duties because of Shina. To get a feel for how important the redhead was to Bashima? Probably. When had Bashima given it away?

He emerged to the sound of waves hitting a cliff-side, a massive black sea churning with whitecaps. The wind darted through him, chilly and uncaring. He flexed his hands and color flew across his body, a rainbow on the dreary sea landscape. He felt a slight pull from his three god-touched, but the temple was close enough for him to push the sensations away. He hoped they were all right, but he couldn't focus on that now.

The temple was impressive, made of gleaming white marble veined with light blue. It was larger than the Temple of the Sun, dominating the cliff it was built into, perched halfway up the cliff face. No ordinary person could reach the main entrance. You'd have to shift. Bashima sneered and did just that.

He hit the main step, and the doors swung open, revealing an odd-looking shade. The woman stared at him, eyes unblinking, hands at her sides. After a moment, she turned around and went further inside, walking along a corridor festooned with glimmering white candles. Unnerved, Bashima followed her, and the doors swung shut behind him with a quiet thud.

The shade led him down hallway after hallway, so Bashima lost his sense of direction quickly. He felt like she doubled back a few times as well, really disorienting him. Since he'd never been to the Time God's new temple, he didn't know what to expect and had no idea of the layout.

Kuroi encouraged caution, even as Bashima shifted away from the temple, begging him to wait for Tengu. That might not have been such a bad idea, but he couldn't wait. Shina was somewhere in the temple, and Bashima wasn't leaving without him.

They finally arrived at the destination, what must be Chronas's throne room. The shade opened the door and stood next to it, face impassive. Bashima wondered if she'd been ordered not to speak to him. She didn't follow him in.

The Time God's throne room was as impressive as the temple's exterior — all white marble, cold and magnificent, but devoid of feeling or emotion. It held no decorations, no emblems. Simple, clean, elegant, and barren.

"I hope you didn't mind my shade," came a voice from the far end of the room. "I've been doing…experiments with them, and their minds don't last long."

The Time God lounged on a high-backed throne made of the same blue-veined white marble. Bashima approached slowly, watching for an attack from the side, listening for an attack from the back. His armor was heavier than the ceremonial set he wore at the summit, and it would protect him from most attacks.

Chronas watched his approach with indifference, bored. His white-blue hair held back by a black crown covered in thin spikes, his cheeks hollow, eyes unfeeling. How had Bashima not noticed the monster that lurked beneath Chronas's courtly smiles? It was right there in front of him.

The Time God wore armor on his chest, legs, and arms, which glistened with swirling patterns of pearls and diamonds. If this wasn't going to end in a fight, Bashima wasn't sure why Chronas would bother with armor. He tensed and stopped walking, a good distance from Chronas. The Time God favored fighting with a sword and short dagger, Bashima recalled—an image of a blood-soaked battlefield in his memory—but the weapons were nowhere in sight.

Neither was Shina.

"You took something that belongs to me," Bashima said. "Return it to me, and I'll leave. If you're lucky, I'll forget the slight."

He had to keep up the ruse that Shina was nothing but a possession. Any god would strike against another if something of theirs was stolen. It was only natural. But to let an enemy know that thing's true value was foolish. The gods were greedy hoarders, not just of precious objects but also people. Some collected shades like they were rare delicacies. There were rumors that far to the west, one god kept a harem filled with human men and women, cycling them out when she pleased.

"Now, now Bashima," said Chronas, leaning back on the throne. "Why should I give up my treasured guest so easily? Perhaps he likes it better here than with you, trapped in that dingy temple all day and night. What a bore."

"What do you want?" Bashima asked, cutting through the bullshit though he doubted Chronas was finished with his little speeches. Now that he had a captive audience, it might be impossible to shut him up.

"Want? Who said I wanted anything?" Chronas looked at his nails.

"You've always wanted my job," Bashima said, lip curling. "But the king bestowed it upon me. Sorry about that, but I can't exactly give it to you."

Chronas laughed, "Oh, we're far past that, Bashima. However, did it even matter that I personally led the gods to Malrias when he was ascendant? Apparently not."

Bashima could feel tension mounting in the room, but he kept his eyes on the other god. He couldn't attack, not without reason. To do so was tantamount to treason. He had to be patient.

"Yeah, you did a great job, spying on the old Sun God for Vaultus," Bashima said. "And you're not too bad on the battlefield either. Not my fault Vaultus didn't pick you, so why are you making it my problem?"

Chronas's eyes flashed with blue light, but he regained his composure quickly.

"I suppose if I'd been a belligerent child, that would have secured me the position, but alas," the Time God said. He stood and walked to the edge of the dais, looking out at Bashima, eyebrow raised, hand on his chin. "You know, there is something I want."

"I'm glad we're getting to the fucking point," Bashima said. "I might fall asleep standing here."

Chronas smiled, but it didn't reach his eyes, and Bashima readied himself for an attack. The Time God clicked his tongue, scolding, and said, "I just want to see you suffer."

Chronas snapped his fingers, and Shina appeared to his left, suspended in the air behind a thin, shimmering barrier. He hung limp, head bowed and arms and legs drooping as though caught on a large hook. His hair fell in red spikes around his face, most of the length sawed off. His upper body covered in bruises and lacerations, dried blood on one of his arms, fresh blood nearly everywhere else. A few drops of blood were suspended in time with him, falling from his body.

Bashima wanted to eviscerate the Time God, unleash all his power, but he might hit Shina in a blast. There was no telling how strong Chronas made the barrier. He'd made Shina his shield.

"Not only have you stolen my property," Bashima seethed, "you've damaged it."

"He didn't, how do they say it, come quietly," Chronas said and flicked the barrier, which sent a ringing bell-like tone through the throne room. "And you can give up the charade. I know you feel *something* for him. You can barely contain your rage."

"Let him go, Chronas," Bashima said, taking a step forward.

"Stop right there, if you please," said Chronas, holding up a hand. "The game is about to get interesting, and I wouldn't want you to miss any of it."

The Time God snapped his fingers again, and another trapped figure appeared to his right. Bashima's breath caught in his throat, and he nearly doubled over.

The other figure frozen in time was Dain.

Chapter Fifteen

"How? Why?" Bashima sputtered, hands dropped, staring at the man he thought he'd never see again. His body shook from the shock; his mouth open in disbelief. "This is a trick," he said, anger growing. His palms flashed with small flames.

"I assure you, it's no trick," said Chronas, sighing. "Though it was difficult hiding his shade when you came calling, so distraught, begging for help, hoping you'd find his emaciated body in the Locker."

"Why would you do this?" Bashima asked, utterly shocked. No god had ever overstepped so far.

Dain looked exactly like he had the day he died. Dressed in an open-collared black tunic and black leggings, his hair for once not in the trademark forward spikes. His body was thinner, but his large build remained intact. No disease could diminish sheer height. Crimson eyes stared out at the room, and Bashima hoped Dain wasn't watching, wasn't able to see.

"*Why?*" Chronas asked, offended. "Why should you have everything you desire, Sun God? Why should someone so caustic, so detestable, get not only the power of the sun but also find the person they're meant to be with? Because that's what he was, right? Your *true love?*"

The Time God's eyes crackled with blue energy, and his hands shone.

"But what is poor Dain supposed to believe when you show up here, pining for that *replacement?*"

The god pointed at Shina who writhed within his time prison, head thrown back, eyes finally open, wide and terrified. Bashima didn't think the redhead could see out of the prison, but even if he could, he doubted Shina could focus past whatever pain the Time God inflicted. Shina stopped moving and slumped down again, chin resting on his chest.

"Stop this, Chronas. The king will—"

"Will what?" Chronas hissed. "What are the lives of two humans to the King of the Gods? As if he has the strength to fight me anyway."

Bashima blanched. Chronas knew. How much, Bashima couldn't be sure. Either way, it didn't matter now. It would take far too long for Vaultus or anyone else to reach the Temple of Time to stop Chronas's demented show. He clenched his fists and stood tall.

"Let them go."

"I don't think so," Chronas said and smiled, teeth gleaming. "I think I'll make you choose. Which one do you want? And don't take all day moaning about how it's not fair and how I'm an evil piece of shit. I could destroy them both right now with a flick of my wrist."

Bashima looked from Dain to Shina. What was he supposed to do? Chronas made a tick-tock sound and wagged a finger.

"Is it really that difficult? Which human means more to you? Your perfect mate or the handsome village boy?"

Bashima felt like a spear had been driven through him. Chronas imprisoned Dain for two thousand years, waiting, watching, preparing for this moment. To torture him. And Bashima served up Shina on a silver platter, first showing him off at the summit then letting him leave the temple's safety. It was all his fault. He didn't know what to do.

What would happen to the man he didn't choose? Bashima didn't want to think about it, but he shuddered and pictured an eternity inside the Locker or expelled from existence entirely.

"Need a little help?" Chronas asked. "Why don't you have a heart-to-heart with the shade?"

He waved a hand, and the barrier disappeared from around Dain. He remained in the air, unable to move his body, but his eyes shined with determination. A broad smile flew across his lips, and he coughed hard, having not spoken for centuries.

"Khresh," he said, voice gravelly but urgent. "Don't listen to this son of a bitch."

"Dain," Bashima said, moving forward as though in a trance.

"No! Don't come any closer," Dain said, coughing harder. "This god is insane. He's not going to let any of us leave here; listen to me."

"You look exactly the same," Bashima said, and tears formed in his eyes. This wasn't a dream, repeating old arguments. Nor was his mind playing tricks on him. Dain was right there, right in front of him, talking to him. He kept inching forward.

"You never listened to a damned thing I said when I was alive! Hear me now!" Dain yelled, and Bashima stopped, surprised. Dain huffed, exhausted. Sweat dripped off his brow. "If you have to choose, don't be a damned fool. Pick the kid."

Bashima's eyes widened. For too long a moment, he'd forgotten Shina was even there. The redhead hung nearby, so close, and Bashima's heart ached.

"Dain," he said, "I can't do this."

"It's hard seeing you like this," Dain said, "You're so lonely, and don't tell me you're not. I know you. I can see it written all over your face."

The shade paused, considering what to say, perhaps wondering how much the Time God would let him say.

"I've pictured only your face the entire time I've been stuck in this hell. I will always love you, Khresh. But you need to choose him. He's alive. He can give you everything you need. I'm already gone, and I lived a fantastic life."

The shade's head turned, and he glared at the Time God, furious. He said, "Don't let this sorry excuse for a god lead you around by the dick." He looked back at Bashima, eyes ablaze. "Fight for him."

Chronas rolled his eyes and threw the barrier back up, silencing Dain. Bashima let out an anguished breath and lurched forward, but Chronas sent up a barrier in his way with a snap of his fingers, throwing Bashima back. He snarled and let fire spears free of his hands, sending them at the barrier, to little effect.

"Such a temper is unbecoming of the Sun God," Chronas said, dropping the barrier when Bashima stopped attacking. "I'm becoming bored with you. Your time is up. Choose."

Bashima looked from Dain to Shina and bit back a sob. He knew what he had to do, but that didn't make it easier. He hated when Dain was right.

He pointed at Shina and whispered goodbye to Dain, who smiled, happy with Bashima's choice.

Chronas snorted, then snapped his fingers again. Dain's shade body erupted in blue flames inside the barrier, and Bashima screamed and hit his knees.

As Dain dissolved into nothingness, Chronas laughed, holding his stomach, face contorted.

"This isn't how I thought this would go at all!" Chronas said, wiping his eyes, teeth flashing. "You chose that?" he asked and pointed at Shina, floating beside him. "That human you barely know over your supposed truest love? So much for two thousand years of mourning, thrown away on some insignificant whelp. Bashima, the reclusive Sun God, who wouldn't come out of his temple because his love was taken away. May he curse the heavens and the hells a billion times that he lost the only person who accepted him for what he is."

Chronas descended the stairs leading up to the throne but stayed at the bottom, mocking eyes gleaming.

"You really are the biggest fool. You made the wrong choice. I might have let you leave with the shade. Old *Dain* had me wrong there, and I'm a little offended by that, but it doesn't matter. He's long gone now."

Chronas waved his hand, and Shina spun around within his barrier. His back was as heavily bruised as his chest, but what caught Bashima's attention almost made him vomit. A massive silvery symbol was scorched into Shina's entire back, flaying his skin. The mark of the God of Time.

"No," Bashima said.

"This is too rich, Bashima," Chronas said, voice sly. "You should see your poor face. It almost makes me feel sorry for you."

Chronas brought Shina down from the dais with a snap and faced him forward. Bashima could see every scratch, cut, and bruise.

"It's a shame he fought the branding," Chronas said. "He wouldn't look so dreadful. My god-touched may have gone a little overboard on the beating, but he'll heal up just fine and then..." the Time God scraped his fingernails down the barrier. "I'm going to enjoy every inch of him."

Bashima flung himself at the Time God, but Chronas was too quick and extended another wall, tossing Bashima backwards. He flipped and landed on his hands and feet, flaming light streaming from his body.

"Come now, I didn't have to force this on him. As you know, the human has to be a willing participant, otherwise the binding doesn't take." Chronas looked Shina over and added, "Let's have it from the human's mouth, shall we?"

He released Shina, who fell to the ground onto his side. His eyes ringed with dark circles, pleading.

"I'm so sorry," Shina groaned and tried to stand. His legs wouldn't support him, and Shina hit the floor again. "He told me he would hurt you if I didn't. I'm sorry, Bashima. Please forgive me." Tears rained down his face, washing some of the blood and dirt away.

"Oh, you'll see that I've succeeded in that, slave. Come here, *now.*"

Shina was dragged to his feet by an invisible hand, forced to kneel at Chronas's side. Bashima looked on in horror. This wasn't what the bond was for—this brutality. What could he do against a god-touched bond if Shina agreed to it? How could Shina go through with it? Chronas must have scared him into it with more than threatening the Sun God...but Bashima didn't think so. That was all it took. He could see it in Shina's devastated face.

"I think he'll fit right in here," Chronas said. He looked down at Shina with disdain. "With the brand, you don't need a leash, but maybe we'll start a trend."

The Time God lashed out and grabbed Shina's chest chain, pulling him up to his feet, and Shina grasped the god's arm, trying to stay upright, straining with pain. "My slave won't need this anymore," Chronas said, tugging the chain, making Shina whimper. "How about it Bashima? Need a souvenir?"

Bashima watched Shina's eyes light up with hatred and knew what was going to happen.

"No! Shina!"

The redhead flung his head back then wrenched it forward and spat right in the Time God's face.

Chronas recoiled, hissing, and grabbed Shina by the throat with his other hand. He threw the redhead across the throne room, Shina's back crunching against a marble pillar. He didn't move from where he fell.

"Shina!" Bashima shouted and blasted across the room, landing next to him. He touched Shina's face, opened his eyelids and didn't see a reaction. Bashima felt for a pulse and found one, but it was distant and faint. There was no way his back wasn't shattered.

"No no no no no, Shina! Wake up! Please wake up." He brushed mangled red hair out of Shina's face, willing him to open his eyes and apologize for the hundredth time. "You've got to open your eyes, idiot. I left the temple, just to come here and get your dumb ass. I left to come for you."

Bashima wanted to pull the redhead into his lap but was afraid it would damage his spine further. What could he do? He was no healer; he was just good at destroying things and ordering the sun around.

"I don't need to be in the temple; I just need to be with you. I heard you before you left when you thought I was sleeping. I want you with me, not just sometimes or when it's convenient."

He sobbed quietly, letting the tears come. Nothing mattered anymore if Shina wasn't with him. It felt like his soul was cracking down the center.

"Please don't leave me. I'm no good alone. You saw me at my absolute worst. You know I can't do this alone."

Bashima wished he could harness every ounce of his power and give it to Shina, fill him with so much sunlight that he couldn't fade away if he tried.

You idiot, Bashima admonished himself, *Shina is the sun. He doesn't need you to shine.*

"Alaric," he whispered, "I...I love you."

Alaric dreamed he was dying.

265

He was on the ground, curled up in a ball, and everything was pain. He smelled a distant sea and heard waves crashing, threatening. But he wasn't afraid of the water anymore. He wasn't afraid of anything. Even though his entire body ached with a long-remembered agony, he felt peace. Would it be so bad if he died? He would be missed, but he'd done so much in a short time. It was worth it.

Dying seemed better than the alternative. If he lived, he was tied to Chronas forever, or until the god grew disinterested and killed him. That was inevitable. He'd seen it. He'd experienced every form of physical pain possible as the god seared his skin, taking his tattoo with a few nasty strokes of the flaming dagger, as Chronas's god-touched kicked him within an inch of his life.

What good was holding on if all he had to look forward to was violation and degradation. He'd seen the hunger burning in Chronas's eyes after the branding was complete, and Alaric lashed out with all his strength. He might have to obey, but he could still fight.

No, he didn't think he wanted to fight anymore.

It was so calm here in the pain.

He heard whispers off in the dark and wished whoever was speaking would stop.

"Be quiet," he said, annoyed. "Everything hurts...part of me wants to let go...and I'm all alone."

The whispers stopped, but Alaric felt a great wind buffet his face, and he opened his eyes. Before him was a great red and gold dragon. Its eyes were like massive rubies, burning with golden highlights. He had sharp silver teeth and smoke streamed from his mouth, but no fire came. Alaric silently thanked the dragon for that. He'd had enough of fire.

"You are not alone," the dragon said, his voice old as the universe. "We are here with you."

"Oh, hello," Alaric said, tired. "I think I'm dying."

The dragon hummed and floated above him, looking down. "You are and you are not."

"That doesn't make sense," Alaric said and closed his eyes. Dragons. Always talking in riddles. He vaguely recalled seeing this beast from another dream. What had it said then?

"You have a choice to make, much like the last time we spoke," the dragon said. "Your human side is gone. The God of Time saw to that. You could let go and let your god-touched body die. Or, you could become infinitely more."

Alaric sighed and reopened his eyes. He could at least be polite. It was nice of the dragon to talk to him as he died.

"I'm sorry, but I don't know what you mean." His body spasmed and Alaric clenched his teeth, biting his lip and drawing blood. "I feel like I'm on fire. It hurts so much."

"I know," the dragon rumbled, voice kind. "You possess a mighty heart, Blood of the Dragon. If you so choose, you may live and become one of us."

"I don't understand," Alaric said. "Riddles. Always riddles."

"We will be with you, Alaric Shina, whatever you choose. The pain will not last long either way. But you must choose now."

"What am I choosing? Please, help me understand."

"Child, there isn't time to explain everything," the dragon said, sympathetic. "Your light is fading."

"Fading..." Alaric said. "Bashima...I can feel him, suffering. He needs me."

The dragon spun in the air, thoughtful. He said, "Mmmmmm your soul bond is strong, but don't return only to claim it. You must do this for yourself. Things will change for you if you arise a son of the dragons. It won't be easy to walk in the world."

"I don't care about that. I can be whatever; it wouldn't matter to him, and it doesn't matter to me. I'll still be me."

The pain intensified, and Alaric thought he might have been stabbed.

"The Time God lied, broke his damn promise." He heaved with the fresh pain in his side. "Bashima needs me. I won't leave him. I have to live."

The chorus of whispers rose in volume, shouting at Alaric, joyful. The dragon winked at him and flew away into the darkness.

Alaric began a chant in his head: *unbreakable, unbreakable, unbreakable.*

"He's not dead," Chronas said. "Well, not yet. I may have thrown him harder than I intended. But can you blame me? Filth dared defile me."

Bashima sat next to Shina's fallen form, holding his hand, crying freely. He could feel the redhead fading away from him, immune to anything Bashima said or wished for. He heard Chronas, like a muffled foghorn somewhere behind him. This was all his fault.

"You motherfucker," Bashima said, putting Shina's hand on his bruised chest. Bashima stroked Shina's cheek, tracing a line of freckles.

"I don't know why you're so hung up on this human," Chronas said, as though he were having a normal conversation with a friend who needed relationship advice. "At least the architect was someone. That boy isn't even close to your equal."

"He's more than my equal," Bashima said and stood, skin glowing. "He's better than me in every way, and if you think I'm letting you keep him, you're fucking mistaken."

"I think Lord Veles is closer to keeping him than you or me," Chronas said, smirking.

Bashima screamed, realizing how damn Tengu must have felt seeing the Fire God attack Oken. It was like an explosion was tearing his body apart, down to the very core of his being. A surge of power went through him, and Bashima launched at the Time God, a dazzling light-trail following him. The Time God tossed up a barrier, but Bashima crashed through, making Chronas's eyes widen.

The Time God's hands were blurs, bringing up shimmering walls only for Bashima to destroy them, his hands creating massive fiery explosions. They danced around the throne room, Chronas retreating from the kamikaze Sun God, his face set in concentration. Bashima knew neither of them had needed to fight in a long time. Both were rusty, but Chronas thought about the Sun God for eons, so his defenses were quick and sharp. And Bashima was tiring. The power boost he'd gotten would give out eventually, just like when Tengu fought Cindras. He needed to end this fast, get Chronas down so he could grab Shina and escape.

He moved in closer, firing off more blasts, not realizing what Chronas was doing.

Just as he went in to strike at Chronas's body, the Time God's hand glowed, and a long, flaming blue sword emerged from the palm. Bashima dodged the sword, grinning.

Nice try, God of Time.

Then he felt a blazing pain in his abdomen and looked down. Chronas had jabbed a short blue dagger into his side where the armor had a small opening, a triumphant smile plastered on his face. Bashima blew out a gust of air and shoved the Time God back, but the dagger stayed in his side, and he crumpled, hitting the floor with a wheeze.

Chronas walked over slowly as Bashima coughed and tried to pull the dagger out, to no avail.

"That won't come out unless I tell it to," the Time God said, making a twisting motion with his hand. The dagger buried itself deeper, and Bashima clenched his teeth. The light dissipated across his skin.

"I never dreamed it would end this perfectly," Chronas said, mocking. He stood next to Bashima, sword in hand, and pointed the blade at the Sun God's throat. "I don't think I can sever your head completely, but I'd love to try."

Before the Time God could strike, a deafening roar filled the throne room, causing both gods to cover their ears. What in the seven hells could make a sound like that? Bashima's ears rang with the sound, threatening to split his head in two. Then, something rushed toward them, a red blur with flaming crimson eyes. Its speed was incredible, covering the throne room in a few bounds, and it went right for Chronas.

The Time God attempted more barriers, each more solid than the last, his face a twisted mire of hate and disbelief.

"You...what is this?" Chronas yelled as the monster struck each wall down, growling, drool spilling from its gaping maw.

Bashima struggled with the dagger in his side, sweat dripping down his forehead. Golden blood seeped from his wound, and he winced, swearing.

The thing stopped attacking Chronas, its head whipping toward Bashima.

Holy fucking hells, Bashima thought.

It was Shina. Taller than the human, this monster was covered in red shard-like scales that shimmered in the throne room's light. His normally sharp teeth jutted from his mouth like knives, and his fingers had transformed into intimidating claws. Even his hair and eyes were rock hard scales, like diamonds.

Bashima's savage grin lit up his eyes. "Holy shit!" he yelled. Shina must have taken that as an "I'm okay," because he redirected his attention to the Time God and bellowed again, which threw Chronas off his feet and sent him flying across the hall.

Shina was on him in an instant, clawing at the barriers Chronas put up as he backed away. He tried the same move on Shina he used on Bashima, keeping his blade hidden until the last moment. As Shina closed in, Chronas thrust the blue sword forward. It would have struck true…if it hadn't shattered on Shina's chest. The monster didn't hesitate. He tore into the Time God, who shrieked in pain.

Bashima watched in horrified fascination as the dagger fell from his side, no longer controlled by Chronas. The Time God might not survive an attack like that.

"Bashi!"

A familiar voice echoed through the hall, and Bashima saw green crackling lightning fly across the floor at Shina, who was blasted off his feet, away from Chronas. Another yellow blast followed Tengu's green, but Bashima didn't see what it did to Shina.

"Veles!" Tengu called.

"It's not working," came an exasperated voice. "It's immune!"

"Shit!" Tengu said. "I was afraid of that. Take care of Chronas, make sure he doesn't try anything. Bashi!"

Bashima had been paying attention to the Forest God and Veles. He didn't realize Shina hurtled toward him. Shina barreled into him, forcing him onto his back on the floor.

"Fuck!" Bashima said, trying to shield himself.

"MINE."

Bashima understood the word that came out of Shina's hardened mouth, but it sounded nothing like the redhead. This voice was ancient and pissed. Shina opened his jaws and bit Bashima where his neck met his shoulder. He did not bite lightly. Bashima struggled against the redhead, trying to push him away. That made Shina bite harder, and his teeth pierced the skin, gold blood running down Bashima's chest. Bashima felt an instant sense of euphoria. He thought he might be aroused…and he went limp.

I wanted to bite you…

"Fucking hells! Get it off him!" That was Alora, and Bashima was sort of glad to hear another friendly voice, even if Shina was currently chomping on him. Bashima saw multiple shadows nearing them, and Shina growled, savage and alert. "What is it?" Alora yelled.

"How the hells should I know?" That was Cabari. "Should I blast it again?" Yellow lightning arced over the ceiling.

"Wait!" Bashima yelled. "It's Shina!"

"You've got to be kidding me," came Alora again.

"What the hells happened?" Cabari asked, not defusing his lightning.

"Let me try something," Bashima said, wincing as Shina dug his teeth in a little farther.

"MINE," Shina grumbled again through his teeth, eyeing the nearby gods. His pupils were gone, irises blown crimson across his entire eyes. Here was what had lurked inside the redhead. He could bite Bashima in half.

"Yeah, fuck, I know. They know. Everyone knows," Bashima said. "I'm yours. I'm okay. Except that you're fucking tearing my neck off my body."

Shina didn't budge, his breath coming rapid and shallow. How the hells was Bashima supposed to make him let go. He relaxed his entire body, which Shina noticed. Bashima lay down, back flush to the floor, and Shina's mouth followed, still attached. Though the pressure was less.

"Hey, Red," Bashima said, and Shina's eye focused on him. Bashima reached up and touched Shina's hardened skin, tracing the scales with his fingers. "It's going to be okay. Just you and me here, all right?" Shina blinked as if he were thinking. Bashima found a soothing tone and said, "It's okay to let go."

Something clicked in Shina's brain, and he gently let go. Bashima sighed heavily and watched the hardened scales melt away into Shina's skin. His hair fell into loose tangles around his face, framing those massive eyes. Once the last scale was gone, Shina blinked, and a small light flared in his eyes, sending them back to normal.

He looked down at Bashima, surprised to see him, then looked at the bloody bite mark on Bashima's shoulder and touched his lips. His fingers came away with golden blood, and Shina gaped at Bashima, horrified with himself. The redhead fainted, dropping bodily onto the Sun God.

"Fuck," Bashima said. "You're fucking heavy."

Chapter Sixteen

Tengu examined Bashima, checking the stab wound from Chronas's dagger and Shina's jagged bite mark. The stab wound hurt like hells, but the bite mark's pain dimmed. It stopped bleeding too.

Shina lay nearby, out cold, body back to its usual size, Alora and Cabari watching him. They were enraged by how beat up Shina was; it seemed that his transformation didn't heal wounds completely, and Alora had to be held back from kicking Chronas's prone form. When they saw the massive brand on Shina's back, the other gods hissed and berated Bashima with questions.

After Veles told them to shut up and take care of Shina, Tengu asked Bashima a few pointed queries under his breath.

"What happened to him?" The Forest God asked, applying a temporary bandage to the bite and the wound in Bashima's side.

"To tell you the truth," Bashima said, "I have no idea. I thought he was dead. Or dying. Then, that thing, Shina, came out of nowhere. I was hoping you might know."

"I have a few ideas, but I'd need to do more research," the Forest God said.

"Dammit, Tengu, you better figure it out fast. What the hells am I supposed to do if it happens again? You saw what he did to Chronas."

"I doubt he'd do that to you," Tengu said, shrugging. "Or to anyone else unless they were threatening you. That's what set him off right?"

"I don't know," Bashima admitted. "I got fucking stabbed, and that's when he roared, almost made my ears bleed."

"Well, you'll have two new scars," said Tengu. "The one from Chronas's dagger might heal completely over time, but the bite…I doubt that will."

"Perfect," Bashima said, huffing. "I'm sure it will be a great conversation starter."

"Don't tell anyone what it is," the Forest God said sharply. His eyes glossed over with green light for a moment. "The only people who know are in this room, and that's where it should stay. Don't even tell Vaultus."

Bashima stared at the Forest God, eyebrow raised. "Okay. But do you really think the moron twins can keep their mouths shut?" He nodded toward Alora and Cabari.

"I do," Tengu said. "If you ask them, they won't tell a soul. You don't have to worry about Veles either, and Shako didn't see what happened."

"Fuck, you brought that asshole with you?" Bashima rubbed his eyes, wincing from the wound in his side.

"We weren't sure what we were walking into," Tengu admitted. "Luckily, he was in the Underworld visiting Jace. He's the only one keeping the Locker closed."

Bashima didn't like Shako, the demigod mimic, but he supposed it was a good idea. Shako could siphon off Chronas's abilities like poison from a wound and keep things in check for a time. It wouldn't be forever. Vaultus would need to appoint a new God of Time.

Veles kept watch over Chronas, whispering some alchemic incantation, but there was no way Chronas would be making trouble anytime soon.

"Mind if I interrupt," asked Veles, walking over. He looked even more exhausted than usual, eyes almost completely red from burst vessels. He crouched beside Tengu and Bashima and said, "We'll need to relieve Shako soon, check the Locker, make sure nothing got out. I'm not sure we got Shako in place in time."

The other two gods nodded at the ruler of the Underworld, and Bashima tried not to think about what could have escaped the Locker if Chronas lost control for too long.

"Also," Veles continued, "there's something wrong with the shades and god-touched we've found. The shade who seems to be the sanest brought that robe and covered up Shina, but she either won't or can't speak."

Shina was indeed covered with his purple robe though it was slashed in many places. Rage filled Bashima again, and Tengu put a hand on his shoulder.

"Easy," he said. "Shina seems okay, for the most part."

"You're fucking joking, right?" Bashima asked, shoving Tengu's hand away. "Look at him! And that brand is still on his back. He's still tied to Chronas."

"I don't think so," the Forest God said, shaking his head. "Otherwise, Chronas would have been able to control him. Their connection is broken."

"Then why is the brand still there?"

"Magical wounds that strong can be impossible to heal. Like the bite mark on your shoulder."

"So he's stuck with it?" Bashima looked away, controlling his temper.

Tengu bit his lip, looking lost for words. He said, "You might be able to transform it, change its shape with your sun power and an alchemic incantation, but it would be really painful."

"I'm not causing him anymore pain than he's already been through," Bashima said.

He stood and caught himself on Tengu's shoulder, steadying himself. He staggered to Shina's unconscious form and sat down beside him, grabbing his hand. Alora patted his uninjured shoulder and Cabari nodded, quiet for once in his life. They stepped away, letting Bashima be with Shina.

Alaric's eyes fluttered open, and he smelled citrus and sage and breathed deeply. He lay on his side in Bashima's bed, and the sun shone brightly outside the windows.

Bashima!

Alaric tried to sit up, but his body cursed him, shoving him back with aches and soreness.

"Ow," he mumbled. His body was covered with bandages and gauze and every inch of it hurt. He touched his cheek, and it throbbed. It felt like his body had been smashed against a shore by powerful waves.

"I bit Bashima," Alaric said to himself, and sobs wracked his poor body, making it hurt more. He tried to stop, but his breath came out in shuddering gasps.

"Shina!"

Matthias came into the room and rushed to the bed. He grabbed Alaric's hand and squeezed lightly.

"It's okay, you're in the temple, everything is okay. Try to breathe with me." Matthias took a deep, measured breath, which Alaric copied, slowing his breathing and heartbeat. He gazed up at the shade, eyes pleading, until he could speak.

"Where is Bashima? Is he all right?"

"The master is in one piece," Matthias said. "Injured from one of the Time God's weapons, but he'll mend. It's you we've been worried about. They tried to give you a healing potion when you all returned, but your body rejected it. You threw it up and have been asleep for five days."

"That long?" Alaric couldn't remember dreaming during that time. His slumber had been thankfully empty of thoughts and symbols and dragons. He raised a bandaged hand, recalling that he'd seen claws spring from his fingers and felt his teeth grow in his jaws.

Matthias nodded. "Master Bashima is working now, but the sun will set in a few hours; then he will come see you. The Forest God is also here with Oken. The others who came to rescue you were here the first night, but they had to attend to their duties and left the next day."

"I barely remember what happened, Matthias," Alaric said and sighed. "Chronas had me by the throat; then everything was blank for a while. Then nothing until now."

"I'm sure it will come back to you," Matthias said and sat beside him in a chair Alaric hadn't noticed before. "I don't think the master has slept well these last few nights. I've found him more often than not sitting in this chair, reading."

Alaric was grateful Matthias told him about Bashima staying with him, but small details were coming back to him, plaguing him. He'd been able to see and hear everything from within the box Chronas trapped him in though his eyes were closed for much of what happened.

"I don't think I can face him, Matthias."

"Who?" Matthias asked, confused.

"The Time God made Bashima choose between me and Dain. And Bashima picked me. I tried to tell him not to, but I was trapped and couldn't talk. I was under the god-touched binding. It was all a trick. Either way Bashima chose, it was a game. I couldn't do anything. He made me listen." Fresh tears welled in Alaric's eyes, and he brushed them away. "He told me awful things," Alaric said. "What he was going to do to me once Bashima took Dain and left. It was worse than anything I could have imagined. He kept…touching me. I was half-crazed from the branding, so I tried to fight back, but he just laughed at me. He ordered his god-touched to beat me. I begged for them to stop, Matthias, but they were like lifeless shells."

Matthias bent forward and rested his forehead on Alaric's hand that he held, and his body shook. "I'm sorry, Shina, I should have gone with you. Found a way to do it."

"You would have been destroyed," Alaric said. "I'm glad I was alone. Wait! What happened to Ichigo?"

Matthias raised his head and smiled. "She came back to the temple, dragging the broken cart behind her. I've never seen a more determined animal. She's doing well." He added the last part quickly, noticing Alaric's shocked face. "She wasn't injured, just very tired. Bashima has a shade taking care of her. Not Emilia, though she pushed hard for the job."

Alaric relaxed a bit. "Emilia isn't worried, is she?"

"Of course she is," said Matthias. "We will let her see you once Master Bashima and Master Cypress have a chance to talk to you. Until then, get some more rest. I know you just woke up, but you need to heal. I'll be right here."

Alaric closed his eyes and squeezed Matthias's hand before falling back to sleep.

When Alaric woke next, the sun was gone, and soft candlelight illuminated the room. No one was in the room with him, but a blanket adorned the chair Matthias used earlier. He smelled something divine nearby, and his stomach rumbled furiously.

As if hearing a distant alarm, the Forest God appeared in the doorway, eyes wide.

"Bashi!" Cypress yelled. "He's awake!"

"Hells, you don't have to yell, Tengu."

Bashima came to the door and stood beside Cypress, expression uncertain. An image of the Forest God approaching him and an injured Bashima flew into Alaric's mind, and he sat up abruptly and growled deep in his throat. Seeing their surprised faces, Alaric covered his mouth and blushed, his entire face going red.

"I'm sorry! I didn't mean to do that!" He dropped his hands and looked at the two gods. Cypress had taken a step back from the doorway, but Bashima stood firm. Was that image from the Temple of Time?

"I'm really hungry," Alaric admitted.

"We can fix that!" Cypress said, voice slightly higher than usual. He disappeared into the sitting room. Bashima stayed in the doorway, and Shina wasn't sure how to interpret his body language or face. It was like the Sun God closed himself off. The Forest God came back, carrying a covered tray. He shoved it in Bashima's hands. "You do it."

"Coward," muttered Bashima. He went to the bed and set up the tray across Alaric's lap then pulled off the cover. Underneath was a veritable meat feast: steak, pork, chicken, rabbit. Alaric heard his stomach call out with urgency and proceeded to inhale the food. He'd never eaten so fast in his life. When it was gone, he looked at the empty plates, amazed.

Bashima stood next to him, very still, eyes huge. Cypress remained by the door, mouth hanging open. Alaric stuck out his bottom lip and said, "I told you I was hungry."

278

"Do you..." Cypress squeaked then cleared his throat and said, "...need more?"

"I don't think so," Alaric said. "That was a lot." He burped loudly and covered his mouth again. "Excuse me." Bashima snorted and sat down hard in the chair next to the bed.

"He's fine," the Sun God said, nonchalant. "You're not going to tear my head off, are you?"

Alaric blanched, horrified. "No! Why would I do that?" His eyes wandered to the bandage on Bashima's shoulder, and his mouth filled with saliva and a faint sweet, metallic taste. "I really bit you, didn't I?"

Bashima looked over at Cypress in the doorway. "Can you get your ass in here?"

"I think it's best that I don't," Cypress said. "We don't know exactly what's going on."

"Whatever," Bashima said. He took the tray off Alaric's lap and set it on the floor. "How do you feel, Red?"

"Like Ichigo threw me going over a jump then ran me over. A bunch of times," Alaric said. "It was bad, huh?" He surveyed his damaged body.

"Yeah, but it looks like your backbone wasn't as broken as I thought. Or you healed part of yourself," said Bashima, not meeting his eyes. His hand wandered to the bandage near his neck, and Alaric's eyes watered. "Wait, don't cry," Bashima said, voice panicked. "It's fine, stopped bleeding almost right away, but it looks like an open wound." If that was supposed to stop Alaric from crying, it wasn't working.

"I don't remember doing it," Alaric said and trembled. Bashima reached for his hand, but Alaric pulled away, crying out, "No don't! What if I do it again?"

Bashima's face shrouded in pain, and he withdrew his hand. "You weren't exactly yourself when you did it," he muttered.

"He's right, Shina," said the Forest God, moving his hands in elaborate motions as he spoke. "Absolutely unprecedented, throwing off Veles's alchemy like nothing, hardly phased by Cabari's lightning, you BROKE Chronas's sword somehow. It's like godly powers have little or no effect on you. Fantastic really, what an ability!"

Both Bashima and Alaric stared at Cypress. He stopped and said, "Ahem, sorry. So, what do you remember?"

Alaric twisted his fingers together, trying to remember. "Um, after Chronas threw me, not much. I can see flashes, lots of white and blue, probably from the marble and Chronas's sword, I guess. It's more feelings than anything. More rage than I've ever felt in my life, and I'm not an angry person, but I wanted to kill something."

Cypress's mouth was a thin line, but he nodded. Bashima stared at Alaric as though searching for something.

"What's wrong with me?" Alaric asked.

"There's nothing wrong with you," said Bashima, disgruntled. "Anyone who says otherwise will hear it from me." He glared at Cypress.

"I've been reading since you've been unconscious," the Forest God said. "There isn't a lot of information on something like this. Even the books my shade brought from the Temple of the Forest had scant clues. Although, it's very similar to a celestial power."

"Tch," Bashima said and drew his legs up onto the chair, crossing them. "Wouldn't we have known if Shina was a celestial? Not that easy to hide."

"I said similar, not *exactly* a celestial power."

"You've lost me," Alaric said. He hated not knowing what happened in the Temple of Time. Hated not knowing what he'd done and why.

Cypress looked excited to launch into a lecture. He said, "You were taught that the gods were the first beings, right? And that we've been around since the world was created."

Alaric nodded, so Cypress went on, "That's not true. There were beings before us called celestials. Titanic powers, way more firepower than us gods. Luckily, most of them were peaceful, mainly focused on creation and all that. They made the first gods. They also made humans."

Alaric couldn't believe what he was hearing. He'd learned nothing even close to that in school and had heard no stories about it. Beings older than the gods?

"I know," Cypress said, hands up. "It sounds ludicrous, but it's true. There aren't many left. Most of them choose to ascend instead of remaining in the corporeal world."

"Means they can die if they want," Bashima said helpfully.

"Gods can die?" Alaric was shocked.

"No, gods can't," Cypress said. "The celestials made us immortal so we could keep the world functioning."

"Then they fucked off to a higher plane of existence or some shit," Bashima said. "Leaving us here to deal with everything they created. And with the celestials who didn't want to ascend."

"That's not what we're trying to accomplish, Bashi," Cypress warned. Bashima waved him off and rolled his eyes. The Forest God said, "Anyway, the celestials were immune to godly powers. For the most part. Which is why I think you might have a similar ability. I've never heard of a celestial-human hybrid, but you're definitely not a god or a demigod."

You have a choice to make…

"I dreamed that a dragon spoke to me," Alaric said. "More than once, actually."

Bashima and Cypress stared at him in surprise and then looked at each other. The Forest God said, "A dragon?" It was like a bolt hit Cypress. He stood still, eyes wide, muttering to himself. "Togarashi? Wow, I thought that was a myth, I mean, it could be real, no reason not to think it's real, especially if Shina did what he did and was indestructible and covered in those scale things."

"Wait, I was covered in scales? Like a snake?" Alaric asked, appalled.

Bashima snapped his fingers at the Forest God. "Tengu! Knock it off. Stop mumbling to yourself."

"Shina," Cypress said, too excited to stay in the doorway. He raced to the bed and leaned close to him, their noses almost touching. "What did the dragon say to you? In the dream?"

"Uh, something about making a choice," he faltered, not wanting to say everything in front of Cypress. His eyes flicked to Bashima, who bit the inside of his cheek, understanding that Alaric was going to hold something back. "He mentioned blood of dragons or something weird like that. Not big on details, the dragon. There were a lot of other voices too, whispering the whole time, like a buzzing in my head."

"Holy shit!" Cypress exclaimed and threw up his arms, causing Bashima to jump in his seat. Alaric drew back, unsure what was so exciting. The Forest God said, "Shina! You're not part celestial, not exactly. In the dawn of time, there were creatures who existed alongside the celestials. They get grouped together, but the creatures had different powers very similar to the celestials." His eyes lit up and his body shook with excitement.

"Seven hells, spit it out already," Bashima said and smacked the Forest God on the back of the head.

"Some of those creatures were dragons!" Cypress said. When neither Bashima nor Alaric said anything, he looked put out. "You're dragon-touched! Your village is named after a celestial dragon, Togarashi, right?"

"Yeah…" Alaric said, disbelieving.

"There are tons of legends about dragons," Cypress said. "Most of them aren't true, of course, but it was well known that dragons chose a place to settle and protect, every inch of it, everything that lived there. They would never leave unless they were killed or ascended. Unfortunately, a lot of them *were* killed. By gods." He winced and leaned away from Alaric. "This was thousands of years ago. Tens of thousands. No one has seen a dragon in what, fifty thousand years?" Cypress asked Bashima, who shrugged.

"I never saw one," the Sun God muttered.

"I haven't either," Cypress said, "but there were stories about people— humans—who would take over protecting their villages if the dragon was slain or ascended. They were entrusted with the village's prosperity, with keeping everyone safe. They were called dragon-touched."

"And they had scales emerge from their bodies? That sounds ridiculous," said Bashima, crossing his arms.

"There isn't a lot of documentation on this, Bashi. And if there were dragon people wandering around, you'd think you'd hear more about it. My best guess, the bloodlines either died out or went dormant if they weren't needed. Basic environmental needs."

The Forest God held out his hands at Alaric. "Maybe it was similar to the god-touched ceremony. Shina said the dragon in his dream told him he had a choice to make. Maybe he took the chance."

At the mention of the god-touched ceremony, Alaric's back itched, and he rubbed back against his pillows and winced. His back was the most painful injury, and he didn't want to think about it.

"And this dragon-touched power...trumps the god-touched ceremony?" Bashima asked, skeptical.

"It seems that way," Cypress said. "Otherwise, there's no way he could have ignored Chronas's verbal or mental orders."

Alaric's back suddenly screamed at him, and he doubled over in pain, grasping the sheets.

"Shit! What's happening?" Bashima asked, standing. He didn't try to touch Alaric, but he was frightened. "Shina! What's wrong?"

The torment ended, and Alaric slumped back on his pillows, sweating and breathing hard. "Bashima?" Alaric asked, exhausted. He put his hand out on the blanket, palm open, and the Sun God took it, kneeling beside the bed.

"I think that's enough for now, Tengu," Bashima said, voice dangerous.

Cypress had already retreated to the doorway. He nodded and sighed, "I agree. I'll do some more research. See if I can find anything about dragon-touched. But I don't think this episode has anything to do with that."

Bashima gave the Forest God a harsh glare, and his green head disappeared.

When they were alone, Bashima rubbed Alaric's hand with his thumb, concerned.

"You're not afraid of me?" Alaric asked, timid and tired.

"What?" Bashima asked, affronted. "I'd never be afraid of your dumb ass." Alaric's lip quivered again, and Bashima grimaced, "Shit, I'm terrible at this. Whenever I got hurt, the hag told me to 'walk it off.'"

That made Alaric smile.

"You shouldn't call your mother a hag."

"Yeah, well, you've never met her." He reached out and smoothed Alaric's hair out of his eyes. "If I could kill that fucker for you, I would."

"I know."

"You put him out of commission for eternity, so there's that." Bashima might have thought that would make Alaric feel better, but it only made him realize he'd been furious enough to want to murder someone. He hadn't thought that darkness was in him.

"Shit, I keep saying the wrong things, huh?"

Alaric tried a small smile, but it died on his lips. "I remember more of the dragon vision or whatever it was. I just didn't want Cypress to know about it."

"I figured," Bashima said, cautious. "Do you want to tell me?"

"I was dying, Bashima." Alaric looked at the Sun God, whose face became a storm cloud. "And I wanted to. It was better than being tied to...him."

Bashima nodded but didn't say anything. His hand became warm, and Alaric said, "Are you mad at me?"

"No," Bashima said, a growl in his voice.

"It was stupid to agree to the god-touched ceremony," Alaric ventured. "But he said he could hurt you enough to affect the sun. And I thought about my parents and everybody here in the temple...what might happen to them if you couldn't control the sun."

Bashima looked away, shivering, but he didn't drop Alaric's hand.

"I thought he might have said something like that," the Sun God finally said. "And he might have been right, but you shouldn't have been in that situation. I'm the one who let you leave here."

"I would have gone back to my village at some point, Bashima. I'm sure he had people watching to see when I did."

"But I could have sent Matthias with you, or I could have gone," Bashima said, sighing. "You were violated by that fucker, and I couldn't do anything."

Alaric's back flared again, and he winced, clawing at Bashima's hand.

"What's wrong?" Bashima asked, alarmed.

"My back..." Alaric said and turned his face away. "I think I want to sleep if that's okay." Alaric was too tired to try and have an important conversation with the Sun God. He needed to say a lot more, but the words refused to form. Maybe sleep would help him get his thoughts in place.

"Yeah, that's okay, whatever you need, Red."

"Can you stay with me?"

"Wouldn't dream of leaving."

A week passed, and Alaric slowly healed although Cypress was impressed with his progress.

"Your cuts are all healed! The bigger one on your arm seems like it might be permanent, but everything else looks good. And your bruises are almost gone." He was mystified whenever he checked on Alaric, green eyes alight with wonder. "You really are extraordinary, Shina!"

They didn't talk about the brand on his back. Cypress checked it daily and changed the bandages. Alaric asked to look at it once, and it looked like someone dumped molten silver all over his back. He saw what remained of his tattoo and nearly threw up. Every so often the brand twinged, like Alaric was being pulled by an invisible chain. He wasn't so sure the Time God's influence was gone.

Bashima stayed by his side at night, sleeping in the chair, and Matthias was with him all day, talking about temple happenings and any news from other gods. Oken came to visit him a few times, when Cypress let him.

"Bell says you're part dragon," he deadpanned one morning.

"Oken!" The Forest God yelled, face in his hands. "You can't talk about that, remember?"

"Not even with Shina? He's the dragon."

Cypress sighed, resigned. "Only if he wants to talk about it. And no one else can know."

"Obviously, Bell, I'm not stupid. That information could be used against him."

"I don't think you're stupid," Cypress said, flustered.

"You two are entertaining as ever," said Alaric, laughing from the bed. "I did all my exercises yesterday, Cypress. Do you think I can walk around a bit?"

"Sure! If Matthias goes with you, that should be fine. Just don't push it. Your legs were pretty banged up, and I don't want you to fall. Bashi would throttle me." Oken patted Cypress's shoulder in sympathy, and the Forest God shook his head. "Let us help you up."

Cypress and Oken helped Alaric out of bed, and he leaned on them, trying out a few steps. Today seemed to be a good day since his legs didn't buckle immediately. Matthias was in the sitting room and watched their progress, eyebrow arched.

"Going on an excursion, are we?" Matthias asked, voice chilly.

"Just down the hall, maybe?" Alaric asked meekly. Matthias was back in peak protector mode, and he disapproved of most movement Alaric attempted. "You can let me go, guys."

Oken let go right away, but Cypress stayed in place, eyeing Matthias.

"Come on, Bell," Oken said. "He can stand up on his own." Alaric said a silent thank you to Oken, and Cypress stepped away. He was shaky, but he stayed up, and Alaric beamed at Matthias.

"Look! Just fine."

"I'll be the judge of that," said Matthias. "If you're set on this, let's go before the master finds out."

"How am I supposed to get better if you all coddle me?" Alaric said, annoyed. He turned around and took some steps and promptly fell over.

"Shina!" Matthias and Cypress yelled at the same time.

"Let him do it on his own," Oken said. "He'll have to eventually."

From his place on the floor, Alaric grumbled at the demigod. His legs felt foreign to him, had failed him. He didn't want Matthias to scold him, so he pushed himself into a seated position and took inventory of his pain. Nothing too bad, just the usual soreness he'd come to expect in the mornings. At least he'd caught himself before his face hit the floor. He didn't need a broken nose added to the list of injuries.

"Nothing damaged," Alaric said, holding up his arms. "Except maybe my pride."

"Oh, good, you don't need that," said Oken, and Alaric burst out laughing, looking at Matthias and Cypress's mortified faces. Alaric fell over and cackled as Matthias and Forest God circled him like worried hens.

"I'm telling the master you let him get out of bed," Matthias said.

"You wouldn't dare," Cypress shot back.

It made Alaric laugh harder, and he finally didn't feel miserable.

Another week passed, and Alaric was able to make a circuit around Bashima's chambers without falling. Matthias walked with him, ready to catch Alaric if he fell, and Alaric vowed to stay on his feet.

"Some great superpower if it makes me like this," Alaric grumbled as he walked past the large windows in the sitting room. Scales and strength were all well and good, but was it worth it to be in constant pain?

"Master Cypress said it was a combination of many factors," Matthias reminded him.

"A huge factor is that I apparently changed into a dragon-beast-man-thing and rampaged around a temple and bit Bashima."

"That is a fairly large factor," Matthias admitted, coughing.

"Don't laugh! It's not funny."

"I have a hard time imagining you rampaging around anything, Shina."

"I'll rampage you," Alaric muttered as Matthias pushed him to go one more lap around the room.

After his torture sessions with Matthias, Alaric was spent. Emilia read to him every afternoon before Bashima came back, and he was always happy to see her. When she read to him, he forgot about his body aching and that he was part monster. She showed no fear toward him, which was a kindness, though he wasn't sure how much they'd told Emilia. She was still young and chatty, and while Alaric trusted that she wouldn't talk about his affliction, he guessed the others didn't share his opinion. As far as she knew, he was just badly wounded.

Every night, Bashima came with dinner, and they talked about his day, which was mostly about the sun being a stubborn bastard that didn't like being told what to do.

"Alora has it easy with the moon," Bashima would say. "Compared to the sun, the moon is a baby bird that can't fly yet."

Alaric laughed at his whining, grateful for the distraction. Because in the middle of the night without fail, the brand would burn. Or at least feel like it was burning. It jolted him awake, doubling him over in pain, covering him in sweat. He tried not to wake Bashima, who brought in a small cot so he could sleep beside Alaric without hurting him. It usually worked, with Bashima stirring but not waking. Sometimes, though, the Sun God leapt off the cot and held Alaric's hand, talking him through the pain. Alaric wanted to tell him to go back to sleep, that it didn't help when Bashima woke up to comfort him. If anything, it made things worse. Alaric was a burden.

Heavy rain woke Alaric one night, a curtain of water pounding down on the window. Lightning flashed, and thunder sounded in the distance. Bashima slept through it, snoring softly on his cot. Alaric sighed, looking at the Sun God's peaceful face. He kept the bite mark covered, mostly to hide it from the shades until they decided how to explain it but also to spare Alaric seeing it. Bashima knew it distressed Alaric, but the bandage only pulled attention to it.

Alaric still had no idea why he'd done it. What could have possessed him to bite Bashima?

Alaric leaned over in bed, reached out, and touched the bandage, which was loose. It peeled away easily, and Bashima didn't stir. Underneath the bandage was an ugly, puckering scar, shaped like a mouth. The puncture marks were an angry red color even in the dim candlelight. Alaric's finger brushed the mark, and he jolted away as if it shocked him. A sizzling energy went through his body, dazzling his nerve endings. Images came cascading into his mind: white, luminous marble veined with delicate light blue markings; bright yellow flames and smoke; his hands growing longer, fingers turning to claws; a bright blue sword at Bashima's throat.

And he heard an ear-splitting roar and desperate pleas.

When he fell back to himself, Alaric looked at his hands, which were normal, then felt his teeth, which were still sharp but not the serrated knives he'd felt growing from his gums.

The rain hit the window hard like waves crashing against a black cliff side.

He needed to get away.

In a daze, Alaric swung his legs out of the bed.

When Bashima woke up, he heard a loud thunderclap and jumped, thinking it was Shina. Shit. He was exhausted. If Shina didn't wake him up in the middle of the night, he dreamt the redhead did, crowding his dreams with worry and fear.

He blinked a few times, cursing Cabari for the weather though the valley was probably due for a big storm. The grass needed rain. He looked over to see if the thunder woke Shina, but the bed was empty.

Bashima leaped up and ran to the sitting room, but the redhead wasn't there either.

"Shina!" Bashima called but got no answer. "Fuck, where would he go?"

Not wanting to disturb the temple if he didn't have to, Bashima searched. He wasn't getting an emotional signal from Shina either, but that could be for a number of reasons. Bashima was trying to regulate his emotional responses to Shina daily, so as not to worry the redhead. He could barely walk yet, no need to add Bashima's emotional baggage to the load. Somehow, Shina was able to pick up on Bashima's slightest moods. It was unnerving but mainly difficult to block out.

Bashima walked from his chambers and checked the library but no Shina. He wasn't in the conservatory or the baths either. Would he go to the kitchens this late? Maybe his room? Bashima wasn't sure why he'd go there, but it was worth a try. Maybe it held comforting familiarity.

A gong went off in Bashima's head, signaling that the main doors were opening.

FUCK.

Bashima raced down the hall, past Shina's room, past the throne room entrance, and saw the main doors standing open, rain cascading onto the front landing, hitting like arrows. Illuminated in the pale light from the main hall, Shina stood, head up, rain coming down on his face. He wore the purple robe from the offering ceremony, hanging limply off his shoulders, its tattered hem dragging on the ground. His feet were bare.

"Shina!"

The redhead turned, and Bashima didn't recognize him. His face was splotchy and despondent, eyes lidded with fatigue, his lips drawn. The fiery red hair was plastered to his head from the rain, which ran down his cheeks in chaotic lines.

Bashima ran forward, and Shina stumbled and landed on his hands and knees, making an odd keening noise. When Bashima reached him, the redhead pushed him away, but Bashima wasn't going to let him sit out in the cold rain. It pelted them both as Shina struggled, saying something Bashima couldn't make out. He managed to drag the redhead to his feet and draped his arm over his shoulder, hauling him inside.

"Leave me alone," Shina said once the doors were closed.

"Like hells," Bashima growled, dripping wet. "What the fuck were you thinking! You could get sick!"

"Can I?" Shina snarled and pushed Bashima hard, sending him slamming against the wall. Startled, Bashima turned to find Shina collapsed on the floor. "Can I even get sick anymore? No one knows because they have no idea what I am."

His eyes took on a scarlet sheen, and Bashima cursed himself. He was getting Shina riled up.

"You're *Shina*, okay? That's all you need to know. That's all I care about."

Shina's head swung toward him, his teeth bared, eyes shining. "I hurt you," he said, voice lower than normal. "I bit you, and it can't be healed."

Bashima put a hand on his shoulder where the bandage should be, but it was gone. Shina must have looked at the bite and freaked out.

"It's fine," Bashima said.

"No, it's not!" Shina yelled, clenching his fists. "Stop saying that! I disfigured you, and that's not fine!"

He bent over, sides heaving, the robe falling in a drenched heap around him. The silver brand shone brightly, and Bashima's soul ached. Shina noticed the distress coming off the Sun God, and his face dissolved into fury.

"I did to you what that monster did to me," he said, then the brand glowed and Shina's back arched. Bashima moved forward, but Shina snapped at him. "Don't come near me! You have no idea what I'll do."

"You won't hurt me," Bashima said. "Please, try to calm down."

"You don't understand," Shina said, the brand losing its luster. Bashima hadn't seen it glow before, not since the temple. Add another item to Tengu's fucking list of research topics. The redhead looked up at him, eyes pleading. "I wish the dragons could take it back. I wish I had died."

Bashima stopped, his heart skipping in his chest, breath leaving his lungs in a gasp. "Don't you dare say that," he ordered. "You don't mean it."

"The dragon said it would be hard, but this isn't what I thought he meant," Shina said, tears running down his face. His eyes went back to normal, so Bashima hoped he was coming out of the fit. There was no telling what might set him off though.

Shina said, "I keep seeing his face. I can feel his hands all over me like I'm covered in spiders. I know what he had planned for me…And when I think about him, my back burns. When I dream at night, he's there. And Dain burns. And *he* laughs."

Bashima didn't know what to do. Shina's suffering was coming off him like thick, black clouds, and Bashima marveled that he hadn't felt it before if it was this bad. Had Shina been shielding himself from Bashima's senses as well?

"Why did you pick me?" Shina asked, begging for an answer but also not wanting to hear it. "Why did you do it? You were supposed to choose him and leave so I knew you'd be safe and happy. Was that too much to ask?"

Bashima flung himself at Shina and kissed him, hands holding onto the back of his head, fingers in his soaked red hair. He released his emotional barriers and let them wash over Shina, his fear, his worry, but also his hope and his love. He shared everything, leaving nothing behind. He let his soul shine out and emitted a soft glow from his skin.

Please, he thought, *Alaric, please, feel this.*

Shina melted and kissed Bashima back, putting his arms around him, tears still streaming down his face, and Bashima felt the gentle push of Shina's soul answering; he was so unsure of himself, who he had become, but Bashima also felt an immense power simmering there, a bright, burning passion encompassed in ruby light. Bashima could lose himself in that strength.

He broke the kiss and grabbed Shina's face, wiping away the tears. He said, "Let me help you."

"Take this brand off me, Bashima. It's eating away at me, and I don't know how long I can fight the urge...to ascend." Shina took Bashima's hands from his face and held them.

Bashima's eyes widened. Fuck, he'd forgotten that celestials possessed that power.

"I'm sorry," Shina said. "I'm trying to fight it. I want to stay here, but it takes all my energy to keep the burning at bay. The dragons warned me that I needed to choose to live for myself, and I only decided to wake up for you."

"I...I don't know what I can do," Bashima said, but his anger was flaring alongside his panic. "Fuck that. Gods dammit, don't you dare fucking leave me, Alaric! I love you, you idiot! You're worth a million gods. Don't let that fucker win. You're stronger than him, stronger than anyone!"

"You called me 'Alaric,'" Shina said, perplexed.

"For fuck sake, yeah I did. Is that all you heard?" Bashima asked, frustrated. "Remember when you spit at not one, but *two* gods? What kind of human does that? It takes someone epic to do that. You want to know why I picked you? Because it was the only choice. Dain knew, and he never even met you. I loved him, and I'll always miss him, but I can't live without you, Red."

Shina blinked a few times as though he hadn't heard a word, then he ran his hands through Bashima's hair and kissed him deeply. Bashima pulled the redhead closer and accidentally grazed his back, causing Shina to flinch away. He needed to do something.

"Tengu said the brand can't be undone," he said, holding Shina's face again. "But I can try to transform it."

"I don't care; just please get this thing off me," Shina said. "Can you turn it into your symbol?"

Bashima pulled away, horrified. "What? You'd just be trading one brand for another."

Shina gave a sad shrug. "It's only fair. I branded you first." He pointed at Bashima's red scar, who reflexively covered it with a hand. "At least people will know we belong together."

Bashima narrowed his eyes. "You want me to cause you horrible pain to try and get rid of horrible pain? That doesn't make sense."

"Wouldn't transforming it hurt no matter what you made? This is my choice. You said you love me. I love you too, and I don't care who knows."

"Okay," Bashima said, barely getting the word out. "When?"

"Now," Shina said.

"Gods, you're so pushy," Bashima said, rubbing his eyes. "Fine but come on; we should go to the throne room where I can concentrate my power."

He pulled Shina to his feet, and the redhead was steadier than he'd been in weeks. He was full of conviction, his eyes bright again. Bashima had reservations about attempting the transformation, but seeing the trust in Shina's eyes was enough.

"This is going to hurt. A lot. You have to tell me if it's too much and I'll stop."

Shina nodded, padding along beside him, robe held closed.

"I mean it, Red," Bashima said, stopping in the center of the throne room. "And if I think it's gone too far, I'll stop."

"I'll trust your judgment," Shina said, and Bashima narrowed his eyes.

"That'll be a first," said the Sun God. "Okay, kneel here." He helped Shina to the floor, and anxiety flashed through his mind.

Shina grasped his hand and squeezed. "I trust you," he said again and faced forward, head bent, exposing his neck.

Bashima took a deep breath and took the purple robe down slowly, showing the hideous silver brand. Fresh anger roiled through him, and he wished he'd been the one to dismantle the Time God. Not only had Chronas terrorized Shina, he'd burned flesh from his body, stolen his tattoo, taken his surety of mind and replaced it with dark anguish.

"I'm sorry," Bashima said, igniting a single finger and starting the transmutation chant. He wished he could close his eyes as he performed the transformation, but it needed his entire attention. He chanted and placed his finger on Shina's shoulder where his tattoo had been. Shina winced but didn't make a sound.

Repeating the chant over and over, Bashima traced the Time God's brand, reshaping it as he went. He couldn't see Shina's face, but his body shook slightly, his fists clenched in the robe's folds. Bashima kept going until his eyes glowed yellow from the effort, his finger leaving a molten gold path across Shina's back as it obliterated the silver brand inch by inch.

As the Sun God finished, his breathing was heavy, and he hit the floor beside the redhead. Bashima reached for Shina's robe and grasped it; then, the redhead's hand found his.

"I..." Shina started, his voice heartbreaking. "I can't feel him anymore."

Bashima let out a rush of air and clenched Shina's hand.

"Thank you," Shina said, then he folded over, Bashima catching his head before it hit the floor.

Chapter Seventeen

Kuroi found them on the throne room floor the next morning, Shina sprawled over Bashima, both of them covered with the purple robe. Raising an eyebrow and sighing heavily, he grabbed the robe, and it was damp, which disgusted him slightly until he realized the entire thing was wet through.

"What in the seven hells?" Kuroi muttered, then pulled it off and gasped, taking several steps back. Where before had been the silver brand, a shining golden mark glared up at him, accusing, Alaric's skin reddened around the edges.

"What have you done?" Kuroi asked, louder than he intended.

Bashima stirred beneath the sleeping Shina and yawned. He kissed Shina's forehead before noticing Kuroi glaring down at him.

"Oh, shit," he said.

"Oh, shit is right," Kuroi hissed, pointing at the golden brand. "What do you think you're doing? He's barely recovered from the Time God!"

"Shhhhh let me get him to my chambers; he's been through a lot." Bashima tried to get up but also felt weakened. "A little help?"

Kuroi fumed as he helped Bashima stand and lift Shina's sleeping form. Focusing on the sun, Bashima breathed deep and absorbed more energy, revitalizing himself. He took Shina in his arms and signaled for Kuroi to follow. Shina's head rested on his shoulder, the faintest smile on his lips.

"Absolute madness," muttered the god-touched man, shaking his head and stomping along after Bashima.

"Can you give it a rest? Hells, I'll explain once I get him in bed," Bashima growled.

"I will most certainly not give it a rest," Kuroi whispered. "He's not only been subjected to every trauma imaginable, but he's also trying to come to terms with what's happened to him. Then you go and add this on top of everything?"

"I know, Kuroi!" Bashima scowled at him and said, "I tried to talk him out of it, but he was losing it last night. He wandered out into the storm wearing that damn robe, no idea how he got a hold of that. I had it stowed away. It was the only thing that calmed him down."

"Yes, I'm sure that branding him irreparably calmed him down," seethed Kuroi.

They reached Bashima's chambers, and Kuroi opened the door for them. Bashima settled Shina on the bed on his stomach with his head lying on his arm and made sure his back wasn't covered. Bashima would have to check that he didn't shove his face into a pillow or something, and he moved most of them to be sure.

"Now," said Kuroi. "Explain."

"You don't have to talk to me like that," Bashima said and stalked into the sitting room.

Kuroi followed him, mutinous. "Perhaps if you were behaving rationally, I wouldn't have to. And don't you dare snap at me, Bashima. I just lost my friend, *again*. You're not the only one who loved Dain, and you're not the only one who cares about Shina."

"I know that, dammit," Bashima said. "I need to get to work in a few minutes. Matthias should be here soon to watch him."

"And make sure he doesn't have a terrible reaction to more trauma? I thought you had better sense," Kuroi said, throwing his hands in the air. "Why did you listen to him? You could have refused."

"No, I couldn't." Bashima got in Kuroi's face, but the god-touched man didn't move. The Sun God said, "You weren't there. You didn't see him. He said he wanted to die, all right. What the fuck was I supposed to do? Let him?"

"You weren't supposed to bind him to you! You could have said no, absolutely not!"

"We didn't do the ceremony. I just transformed the brand with a transmutation incantation." Bashima sighed and stepped back. "Tengu said the bond was broken between Shina and Chronas, but he felt burning pain every night. It was driving him mad and last night was apparently the last straw."

Bashima stretched his shoulder, still twinging from when Shina shoved him against the wall. "He asked me to help him. I didn't want to do it, but I think it worked."

Kuroi looked at the bite on Bashima's neck, and the Sun God wouldn't meet his eyes.

"We'll just have to see, won't we?" Kuroi said. "Lord Veles made contact. He'd like to meet with you later this evening. I'll tell him to be here as soon as the sun sets." He spun on his heel and shifted away.

Alaric dreamed he was a dragon. Though he had no wings, he flew above a sea of tufted clouds, the wind rushing past his face, and swooped down into one, shooting out the bottom, covered in dew. He spun in the air, scattering droplets and laughing. This was wonderful. The sun reflected off his scales, which were varying shades of red, mainly deep ruby and garnet like his eyes, and when he concentrated, smoke came out his nose, tickling him.

He was dragon-shaped in the dream though he knew his dragon-touched form was different, at least according to Bashima. And he would know because Alaric literally almost took a chunk out of him.

In the dream, Alaric looked almost identical to the dragon guide from his other dreams though that dragon had red and gold scales and was much bigger.

"Maybe I'm a baby dragon," Alaric said.

A shadow fell over him, and Alaric flipped to float on his back, looking up. A large, friendly face gazed down, the red and gold dragon flying parallel above him.

"Hello!" Alaric said and twisted in the air. "I can cloud dance on my own now!"

"Indeed," said the dragon, smiling. He dipped down to fly beside Alaric, his body undulating with the wind, which buffeted Alaric around. "You will eventually get the hang of it," the dragon said, chuckling.

"So, Cypress is right?" Alaric asked. "I am a dragon?"

He rumbled with laughter and zipped around Alaric in a lively figure eight, scales dazzling in the sun. "Oh, my no, not a dragon completely. Blood of the Dragon and son of dragons, yes. My blood as it happens."

Alaric's eyes widened, and he fell a short distance in the sky. The dragon swooped below him and propped him up with his giant head. Alaric leveled himself out and said, "You're Togarashi?"

"I am. I ascended thousands of years ago though my blood still runs true in your village. Of course, no one has activated in some time." That same rumbling laugh cascaded through the sky. "Your village is much-favored by a certain explosive deity, and they haven't needed protection since the village captured his attention. I have excellent taste in locations."

"I was activated?"

"Of course, similar to the god-touched, dragon-touched people only arise when needed or when activated."

"So…what activated me?"

The dragon raised an eyebrow and laughed again, saying, "I believe you're a bit bashful about the topic. Of course, your soul bond certainly helped things along."

"You said that before," said Alaric. He felt the scales on his face getting warmer; he was blushing! "About a soul bond."

"It is an interesting confluence of many factors, how you came to be," the dragon said. "In order to keep your human body alive after certain 'sexual cautions' were ignored, your blood tried to counteract the foreign substance. In doing so, part of Bashima's power was absorbed into you. Not only did your dragon blood crave, hmm, 'completion' when it was activated, but your soul bond called out to its mate, once you'd met him, of course."

The dragon winked at Alaric then paused, considering what to say next.

"Not everyone has a soul bond, and not every soul bond is completed. There is always a choice, young one. You could have lived your entire life without meeting your bond partner. You could have also denied him. But he is very handsome, and I imagine a deft lover."

Alaric choked and dipped in the air again, recovering before the dragon had to assist.

"Humans," said the dragon, "always so squeamish."

"You're saying that Bashima and I are...soul mates? That's just a fantasy, Togarashi."

Alaric couldn't believe what the dragon was implying. Sure, he understood that he'd activated his dragon ability with "too much sex" as Emilia had mentioned so long ago, but soul mates? That was something out of a romance epic.

"Weren't dragons just a fantasy a few months ago?"

"That's different."

"Then, how can you explain that you sometimes feel what he's feeling, hmm? When you were faced with death in the Temple of Time, you not only experienced your own agony, you felt his as well. It pulled you back to life though I hoped you'd choose to live because you valued yourself."

Alaric hung his head and clicked his claws—claws!—together. "I thought you might lecture me about that if I ever found you again."

"Lecture? There's nothing wrong with choosing to live to save another. I'm sure he was grateful. And I see you're moving along on the self-worth."

They flew in silence for a while, letting the wind carry them on different paths, until they were over a dark sea. The air suddenly smelled like salt and turned cold. Alaric stopped, not wanting to go further.

"Wait," he said. "I'm...afraid."

"Of what?"

"Will you be angry if I say 'everything?'" Alaric looked down at the water, churning below. How had he thought it was clear blue the first time he saw it in a dream? It was inky and impenetrable, devoid of life.

"I would be alarmed if you weren't afraid, but you don't fear as much as you think."

"I'm going to live a long time now, right?" Alaric asked, trying to give reason to his fears.

The dragon nodded, whiskers fluttering. His eyes glimmered in the dimming sunlight.

Alaric went on, "I can fend for myself, you know, go back to my village, protect it like you used to, but..."

"But you don't want to be alone?" The dragon caught onto Alaric's thoughts quickly.

"What if I can't be with Bashima? Because I can't control what's inside me?" Alaric asked.

"Control? You'll learn that quickly. The initial shock can be difficult," the dragon said, "but it doesn't take long for your body and mind to adapt. Especially since the god-touched bond has been completely obliterated."

"But I bit Bashima, scarred him."

"Of course you did," the dragon said as though Alaric had lost his mind. "He's your chosen mate. It lets other dragons know to stay away because he's yours and you're his. You won't do it again, obviously. All dragons act this way."

"What?" Alaric asked, perplexed. "You could have warned me!"

"I did," the dragon said, pulling in front of Alaric. "I told you it would be difficult if you chose to live and accept the dragon part of you."

"You left out some important details!"

"There really wasn't time," said the dragon, shrugging. "The claiming—it's an instinct, completely normal. I suppose I should have taken it into account that seeing your soul bond partner in danger might send you out of control." He clicked a claw against his chin.

"You suppose?" Alaric said, irritated. "I could have really hurt him."

"Unlikely," the dragon said. "You would not hurt your mate. Besides the light biting, that is. He should be proud! What god can say they've been claimed by a dragon? None, I should think." The dragon puffed out his chest. "None of those jumped-up celestials either."

"Has anyone ever said you're exhausting?"

"Constantly," the dragon said, flicking his tail. "Is there anything else you'd like to know? The sun is fading, and so is your time here."

"Is there anyone who can tell me more about being dragon-touched? Are there any others in the world?" Alaric asked. "Not that I don't like talking to you, but you're an actual dragon. You're used to all the powers and long life and stuff."

"Hoom," the dragon said, "there is one other, I believe. In the south. He is son of the Steel Belly Dragon, Kamaishi."

"Only one?" Alaric asked, crestfallen. He'd hoped there would be more, even just a few.

"Just as dragons are gone from the world, so does their blood diminish. Unless it's needed, of course." The dragon looked wistful, lost in thought. He said, "The other dragon-touched is named Daruk, and you will find him in Kamaishi village if you choose to search for him."

"Thank you, Togarashi," Alaric said, inclining his head. He wished the dragon wasn't so cryptic, but he was the only guide Alaric had.

"A dragon bows to no one, young one," the dragon said. "Unless they really deserve it." He winked again and did a zigzag with his long body, making Alaric smirk.

No bowing, he thought. *Why does everyone keep telling me that?*

"Before you go," the dragon said, holding up a claw, "remember to keep your true nature a secret. If it was discovered that you are Blood of the Dragon, you would be hunted. Rare and beautiful creatures were the dragons, and gods and humans have the tendency to covet both those qualities."

"All right," Alaric said.

Togarashi, the Ruby Dragon, smiled at Alaric and flew up into the sky. He joined a massive flight of dragons above, and Alaric marveled at their number, thousands of dragons in many colors and sizes. As he watched, the dragons dove down and enveloped him, flying in a tight circle around him. They all smiled, eyes shining, welcoming him with whispers and smoke.

"And I said whatever you have to say, Shina needs to hear it too."

Alaric cracked an eyelid. That voice was so cranky.

"I hardly think that's necessary," said someone with a low, melodious voice. He sounded exasperated and weary. Alaric recognized it.

He shook the dragon dream from his mind and looked at his hands. No claws. That was good. He felt okay, no pain besides the usual aches, and when he prodded the place in his mind where Chronas had lived, he found nothing. His influence was indeed gone. Alaric shuddered when he thought of the Time God, but it wasn't as agonizing as before. He was able to quiet that part of himself.

"I think it is," said Bashima, walking into the bedroom. Light flew up and down his arms, but his palms didn't ignite. Annoyed but not threatened. Behind him came a god with long dark hair tied up in a knot at the back of his head, gray skin, a scarf draped across his shoulders. The God of the Dead, Lord Veles.

"Fucking hells, Bashima," Veles said and rubbed his eyes, sighing. "What did you do to him?"

"Good, you're awake," Bashima said to Alaric, ignoring Veles. "How do you feel?" He came to the bedside and tucked some hair behind Alaric's ear, eyes soft.

Alaric sat up fully, hiding his back from them. "Pretty good, I think," he said and stretched his arms. "It hurts, but nothing like the...other one."

"He needed me to get rid of Chronas's brand, so I did. I'd appreciate if you laid off the commentary," Bashima said to Veles and slumped in his chair next to the bed. "Now, you can tell me what you came all this way to say."

Veles glanced at Alaric, who tried for a smile that came out a nervous grimace with too much teeth. "I'm really okay, sir."

Veles arched an eyebrow and Bashima laughed.

"You don't have to call him sir. Veles, what is it? I haven't eaten all day and neither has Shina."

302

"We found out a few things from one of Chronas's god-touched," Veles said and crossed his arms.

Alaric looked at Bashima, slightly panicked. He thought the Time God's servants couldn't speak. The ones he'd seen were like blank slates.

The Sun God leaned his chin into his palm and said, "Anything useful?"

"It was difficult," Veles said. "Jace and Leon were only able to get so much."

Bashima cut in, glancing at Alaric, "Veles's kid can do a bit of mind reading, and Leon is a freak but is really good at interrogation. He's a Truth Talker. Never bring him here by the way." He pointed at Veles, who rolled his eyes.

"This is where things get decidedly strange," Veles said. He glanced at Alaric again and took a deep breath. "The god-touched said he was a tribute but not for the Time God. He worships the Sun God."

Alaric sat up straighter, eyes wide, and he looked at Bashima, and said, "A tribute from the Temple of the Sun? Are you sure?"

Veles looked offended but answered, "Obviously, we're sure. You can't lie your way around a Truth Talker. Besides, why would he lie? His master is in no shape to order him."

Alaric flinched and pulled the blanket up, covering more of himself.

"Shina told me that tributes to my temple have gone missing in the past," Bashima explained, reaching for Alaric's hand. He grabbed the Sun God's proffered hand tightly.

"The thing is," Veles said, noticeably looking away from them, as though he caught them in an indecent moment, "he said that *all* of Chronas's god-touched are tributes from the Sun God. Those that didn't die. He's been experimenting, seeing how far his god-touched could function away from him. Same with the shades. He did alchemic distance spells on them then let the spells run out, waiting to see how long it took for each shade to almost disappear. It would have driven them insane very quickly to be away from their assigned temple. Or from Chronas if they were god-touched." Veles looked uncomfortable and angry. The shades were his responsibility. "Which is probably how he grabbed Shina. Sent his god-touched after the boy. There's no way you wouldn't have noticed someone with Chronas's power lurking around."

"Hells," Bashima said, alarmed. "No one deserves that. Those poor tributes."

"Like I said, Chronas is in no position to hurt anyone right now. It's doubtful that he'll overcome his…injuries."

Alaric felt indignance surge within him. He was done feeling guilty for hurting the Time God. Veles kept looking at him like he was a monster, and he might be, but he'd only attacked the god who abused him.

"Lord Veles, I feel absolutely no remorse for what I did to him."

The God of the Dead observed Alaric as if he were an interesting museum exhibit, but Alaric saw a faint hint of a smile.

"I wouldn't either," Veles said, "but word will get out that he's out of commission. In the meantime, I've spoken to Vaultus and my husband. His daughter Nim has potential to control time. She will be trained and observed and will eventually take over the job. Until she's ready, Shako will assist in the duties, mainly keeping the Locker closed."

"Can a demigod do the job?" Bashima asked, perplexed.

"I suppose we'll see," said Veles, smiling proudly. "But she's the most viable option at the moment. I don't think we need to worry; she's incredibly powerful."

Alaric sat in silent awe of Veles. He was willing to put forward his husband's child, one with which he didn't share blood, and he looked proud. Thinking about what Jace said at the summit, how his stepfather didn't like him, filled Alaric with sadness. At least the girl Nim didn't have to contend with that treatment.

"About the Locker," Veles said, voice tense.

"What about it?" Bashima said, and Alaric felt the Sun God's palm start sweating.

"There were escapes. When Chronas lost control." Veles leveled his gaze at Alaric. "I don't blame you for what you did, Shina. He deserved what he got, but this could be…" He shook his head, looked at Bashima and said, "Mainly shades got out. Easy enough to find and put back in the Locker. But a few demigods escaped. And one celestial."

"Well, I think that's enough for tonight," Bashima said and stood, ushering Veles out of the bedroom. "Are you sure?" Alaric heard him ask before they were out of earshot.

He waited for Bashima to return, wondering what Veles meant. Wouldn't a celestial be dangerous if it escaped the Locker? But he didn't have the energy to worry about hypotheticals.

When Bashima came back, Alaric waited until he'd sat down in the chair, his blond hair drooping, eyes far away. Alaric said, "The tributes. Chronas took them."

"Seems that way," Bashima said. "And I had no idea."

"It's not your fault." Alaric motioned him over, wincing as his healing skin pulled on the new brand.

"Are you going to be okay?" Bashima asked, eyes shining.

Alaric threw the blanket back and said, "Come lay with me."

Bashima didn't need telling twice though he was careful not to touch Alaric's back. They curled up under the blanket, facing each other. "This is nice," Alaric said. "We haven't been in the same bed in..."

"Too fucking long," Bashima growled.

Alaric pulled the Sun God close, and he draped his arm over Alaric's hip, letting his forehead meet Alaric's. Bashima sighed and said, "You feel really warm now."

Alaric laughed, "You won't yell at me about cold feet anymore."

They lay together for a while, not talking, just breathing together. Alaric thought about what the dragon said, concerning soul bonds. He didn't care if it was real or not; he loved Bashima, bond or no bond. Strange dragon mating ritual or not. He giggled and Bashima looked at him, orange eyes flashing.

"What's so funny?"

Alaric reached out and touched the uncovered bite mark on Bashima's shoulder, and the Sun God melted when he did. Alaric felt a rush of passion fly through him, and he imagined flipping Bashima around and grinding into him until they both passed out. But his body was too weary and weak to respond in the way he wanted.

"Holy shit," Bashima said. Alaric leaned in and kissed him softly, cupping his chin with his hand. Bashima kissed back, harder and urgent, but he backed away, knowing Alaric wasn't ready for anything beyond kissing at the moment. "What was that? I'm nearly hard, fuck."

"Sorry, I just wanted to check something," Alaric said, and Bashima raised an eyebrow. "I'll tell you tomorrow." He kissed Bashima's nose and closed his eyes, falling asleep with his head against the Sun God's chest.

Chapter Eighteen

Shina was still weak, but Bashima sensed a revitalized vigor within the redhead, and his smiles came more readily. Bashima hadn't realized how much he missed that sharp-toothed grin until he hadn't seen it for weeks. Shina was able to move around Bashima's chambers with ease and ventured to other parts of the temple, supervised by either Matthias or Oken or both. They squabbled over how much help Shina needed, and the redhead often left them behind, arguing about speed and recovery time.

Bashima and Tengu met to discuss the cover story for the Temple of Time Incident, which was what fucking Tengu called it. Every time the Forest God said it, Bashima rolled his eyes and smacked him. Which didn't deter him in the least.

They met with Shina one night in Bashima's sitting room to go over the basics and confirmed that the other gods received the story and agreed to it.

"Veles, Alora, and Cabari were the only ones who saw you transformed, and they agreed to say it was part of Chronas's god-touched ceremony, just a side effect. You bit Bashima and didn't know what you were doing. Things like that can happen," Tengu said. "Like with Oken's mother."

"And what about the god-touched connection?" Shina asked. "How did it break?"

"Since it's never happened before, there isn't much we can say about that," Bashima said. "Chronas most likely won't wake up, so it doesn't matter. He wouldn't be around to control you, which has to be done consciously. We just won't bring it up. If people see my brand on your back, they'll assume I was able to transfer your loyalty to me."

"And if he wakes up?" Shina whispered.

Damn Tengu twiddled his thumbs, letting Bashima answer.

"We'll tackle that if it happens," Bashima said, taking Shina's hand.

"Speaking of the, uh, new brand," said Tengu, stammering. "How is it feeling? Any soreness?"

Bashima glared at the Forest God. He was grateful Tengu was around to help with everything, but he asked the worst questions at the worst times.

Shina was cheerful about the whole situation. "I barely feel it," he said and stretched his back. He was finally able to wear light, soft tunics, and he'd chosen one of Bashima's favorite colors—the dark forest green. Although it matched Tengu a little too much for his liking.

"That's good," Tengu said. "You'll probably feel some residual effects from it, get bits of Bashi's emotions now and again. The transmutation incantation he did to change the brand was Creative Alchemy, which leaves behind a trace of the alchemist or god that uses it. Like in Kuroi's paintings or the temple…"

Bashima glowered at the Forest God again, trying to sear him from the inside out.

"Oh," Shina said, "I thought that was because of the soul bond thing."

Fucking Tengu spit tea all over the floor and himself, and Bashima turned his head slowly to look at the redhead. "What did you say?"

Shina asked Tengu if he needed help, and the Forest God shook him off, sputtering. Shina said, "Is it supposed to be a secret or something? The dragon told me about it."

"Dragon?" Tengu asked from the floor where he wiped up the spilled tea.

"From my dream vision things?" Shina said, turning bright red. "Now that I said it out loud, it sounds really dumb. I told the dragon it wasn't real, but he was pretty adamant about it. He said I bit you because you're my mate, and I was claiming you and that's normal for a dragon. I guess you kind of claimed *me* with the brand because now I can feel you almost all the time unless I concentrate on not doing that."

Both Bashima and Tengu stared at him, shocked. "Now I look like an idiot," Shina said and rumpled his hair.

Tengu cleared his throat and said, "I think Oken needs me. I better be off. We can talk more about things later, Bashi." He gave Shina a curious look and left the room, off to hide with Zebra Head.

Bashima and Shina sat in awkward silence. Bashima opened his mouth to speak but had no idea how to start the conversation, and Shina looked embarrassed. He fiddled with a piece of his hair and wouldn't meet Bashima's eyes.

"So," Bashima finally said, "your dragon friend said we're soul-bonded?"

"Um, yeah," Shina said, voice quiet. He drew his knees up to his chest on the sofa and rested his chin on them. "He's not very helpful. I don't think he's talked to a human in a long time, seemed to think I should know everything about dragons. He was shocked that I had no idea why I bit you."

"And you bit me because…explain it slowly."

Shina's entire face and neck flushed, and he hid his face behind his knees. "He called it 'claiming,' when a dragon bites its chosen mate to tell other dragons to back off. Signals that they're off the market, I guess. He mentioned that seeing you in danger made me lose control. I think I was reacting to all those other gods in the room or something when I did it. I didn't like them being near you when I hadn't claimed you yet."

Bashima remembered the terrifying voice saying, "MINE." He touched the uncovered bite mark on his shoulder and said, "I suppose I'm good and claimed then."

"It's okay," Shina said sadly. "You don't have to be tied to me. The dragon said it was a choice. But now you'll have that scar forever."

"And you won't have that brand forever?" Bashima asked, voice gruff. "I'd say we're tied together no matter what, whether soul bonds are real or not."

"I don't want you to be stuck with me because of something I don't remember doing," Shina said, getting angry. Bashima could feel the tension rising, could see the hairs standing up on Shina's arms. A jolt went through him when he pictured drawing his finger across the redhead's back, the molten gold destroying Chronas's silver, staking his own claim.

When he refocused on the redhead, Shina was perched on the sofa next to him, intense look on his face, pupils dilated. "You smell really good right now," Shina said, not blinking.

Now that Bashima thought about it, Shina smelled divine, like summer rainfall and smoke. Bashima felt the sun's power build up within him and crackle across his skin, enveloping him in orange and yellow light.

"I'm having a hard time shielding from you right now," Shina said. "You're sending out...a lot."

Bashima thought Shina looked like a large cat readying to pounce on its prey, which turned him on to a ridiculous degree. The redhead made a loud purring sound, desire coming off him in waves, and Bashima couldn't take it anymore. He launched himself at Shina, whose face broke into a feral grin.

Even in his human form, Bashima discovered that Shina possessed strength almost equal to his own. It seemed like he was over his injuries because he pushed Bashima back onto the sofa with ease and straddled his hips, dipping his head to lick the bite mark on Bashima's shoulder. Which sent another wave of intensity pouring into him, making Bashima gasp and jerk his hips up.

Shina ground his hips down and snarled into Bashima's ear, "Mine." Not in the scary dragon voice but still possessive and intent.

Bashima grinned and said, "No, *you're* mine," and tossed Shina off the sofa and onto the floor, landing on top of him and pressing his mouth to the redhead's, not caring if he nicked his lips or tongue on Shina's teeth. Shina kissed back with an intensity Bashima hadn't experienced yet, like it was their first kiss and the redhead thought he might try to escape.

Shina wrapped his legs around the Sun God and flipped him over, pressing his entire body down, sniffing up Bashima's neck and nibbling at his ear. Shina was always an impatient lover, but now he was voracious, and Bashima wasn't quite sure how to deal with it or how much strength he could use. Deciding to test it, he planted his hands against the floor and made a small explosion, sending them careening into the sofa with so much force that it slammed against the wall, shaking the windows. Shina wasn't phased in the slightest.

His eyes turned from human to dragon in an instant, blowing full crimson. He grabbed Bashima's tunic and tore it apart, and the Sun God lost whatever composure he had left. Bashima snarled and ripped Shina's shirt off, grasping the gold chest chain and tugging on it, sending Shina into a spiral. His desire struck Bashima like a hammer, and they cascaded together, lips meeting, tongues demanding, hands everywhere. They pulled at each other's soft trousers, vexed that trousers even existed.

Bashima wasn't prepared for Shina to succeed first, and he dove onto the Sun God's rapidly filling cock, sharp teeth at bay but still teasing like needles, driving Bashima forward. For not having done this before, Shina excelled. Unafraid of being poisoned by Bashima's cum, he bobbed up and down along Bashima's length, laving his tongue on the underside and salivating. He grabbed Bashima's hip to hold him in place, and the Sun God tipped his head back and grabbed Shina's red hair, trying not to pull too hard but lost in the sensations. It didn't take long for Shina to bring him close to coming, but then the redhead pulled back and attacked his lips again, grinding his also hardened dick against Bashima's.

"Fuck," Bashima whispered around Shina's mouth, and the redhead grinned, ridding himself of his trousers.

"That's the idea," Shina said, kissing harder, hands searching Bashima's body, grabbing under his hip and raising the Sun God up to meet him. "Oil," Shina commanded in a deep voice and Bashima snapped his fingers, bringing the sea-scented phial into his hand. "I need you to fuck me first, okay?" Shina said and Bashima nodded vigorously. "Because I'm about to destroy you but I need you too," he said.

Bashima's eyes blazed as he dumped oil on his hands. Shina shook his head and said, "No now."

The Sun God pitched Shina over, using a little too much strength, sending him against the table, which upended and went skittering across the floor. Shina landed in a crouch, reflexes prepared, his hair falling into his eyes. He smiled and beckoned Bashima to him. The Sun God stood and circled the redhead, breathing hard, getting the impression that Shina wanted to be overpowered. The dragon wanted a worthy mate. Shina stayed in his crouch, eyes watchful. Bashima's skin flared with light, aroused and anticipating what the redhead might do.

Shina wanted Bashima to earn it, so he would. He increased the friction in his palms and exploded forward in a blaze of fire. The redhead, thinking he knew what the Sun God was up to, moved to meet him, but Bashima had the advantage of maneuverability. He redirected another explosive blaze from his hands and flipped over Shina, landing behind him. He tackled the redhead, laying him out on the floor, making him growl and moan and press back against him.

Bashima stroked a hand down the golden brand on Shina's shoulder, and the redhead arched his back, letting out a soft cry. Bashima tapped into Shina's mind, feeling the crashing waves of yearning. It was intoxicating. Shina angled himself up, and Bashima wasted no time, pressing his hips home. He felt their connection like electricity flowing through every part of their bodies and almost came immediately. He held back, biting his tongue, knowing he wouldn't last long. He remembered Shina's mouth, his perfect lips.

"Come inside me," ordered Shina, and Bashima was helpless to deny him. He thrust deep, not needing much time to reach his climax. He closed his eyes at his release, only to be met with a rumbling beneath him. Opening his eyes, Bashima saw the golden brand ignite with light and color, illuminating the room.

"Shina!" Bashima said, and the redhead crumpled to the floor, the Sun God on top of him. He wasn't dazed for long. Bashima was upended onto his back, unsure how it happened. Shina loomed above him, the brand gleaming behind him, eyes full red and glittering.

Shina reached for the oil phial nearby and unstoppered it, pouring oil generously on his hand, rubbing it between his fingers, feeling its consistency. Bashima thought about tossing him off again, but he wanted Shina too much. He hadn't realized how much until the redhead was on top of him, possessive look in his eyes.

He wasn't quite as gentle as Bashima had been their first time, but the Sun God was ready. This Shina was at the apex of his need and want, his hunger built from months of not being the one in control. Bashima dug his hands into Shina's skin, the redhead's grin fierce and commanding.

Bashima reached up and brought Shina's mouth back to his own, tongue thrusting, trying to claim some space. Shina's hips rolled forward, but he waited, feeling where the Sun God's pleasure lay. It didn't take him long to find it, and Bashima's eyes widened as he strained into the touch. Shina kissed Bashima deeply, asking, "Are you ready?"

"Fuck yes," Bashima rasped and rolled his hips up. Shina met him like he'd been waiting to bed the Sun God his entire life. He nearly collapsed into Bashima, exhaling in relief, and stayed motionless for a moment. Then he picked up a steady rhythm, holding up Bashima's thigh so he could go even deeper, and Bashima held onto him, panting against his shoulder.

"Fuck, Shina, hells," he said, biting the redhead's shoulder, which only encouraged him.

Shina was bigger than Bashima, but he fit with the Sun God as if he were made to be there. The redhead's skin felt hot, giving off heat like an open flame. Bashima bit down harder as Shina pulsed faster, holding up Bashima's hips with ease. So strong. Dragon strength.

When he hit Bashima's pleasure center again, the Sun God couldn't control the light inside anymore. It came pouring out, lighting his skin in a dazzling display, shining in Shina's eyes, melding with the golden light coming from the brand on his back.

"Fuck, I love you so much," Bashima whispered hoarsely in Shina's ear, pleasure radiating through his entire being. The redhead's body shuddered, and he moaned, releasing inside Bashima with incredible force. The Sun God braced himself, accepting all of Shina, hugging him closer, rocking together.

Shina finally let go of Bashima's hips and let them sink to the floor together.

"That was incredible," Bashima said, breathing hard, sweat pouring off his face. His hair was wet from the heat Shina put out; he was like a damn furnace. Shina lay on top of him, also spent. His back's glow dimmed slowly, and Bashima's light also faded.

"I don't think I can move," Shina said, groaning happily. Bashima wrapped his arms around the redhead and rubbed his back in small circles, and Shina sighed. Bashima wasn't sure how mobile he would be either, and Shina was still inside of him, filling him completely.

The Sun God surveyed the room. They hadn't completely destroyed anything, but all the furniture was overturned, and the sofa cushions were shredded. When did that happen?

Their clothes lay in tatters on the floor, and Bashima thought to order Shina more tunics like the dark green one. It was his best color.

"No one has ever been able to throw me around before," Bashima said. "You've gotten really strong."

"You didn't seem to mind," Shina said, chuckling. He slid himself out slowly and rested his chin on Bashima's chest, eyes heavily lidded but shining. Bashima missed the redhead inside him, but he knew that wouldn't be their last time together, so he held in his displeasure.

"I didn't," Bashima said, "just wasn't expecting it."

"So," Shina said, "we did…that…" He laughed and looked around. "Kuroi is going to kill us."

"Pretty great way to go out," Bashima said and nuzzled Shina's head. The redhead looked pensive as though something still weighed on him. Not sad, just thoughtful.

"I can be your equal now," Shina said. "I'm strong enough to deserve you." He sighed as though a weight had been lifted. "I'm someone now."

Chronas's hateful words tumbled through Bashima's mind, *At least the architect was someone. This boy isn't even close to your equal.* He felt a fresh wave of anger for the Time God. Who knew what else Chronas said to Shina before the branding. Or after.

"Hey," he said to Shina, touching his cheek. "Can you sit up for a second?"

Shina's confused look was so damn cute that Bashima almost dragged him down into another kiss.

"Stay right here," he said and stood and padded to the bedroom. He went to the bedside table, which was now full of medical supplies for Shina, books he might like, and a vase of fire lilies. Gone were the two small paintings that tormented Bashima as much as they brought comfort. He gave them to Kuroi, who agreed they belonged with the artist.

Bashima didn't mind. He could hold Dain in his heart. Shina deserved his soul.

He went back into the sitting room, finding Shina sitting cross-legged on the floor where he'd left him, head tilted to the side, eyes large and expressive as ever. This version of Shina was miles away from the sexually confident redhead Bashima just grappled with, but he loved both. Shina contained multitudes.

Bashima sat down across from him, moving closer until their knees touched. He reached for Shina's hand and opened it, rubbing the palm with his thumb. Shina hummed in appreciation, then Bashima placed a small box in his hand.

"I guess Kuroi knew before we did," Bashima said.

Shina looked at him, eyes widening to epic proportions. His hands shook as he opened the box, revealing the white gold pin Kuroi made for him. The dragon and the Sun God's symbol glittered up at him. Tears formed in his eyes, and Bashima hoped they were happy tears.

"I need you to listen to me, Shina," Bashima said, voice firm, "You were someone before you had this power. Does it make things easier for us? Yes and no. Are things ever certain? Usually not. But never doubt that you're worth just as much as me, if not more so."

"Bashima..."

"I wasn't done," Bashima said. "I want you to call me Khresh. That's as much my real name as anything. What humans call a 'given name,' I guess. I want you to move in here with me. I want to spend all the time we have with you together. But mostly, I want to marry you."

Shina looked like he'd been struck by lightning and wasn't perceiving the world around him anymore. Had Bashima stunned him with too much at once?

Shit, he was so terrible at this. He kept silent, waiting for a response, watching the gears turn in the redhead's mind. Waiting was agonizing.

"I want to marry you too," Shina said quietly. Stars danced in his eyes, and tears dripped off his long lashes. Bashima leaned in and kissed the tears away. Shina set down the pin and pulled the Sun God nearer until their legs were intertwined, hugging him close.

Chapter Nineteen

"You look great," Bashima said, wrapping his arms around Alaric's waist and resting his chin on Alaric's shoulder. His eyes scraped down Alaric's body in the mirror.

Looking at his reflection, Alaric had to agree. His hair had grown back, thick and lustrous and very red. Matthias was glad his hair-dying days were over, and Alaric told him they'd find other ways to hang out. The shade wasn't worried.

Emilia helped with his hair that morning, leaving most of it long and loose but spiking up a few pieces in the front. A big chunk swept down across his forehead, which Emilia said made him look dashing. After demanding to be part of the wedding, Alaric said she could be his personal attendant, and she'd beamed. Besides doing his hair, Emilia also traced the kohl for his eyes, making Alaric recall their first days together. It felt like a lifetime ago.

Matthias helped him dress in a more traditional outfit for the ceremony, much different from his usual attire. Alaric was draped in a lavender billowy toga that hung off one shoulder and covered about half his chest, showing off the golden chain that Bashima loved. He'd chosen golden bicep bands to match Bashima's but left his forearms bare. To save his modesty—though the Sun God had voted for see-through everything—the translucent top transitioned gradually to full coverage. The toga hit him around knee-length, showing off his legs with a strategic slit up to mid-thigh. The guests would still get quite an eyeful of Alaric's entire body, but he told himself that at least his "important bits," as Emilia called them, were covered. He left his legs bare of decoration but wore sandals that strapped up his calves.

"Do I have to wear the crown?" Alaric asked, fiddling with it. Though lighter than he expected, the headpiece was enormous, a golden band secured over his hair with a massive dark gold sunburst forming a corona at the back of his head. Bashima had a matching one but hadn't put it on yet. He grinned at Alaric in the mirror, orange eyes mischievous.

"Just for the ceremony, I promise," the Sun God said. "Vaultus is wild for traditional shit."

"Fine, if it's for the King of the Gods," Alaric said, voice dramatic.

He turned around and faced his husband-to-be, who also looked fantastic. He'd chosen the ceremonial armor from the summit with a few artistic upgrades from Kuroi. His skin shone, lit from within by power and happiness.

Alaric whistled and said, "Can we skip the ceremony and go straight to the honeymoon?"

Bashima laughed and said, "You think I didn't lobby for that? My so-called 'friends' would have crashed into our bedroom and thrown a damn party whether we wanted one or not."

"I suppose my parents are coming all this way too," Alaric said, sighing.

"Don't remind me," Bashima said, nerves showing.

"Hey, it's only fair. I have to meet yours," Alaric reminded him.

After Bashima's proposal, Alaric finally made the trip back to his village. Bashima constructed a long-term travel charm for Matthias so the shade could accompany him. He wasn't taking any chances. Bashima wanted to send an entire army, but Alaric told him that was overkill.

Cypress offered to keep watch via the forest trees, which Bashima agreed to, saying, "If anything happens to him and your damn trees miss it, I'm coming straight to your temple and kicking your ass."

Cypress laughed as though that was an impossibility.

When Alaric returned home, it was a spectacle as he expected. The entire village was alerted when a young girl spotted him coming up the main road with Matthias, both of them walking next to Ichigo, who towed the repaired cart.

His parents dissolved into giant teary puddles, covering him with hugs and kisses and various oaths of love. They welcomed Matthias to stay in their home but were immediately suspicious and demanded answers once the villagers stopped celebrating and gawking. They weren't pleased when Alaric said he would be leaving again in only one week.

Alaric tried to explain everything that happened since the tribute ceremony, leaving out the gory details, such as Bashima's initial behavior, how frightened he'd been, the other gods and the summit, and his kidnapping by the Time God. He showed them the brand on his back, which would have been difficult to hide and explained that it was part of a binding ceremony that tied him and the Sun God together.

His father was enraged that someone, even a god, had branded his son, and he'd yelled for quite a long time, scaring Matthias and surprising Alaric. Alaric's mother got him to calm down long enough for Alaric to say that he also marked the god as his own and that they were to be married, which made his parents gape. How could a human entice a god into marriage? Matthias blushed at the question, which silenced both parents and made Alaric collapse into a giggling fit.

"I'm a very charming person," Alaric said, which closed the topic to further discussion. They were, of course, invited to the wedding, which would take place in a month.

"Invited to a god's wedding?" his mother shrieked and launched into planning her wardrobe and what gifts they should bring. "Obviously, we need another offering," she'd said. "It would be disrespectful not to bring something."

While his mother panicked about logistics, Alaric's father took him aside.

"Were you tricked into this?" he asked, Alaric's mother badgering poor Matthias with questions in the background.

"No!" Alaric said. "I want to be with him more than anything."

"But how is this possible?" his father asked. "You're mortal, and he's a god. Those relationships never work out."

Alaric wanted to wait to talk about his newfound abilities and longer lifespan, but his father was too perceptive. He needed to help them understand his decision as best he could without revealing things that would worry them. So, he collected his mother and sat them down.

"Mom," Alaric said, "besides the village being named after a dragon, were you ever told stories about the village being protected by a dragon? Or anything else about dragons?"

His father looked confused, but his mother nodded.

"Oh yes, when I was a girl, my grandmother talked about dragons a lot. She loved the old epics and claimed our village was founded by a dragon. I've told you that before. She said it's where the red eye trait comes from, that our family has dragon blood, but I never thought much about it. Old people enjoy their tales, you know."

"Well," Alaric said, looking at Matthias who shrugged. He had advised Alaric not to say anything. "As it turns out, she wasn't wrong. We do have dragon blood, going back thousands of years."

"I'm sorry, what?" she'd asked, blinking rapidly.

"I sort of accidentally found out," Alaric said. "And now I'm going to live...much longer than a normal human."

"How much longer?" his father asked, perturbed.

"Possibly...forever?"

Both were stunned, looking him over, searching for a recent head injury perhaps.

"How do you accidentally find out that you're immortal?" his father asked, face stern.

"It has to do with the dragon thing," Alaric said, flushing. "I can sort of show you..."

He rolled up his sleeve and concentrated. He'd been practicing making the scales appear on his body by thinking about them and had moderate success. He couldn't transform completely yet, but he could harden his hands and arms without much effort. He bit his lower lip, focusing on his forearm, willing the scales to appear. After a few moments, his parents thinking he'd lost his mind, glimmering red scales appeared on his arm, moving up to his bicep and down to his wrist. When the arm was covered, Alaric turned it over, proud of his control. The last time he'd tried at the temple, the scales hadn't all come in and instead appeared randomly all over his body.

"See?" Alaric said, tapping on a hard scale. His parents paled like they might faint. "I'm still me," Alaric said, allowing the scales to fade back into his skin. "Just with a few extra details..."

"You're a dragon then?" his mother asked, voice high and unsure.

"Not quite, just some perks from the dragon blood," Alaric said. "Longevity is one of them. Increased strength. Impenetrable skin...Oh! And my hair grows in red now too!"

Matthias put his face in his hands and sighed.

"What?" Alaric asked. "I know it's weird and hard to understand, but I've accepted it. And Bashima doesn't care that I'm different."

"Alaric..." his father started, but his mother cut him off.

"Does this mean you can't be hurt?" she asked.

"When I'm in my armored form, I think it's pretty tough to hurt me, yeah."

"Then, I'm okay with it," she said and touched his arm where the scales had been. "It's like something out of a fairy tale, and my son is a dragon." She smiled at him, tears in her eyes. "When you didn't come home, we thought the worst. Do I wish you told us sooner where you were? Yes, and I'll be angry about that for as long as I live. But you're safe now, and I can tell that you're set on this wedding."

"Even though this god basically kept our son prisoner for months?" his father grumbled. Matthias sunk lower in his chair, sipping his tea.

"I knew you wouldn't be completely okay with this," Alaric said, but he grabbed his father's hand and looked him in the eyes. "But it's what I want. I've never wanted anything more. I didn't think this was where my life would go, but I'm not giving him up."

His father took a deep breath and sat back, pulling his hand free. "I know I won't be able to talk you out of it, not with your stubborn streak. Let's take this week to get reacquainted with each other." He'd stood up and left the room, muttering, "Couldn't even come here and explain himself."

Alaric warned his parents not to mention the dragon thing to anyone, and his mother laughed, saying, "Who in their right mind would believe us? Wrapping their heads around you getting married to the Sun God will be quite enough for the village gossips."

Now, they stood in front of each other, Sun God and Blood of Dragons, nervous about meeting each other's parents. They laughed together, and Bashima said, "I'm ready to get dirty looks from your parents. I deserve it. I better finish getting ready. Kuroi's been on my ass all morning. Just wanted to get away for a second to see you." He leaned in for a quick kiss, then shifted away, grinning.

Matthias came back in, saying, "Was Master Bashima just here? Kuroi was looking for him."

"He was," Alaric laughed. "Wanted to tell me again that my outfit should be transparent."

Matthias rolled his eyes. He said, "Hardly fashionable, and he would hate if other people got to see *all* of you." He muttered about jealous gods and looked Alaric over. "Almost everyone is here. The king and queen are waiting to greet you before the ceremony."

Alaric bit his lip. Just because he'd met the king and queen didn't mean he wasn't anxious. He was joining their elite club, and as far as they knew, he was god-touched. An odd choice for a god to marry a god-touched, but they'd given their approval, knowing Bashima would do as he liked whatever their answer.

"I think this is as good as it's going to get, Matthias," Alaric said, taking one more glance in the mirror. "Ready?" Matthias smiled, grasped Alaric's arm, and shifted them down to the valley.

Bashima insisted on an outdoor wedding.

"The fewer of those assholes in our temple, the better. My mother insisted on staying over, and I couldn't turn down Vaultus and Hastia, so then Tengu gets to stay. But that's it. No one else."

Alaric agreed, but he knew Alora, Garyn, and Cabari would find a way to stay over as well. "Cypress would be staying anyway," Alaric reminded Bashima, teasing. "It's your own fault for letting Oken keep his room here."

322

"Ugh, don't remind me," Bashima had said.

Matthias shifted himself and Alaric to the temporary pavilion near the base of the mountain to the wedding party private tent. Kuroi called it a tent, but it was massive as a dining hall with plenty of room for Bashima and Alaric and their attendants. No one else was allowed inside, supposedly.

"So," a crisp voice said when they appeared, "you're the boy who's stealing my son away."

Matthias bowed his head and whispered, "Good luck," to Alaric before backing away.

"Traitor," Alaric mumbled, then faced Bashima's mother.

She was the most beautiful woman Alaric had ever seen, and Bashima looked just like her. Her skin was flawless and luminous as though she could also harness the power of the sun, and her blond hair shone like sun-drenched wheat just like her son's. She looked Alaric over with dark orange eyes, her perfect lips an unreadable line. She wore an expertly fitted gown that flowed around her body like water, and a crown of delicate beaten gold roses sat in her hair.

"Sigrid, we agreed not to frighten the young man," said the god next to Bashima's mother, who had to be his father. He had disheveled brown hair, less chaotic than son's, and kind brown eyes. He was much taller than his petite wife and broad across the shoulders and torso, where Bashima had a slimmer waist and narrower hips, and he wore a set of armor in earth colors: browns, deep greens, and golds.

Bashima's mother crossed her arms, lifting her chin, haughtier than even the Sun God. Alaric gulped and attempted a smile, which enticed Bashima's father to approach, grinning, hand out. He grasped Alaric's hand and shook, grip strong but not overpowering.

"It's wonderful to meet you, Shina. I'm Khresh's father, Samsan. My lovely wife, Sigrid." His voice and smile were warm and inviting, and Alaric relaxed. At least Bashima's father would be easy to get along with.

"Nice to meet you as well," Alaric said.

"At least this one is prettier than the other one," Sigrid said, eyebrow arched as she approached. Alaric blushed and choked on air. Bashima warned him that his mother was temperamental and rude. She put her hand out, disdainful, and Alaric leaned down, taking it gently in his own hand, and kissed it. She sighed and added, "And I suppose your manner is pleasing."

A growl came from the tent's entrance and Bashima stomped inside. "Try not to rip his heart out and eat it, hag." Alaric felt a wave of annoyance coming off the Sun God, and he bit back a giggle. "What the hells are you doing in here?"

"Ah, there's my loving son," Sigrid said, voice dripping with sarcasm.

"Hello, Khresh," Samsan said with a small wave.

"Dad, I asked you to do one thing," Bashima said when he reached them, pulling Alaric away from his mother. "And you've already failed."

Samsan looked around the tent, anywhere but at his son. "Lovely pavilion, don't you think? The size of this tent is perfect." His voice trailed off when he finally looked at Bashima and saw his expression.

"They were just introducing themselves," Alaric said, conciliatory.

"It's never 'just' anything with her."

"I'm standing right here," Sigrid said and rolled her eyes.

Alaric spied Matthias out of the corner of his eye, mouth closed, body shaking with laughter. Alaric made a "help me" face, but the shade shook his head slightly.

"Conveniently right where you're not supposed to be," Bashima said, but his mother shrugged regally, not caring in the least what Bashima wanted.

"Let me look at you," she said and made a turning motion with her finger. Shocking Alaric, Bashima paused for only a moment before turning slowly, his expression stormy yet resigned. "You as well, human."

Bashima grabbed Alaric before he could comply and said, "He's not human anymore, you old witch. Stop being such an asshole."

"I wanted to see what finally made you settle down and start taking your life seriously," she said, flipping her hand. Alaric wanted to scream; they were so alike. He knew Bashima would hate the comparison, so he filed the fact away for another time. She eyed him and said, "I don't have all day," and made the spinning motion again.

Alaric listened and turned slowly, blush growing by the second. Samsan gasped when he saw Alaric's back and Sigrid clicked her tongue.

"Did you have to go so overboard, son?" she asked, voice sharp.

"I already told you what happened," Bashima said, seething through his teeth.

"It's okay," Alaric said. "I'm sure it will shock a lot of people." He put his hand on Bashima's shoulder and said, "I asked him to do it to get rid of the Time God's mark. It's not his fault, and I really don't mind."

Especially when I marked your son first, he thought.

As though reading his mind, Sigrid's eyes flashed to the scar on Bashima's shoulder, which was mostly covered by his armor. She ran her tongue over her teeth and said, "I never expect thoughtfulness from my son, so perhaps you've rubbed off on him."

Kuroi chose the perfect moment to enter the tent, Tika in tow, who carried Bashima's crown and looked harried.

"Master Bashima," Kuroi said. "Really, we've been chasing you around all morning. Vaultus and Hastia are ready to receive you. Mistress Sigrid, Master Samsan." He inclined his head to Bashima's parents, unfazed that they'd infiltrated the private tent. "Shina, your parents are here. I've assigned three shades to them, and Draiden has volunteered to chaperone. Heavens know what the other gods will do when they see humans here."

Kuroi flew from the tent, muttering. Tika narrowed her eyes at Bashima and held out the crown. "Shina is wearing his," she said archly.

Bashima groaned. "Fine." He took the crown and jammed it over his hair. Shina moved in quickly to fix the blond explosion before his mother could. Bashima didn't budge as Alaric adjusted the crown until it sat correctly. He saw the approving look in Sigrid's eyes and grinned.

One point for Alaric, he thought.

Matthias moved forward to stand behind Alaric, and Tika took her place behind Bashima. Kuroi had drilled the schedule into both Alaric and Bashima, but Alaric couldn't help but take the Sun God's hand for a moment before they proceeded from the tent. Bashima raised his arm and kissed the back of Alaric's hand, winking, and they walked through the entrance, Bashima's parents following behind the two shade attendants.

The air was light and crisp, a warm breeze playing across their skin. King Vaultus and Queen Hastia waited outside. They had to drop each other's hands to greet the king and queen.

"Bashima, my boy!" Vaultus boomed, embracing the Sun God, his massive form hiding his infirmities well.

Hastia took Alaric's hands and smiled up at him, saying, "I had a feeling when I met you that this day would come."

"I think everyone knew before I did," Alaric admitted, shy. The queen's bright green eyes danced as she moved to greet the Sun God.

Vaultus clasped Alaric's hand and shook smartly, beaming down at him. He said, "I never thought I'd see the day that young Bashima left his temple." The king's eyes glistened, and Alaric was alarmed.

"King Vaultus," he asked, "Are you all right?"

"I haven't been this happy in a long time, Shina," he said and inclined his head. "Just make sure he doesn't try to boss you around."

"I don't think you have to worry about that, your majesty," Alaric said and laughed. The king's voice boomed across the valley, and he rubbed his eyes, moving to congratulate Samsan.

Hastia and Sigrid embraced warmly, which surprised Alaric. Then he heard a tremulous voice behind him, "They've been friends since they were very young."

Cypress stood with Oken at his side, curly green hair a cloud around his head. He wore an impressive set of armor filigreed with intricate leaves, vines, and flowers.

Oken had a big smile on his face. He said, "I'm happy you can walk again, Shina." Cypress's eyes bugged out, and Alaric bit his lip, trying not to laugh.

"Thank you, Oken," Alaric said. "That means a lot."

"It's us who should thank you for marrying Bashima," the demigod said, leaning in and glancing at the Sun God, who was in animated conversation with Hastia and his mother. Oken went on, "He was really difficult to be around until you came along. Although he's still fairly difficult..." He trailed off when Cypress gave him a pleading look. "Did I say the wrong thing?"

Alaric pulled the demigod into a hug, which Oken wasn't expecting. When he let go, Oken looked alarmed but also pleased. "We got you a nice gift," he said, blocking one side of his mouth as though telling a secret.

Draiden chose the perfect moment to walk up, Alaric's bewildered parents in tow. He'd never seen his mother and father look finer, both dressed in fashionable formal wear that one of Bashima's shades designed. He was amazed his father agreed to wear the ornate suit, but it fit him perfectly, and he stood tall and proud, towering over many of the gods.

Draiden cleared his throat and announced, "May I present Master Shina's parents, Shurui and Ganjo." He gestured them forward, Alaric's mother's arm linked with his father's. Her rosy cheeks and ready smile could pull anyone in, and Queen Hastia held Sigrid's hand and stepped forward.

"How lovely that you could come today. I am Hastia, Goddess of Spring, and this is Sigrid, Goddess of Youth and Bashima's mother," Hastia said, taking Alaric's mother's hand. She looked at Alaric who nodded, encouraging, and disengaged from her husband to converse with the two women. Alaric heard his mother say to Sigrid, awed, "Your son is so handsome. I don't think I've seen his equal." Which must have been the perfect thing to say because Sigrid's face thawed.

Vaultus and Samsan crowded around Alaric's father, exclaiming their adoration for Shina, and applauded him raising such a fine son. Alaric's father spared him a quick glance and smile then spoke with the gods easily.

Before long, Kuroi returned, looking no less stressed than before. He lectured them about the timeline, reminding them that staying on task was key. He ordered Matthias and Tika to make sure Alaric and Bashima were ready, then asked the king, queen, and parents to follow him to their places. Cypress and Oken wished them luck, then went to sit down as well.

It was only Bashima and Alaric with their attendants, waiting for their music cue to enter the pavilion.

"It's not too late to run, is it?" Bashima asked. He already looked spent from the social interactions. While Alaric was ready to talk with everyone, dance into the evening, and show off the Sun God at his side. Seeing his parents put him in the mood to have a good time and mingle with their guests.

"It's only one day," Alaric said and touched Bashima's cheek. The Sun God leaned into his hand and sighed.

"Fine," he said. "I'm only doing this because you want to. Talk all you want about eloping, I knew you'd want a party." He beckoned to Tika, who came forward with a small box. Bashima took the white gold pin from the box and fastened it on Alaric's toga near the shoulder. "You're mine, and I'm yours," he said firmly.

Alaric leaned in and planted a soft kiss on Bashima's lips. He whispered in the Sun God's ear, "I'm going to do such bad things to you tonight."

Yellow light crackled in Bashima's eyes, and he grinned, showing sharp canines. "Can't fucking wait."

Epilogue

Alaric was right. Not only did more people stay overnight than Bashima wanted, they were loud and obnoxious about it. Alora and Garyn got extremely drunk and shifted to "their" room in the temple without asking. The Lightning God made perhaps the most embarrassing toast in the history of the world before toppling off the pavilion stage. Luckily, Jace caught him, which might have been Cabari's plan. Cabari talked Jace into staying over much to Lord Veles's dismay.

Alaric was sure he'd heard the Lord of the Underworld mutter, "I told him no loud blonds," before he'd left with his husband, the original loud blond himself.

Bashima's and Alaric's parents stayed, getting along famously, which concerned Bashima but delighted Alaric. The Sun God had gotten chilly glares from Alaric's father, but as the day went on and they'd spoken quietly together, Alaric's father loosened up and enjoyed the party.

King Vaultus and Queen Hastia retired early, Hastia claiming weariness. Kuroi led them to the temple, Cypress watching as they left. Kuroi returned sometime later, his expression stoic, but Alaric knew him too well. Kuroi was concerned about the king.

The Forest God whispered something to Oken, and they'd said good night not long after.

That would have to be a talk for another time.

329

Alaric discovered, both to his delight and annoyance, that alcohol didn't have much effect on him now even the strong wine the gods drank. Bashima wasn't much for liquor either, but he stared in fascination as Alaric downed goblet after goblet of wine and nectar.

Alaric was glad for his clear head later.

Once the other guests left and those staying in the temple turned in, they went to the stable and visited Ichigo and Yoru. After feeding the horses pilfered treats from the wedding feast, Bashima and Alaric walked out into the valley.

The night sky was clear and dappled with stars, the moon high and bright.

"Husband," Bashima said, glancing sidelong at Alaric, smirking.

"Husband," Alaric agreed, huge smile spreading across his face. He'd wanted to share something with Bashima for a while but decided to save it for a special time. What better day than their wedding?

Alaric faced Bashima and grabbed his hands, clasping them tightly. The Sun God raised an eyebrow at his new husband and said, "What are you up to, Red?"

"I need to show you something," Alaric said. The wind tugged at their clothes, tousling their hair. Alaric heard chimes somewhere in the distance, calling the shades back to the temple. The pavilion and tents would be dismantled tomorrow after everyone had time to rest.

He took a deep breath and said, "Hold on, Khresh."

Bashima made a face and said, "Wouldn't dream of letting go."

Alaric smiled, red light playing in his eyes. The golden brand glowed on his back as he concentrated, thinking of being weightless and free. Bashima's eyes widened, and his grip on Alaric's hand tightened. Alaric closed his eyes, took a deep breath, and pushed off from the ground.

They took off, floating up into the air, leaving the ground behind. Bashima's skin came alive with color, his eyes glimmering. He didn't look down to check their ascent. He didn't check their surroundings. The Sun God gazed at Alaric until he opened his eyes and sighed. It was the most wonderful feeling in the world.

Alaric said, "The dragons call this cloud dancing. I wasn't sure I'd be able to do it."

"Of course, you can," Bashima said as though he had zero doubts in Alaric's abilities. "You're the most incredible person in the world."

Alaric tugged on Bashima's hands, bringing him closer. He leaned forward, and Bashima met him, closing his eyes as they kissed. Soon they were intertwined, clinging to each other, spinning in slow spirals through the air.

"I love you," Bashima said, and Alaric hugged him tighter.

"They'll have to change the beginning of the story," Alaric said and began lowering them to the ground to begin their life together.

Nothing is eternal but the gods...and perhaps, love.

This book has a crazy life story, and there are so many people to thank.

Firstly, to my parents and brother, who humor me whenever I talk about writing and books. I wouldn't be here without your patience. To my very enthusiastic friend Eva, who introduced me to a little thing called Boys Love, aka MLM. This book truly would not exist without you planting the idea in my head then fervently asking for more chapters. All the times you called me mean for doing terrible things to the characters kept me going.

To Christine, for giving me the courage to try and make a "silly little story" into a novel, even if she has to close her eyes through certain parts. My poor friends, who had to listen to me go on and on about how much I loved BL and MLM stories, though a few might have tried it by now.

To my relentless editor Misty, who enjoyed the story so much that she needed the second installment immediately. To all the wonderful people at Between the Lines Publishing for taking a chance on this book and making it a reality.

Lastly, to my readers, whose comments and encouragement are the fuel to my authorly fire.

Colleen McMillàn is a Minnesota native who currently lives in the Twin Cities with her cantankerous cat, Duncan. She also likes to call Paris her second home, but don't tell the Parisians. She was educated at the University of Wisconsin, River Falls and received her master's degree in creative writing at the University of Kent, Canterbury in England.

Twitter: @Colleen40303158
Facebook: @ColleenMcMillanAuthor